C000254055

HE..
REVENGE

BOOKS BY EMMA TALLON

Runaway Girl
Dangerous Girl
Boss Girl
Fierce Girl
Reckless Girl
Fearless Girl
Ruthless Girl

EMMA TALLON

HER REVENGE

bookouture

Published by Bookouture in 2021

An imprint of Storyfire Ltd.
Carmelite House
50 Victoria Embankment
London EC4Y 0DZ

www.bookouture.com

Copyright © Emma Tallon, 2021

Emma Tallon has asserted her right to be identified
as the author of this work.

All rights reserved.
No part of this publication may be reproduced,
stored in any retrieval system, or transmitted, in any form or by
any means, electronic, mechanical, photocopying, recording or
otherwise, without the prior written permission of the publishers.

ISBN: 978-1-83888-144-3
eBook ISBN: 978-1-83888-143-6

This book is a work of fiction. Names, characters, businesses,
organizations, places and events other than those clearly in the
public domain, are either the product of the author's imagination
or are used fictitiously. Any resemblance to actual persons, living or
dead, events or locales is entirely coincidental.

For my little pickle and my little doll, the two loves of my life,
Christian and Charlotte Xx

PROLOGUE

The sound of screaming woke the little girl up. She rubbed the sleep from her eyes, confused. It was still dark; it wasn't morning yet. The sound of her father's voice wafted up the stairs, urgent, breathless. He was saying something, but Scarlet couldn't hear what it was. She swung her skinny legs over the side of the bed and slipped off, silently padding across the room and out into the hallway. Carefully she crept towards the glow of the downstairs light that bathed the stairs and sat down on the top step, hugging her knees to her chest as she peered through the bannisters.

Her father paced the hallway below, agitated, his gait unusually awkward. As he swung around to address someone, Scarlet stifled a gasp. He was holding his hand over a large dark patch of blood. As she watched, it seeped out and flooded down his shirt and he groaned in pain.

Is Daddy dying? she wondered in horror.

Her mother came into view; her pale skin was tinged with grey, and terror coloured her eyes. She wailed but quickly put her hands to her mouth as her husband shushed her.

'You'll wake Scarlet, woman,' he berated.

'You need to lie down… Christ, Ronan. You need a hospital,' she whimpered.

'No, no hospitals, love.' He touched her hair in comfort. 'Lil will be here any minute. She'll fix this.' He swung towards the front door, irritation flashing across his face. 'Jesus, where is she?' He wavered, light-headed from the blood loss.

'I'm here,' came a quiet, strong voice from the kitchen.

'Lil,' Ronan breathed in relief.

Lily Drew came into view, followed by her twin sons, and Scarlet pulled back into the shadows, unable to peel her eyes away from the scene below. Her aunt Lily slowly walked in a circle, pausing to stare into the lounge for a moment.

'Cath, put him on the kitchen table, get a bottle of vodka, some clean towels and your sewing kit,' she instructed.

Scarlet heard her mother gasp and begin to protest, but Aunt Lily cut her off with a dangerous flash of her eyes.

'There's no time for dithering. Do it,' she said, her tone stern.

'Lil...' Ronan paused as Cath began to lead him away. 'What are we going to do with *him*?'

Who? Scarlet's childish curiosity got the better of her and she crept down another couple of stairs, keeping close to the wall, so she could see into the lounge. Her eyes widened as she clocked the man trussed up in a heap by the fireplace. There was a gag in his mouth, but as she watched, he wriggled and writhed, trying to free himself from his bindings. His eyes met hers and a shiver of cold fear ran through her body.

'He's seen too much,' Lily replied. 'There would be too much comeback from this.'

Ronan nodded. One of the twins reached into his inner jacket pocket and pulled out a gun. Twisting a silencer onto the end, he handed it to his mother without a word. She stood before the man in the fireplace, staring down at him in contempt.

'Did you really think you could take out Ronan Drew? Did you really think even if you had, that you would be allowed to walk away from it?' she growled.

Something in her tone sent icy chills up Scarlet's spine. She knew she shouldn't be here. Whatever was happening, this wasn't for her eyes. But she couldn't seem to move.

'You stupid fool,' Lily continued, her lip curling in contempt. 'I don't suffer fools. And I certainly don't let them walk away once they've tried to mess with my family.'

She stepped closer and raised her arm, pointing the gun at his head. The man bucked and tried to back away, terror replacing the anger that had been in his eyes before. He looked to Scarlet, pleading silently for the little girl to help him, but all she could do was stare, frozen in terrified confusion.

A second later Lily pulled the trigger, the dulled sound of the shot echoing off the walls and making Scarlet jump in shock. The man slumped back, and blood sprayed across the rose-coloured carpet that was Cath's pride and joy. Scarlet opened her mouth to scream but no sound came out.

Lily handed the gun back to her son and stared down at the dead man on the floor. 'Wrap him and get him out of here,' she said, eying the carpet with a slightly regretful look. 'They needed to redecorate in here anyway,' she muttered.

As she moved to find out how her brother was doing, she caught sight of her niece cowering on the stairs. After a pause she went and sat down next to her, wrapping her arm around her thin, shaking shoulders. 'Close the door, Connor,' she called to her nearest son.

Moving into Scarlet's line of sight, Lily smiled kindly. 'Come now, my little doll. Don't you worry,' she crooned, comfortingly. She sighed and pulled her closer. 'That was a very bad man who tried to hurt your daddy. That's why I had to do that, to keep everyone safe. But Daddy's going to be just fine.' She reached up with her free hand and smoothed Scarlet's hair. 'And as for all that mess in there, Aunt Lily will take care of it. Aunt Lily takes care of all of you, remember? I'll never let anyone hurt you. Any of you. You're safe, I promise.'

The little girl frowned at this and bit her lip.

'What is it, little doll?' Lily asked.

She sniffed and stared at the now closed door to the lounge and then back up at her aunt. 'Who looks after you, Aunt Lily? What if someone comes to hurt you?'

Lily pulled a wry smile and kissed her forehead. 'I don't need anybody to look after me,' she replied. 'I'm very strong, my love. No one can hurt me.'

Scarlet stared back at the door again, her wide blue eyes serious. 'Well, then I want to be like you when I grow up, Aunt Lily. I want to be strong so no one can hurt me either. Not ever.'

CHAPTER ONE

Ten years later

Scarlet stared up from where she lay on her bed, through the Velux window above and into the sky. Her friend Natalie lay next to her, gushing about her boyfriend Scott, as if their month-long relationship was the greatest love story of all time. She tuned her out, bored of hearing how wonderful Scott was and about all the plans they'd made for their future.

Today was the day they were graduating from sixth form. It was a day of celebration for everyone in their year. Some of her peers were heading off to university. Some of them had jobs lined up or were setting off on travel adventures. Scarlet had an offer from her first choice of university, St Andrews, to study business. It was something her mother was thrilled about, but although on the outside her father was too, she knew it would be a huge disappointment to him if she didn't join the family business. He and her aunt Lily had been waiting on the sidelines to see what she would do, their fevered hope almost tangible.

She had always been ahead of the rest of the class and passed her A levels with flying colours. Her university acceptance had come quickly and she'd immediately responded to accept her place, but she'd held off admitting this to her family, keeping this secret close to her chest. Not even Natalie knew yet. She'd avoided all talk of the future with everyone, claiming she needed time to think.

For now she just wanted to enjoy graduating from high school. She still had all summer to work up the courage to tell her dad.

The decision to take this path hadn't been an easy one. She'd spent her whole life on the edges of the world her father and his side of the family inhabited. It had been hammered into her from an early age that the most important thing in life was the family. Nothing mattered more than that. The family firm had been built by her father and aunt from nothing up to the thriving enterprise it was today. They had built it with blood, sweat and tears, to be carried on by the next generation. It had all been for them, for their future, and Scarlet knew it. So it was difficult to turn away from it.

The only person she knew would support her decision whole-heartedly was her mother, Cath. Because the family business was not all it appeared to be on the surface. Her father ran a factory with Aunt Lily, which created small plastic parts for pipework, but although this was successful enough, the business ran much deeper and darker than that. The factory was also a front, a legal channel to funnel the real money they made from their less legal enterprises. And of those there were many. The money was good but the risks were high, and Cath wanted nothing more than to steer her daughter as far away from it as she could.

Cath herself had nothing to do with the family business. She supported her husband, turned the other way, lied for him when required and kept her mouth shut, because she loved him fiercely. But she had never actually approved of what he did. So when the time came when Scarlet could put off revealing her decision no longer, she knew that at least she'd have her mother on side. It was a small comfort against her torn loyalty and the pain and disappointment she was going to cause, but a comfort all the same.

She glanced down at the clock on her wall and sat up. 'Hey…' She cut Natalie off, mid gush. 'We're going to be late if we don't leave soon. Come on, grab your cap.' She stood, picked her own graduation cap up off the desk and carefully positioned it on top of her long raven hair. In the mirror, grey-blue eyes stared back at her from a pale, heart-shaped face. She pinched her cheeks in an attempt to give them some colour, but it didn't do much. With a look of resignation she quickly applied some Vaseline to her full lips and ran her fingers through the ends of her hair before turning towards the door. 'Come on, let's go.'

The young women made their way downstairs, Natalie following behind Scarlet.

'Ladies!' As they entered the large kitchen which was the heart of the house, Ronan greeted them with two glasses of champagne. 'I think today's activities call for a little celebration, wouldn't you say?'

At six feet three with a broad frame and a face that told of many boxing matches lost, Ronan was a formidable-looking man. As dangerous as he appeared – indeed, was – to his enemies though, he had a huge heart with which he loved his family dearly. For his wife and daughter, he would do just about anything.

Scarlet and Natalie took their glasses and raised them to meet his. Cath hurried forward to join them from the counter where she'd been checking the roast she had in for later and Ronan wrapped his arm around her shoulders as they all chinked their glasses together.

'Cheers to the both of you for all your achievements in high school, and for the future…' He raised his glass higher. 'A wish my family have always bestowed on those we love – may the road rise up to meet you, may the wind be always at your back and may the sun shine warm upon your face.'

Scarlet smiled up at Ronan warmly. 'Slainte,' she said, taking a sip of her champagne.

'Slainte,' he repeated back to her.

Both Ronan and Cath had moved over to London from Ireland with their families when they were just children. In the same boat as outsiders initially, they had stuck together, and eventually fallen in love and married. They had lived in London most of their lives, but they still retained a slight accent, and they held on with pride to their Irish roots.

'Good lord, is that the time?' Cath suddenly exclaimed. She patted her dark hair, done up especially for the occasion, and smoothed down the blue dress she'd bought to match the colour of her daughter's graduation gown. 'We'd better make a move or we'll be late. And we can't have that now. Not on the day you girls are graduating. Come on now, Natalie, you'd best run home to your parents – they'll be wondering where you are.'

'Yes, Mrs Drew. Thanks for the drink, Mr Drew.' Natalie swigged some of the champagne from her glass and shot a grin at Scarlet. 'See you there, Scar.' She hurried off, and Scarlet took another sip of her drink.

Ronan smiled down at Scarlet as he pulled Cath into his embrace once more. 'We're both so proud of you, Scarlet,' he said, emotion colouring his tone. 'You have no idea what today means to us. I never finished school. Never really went at all actually. Something I always regretted.'

'But you still did very well regardless, Dad,' Scarlet replied. 'Look at all you've achieved.' She pointedly looked around at the spacious, white marble kitchen. Their house was large and opulent, a testament to how well Ronan Drew had done in his life.

'Well, yes, but I wouldn't have managed to build all this on me own,' he replied. 'If it weren't for your aunt Lily's idea for the factory...'

'Ronan.' Cath put a hand on his arm. 'Come now, today is about Scarlet.'

'You're right, of course,' Ronan conceded. 'Let's go.'

Scarlet turned and led the way out towards the car, her heart sinking at the mention of the factory. Her father was going to be crushed when she told him his only child was walking away from it. His only heir. She resolved to spend as much time as she could with him over the summer to soften the disappointing news. Perhaps she'd agree to work in the factory for a few weeks. As she thought this, her heart lifted slightly. This would be something she could give him at least, some quality time. Plus, the extra money she earned would come in handy when she got to Scotland.

As they reached the car, she smiled at him, her decision made, and sent up a silent prayer that this quality time would be enough to soften the blow.

CHAPTER TWO

Ronan made his way through the crowded school hall to the front row of the parents' section. As he passed, several of the parents and teachers greeted him and nodded their respect. Even at the school, the notorious Ronan Drew was treated like a local celebrity. Whilst people were aware of his line of work or at the very least had heard rumours, they were also aware of the generous donations he'd made around the community. The area was a better place thanks to the work he'd done over the years.

Ronan sidled down the row of chairs to where his sister, Lily, was already waiting with her twin sons. She watched with keen brown eyes as her niece found her seat among her friends.

'She's grown into a true beauty, that one,' she said as her brother took his place next to her.

'She has indeed,' he replied, leaning sideways to peck her on the cheek.

Lily turned towards them both. 'How are you keeping, Cath?' she asked politely.

'Well, thank you, Lil. You're all joining us for lunch after this, aren't you?'

'Of course – wouldn't miss it for the world.' Lily turned her gaze back to the front and pushed her natural tight blonde curls back off her face. She was a tidy person by nature, her outfit and make-up impeccable, but no matter what she did, her hair would not be tamed. It was something she'd had to come to terms with years before, but it still irritated her. She leaned sideways towards her son Connor. 'Did you get the new schedule from Rus?' she asked quietly.

'Yeah,' he murmured. 'There's a load of Louis coming in from the mainland next Thursday that looks worth pursuing.'

Lily pursed her deep red lips. 'How many?'

'Just the one truck.'

Cillian leaned across his brother to whisper to their mother. 'We've got to hit this one, 'cause Connor's promised his new bird a handbag.'

Connor swiped at his brother, and Cillian moved back into his own space with a chuckle. Lily's dark eyes flashed with annoyance.

'You give that cheap tart anything off that truck and I'll give you what for, Connor Drew,' she said sharply. 'You know damn well we can't chance the goods being traced back to us. They need to be moved quickly.'

Connor shot his brother a murderous look but didn't argue, knowing it was the wiser course of action.

The twins were identical, even down to their choice of haircut and suit. They dressed, moved and spoke in the same way, to the point that often the only person who could tell them apart at a glance was their mother. They were also the very best of friends and had each other's back through thick and thin. The main difference between them was that Connor was the more serious of the two, while Cillian was usually the ringleader in their less sensible ventures. Blessed with the thick dark hair of their father and their mother's brown eyes, they were handsome young men, which, partnered with their family name, ensured they suffered no lack of female attention.

Everyone sat down as the graduation ceremony began and waited patiently through the lengthy speech about what bright futures the headteacher was imagining for them all. Eventually, the students began being called up.

''Ere she goes, look,' Connor whispered with a smile. 'Our little Scarlet.'

'Not so little anymore,' Lily reminded him. Her boys were seven years older than their cousin and had always looked out for her. She glanced sideways at Ronan. 'So,' she said, testing the water, 'when's she coming to the office to talk through her options?'

Cath immediately leaned across her husband with a glare. 'She is *not* joining the family business,' she hissed.

'Don't you think *she* should be the one to decide what she's doing?' Lily shot back.

'I'm her *mother*,' Cath responded.

'She's eighteen years old, Cath,' Lily replied.

'An eighteen-year-old with a place at St Andrews University,' Cath said, folding her arms.

'Which I'm as proud of as you, but the girl doesn't need a piece of paper to show how smart she is,' Lily replied.

'Ladies,' Ronan's gruff voice cut through the tension. 'Let's just celebrate this right now, shall we?' He nodded towards the stage, where Scarlet stood with a smile on her face and her head held proudly as she accepted her scroll.

Lily settled back and clapped as her niece posed for the camera then made her way back to her seat.

Cath had been against their way of life from the start. She'd never tried to stop Ronan doing what they did – she loved and respected him too much. Lily had to grudgingly give her that. But now she wanted to keep Scarlet away from it too. She wanted to turn her into a straight shooter and protect her from all the badness in the world. But no one could be protected from this world. And Scarlet was unusually intelligent for someone her age.

Recently, whenever Cath wasn't in hearing range, Lily had turned her conversations with Scarlet towards the factory, and the girl had come up with some incredible ideas to streamline and modernise. Curious, Lily had tried one or two of them out. They had almost immediately improved efficiency, and Lily had been impressed. As young as she was, with her sharp brain and thirst for business, Scarlet would be a great asset.

Lily breathed in deeply and smiled at her niece as she looked over towards them. She would just have to bide her time and wait and see what happened.

CHAPTER THREE

Drawing on the slim cigarette in her hand, Lily breathed in the smoke and blew it out slowly. She stood at the back of the office, leaning against a tall filing cabinet, her arms folded across her chest as she watched the conversation unfolding in front of her.

Ronan was at the desk, listening, with a grave expression, to the man seated opposite.

'I really don't know what you're talking about, Ronan. I-I turned the money over to Cillian, same way I always have done.' He swallowed, his Adam's apple bobbing up and down as his wide eyes darted worriedly between Ronan and Lily.

'Except that money was a few hundred quid light this month, weren't it, Dan?' Ronan asked with a growl.

'W-Was it?' Dan swallowed again. 'Nah, it couldn't have been. I counted it myself, I swear.'

'Oh, you swear, do you?' Ronan laughed and turned to Lily. 'He swears, Lil. So he must be telling the truth.'

Lily smirked coldly and took another drag of her cigarette. ''Course he is,' she said, her tone laced with sarcasm.

The smile dropped from Ronan's face as he turned back to Dan and was replaced by a thunderous expression. 'You can swear on Mother Teresa's grave for all I care, it still counts about as much as pig shit in a pie competition. Your bag was short this month and I ain't fuckin' happy about it.' Ronan slammed his hand down on the desk and Dan jumped. 'You know it's really simple. You're given a set amount of money to launder through that takeaway of yours each month. You push it through for me and you get to keep ten per cent for your troubles. I even threw in free protection to sweeten it for you. And it works for everyone. Or at least it always *did* work, up until this month, when you decided to put your sticky little fingers in the cookie jar and help yourself to some of my cash. Did you really think it wouldn't be noticed?'

A bead of sweat formed on Dan's forehead and began to trickle down his face.

'I-I really didn't, Ronan; you've got to believe me. Why would I want to cross you?' He tried to smile but it came out as a frightened grimace. 'M-Maybe it got lost in transit? Or – or maybe one of the men who collect it took a little for themselves?'

Lily stood up abruptly, fury flashing across her face. She crossed the small office as quick as lightning and grabbed Dan's face in her hand, squeezing viciously as she snarled down at him. 'What did you just say?'

'Th-That it got lost in transit?' Dan squeaked.

'After that,' she prompted, her tone low and deadly.

'One of the men who collect might have taken it?'

Lily's grip tightened and he cried out in pain as her nails dug into his cheeks. 'My boys are not thieves, Daniel,' she said, her calm voice at odds with the heated anger still radiating from her expression. 'They are many, many things, but not that. And if I ever hear that you've said that again, I'll make you regret it in ways you can't even imagine. Do you understand?'

'Yes – yes!' Dan cried, wincing.

'Good.' Lily released his face and returned to where she'd been standing, repositioning herself as if nothing had happened.

Dan rubbed his face and glanced over at her warily. He hadn't realised the twins were her sons. It wasn't a mistake he would make again.

Ronan tapped his fingers on the desk between them as he watched the other man for a few moments. 'You've got three hours to deliver the money that was short to this office. If you do not deliver within this time, you'll be gifted with two broken legs and our business will be fully terminated. If you *do* deliver, I will put this down to an oversight on this one occasion. However, if it is ever repeated, I will do a lot worse than break your legs. Do we have an understanding?'

Dan dropped his gaze and nodded, shaking in his seat. He never should have tried to skim from these people. He wished he'd never listened to his girlfriend; her and her stupid ideas. It wasn't something he would ever attempt to do again.

'Get out of my sight,' Ronan spat, disgusted by the man. He watched as Dan hurried to the door. 'Oh, and Daniel? Our protection is no longer available to you. Take that as your payment for this *misunderstanding*. The next time you have problems with rivals or groups of lads causing trouble, you're on your own.'

Dan nodded, the devastation clear on his face. Their protection had been a godsend for him and his little takeaway, nestled in the middle of the bad end of a dodgy estate. Losing it was going to cost him big time. He slipped out of the office before Ronan could change his mind and impose a heavier sentence.

As the door closed, Ronan sighed and Lily took the now-empty seat opposite him. She pursed her lips and stubbed her cigarette out in the ashtray.

'You let him off too lightly,' she said.

'I know, but we need him,' Ronan replied. 'He launders too much for us.'

'If he thinks he can get off that lightly, he may try it again.'

'What do you suggest?'

Lily pondered for a moment. 'You've taken away his protection. Wait a few weeks then send some kids round there to mess the place up a little. Get them to leave him a warning, make it clear it's from you. Shake him up.'

Ronan nodded. 'OK.' He eyed her subtly. 'You alright?'

'I'm fine, little brother,' she replied, giving him a quick smile. 'I'm fine.'

Ronan smiled back fondly. Lily was, by nature, a calm and collected person with a shell as hard as steel. There wasn't much that rattled her. If anything, he was the one more likely to lose his head in situations like this. But to Lily, the most important thing in the world was her family. Everything she did, she did for them. She loved and protected them fiercely and no matter what happened or what any of them did, she would never hear a bad word said about them from an outsider.

He knew it stemmed from their childhood, this strong bond to the rest of the family. When he was only eight, their parents had died in a car crash and they'd been left alone in the world. Lily had been fourteen at the time, too young to legally care for him. The authorities had tried to take them away and split them up, but Lily had been too quick for them. She'd packed up their things and snuck him away before they'd made concrete arrangements, taking him into hiding until they gave up looking for them. Luckily for them, in the East End, children like them slipped through the cracks all the time, so it hadn't taken too long for the search to die down.

She'd found a cheap room and taken on whatever work she could to pay the rent and keep them fed. She looked after him and made him feel safe, holding him close when he had nightmares and hiding the harsher reality of their existence from him as much as she could. In her spare time, she taught him from old textbooks she found cheap in charity shops, since he couldn't go to school anymore. He was her little brother, and she knew her parents would have wanted her to love and protect him, no matter what.

It hadn't been an easy time for either of them, but they'd made it through relatively unscathed, together, and had built up everything they had today side by side. Ronan was forever grateful for all his sister had done for him. They may not have grown up with luxuries or with anyone else, but they had always had each other, and that was all that mattered. He knew that the need for her to protect those she loved was so deeply ingrained now that she could never change. Not that he would ever want her to. She was as hard as nails on the outside, but underneath she was the most loving person he had ever known. It was a rare and wonderful combination.

'When's Scarlet coming in?' Lily asked, pulling another cigarette out of the box on the desk and lighting up. She took a drag and blew out the smoke, pushing her tight blonde curls out of her face. Scarlet had still not made a decision about what she wanted to do long term, but she'd asked if she could work in the office for a few weeks over the summer to make some extra cash. Lily had taken this as a sign that the girl was wavering. If she wanted to be in here for the summer, maybe they could persuade her to stay on for good.

'In a few days. She's just taking a little break after finishing all her exams before she starts,' he replied.

'Cath still not keen?' Lily asked.

'No.' He pulled a face. 'I've told her that it's just for a few weeks, nothing's decided. And it's only the factory Scarlet's getting into. Just because she's here doesn't mean she has to be involved with everything else.'

Lily tilted her head to the side and raised her eyebrows at him.

'Well…' He waved his hand dismissively. 'If she's only here for the summer, I mean. She still hasn't confirmed what she wants to do yet, either way.'

'Everything is linked into this place, Ronan. All of it. Unless you put her on post duty and nothing else, she'll have to under-stand how it all works at the very least. And actually,' she added, 'it will be dangerous if she doesn't. If she's in the know, she'll be able to cover things up properly if anyone comes snooping. If she's not, she could accidentally slip up. Knowledge is power, after all.'

Ronan exhaled heavily. After several heated discussions with Cath about Scarlet coming here at all, she'd had no choice but to relent – but not before making him swear that he'd keep their daughter away from their more nefarious enterprises. He'd been loath to promise her this, knowing it would be impossible, but she'd refused to let it go. Now he felt trapped between a rock and a hard place. Lily was right. It was stupid to allow Scarlet into the business and yet keep her in the dark, even for a few weeks. It could cause all sorts of problems, and Scarlet herself would just end up confused and frustrated. But what choice did he have? If she decided to stay on, and he hoped she would, at that point he would have to go against his wife's wishes and open up his world to Scarlet. And as elated as he'd be to bring his daughter into the fold, the argument wasn't something he was looking forward to. But for now he could keep the peace for just a little while longer. He rubbed his forehead.

'We can cross that bridge later,' he said. 'There's enough to keep her busy just on the paperwork side of things. Orders, updating client details, she can help with the accounts…' he reeled off.

'OK.' Lily dropped it. She knew when to push and when not to, and she knew that right now Cath was putting a lot of pressure on her brother. She turned her attention back to Dan.

'You know, we need to be able to pull our business instantaneously, if the need arises,' she said, giving Ronan a serious look. 'We shouldn't have to be careful because we *need* someone like Dan. It makes us look weak.'

'There's too much going through there to place elsewhere though,' Ronan replied. 'If we push that amount through the others suddenly, it will flag up. Even if we spread it thin. We're pushing the limits as it is. I don't know any other takeaway that banks that sort of cash each week.'

Lily put the cigarette to her deep red lips and took another slow drag. 'Then we need to look at expanding.'

'The factory isn't set up to take on any more contracts,' Ronan said, shaking his head.

'That's fine,' Lily argued, sitting forward. 'We can plough some money into more machinery.'

'There's no space.'

'There is if we move what we have around and clear out that big back store. That's wasted space,' Lily responded.

'Then we'd have more legitimate money coming in, which would bring more work but still nowhere new to launder the excess from elsewhere. It doesn't solve the problem,' Ronan said exasperatedly. He sat back in his chair and frowned.

'I wasn't talking about keeping it straight. We wouldn't need to actually bring on the new contracts, just make it look like we have. Which means we can launder more cash straight through here,' Lily replied.

Ronan shook his head. 'No, this place was supposed to stay more clean than dirty. There isn't too much going through it right now – if we get investigated we can hide what we don't want them to see. If we do that, it increases the risk too much.'

'You have to take some risk to grow, Ronan,' Lily pushed.

'Some, yes. But that's too much. I think we're better off just finding a couple more small businesses we can set up the laundry through.'

Lily sighed. Ronan didn't like change; he never had. It had always been her who had dragged them up, level by level. And every time, once she'd forced him out of his comfort zone, he'd executed things perfectly. He was brilliant, when he put his mind to it. But he hated her idea, and she couldn't think of any other viable options right now.

It was times like these she wished she could pull Scarlet into the conversation. She was young and green, yes, but the girl had a head full of fresh new ideas. Ideas that were sharp and creative. The ideas Lily had implemented of hers within the factory had been nothing less than brilliant. Scarlet was a problem solver, and that was exactly what the firm needed right now.

Her phone began to vibrate across the desk between them and she glanced at the screen. 'We'll revisit this conversation,' she said, giving him a hard look. Standing up, she quickly grabbed her car keys and answered the phone. 'Cillian, what is it?'

'You need to get over here now,' came the urgent voice of her son. 'Things have gone tits up. It's bad, Mum. And when I say bad... I mean really fucking bad.'

CHAPTER FOUR

Lily turned off the road and down the dirt track that led towards the large old barn set in the middle of nowhere. They rented it from the farmer who owned the land for cash and gave no names, ensuring there was no paperwork. With no other buildings around for a couple of miles and the barn set back from the road behind a copse of trees, it was the perfect place for them to hold stolen goods until the heat died down and they could sell them on.

This was a lucrative business for them, the stealing and selling on of high-end goods. Lily had gained enough contacts over the years to be able to easily source the highly guarded planned routes for truckers transporting goods into and around the country. She carefully selected the trucks, planned out all the details, then her sons pulled the heists. It was a well-oiled operation.

Sometimes they were able to get in and out of the back whilst the trucker slept. This was the easiest way, but not always possible. Other times they would stage some sort of road block and hold the driver at knife point whilst they ransacked the back. Occasionally, if the truck was small and the load was too large to move quickly, they would take the whole vehicle. This was rare, as getting rid of the truck was a mission in itself. But sometimes it was worth it. Today had been one of these instances. The truck was small, but it had been full to the brim with Louis Vuitton handbags and shoes. These sold like hotcakes on the black market, and with the route being so rural, it had been too good an opportunity to miss.

The plan had been simple. Cillian was to stage a breakdown in the middle of the road and when the truck stopped and the driver got out, Connor would grab him from behind, tie him up and leave him a few metres into the nearby woods. It was so out of the way, the chances of anyone coming across him were slim to none. They would then come back later to release him, of course, but only after they'd successfully hidden the goods and disposed of the truck. The driver would then make his long, slow way to the nearest sign of civilisation and report the heist to the police. But with no truck left to scour for evidence and the only description he'd be able to give being two men all in black with balaclavas, the case would go cold. It always did. However this time, there had been a problem.

Lily didn't know what the problem was as yet. None of them ever discussed business over the phone, just in case anyone was listening in.

She pulled the car in behind the treeline and glanced back towards the road, double checking no one else was nearby. She flicked her curls back over her shoulder and locked her jaw before walking purposefully towards the barn, avoiding the more uneven ground and muddy patches in order to protect her black patent high heels.

As she reached the door of the barn, Connor ran over and pushed her back outside.

'What the hell!' Lily exclaimed. 'What are you playing at?' She pulled back and straightened herself, looking at her son crossly.

'Sorry, Mum,' he said, glancing back in.

'Why have you still got your mask on?' she asked, looking him up and down with a frown.

'You'll see,' he said heavily. 'You need one on too.' He handed her a balaclava and she raised an eyebrow at him, unimpressed. 'Go on, please.'

She tutted and pulled it over her head, but no matter how much she tried to tuck them in, her wild curls still stuck out the bottom. Connor made a sound of annoyance and disappeared back into the barn. A few seconds later he reappeared holding a black zip-up hoody.

'Here, shove this on and pull up the hood. That should do it.'

'You are joking?' Lily looked down at her outfit pointedly. At forty-five, Lily was as fashion conscious as she had been twenty years before. Her slim legs were encased in a knee-length black leather pencil skirt which was paired with a thin black turtleneck. It was a suitably sleek and daring look.

'Nope. No jokes today. Unfortunately,' he added in an irate tone. Connor held out the offending jumper and waited. With a look of disgust, Lily grabbed it and shoved it on, doing up the zip and pulling the hood up to hide her bright gold hair. The jumper swamped her slight frame and hung almost to her knees, accentuating her shortness, but Connor knew better than to point this out. 'OK, let's go.'

'So now you've got me dressed like a teenage reprobate, what's going on?'

'It's easier to just show you.'

Connor led the way into the barn and Lily followed, pausing just inside to allow her eyes to adjust to the dim light within. The truck had been backed up into the barn so that the brothers could unload the contents along the back wall, but instead of a tidy pile of designer goods, all Lily could see was Cillian sat on a wooden stool, staring into the open back of the truck.

The fact the truck was still here was a problem in itself. The longer it was in their possession, the higher the risk. They needed to solve whatever the problem was and get rid of it quickly.

'What are you doing?' she asked. 'Why haven't you started unloading?' She walked towards him. 'Is it not what we were expecting? And what is that smell…' The thin, mewling cry of a baby pierced the air and stopped Lily dead in her tracks. Her dark eyes widened. 'What in the devil's name—'

'No, Mum,' Connor said heavily. 'It ain't what we were expecting at all.'

CHAPTER FIVE

'Jesus Christ,' Lily gasped as she looked around the door into the truck. Her hands flew to her mouth.

In between the stacked boxes holding the goods they'd been aiming for, several bodies lay unmoving. After taking a moment to process her shock, Lily took stock of what they were dealing with. A man and a woman lay together slightly twisted, face down. The woman's hand was gripping that of a boy who was maybe twelve or thirteen, and the fourth body belonged to a teenage girl not much older.

'The baby?' Lily asked.

Cillian pointed towards the back and Lily shifted to look around one of the boxes. At the very back of the truck, huddled in the corner, was a little girl no more than four or five years old. Her big brown eyes stared back into Lily's, terrified. In her arms, wrapped in a dirty blanket, she clutched the baby Lily had heard cry out.

Tears stung the back of Lily's eyes and she glanced away for a moment to dispel them. She placed her hands on her hips and turned in a slow circle taking deep breaths, before returning her gaze to the truck.

'Hey,' she called softly to the girl, leaning in. Before she could say any more, the girl began to scream and tried to push further back into the corner, gripping the baby as tightly as she could. The baby began to cry, distressed at the tight hold. Lily held her hands up and stepped back. 'OK, it's OK,' she crooned. 'I won't hurt you.'

'We've tried getting to her but she just screams like that every time we go near,' Connor said.

'Well of course she does,' Lily answered, eying her sons. 'Look at us. You'd be scared too, especially after all she must have been through.' After a second of deliberation, Lily discarded the hoody and pulled off the balaclava.

'Mum!' Cillian started.

'It's fine, she's too young to give over any information that's solid enough to incriminate us. What can she say? Some blonde lady talked to her somewhere she don't know in a language she likely don't speak? She probably don't even realise the truck's been nicked. Keep yours on though. A blonde lady with twins to your description ain't so common.'

Shaking out her hair she peered back through the dark truck at the girl and smiled. 'It's OK,' she said softly. She picked up a bottle of water and kicked off her shoes, then pulled herself up into the truck. The girl wailed in fright once more, but this time Lily didn't pause. Carefully stepping around the dead bodies strewn across the floor, she made her way to the back. As she moved, she tried not to breathe in through her nose. The stench was overwhelming.

She kneeled down a couple of feet away from the trembling child and put the water down in front of her. She could see the girl's lips were dry, and her sunken eyes latched onto the water.

'Hey, little love.' Lily pulled her attention back up and then gestured towards the baby. 'Can I see?' She held her arms out and the girl pulled the infant back with fresh wariness. 'It's OK.' Lily bit her lip and looked back at the body of the woman on the floor. She pointed to the baby and then the mother, then pointed at her sons and herself. 'I'm a mummy too. Those are my babies. Let me see, eh?' She held her arms out once more and waited, giving the girl an encouraging smile.

Tears fell from the child's eyes as she fought with her desperate need to drink the water against the need to protect her younger sibling. Eventually, her thirst won out and she nervously relaxed her grip. Lily slowly reached forward and took the baby from her, freeing the little girl's arms up to grab the bottle of water. She gulped it down noisily whilst Lily unwrapped the dirty blanket holding the baby.

Lily swallowed the wave of pity that came over her as she uncovered the little mite. The only thing he wore was a nappy which was so full that he'd soiled through it and into the blanket. His ribs jutted out of his tiny chest, and his cry as she checked him over was weak. He needed milk, and soon, if he was going to survive much longer.

Tossing the blanket into another corner, she called back over her shoulder. 'Pass me that hoody.'

Connor threw it in and she wrapped it around the baby. The girl had finished the water and was now staring at her silently. Lily stood up, the baby still in her arms, and the girl started to panic.

'It's OK.' She held her hand out. 'Come on. Come with me.'

The girl tentatively placed her hand in Lily's, and slowly Lily guided her out of the truck. As they passed the bodies of the people she presumed were the girl's family, Lily pulled her in under her arm and put her hand over her eyes. 'Don't look, my little love. They're sleeping now,' she said gently.

Lily jumped down with the baby and then turned to help the girl to the floor. She gave the baby back to her and sat her down on a stool out of the way as she tried to think over what she was going to do.

Watching the sorry pair, Lily's heart bled for them. The girl was skin and bones, her face sunken with hunger, and she looked like she was about to pass out. She guessed the only reason they were the last ones alive was that the parents had probably given the youngest ones the last of the food and water. They were clearly migrants who had managed to hide in the truck in the hope they would make it here for a better life, though where from was anyone's guess.

'I need to get them home,' she decided out loud.

'Home?' Cillian questioned with a frown. 'And then what?'

'And then I'll feed them, bath them, get them in some clean clothes and let them sleep in a warm bed,' Lily replied. 'And when they're in less of a bad way, I'll take them to a hospital and leave them somewhere safe where the authorities can take them into care.'

'Can't you just take them there now?' he asked. This was a stupid idea to his mind. Just another risk they didn't need to be taking.

'Cillian Drew,' Lily snapped, 'look at the state of them. They're this close to either their hearts giving out or dying of pure terror. They've lost everything in the world. Some comfort and care is little enough to give, and it's the right thing to do. And you should thank the good Lord that *you* weren't ever in a situation like this. The only real difference between you and them is where you were born, you know.' She eyed him with a hard look, and he had the grace to glance away in shame.

'Of course,' he agreed. 'What do you need for them? Me and Connor can go do a shop.'

Lily nodded. This was more like the boy she'd raised. 'I'll make you a list. Then you can stick around and watch them while they sleep so I can go and see Ray.'

'What do you need Ray for?' Connor asked with a small growl of annoyance. Ray Renshaw was their mother's long-term casual romance. He ran most of South London and was a force to be reckoned with, which was the only reason the brothers hadn't seen him off over the years.

'We need a clean-up crew,' Lily replied, ignoring the underlying tone in her son's voice. She glanced back into the lorry and shook her head. 'We need this dealt with.'

The brothers looked at each other. 'We'll clean it up – you don't need Ray,' Cillian said.

'No, I don't want you touching this.'

'Oh, come on, it ain't like we haven't dealt with a body before. And no one will be looking for these ones,' Connor protested.

'I'm well aware of your past experiences with bodies, Connor,' Lily replied, her patience waning. 'And if this was just the one body it would be fine. Two, sure, OK. We'd figure it out. But there are four bodies in there. *Four*,' she repeated sharply. 'I'm asking Ray to lend us a clean-up crew and that will be the end of it. Are we clear?'

Connor sighed irritably and began shutting up the truck. Cillian saluted with a wry smile. When their mother used that calm tone with a sharp edge, there was to be no further argument. They all knew who was in charge here.

'Good.' Walking back over to the girl, she placed a hand on her shoulder before gently taking the baby. 'Come,' she beckoned, waiting for her to follow.

As she walked the orphaned children out to her car, Lily exhaled heavily. This was not how this heist was supposed to have gone down. Even if she could sort the bodies out quickly, they still needed to get rid of the truck in good enough time to go and release the driver from where they'd left him tied up. The clock was ticking, and the risk increased with every second. Glancing up to the skies, she said a silent prayer that she could sort this latest nightmare out without any more surprises.

CHAPTER SIX

Lily stepped out of the taxi and stared up at the large dark brick building. The St Heliers Tavern was notorious, not just in the local area but throughout London. If you weren't part of the underworld – and on the right side of that underworld – it was far from safe to set foot inside. For Lily Drew though, it was just another day in the life. Stepping forward, she approached the front door and marched in.

The chatter inside the busy pub paused for a moment, before resuming as its current inhabitants registered her as one of their own. She smiled at the barman, who inclined his head to the side to indicate Ray was in his usual booth. With a nod of thanks, Lily made her way over to the end of the pub where she knew she would find him.

She heard him before she saw him through the crowds of people. It was Friday night, the busiest night of the week for this particular venue. As she caught a glimpse, she could see he was entertaining at his table – two of his men and a few young women sat around him, hanging off his every word as he shared his latest joke.

'And then he said...' Ray's craggy voice tailed off as he caught sight of Lily. His rugged face lit up. 'Well, if it ain't my siren of the underworld,' he said with a grin. 'Lily Drew.'

'Hello, Ray,' she said, reaching the table. She waited.

'Right, go on then,' Ray said to the group of people around him. 'Fuck off.'

No one needed to be told twice. The group dispersed and Ray rose to greet Lily properly.

'You're a sight for sore eyes,' he said, leaning forward to kiss her.

She turned her head to the side, ensuring the kiss landed on her cheek, then allowed him to lead her to a seat. 'Your view seemed to be well enough without me,' she replied, getting comfortable.

'No view is ever well enough without you in it, Lil.' Ray smiled – a warm, genuine smile.

Ray had been in love with Lily, and indeed she him, for many years and the two of them shared a relationship of sorts. But Lily always kept him carefully at arm's length and refused to call what they had anything more than a friendship with benefits. It had been this way for as long as she could remember, despite his ongoing and unsuccessful attempts to turn it into something more. He never gave up trying though, and every time she pushed him back he would gracefully retreat and claim in good humour that tying her down and making an honest – or at least fairly honest – woman of her was one of the few failures of his life.

'So…' Ray signalled to the barman. 'To what do I owe the pleasure this evening?'

Lily smiled back at him. He was in a good mood, as she'd hoped. 'It's not a social call, I'm afraid. I need your help with something.'

'What do you need?' Ray sat back and rested his arm across the back of the booth. If he was surprised, he hid it well. Fiercely independent, Lily very rarely asked for help. And when she did, it was serious.

Lily briefly took in his appearance with a look of approval. Ray always looked good. He was dressed impeccably, his black suit teamed with a crisp white shirt, its top two buttons open, a hint of chest hair peeping out at the top. His strong jaw was shaded with stubble, and his blue eyes twinkled under a pair of dark eyebrows.

She wasn't fooled by the calm appearance he displayed. She knew Ray better than anyone. His mood could swing on a sixpence if something was to rile him. He was as dangerous as they came, but he was also loyal to a fault to those he cared about. And she was lucky enough to fall into that category. Although she'd witnessed the hurricane of destruction that Ray Renshaw could create in a rage, she had never been in the line of fire.

'I need you to lend me a clean-up crew,' she said quietly, her eyes sliding sideways as she spoke, checking they weren't being overheard.

Ray's eyebrows rose in surprise. That wasn't what he'd been expecting. 'Why?' he asked.

Lily crossed her slim legs and pulled out her cigarettes as the barman reached the table with their drinks. She lit up and took a long drag, blowing the smoke out in a thin line as he walked back to the bar. She leaned forward and picked up the glass of white wine, taking a sip before she spoke.

'The boys picked up a truck earlier today—' she started.

'Oh right, what have they done then?' Ray asked with a deep laugh.

Lily's eyes flashed and she sat up straight. 'They've not done a thing,' she replied sharply, not liking his tone. Ray's laugh trailed off and he nodded for her to continue. She relaxed her shoulders. 'It was a big load, small lorry, so they took the lot. But some illegals had snuck in the back and copped it en route. I've got four bodies that need disposing of.' She didn't mention the children she'd taken back to her house. There was no need. It didn't concern Ray. It didn't concern anyone outside of their family.

Ray gave a long, low whistle, then took a sip of his brandy. 'How are you planning to get shot of the truck?' he asked.

'Chop shop. Can't exactly send it with them still inside,' she answered.

'No.' Ray rubbed his hand over his lip as he thought it through.

'It's a big ask,' Lily said, leaning forward. 'But you know I wouldn't come to you if I didn't need to. And I'll make it worth your while.'

Ray waved his hand dismissively. 'I'm not going to charge for helping you out, Lil.' He rolled his eyes. 'You're my woman, for God's sake.'

'Good friend,' Lily corrected.

'Ahh, Lil, you kill me. You really do,' Ray said, shaking his head. ''Course I'll lend you a crew. How soon do you need this sorted?'

'Tonight. The driver's still tied up.'

'Fuck's sake.' Ray ran his hand through his hair and then laughed. 'Well, there's one thing I can always say about you, Lily Drew.' He stared at her fondly. 'You never let things get boring.'

CHAPTER SEVEN

Lily returned home with a tight knot of anxiety in her stomach. She'd given Ray the location and he'd sent the crew over to take the bodies away and dispose of them. How she didn't know – or care. She trusted Ray and knew that his men were efficient enough to deal with the situation swiftly and securely. But the truck had been sitting in the barn for hours longer that it was supposed to have been. And the driver was still tied up in the woods. At least she hoped he was. Every second that went by was one more second that someone could happen across the man and release him. It was unlikely, but not impossible.

She hung her keys on the hook behind the front door as she closed it and entered the lounge where her sons sat waiting.

'Have they woken?' she asked.

'The baby did, but I gave him more milk like you said and he went back down,' Cillian answered. 'The girl hasn't stirred at all.'

'Good – she needs rest, poor mite. Listen, you stay here with them. Connor, you come with me. We've got a lot to do.' Without waiting to hear the protest she knew would escape Cillian's lips, she turned and marched back out.

An hour later, Lily and Connor pulled up to the barn and cut the engine. They stepped out. It was dark, the moon hidden by thick cloud, and without the artificial lights they were used to in the city, they had to squint to make out Ronan's broad figure as he ambled towards them.

'They've just left, about ten minutes ago,' he said as he reached them. 'It's clear – the truck can go. Steve's at the chop shop waiting; he just needs a five-minute heads up to get the gate open as it's all locked up for the night.'

'OK.' Lily nodded and walked into the barn.

The truck sat where they'd left it earlier, clear now the goods had been stacked neatly against the back wall by Ronan and the bodies and accompanying items had been removed by Ray's men.

'Connor, take my car and get to the driver. I'll confirm when the drop-off is done and you can set him loose,' Lily ordered. 'Ronan, do you want to drive the truck and I'll follow in your car?'

'Sure,' he replied. 'I've switched the plates already, so let's get on the road.' He checked his watch with a frown then jumped up into the cab of the truck.

Lily nodded to Connor. 'You stay in touch now,' she said. 'And hurry.'

'Will do.'

As Connor jogged back out to the car, a heavy feeling settled in her stomach. Was the worst of the night over? She prayed to the heavens that it was.

*

Connor pulled off the road onto the grass verge of the narrow country lane and stepped out, pulling the balaclava back over his head. He rubbed his arms as the chill of the evening seeped through his clothes then walked briskly down the road a few metres before entering the dark wood. Pulling out his phone, he turned on the torch, unable to see anything at all under the canopy of leaves blocking out what little light the cloudy night provided. He shone it around, trying to find the marks he'd left earlier to lead him back to the driver. Eventually, after checking several trees, he found what he was looking for and tramped deeper into the woods. The dried leaves and twigs underfoot crackled as he moved, which he knew would alert the driver to his presence. He waited for the expected call of help. This was about the time they all started calling for help. But no sound came, and Connor frowned.

He paused for a moment and listened. Perhaps due to the late hour and the darkness that engulfed them, the driver was too scared to call out. Usually, they wouldn't have left him alone and bound for so long. It was normally still light when they released them.

'Oi,' he called out, making his voice intentionally gruff so it was less recognisable.

Silence.

'It's time to go,' he called again.

Still no reply. He tutted in annoyance and continued towards where he thought he remembered leaving the man.

He turned the phone slowly, shining the torch on each tree until he found the rope they'd left tied around the trunk. Making his way over, he flicked out his knife, ready to cut through it and let the man trussed up around the other side go free. Once or twice they'd tried their luck when they'd been freed, but most of the time they just ran for the hills straight away. This guy wouldn't be any trouble, he wagered. He was a lot older and weedy to boot.

'Come on then, let's get these off you...' Connor tailed off and his jaw dropped in horror as he rounded the tree to where he'd left the driver hours before.

The rope was still secured to the tree trunk, but the man whose wrists and ankles had been bound by it was gone. He kneeled down next to the frayed end and picked it up, aghast.

'What the fuck?' he breathed. As his gaze dropped, it landed on a small flat stone with a sharp edge. His mind quickly pieced together what must have happened and he groaned.

Quickly, Connor used the knife in his hand to saw through the remaining rope. He had no idea how long he had before the police arrived here to sweep the scene for evidence, and he certainly wasn't leaving it behind as a gift. Pulling it away from the tree, he grabbed the stone for good measure and began to run through the trees, back the way he'd come. The ground was uneven and he stumbled but soon righted himself without stopping. He needed to get out of here – and quickly.

Reaching the car, he slid to a stop and flung the door open before jumping in and turning the key faster than he ever had before in his life. The big black Mercedes roared to life, and he slammed his foot down on the accelerator, turning it around with a kick of the back wheels before screeching off down the road.

Racing away, he paid no mind to the speed limit, knowing only that he needed to put as much distance as he could between that place and himself before the police swarmed in. He tapped at the backlit screen in the centre console and found his mother's number.

'Come on, come on, come *on*,' he muttered, his tone laden with frustration. He had no idea how long it had been since the driver had escaped – he hadn't yet led the police back to the woods, but that didn't mean he hadn't already reported it. He could be there in the station now, telling them everything about the hijacking and his subsequent kidnapping. They could already have sent out an alert about the truck. It would be the first thing they did. And if they'd already done that, every police patrol within a hundred miles would be on the lookout for it.

Lily finally picked up. 'Connor.' Her calm voice filled the car as she greeted him.

'He's not there,' Connor yelled, his panic finally coming to the fore. 'The truck's hot – get the fuck off the road *now!*'

CHAPTER EIGHT

Lily's dark eyes widened and her hands gripped the steering wheel tighter as she heard Connor's panicked warning come down the line. She ended the call without wasting time answering him and immediately dialled Ronan's number, her red lips forming a grim line. The phone began to ring, and she waited for him to pick up.

'Come on, Ronan,' she whispered, staring at the tail of the truck. She backed off slightly and checked all her mirrors once more for any sign of the police. They were coming into a more built-up area now, where there was traffic and cameras, and despite the fact they'd changed the number plate to avoid being picked up on that, if the police were already alerted to a stolen truck of this description, they could still be pulled over.

'What's up, Lil?' Ronan finally answered.

'The driver's gone and we don't know how long he's been gone for, so the truck may already have been reported,' she said quickly.

'Shit,' Ronan cursed.

There was a long silence and Lily waited for him to think things over. It was ultimately his decision as to how they would handle this, as he was the one in the hot seat. 'It's too late to turn back,' he said eventually. 'If we turn around, we'd spend more time getting this back into hiding than we would if we just deliver it. We're going to have to risk it.'

'You're sure?' Lily asked. 'We could find a quiet car park and hide out until the search dies down.'

'We'd be sitting ducks. They'll search the car parks and our DNA will be all over this. It needs to be destroyed tonight.'

Lily nodded to herself in the darkness. Ronan was right. 'OK, let's just get there.'

They turned onto the slip road that led them to the South Circular, a busy road teeming with police cars at the best of times, but one they could no longer avoid at this point in their journey. Lily's hands tightened once more on the wheel and her heart began to race. 'This is it now, Ronan,' she said heavily. 'The final stretch. Just a couple of junctions and we're there.'

'I hope to God that's all there is to it,' he replied quietly.

Lily exhaled slowly. She could hear the tension in her brother's voice. He was worried and rightly so. They were more vulnerable than they had ever been right now, and every second that passed felt like a minute.

They joined the busy dual carriageway, and Lily carefully edged out into the second lane, coming up alongside the truck. She slowed slightly, so as not to leave him behind. 'Hey,' she said, glancing sideways at him with what she hoped was an encouraging smile. 'Nearly there. I'm going to go now and ring Steve, OK? Let him know to open up ready for us.'

'Sure, tell him that… Shit!'

Lily glanced sideways at him again and saw him staring into the wing mirror with an expression of horror. She looked through her rear-view and saw what he'd spotted. A patrol car had just pulled up behind her.

'It's going to be OK, Ronan,' she said, her tone much calmer and more confident than she felt. 'They're not looking at us.' But as she said this, one of them began eyeing the truck.

'They're looking, Lily,' Ronan replied, his tone becoming urgent. 'They're definitely fucking looking.'

'Alright, just calm down,' she said, watching the car. They were indeed looking at the truck and had begun chatting between themselves. 'It's going to be OK.' But even as she said it, she wasn't so sure this was true.

Up ahead was a set of traffic lights, and as they approached the junction, the lights turned red. They had no choice but to slow both vehicles, and Ronan began almost incoherently cursing in panic. Lily glanced back at the patrol car again and watched as one of them looked down towards the screen in his hands. He was about to run the plates, she realised. And if he ran the plates, he would see that they were fake and then Ronan would definitely be pulled over, whether it had been reported yet or not. She swore under her breath and made a swift decision.

'Ronan, just call Steve and get the truck there,' she ordered. 'I've got you covered.' Without waiting for a reply, she ended the call and put the car into gear. Slamming her foot down on the accelerator, she pulled the car forward with a screech of the wheels and sped through the red light and on down the road.

As expected, the patrol car immediately set off after her, blue lights and siren coming on a moment later. She watched them in her rear-view as she continued picking up speed. As Ronan and the truck became smaller in the distance, she slowed and turned down a side road, pulling to a stop a few metres down as the patrol car caught up.

She switched off the engine and got out of the car. 'Is everything OK, officers?' she asked, giving a broad smile as they ran over.

CHAPTER NINE

Scarlet stared down at the St Andrews prospectus once more, studying the eager happy faces of the students on the cover as she lay on top of the bed. They looked so happy. She let herself imagine them all going for lunch together and heading to the vaulted library to study as exams loomed. But then she let the image go. They were models, just posing for the brochure. Dropping the pages, she stared off into the distance and began to picture herself instead making new friends and new memories, and her mouth curled up into a smile.

Her back began to ache so she sat up, twisting her legs up underneath her. Her gaze came to rest on a picture of her family that she kept by the bed and her smile softened. Going to St Andrews meant leaving them. The thought sent a stab of pain through her heart and she sighed. How was she going to take this next step in her life without the people who meant the most by her side? They wouldn't even be around the corner; they would be in a whole different country.

She looked down at the prospectus again and the smiling faces suddenly didn't appear so welcoming. *What would the people be like?* she wondered. St Andrews was one of the most prestigious universities in the UK. She had earned her place through impeccable grades, but it was a place where royalty had been. How on earth was she supposed to fit in with people like that? Scarlet Drew, a girl from the East End whose father ran a criminal empire. Would they see the darkness inside her?

Memories flickered. The memory of her father teaching her the rules of surviving the underworld. The memory of Aunt Lily pulling the trigger on the man in the lounge. As that played out in her mind, the shot rang out as loudly in her head as it had that day. She wasn't normal like the other students. She lived in a world and had seen things that none of them would have ever experienced. Would that be obvious? The other students might be naïve and kind, or they might rally against the obvious outsider. And she'd be going in alone. It wouldn't be like walking into the family business.

Once more the reminder of all she was throwing away came forth and she sighed. It was everything her father wanted, her to take her rightful place alongside him and her aunt and cousins. And she'd fit right in, among people who loved her, in a world she already understood. But despite how easy that would be, she couldn't let go of her curiosity. She needed to go to St Andrews. She needed to start her own adventure and carve her own path in life. Whatever that may be. But first she needed to find the courage to tell her father.

Scarlet rubbed her forehead, pushed her long dark hair back and stared into the mirror on the wall. A pair of solemn grey-blue eyes stared back at her. Then her vision split, presenting two versions of herself side by side. The two versions that lived inside her body, that tore at her heart so. They both looked exactly the same as she studied them, except for one thing – their choice of weapon. In one's hand there was a degree – a first, with honours listed after her name. And in the other's was a gun.

CHAPTER TEN

The double doors opened in front of Lily, revealing the bright summer sunshine. Cillian was waiting in his car in the side street nearby. She opened the door and slipped in beside him, discarding the hat and scarf that had been carefully hiding her identity as he drove off into the busy London traffic.

'All OK?' he asked.

'Fine,' she replied.

She turned to look out of the window, swallowing the lump in her throat as the feeling of the trusting little girl's hand still lingered on her palm. She had just dropped the two children off in the waiting room of the children's hospital, wrapped up warm in new clothes, with full stomachs, a bag of supplies and a note explaining that they had been found on the side of a road alone and that they spoke no English. It had been one of the hardest things she'd ever done, leaving them alone, but they would be noticed soon enough and given the help they needed. She prayed they would be kept together and given a loving home someday.

The feel of the little girl's hand in hers had also brought forth memories of holding another little hand. Her daughter, Ruby, had once been a sweet, innocent child too. She had looked up to her with the same trust and held on tight, never pulling away. But that had been a very long time ago. And the woman she had grown into was a complete stranger to Lily.

Ruby Drew was a year younger than the twins, but unlike her brothers, who Lily saw every day, Ruby only turned up when she wanted something. And even then it was usually with an insult or an argument. Her choices in life were a constant source of heartache for Lily, but after years of trying – and failing – to help her, she'd had to accept that Ruby was a soul who was determinedly set on a path of self-destruction and nothing she could do would stop her.

'Come on, let's pick up your brother,' she said, pushing thoughts of Ruby back out of her mind. They only led to worry, and worrying never seemed to help in this particular case. 'We've got work to do, sorting out last night's haul. I think a lot of it will have to go through the back doors,' she mused, purposely pushing her mind towards work.

'You don't want it going through the markets?' Cillian asked resentfully.

Most of the items they stole were carefully filtered down through a string of market stalls they owned, but some things were better suited to other black-market channels. Certain shops had a secret back room reserved for select customers who were in the know. High-end goods tended to trade better here and reach a higher price, though they didn't own these places so they lost a percentage to the trader. This was a safer option, and they did well out of it, but Cillian resented handing over so much of their profit to someone else after they'd done all the hard work and taken the majority of the risks. He made no secret of his feelings either, and so Lily shot him a look to let him know she'd noted his tone.

'You know it's too high-end for that.'

'Mm.' Cillian grumbled, but didn't bother complaining. It wouldn't get him anywhere. 'By the way, I think Connor's having a lie-in today,' he said. 'It was a late night,' he added, seeing his mother's eyebrows shoot upwards.

'Yes, it was. For all of us,' she replied. 'He can rest tomorrow, when the work is done. Today we need to move – he knows that.'

'Yeah, but, I mean…' Cillian's chiselled jaw opened and shut as he tried to locate a good excuse for his brother so Lily would leave him in peace, but he couldn't seem to find one.

Lily glanced sideways at her handsome son and eyed his face critically. 'What's going on with this constant five o'clock shadow you've got going on lately?' she asked. 'Has your razor broken?'

'It's called *designer stubble*, and the girls laaaave it.' He raised his eyebrows with a wink and a cocky smile.

'Oh yeah?' Lily laughed, the lines around her eyes crinkling up prettily. 'Who told you that then?'

'Loads of 'em, Mum,' he replied. 'That Tracey from the hairdresser's—'

'The redhead you finished with a few weeks ago?' Lily interjected.

'Yep, her. Then there's Sandy from the bar at Ronnie's, Chastity, Connor's bit of stuff—'

'Chastity,' Lily snorted derisively. 'That girl wouldn't know the meaning of the word if it hit her in the face with a— Oh!' She rounded on Cillian as the penny suddenly dropped. 'That's what he's really doing this morning, ain't it?' she demanded. 'He's got that bit of skirt round wasting his time when he should be out bloody working!'

Cillian groaned as he realised he'd accidentally dropped his brother right in it. There was a lot that Lily would forgive her sons, but not neglecting the business in favour of a girl. Never that. Especially this one.

Chastity had a reputation around the estate she lived on for being not only an easy ride, but a class A gold-digger too, something that had been brought to Lily's attention when she'd set her sights on Connor. She'd left behind a string of ex-boyfriends who had been rinsed and dumped as soon as their pockets were empty, along with a few who swore blind she'd robbed them in the process. But Connor seemed unfazed by this for some reason Lily couldn't fathom.

'Right. Put your foot down and get us there now. I'm not having that flash-in-the-pan stopping him from helping out today,' Lily ordered, annoyed.

Both her boys had always kept up a steady, fast-moving string of girls, and they were *always* the wrong sort in her opinion. But the fact they got bored easily meant that she never had to endure any one of them for too long. Unfortunately though, despite Lily's findings, Chastity had been around for a little longer than most.

'Yes, Mum.'

Ten minutes later they pulled up outside Connor's block of flats. Lily marched into the building and went up via the lift to her son's floor. Pulling her key out of her purse, she unlocked the door and Cillian groaned behind her.

'Come on, Mum, at least knock...'

'I certainly will not,' Lily responded indignantly, pursing her red lips together.

The door swung open into Connor's open-plan living room and she stalked in, pulling herself up to full height. Connor froze on his way into the lounge from the kitchen carrying two cups of tea in nothing but his boxers. His brown eyes widened in guilty shock as he saw his mother standing there, her expression furious.

'Hello, Mum,' he said flatly.

'Don't you *hello* me,' Lily replied, placing her hands on her slender hips. 'Getting your brother to tell me how tired you are when there's work to be done, and really you're here entertaining.'

She purposely ignored the half-naked blonde curled up on her son's sofa.

'Oh, come on, Mum, it's Saturday, for God's sake,' he complained with an edge of annoyance. He shot Cillian a murderous look. He really was tired after all the events of the previous night and could have done with the morning off.

'Exactly,' she countered. 'Which is the best day of the week for eager shoppers.' She gave him a meaningful look. As much as she knew Chastity was aware of their general business, she didn't want to say too much in front of the girl. She could already see the calculated gleam in the girl's eye as she watched her in her peripheral vision. 'So we need to get things moving now, before the rush of the day.'

Connor sighed. There was no point fighting it – she was right. They needed to get all the designer shoes and handbags in the back doors of the black-market shops before midday if they hoped to shift them on quickly. And he knew this would be the plan without needing to ask. Their haul was too highbrow for the markets.

Lily saw the resignation sink in and relaxed her shoulders. 'Right. Get dressed then – we don't have all day.'

'*Actually*, Mrs Drew,' Chastity piped up from the couch in a girlish tone that irritated Lily straight away, 'we're going out shopping today, aren't we, babe?' She gave Lily a smug smile. 'There's a gorgeous bracelet I've seen that I want to show Connor.'

'Oh yeah,' Lily said drily. 'And why's that then?'

Chastity blinked. 'Why's what?'

'Why do you want to show Connor?' Lily raised an eyebrow and waited.

'Well, because I like it,' she replied, glancing over to Connor in the hope he would chime in.

'Then go buy it and show it off to him later,' Lily said sharply. 'Though I can't imagine he'd be much interested in seeing it – he doesn't wear bracelets himself.'

Chastity's cheeks flooded with colour as Lily called her out. She'd obviously wanted to show Connor in the hope that he would buy it for her because it was far too expensive a piece for her own wallet.

Cillian walked over to the window and looked out across the smoky rooftops below as they waited for Connor to dress. Lily folded her arms and began pacing, keeping one subtle eye on the scantily covered girl on the sofa. Chastity was watching her with a sly gaze. Lily knew what was going through her mind. She saw her as a threat to her set-up with Connor. Lily was the only thing that could get in the way of her access to his wallet, like it had today. Which meant that she was about to go one of two ways. Either she would fight, make some sort of stand and try to pitch Connor against her, or she would try to befriend her to carve out some sort of position for herself in their family, in order to cement her ongoing access to his wallet. Neither of which would work, but Lily was curious to see which option she would choose.

Connor reappeared doing up the last button of his shirt and made a beeline for his suit jacket hanging by the door. Cillian immediately fell into step beside him, and Lily waited for Connor to shrug on the jacket.

'Mrs Drew,' Chastity began, her tone loaded.

Here we go, Lily thought.

'I was thinking…' She smiled, the sweetness of the action so fake Lily almost rolled her eyes. 'Why don't I cook us all a nice roast dinner tomorrow, here at Connor's flat. We could all sit down and get to know each other better, couldn't we?'

Her naturally whiny tone set Lily's teeth on edge and she tried not to grind them. She looked at Connor, who hid a smile and ducked out before she answered. He knew exactly how this was going to go. She turned to Chastity as her boys disappeared through the door.

'Sundays are reserved for family, sweetheart,' she said, her expression cold. Following her sons, she called back over her shoulder. 'So fuck off back to yours.'

CHAPTER ELEVEN

As Ronan pulled into his sister's drive, he welcomed the relief he knew would come once they walked into Lily's house for the weekly family get-together. Cath wouldn't carry on in there, or at least he hoped she wouldn't. She'd been unrelentingly vocal on the drive over about Scarlet spending the summer working at the factory.

It was tradition in their family to all get together for Sunday lunch after church each week, no matter what was going on. The only person who was routinely absent was Ruby, but other than her, everyone was expected to be in attendance unless they had a very good reason not to be. It was an important tradition to Ronan and Lily. After their parents had died, family time had become more precious than ever. So now, each Sunday, Lily and Cath took it in turns to host.

'Lil! Crack that open, will ya?' Ronan greeted his sister heartily as she opened the door and handed her a bottle of red wine. 'Alright, you two?' he said, once in the large kitchen where he knew the twins would likely be hanging around in the wait for lunch.

'Pukka, thanks, Uncle Ro,' Cillian answered through a mouthful of bread.

Lily walked in with the wine and slapped his hand as he reached for another slice. 'Get off it, you gannet. Here, open this and pour a glass for your uncle. See what everyone else wants to drink too.' She made her way back around the large white marble counter and continued mixing up the gravy.

''Ello, Scar,' Cillian called warmly as their cousin entered.

Scarlet smiled broadly as she joined him, and Cath came in quietly behind her, pursing her lips and throwing Lily a tight smile as she hung her coat and tried to let go of her worries for a while.

'Hey, Cillian,' Scarlet replied. 'Hey, Connor. No Ruby today?' she asked, looking around warily.

'No, no Ruby,' Lily responded without looking up.

Scarlet visibly relaxed and sat down on one of the breakfast stools dotted along the large kitchen island. She never voiced it aloud, but Ronan knew she couldn't stand her cousin Ruby. She didn't rock up to family Sundays very often, but when she did, she always created unnecessary drama and ruined the lunch for everyone.

'So, you all set to start at the factory tomorrow then?' Connor asked.

'Yeah, all set,' Scarlet replied eagerly. 'Looking forward to jumping in and making some extra cash.'

'I'll take a glass of that wine, Cillian,' Cath said suddenly, gesturing at the bottle in his hand.

'Me too,' Lily chimed in. She smiled at Cath. 'We can have a toast to the next exciting chapter in the family. No more kids at school now, eh, Cath? Feels a bit crazy that they're all grown up.'

Cath couldn't help but smile fondly, clearly remembering all the children when they were younger. 'Yeah, is a bit weird, ain't it? No more homework, no more toys to trip over at every turn…'

'Still…' Lily took the freshly poured glasses from Cillian and handed one to Cath, chinking hers to it. 'There's still all their bloody washing to keep us busy, eh?'

They both cackled with amusement, the sound of their laughter filling the room, and Ronan smiled. The bee in his wife's bonnet had been subdued. For now, at least. His gaze moved to his sister and he caught the wink she shot him. He nodded subtly in gratitude. They always had each other's back, him and Lily. Even in the little things.

'Right.' Cath took a swig of her wine and placed it back down on the counter. 'Come on, Scarlet, let's help your aunt get all this to the table.' She picked up a plate of vegetables and Scarlet dutifully followed suit.

As they walked away, Lily went back to adding the finishing touches, so Ronan turned his head to work. 'So, how'd we do yesterday?'

'Very well once we actually got there.' Lily shot Connor a look and he swiftly busied himself with laying the table. 'More than half the stock is already gone. About another twenty per cent is aside on a promise, and the rest is such good stuff I doubt it will sit through another weekend. Should all be gone and the money in our pocket by next Sunday.'

'Christ, that's good,' Ronan replied, raising his dark eyebrows in surprise.

'It was a perfect haul. Well, other than the obvious issues,' she added. 'There was no shit to get rid of, all popular items.'

'Good, good.' Ronan nodded and his eyebrows knitted together as he thought over the implications of this.

Lily read his expression and followed his thought process correctly. 'Ro, we need to talk about expanding the factory.'

'Lil, I've told you, I don't want to keep shitting on our own doorstep.' Ronan exhaled heavily and ran a hand back through his hair, agitated.

'We can't keep pushing through so many little businesses, and we've tapped out pretty much all the viable locals anyway,' Lily argued. 'I *know* you don't want the added risk, but unless you want to downsize our business then we *have* to come up with a decent laundry for the excess.' She held her hands out to the side, exasperated. 'There are no other options, Ronan.' She glanced through at Scarlet as her niece laid the potatoes on the table. She so greatly wanted to pick that sharp mind of hers; she may even have an answer in there that neither of them had considered. But unless Scarlet chose to join them, her smart brain and all of its brilliant ideas would be leaving them very soon.

Ronan sighed and looked away, biting the inside of his cheek. She was right – they had to do something and it couldn't be a short-term fix. It wasn't that he'd been ignoring the problem, he just didn't want to dirty the factory any more than they already were. 'I know,' he said. 'Look, I have an idea, but I need to look into it more before we sit and discuss it. Give me a few days and then we'll revisit this. OK?'

Lily raised her eyebrows and gave him a long, hard look. 'OK,' she replied. 'As long as we do, Ronan. Because we're vulnerable with that much cash sitting around. I don't like it. We need it filtered off with a paper trail as soon as possible.'

'I hear you,' Ronan replied, picking up the gravy and walking through to the dining room. 'Now, come on. It's Sunday. Let's focus on what's important, yeah?'

'Of course.'

*

Lily sighed inwardly as she watched Ronan's retreating back. He was right: family was the most important thing in the world, especially on a Sunday. But what Ronan didn't seem to grasp was that this was exactly why she needed to focus on work at all times and never stop, not for anything. Because everything they did to get and to hide their money was *for* the family.

CHAPTER TWELVE

Hours later, Lily stood at the front door, waving off the last of the family. They had eaten, drunk, laughed and talked; all in all it had been a very enjoyable afternoon and evening.

The twins had had them all in stitches with their terrible tales, and the rather embellished version of Lily's rejection of Chastity's Sunday dinner offer had become the favourite funny story of the night. Now they were all finally leaving to go home and Lily was ready to unwind and go to bed. She waved until the last pair of tail-lights disappeared around the corner and then began to turn, until a parked car in the distance caught her eye.

She squinted to make out the number plate, then a knowing smile crept up on her red lips. Thoughts of heading to bed abandoned, she turned and walked into the house, locking the door behind her.

*

Ray sat in the dark in the large armchair in the corner of the office and waited, a glass of whisky in his hand. He heard the door close and then smiled in amusement as he listened to her methodically searching the downstairs rooms for him. Eventually, she reached the office. The light went on and there she was in all her glory, hands on hips and chin held high in natural defiance. A thrill rippled through him, as it always did. The same way it had for nearly thirty years.

His gaze roamed over her, drinking her in like she was the last glass of water in the desert. She wore one of her customary black-knee-length-leather-skirt-and-black-top ensembles. Her signature look. It was classic, timeless; yet daring and forward. Much like she was herself. Her mass of wild blonde curls stood proud and glorious, paying no mind to gravity. He knew she wasn't a fan of her hair, untameable as it was. But he loved it. The feel of it beneath his fingers and the sight of it on the pillow beside him gave him great joy.

His gaze finally rested on her face. Her perfect red lips held a hint of a smile, and her dark brown eyes bore into him, concealing a hundred secrets that he would never know. Maybe this was why he could never get enough of her. Because she was the one woman he would never truly see laid bare.

'And what, may I ask, do you think you're doing sneaking into my house as though we're kids again?' she asked, her tone loaded with amusement.

Ray smiled, his rugged face crinkling up handsomely with the action. 'Don't you remember, when you used to make me sneak in when we were young, so that Ronan wouldn't see me?'

Lily laughed. 'I do,' she replied. 'Though I think it's safe to assume he knows about you now,' she added.

'Of course, but it's much more fun to act like he doesn't.'

They stared at each other across the room for a few moments, the invisible connection they'd always had pulling them together.

'Did everything go OK on Friday, after my clean-up crew left?' Ray asked.

'It did.' Lily crossed to the side of the room where her drinks trolley sat and poured herself a brandy. 'There were a couple of hiccups, but it all worked out.'

'Hiccups?' he asked.

'Nothing major,' she replied. 'I earned three points on my licence, but it was a small price to pay, considering. Everything is nicely under control.' She placed the stopper back in the crystal bottle of brandy and moved to sit down in the chair nearest Ray.

'As always,' he said wryly. 'I think I've yet to see the day when Lily Drew doesn't have things *nicely under control*.'

'What can I say?' She shrugged. 'That's just how I roll.'

He laughed. 'It is. I wish you'd roll a little closer to me though.' He narrowed his eyes with a smile, testing the water. 'You know I'm still determined to make a slightly more honest woman out of you one day.'

'And I'm still determined to stay as independently dishonest as they come,' Lily immediately replied, her words as smooth as glass.

Ray nodded slowly and then let his mask drop, revealing an expression of raw honesty. 'Come on, Lil,' he said. 'I don't get it. We've spent years doing this dance. You know I love you. You know I'd move heaven and earth for you. You're the only woman I have ever seen as an equal, the only person I've ever wanted to share my life with. And I know you feel the same. This thing we have... Are we really going to go on through life not properly grabbing hold of it, not ever taking some enjoyment for ourselves?'

Lily looked down into her glass, her heart dropping. She hated it when he did this. It was hard for both of them, because the truth was, she felt exactly the same. They shared something neither of them had ever felt with anyone else. If she'd believed in the concept of soulmates, then he would have been hers. But whilst they could enjoy each other from a distance, she could never commit to him. Not in the way he wanted. Ray wanted it all, the whole shebang: marriage, a home together, a shared life. But that meant she would have to share *his* life. Not the other way around. Ray ran a much bigger firm than hers and he couldn't leave it. But on the flipside, she couldn't leave hers either. Ronan wouldn't be able to drive their firm to where it needed to be on his own, and there was no one to take over from her. Not yet anyway. If she gave in to her own selfish desires and left this family to float without her undivided attention, it would sink. And she hadn't spent her entire life building it up for it to fail.

'Ray,' she said softly, 'you know I can't leave.'

'But you wouldn't *be* leaving, Lil,' he pressed. 'You'd still be able to work as much as you like. Just because you'd move south of the river, that doesn't mean you would be abandoning your family.'

'We both know if I'm down there, with my skills, as your wife, you'll want me working alongside you. Come on, admit it, you would.'

Ray tilted his head to the side. 'I won't deny it would be great having you around for that too, but nothing else needs to change, Lil. We'd just be grabbing happiness with both hands for once, rather than snippets of time here and there when we can.'

'You know where I stand, Ray,' she replied firmly. 'And I won't be swayed. Maybe one day things will be different. Maybe one day I'll retire. But right now, I can't.'

Ray took a deep breath and sighed, then took a long drink of his whisky. He shouldn't have bought it up. It wasn't why he'd come, to try and convince her for the hundredth time to give in. He knew there was no point, not now anyway. He should have just stayed quiet and enjoyed his time with her. Now she was tense and annoyed.

It was his own fault they weren't properly together, he knew. And it was something he berated himself for daily. He had been in love with her since they were giddy teens; indeed she'd been his first love. His only love, looking back. She had adored him too. She'd always put her younger brother first, but other than Ronan, Ray had been the light of her life. But he had been young and hot-blooded and hadn't wanted to settle down and play family, which was what Lily had wanted and needed. So he had kept things light and played the field.

It shouldn't have come as a shock to him when she met someone else and settled down with him instead. He had watched from a distance as she'd set up home and had the twins and then Ruby. He'd hated Alfie, the kids' dad, with a jealous passion. Then one day Alfie up and left, having taken up with some skirt that took his fancy more than Lily. He left Lily and the kids to fend for themselves, no thought for anyone other than himself, and he was never seen again.

Ray had swooped back in, ready to be her shoulder to cry on, but she hadn't cried. Not in front of him anyway. She'd put her hard face on and just worked more furiously than ever to give the kids everything they needed. If anything the experience had just made her stronger, and although their romantic relationship had eventually blossomed again, she'd never allowed him the chance to get too close.

'Anyway,' he said, changing the subject. 'That actually wasn't why I came. I've been hearing rumblings about Harry Snow wanting to make waves with you and Ronan.'

'Oh?' Lily sat up, her irritation forgotten.

'He's been talking about poking around your turf, trying to take over some market space. Not just with you, all round. But it would affect you more than most, I guess.' He shrugged and took another sip of whisky. 'You might want to have a look into that. Approach him head-on. He's a weaselly fucker, likes to go round the houses but don't like having to deal with things face to face.'

'Yeah, I know.' Lily stared off into space, lost in thought.

Ray downed the rest of his whisky. Harry Snow was a savvy businessman and had next to no scruples, which served him well. He wasn't a particularly popular man, but he had some very large businesses which fed into many of the firms and so people put up with his odd ways. In turn, he hated people. He hated having to deal with them, had developed a nervous tic whenever forced to engage in conversation with another person, as though it physically hurt him. Perhaps if Lily used that to her advantage, she could sway his interests away from her area without having to get heavy-handed? Ray wanted to offer to sort it all out for her, but he knew that she would just decline. He could count on one hand the times she'd come to him for help, and it had only been when her back had been so up against a wall that she'd had absolutely no other option.

'Well,' he said, standing up. 'You know where I am if you need me.'

'I know where you are?' she replied, her gaze turning sharply towards him. She stood up and shot him a challenging smile. 'I'm rather hoping for the next few hours at least you'll be upstairs.' She turned and left the room, her petite behind swaying from side to side provocatively.

Ray watched her with an appreciative smile. It didn't matter how many years passed, she still knew how to get him exactly where she wanted him.

'Well?' she called back over her shoulder. 'Are you coming?'

Shrugging off his jacket, he followed her upstairs. He didn't need to be asked twice.

CHAPTER THIRTEEN

Scarlet checked her make-up in the rear-view mirror one last time. She felt very smart today. Smarter than she had ever felt before. But then she'd had no need to dress like this until now. At the weekend she'd gone and bought her first ever suit, a smart grey trouser suit with a fitted jacket and a small black ruffle along the edge of the pockets. She wore this now, with a black polo neck and her favourite pair of black heels to match. Her pale skin was flawless already with youth so she didn't usually wear much make-up, but today she'd applied some eyeliner and mascara to her grey-blue eyes and pillar-box-red lipstick to finish the look. With her dark wavy hair loose around her shoulders, she felt like a million pounds.

Stepping out of the car, she looked up at the imposing industrial building and a smile brightened her face. She'd lost count of the number of times she'd been in here over the years, but this time she wasn't entering as a child just visiting her father, she was entering as a young woman ready to work alongside him. And the thought warmed her. She was close to her dad. Leaving him at the end of summer was going to be the hardest part of all. She swallowed a small lump that rose in her throat at the thought.

Having heard her car pull up, Ronan came to the door to meet her. As he opened it for her, he paused and a fond smile crept up on his face.

'What?' she asked, feeling self-conscious.

'Nothing, it's just…' He smiled almost sadly. 'You look so grown up.'

'Well, that's probably because I am,' she said with a small laugh. 'You wouldn't want me helping on the accounts if I wasn't, would you?'

'This is true,' Ronan replied, following her inside. 'Come on then – let's start in the office. You don't need a tour; you know where everything is.'

They made their way across the busy factory floor, past the machines and the people who worked them, some of whom tipped their hats to Scarlet as she passed. They all knew who she was. They reached the metal stairs and climbed up to the two offices above. From one of the windows Scarlet could see Aunt Lily on the phone. She waved and Lily smiled back briefly before turning away with a frown as she talked urgently down the line.

'Er, we'll see your aunt in a minute. She's just dealing with something.'

Scarlet glanced at Ronan and could tell from his face that Lily's call was probably not one for the legitimate side of their business. She pursed her lips and filed this away in her mind. Her mother had been adamant that if she was going to work in the factory over the summer that she had to be kept strictly on the legitimate side of things. Scarlet wasn't sure how she felt about this demand. She had grown up in her father's world, much as Cath tried to ignore it, and she knew exactly who her family were. What was the point in pretending otherwise? It wasn't as though they'd put her on anything big – there was only so much of the underworld they could allow someone who wasn't all in to become involved with.

'Here we are. I figure for now you can move between our offices, as we're rarely both in at the same time. Then we'll figure out what do to about a proper desk for you later on if we need it. That alright with you?' Ronan asked, his tone hopeful as they stepped into his office.

Scarlet looked down. Even now she could see the hope in his eyes, spurred on by her lack of confirmation. She felt bad then.

She'd been trying to spare him the pain for a while longer by keeping her decision to herself, but perhaps it was just drawing out the agony. She resolved to find the time to break the news to him over the next few days.

'That's fine. So where do I start?' she asked, looking around.

Ronan's office was the same as Lily's – square, purpose-built, practical. But they each had a few luxuries in there which warmed up the place. Ronan had an old-fashioned, oversized mahogany desk. He'd told them the story time and again about how he'd found it in an old antique store one winter and had fallen in love with it. Behind it stood a comfortable red leather chair. Several pictures of them all lined the wall to the side. In contrast, her aunt's desk was of a sleek modern design and everything matched perfectly.

'Well, for now I could do with you jumping in on sorting out the paperwork. The hard-copy files for our customers are a total shambles. I need everything organised into sections and then date order. It's boring, I know,' Ronan said with a grimace, 'but it needs doing and to be honest, it's the best way to start learning about how we work here. You'll get to see who our regular customers are and the sort of levels they order in.'

Scarlet nodded and glanced to the side of the office.

'So all of these files in here?' she asked, gesturing towards the wall of filing cabinets.

'The first three rows. Listen, you go ahead and start – use my desk.' Ronan glanced out of his window distractedly. 'I need to go talk to Lil about some things, then I'll make us a coffee.' He began walking out. 'And we'll go for lunch today, yeah? I'll take you somewhere special to celebrate your first day.' He grinned at her as he left and the door slowly shut behind him.

As the room became quiet, the only noise creeping through from outside the rhythmic hum of the machinery, Scarlet placed her hands on her hips and looked around feeling slightly disappointed.

She'd hoped they would be working together during her time here, not apart. That was the main reason she'd suggested it – to gain more quality time with her dad. But still, she was here to make some extra money too, and he'd promised to take her to lunch so it wasn't all bad. She nodded to herself and turned in a slow circle, assessing the room and mentally processing the task ahead of her.

Snapping herself into work mode, she marched forward and opened the first filing cabinet. It might be boring, but if she was going to be stuck organising files then she was going to do a damn good job of it.

CHAPTER FOURTEEN

Ronan quietly closed the door to Lily's office. He sat down in one of the chairs to the side and waited.

'Right. Leave this with me; I'll see what we can do.' She ended the call and turned to Ronan with an irritated sigh. 'That was Sonia. They've closed down the chippy, citing health hazards.'

'Ah, shit.' Ronan closed his eyes with a groan.

'Yeah, not what we need right now. That's *that* laundry stopped for at least a week, best-case scenario. Plus they're a protection client, so we need to try and get them back open.' She twisted her mouth to one side.

'Dean…'

'Got promoted last month and we haven't tapped up his replacement,' Lily said, cutting him off.

Dean was the local health inspector, who wasn't averse to taking cash bribes any time they needed somewhere to be avoided or reopened off the back of a bad review. Or at least he had been until his promotion.

'Who's the new guy? I could go over today, talk to him?' Ronan suggested.

'No, don't worry. I already befriended him in a bar last week. I just haven't got round to finding out whether or not he's up for a bribe – we got interrupted. I'll arrange a drink and get to the point tonight,' she replied, walking around her desk and sitting in her chair.

She crossed one slim leg over the other, lit a cigarette and relaxed back in the chair, resting her wrists on the arms. 'So' – she took a drag and blew out a thin line of smoke – 'what are you starting Scarlet on?'

'Sorting out the files.'

'The files?' Lily pulled a face. 'Really? The girl dragged herself out of bed to do something you could get a minimum-wage admin assistant to do?'

'She's only here for the summer at the moment, Lil. Plus, whether she stays on or not, I think it's important to start at the bottom and learn how things work that way. We certainly had to,' Ronan responded.

'We didn't have a choice,' Lily replied, looking away through the wall to a distant memory. 'Or parents to help us out. And plus, if you're trying to entice her to stay rather than go off to this fancy university of hers, boring her to death isn't going to do you any favours.'

'I know, but there's no point dazzling her with a false front either,' he replied. 'I don't want to trick her into staying, only for her to realise later that it ain't all fun and games.' He sighed. 'I want her here just as much as you. I didn't spend my whole life slaving away, building this business up with blood, sweat and tears to not pass it on to my only child, but at the same time, I can't force her to stay. She has to want to stay. She has to want to be a part of this.'

'We ain't going to be around forever, Ronan,' Lily said quietly. 'And this place is going to need them all, to survive.'

'I know,' Ronan agreed. 'I know.' He was silent for a moment. 'Look, she still hasn't decided what she's doing yet. I'm hoping that being here, even just on the files, will show her all there is in store – all that I've built up for her.'

'I really hope you're right, Ronan,' Lily replied, taking another drag on her cigarette. 'For all our sakes.'

*

Outside the office, just beyond the slightly open door, Scarlet quietly retreated into her father's office. She shut the door again silently and put her hands to her face as the guilt piled down hard upon her shoulders. How on earth was she going to tell him now?

*

Nipping down the stairs to the small kitchen, Ronan set the coffee pot on its stand and waited for it to come to a boil. Pulling his phone out of his pocket, he typed out a quick message confirming his afternoon meeting. He paused, his expression thoughtful as he wondered once more whether he should tell Lily what he was planning. But he dismissed the idea almost immediately. She wouldn't like the idea at all. It was a long shot. Chances were it would come to nothing, and she had enough on her plate to think about already. No, he'd see if it panned out first before he brought her into the loop.

The light on the coffee machine flickered on and Ronan grabbed two cups and began to pour. Suddenly, he desperately hoped that his meeting paid off. If it did, if fair terms could be agreed and a mutual understanding met, this could sort out their larger money-laundering issues once and for all – which would mean Lily could relax and let go of the idea of pushing more money through the factory for good.

CHAPTER FIFTEEN

Scarlet watched her father across the table in the restaurant he'd taken her to for lunch. Her taut nerves jangled as she tried to work out how to tell him the plans she'd already put into motion. It was going to kill him – she knew this. It would be better for all concerned if she just got it out now, if she was just honest and open and ripped the Band-Aid off quickly. But right now there didn't seem to be an obvious way into the conversation; her father was unusually distracted. She picked up her sparkling water and took a sip, then glanced down at the menu.

'So, what's up?' she asked.

'Hm?' He looked up at her in question.

'You've barely said two words since we left the office. You OK?' She watched him, concerned. He was never quiet. Even when he was juggling a million things, he was still jovial and on the ball, always talking, always joking in his deep booming voice.

'I'm fine,' he answered, plastering on a wide grin. 'Just thinking about a meeting I've got this afternoon.'

'Oh?' Scarlet raised her eyebrow in interest. 'What meeting?' Perhaps she could tag along. After a morning wading through the mess of files they'd left unorganised for so many years, she could do with something a little different for a while.

'Ah, nothing interesting, just a client I want to talk to about something.' Ronan dismissed it with a wave of his hand.

Scarlet leaned in, interested. 'Well, why don't I come with you? You know, take notes maybe, keep you company?' The meeting might provide her with the opportunity she needed, if she couldn't find a way to tell him over lunch.

'No.' Ronan's reply came a little too fast and strong and Scarlet frowned. 'I mean…' He softened his tone. 'It's nothing that would interest you, and nor would it make much sense.'

'I'm not stupid,' Scarlet retorted. 'I pick things up pretty quickly.'

'Well, it's not…' He floundered for a moment. 'It's just not suitable for you to come to this one, OK?'

Scarlet bit her bottom lip as it clicked that the meeting was for the other side of the business. 'Ah. I see.' She smiled and busied herself with her napkin.

Ronan locked his jaw, clearly debating whether or not to say what was on his mind. For a few moments it seemed as though he'd decided against it, but then he began to speak.

'You know, when Lily and I started out, we knew nothing about this life. Not really,' he said. 'And it wasn't easy, none of it, but especially in the early days. If it wasn't for Lil, we wouldn't have made it this far at all, that's for sure. She's got bigger balls made of harder steel than any man I know,' he admitted with a crooked smile. 'And I see so much of her determination and strength in you. She does too – I can tell. There's a fire running through the veins of the women in this family, more so than us men, if I'm honest.' He glanced at her. 'But more than that, you're smart, Scarlet. *Really* smart,' he said with feeling. 'And if you joined us, you'd be an asset, of course you would. If fact if you joined us, I have no doubt you'd end up more a force to be reckoned with than even me, one day. I'd be proud to have you by my side.' He smiled at her.

Scarlet nodded, her heart sinking as he finally made his subtle plea. 'I know.' She looked down at the menu.

Ronan exhaled slowly. 'But of course,' he said, 'the most important thing to me is your happiness.' He swallowed and shifted in his seat. 'Whatever you decide to do, I'll be proud of you, my little Scar.' He studied her for a moment. 'I always have been and I always will be. Remember that.'

Scarlet swallowed the lump of emotion that had gathered in her throat. 'Thanks, Dad,' she said. She looked up with a quick smile. 'Let's eat, shall we? I'm bloody starving.'

''Course. Come on then – what you having?'

Scarlet forced herself to choose some food and settled in to listen as Ronan began to tell her a funny story about a client he'd taken here. He was getting to the climax of it when something snapped inside her and a wave of determination set in.

'Dad?' she said suddenly, unable to keep her secret any longer.

'Hm?' he looked at her questioningly.

'I, um…' She took a deep breath and licked her lips. They felt dry.

'Can I take your order?'

She blinked up at the waiter who had intruded at the exact moment she'd finally worked up the courage.

'Yeah, I'll have the…'

Ronan began to order and her courage slipped away. She just couldn't hurt him, she realised resignedly. Not today at least. She'd just have to find a way to do it tomorrow.

CHAPTER SIXTEEN

Scarlet awoke to the sound of a bell ringing somewhere and rubbed her eyes with a frown. Surely it wasn't morning already, she thought, the fuzzy tug of sleep threatening to overtake her. It hadn't sounded like her alarm, but what else could it have been?

The bell rang again and this time she rolled over to check the time on the small blue screen of her digital bedside clock. It was just past two in the morning. Who on earth was ringing their doorbell at this hour?

She heard her parents' bedroom door opening and the soft pattering of her mother's footsteps descending the stairs. She sat up and rubbed her eyes once more, slipping her feet into her slippers and reaching out for her dressing down. Whoever it was, they were going to get the bollocking of their lives once her dad got down there. Unless it was a matter of life and death, no one was welcome to put in an urgent call at his home in the middle of the night. Then again, she considered, as she entered the hallway, perhaps it *was* a matter of life or death. You never knew in their line of work.

Cath opened the door and Scarlet listened to the voices as the sound carried up the stairs. She leaned on the wall just out of sight, not having decided yet whether or not she was interested in joining the situation.

'Hello? Oh, Officer… What – what is it?' Cath said, worry flooding her tone immediately. 'What do you want?'

Scarlet froze and her eyes widened. Why were they here? Were they going to arrest her dad? But he wasn't here, she remembered suddenly. He hadn't been in when they'd both hit the sack hours before and she hadn't heard him come in since. This wasn't unusual; he was often out through the night, dealing with what her mother referred to as *his other work*. So whatever they wanted to arrest him for, they would be out of luck tonight. She nearly turned to get her phone to warn him but paused, deciding to wait and hear what they had to say first. The more information she could give him, the better.

'Madam, may we come in?' a male voice asked.

'That depends,' Cath replied in a clipped tone. 'Do you have a warrant?'

Scarlet's mouth curled up into a grin. Her mother may hate what her father did for a living, but she loved him fiercely and would protect him with every ounce of strength she had.

'We don't need a warrant tonight, madam,' the officer replied tiredly. 'We just need to talk to you for a moment. It's about your husband.'

'Well, yes, I gathered that,' Cath replied sarcastically. 'But unless you have a warrant, or arrest me and take me in, I have nothing to say to you.'

'I don't think you understand what we're here for. We're not here to accuse your husband of anything.'

'Well, damn right,' she interrupted indignantly. ''Cause he ain't done nothing.'

'We're here because we have some news for you. About your husband.'

There was a silence and Scarlet crept forward, a frown forming on her forehead.

'What do you mean?' Cath asked, doubt creeping into her tone.

'Look, please can we come in, Mrs Drew? We're not here to cause problems, we just have some news, but I think you might need to sit down,' another voice said gently, this one female.

Scarlet felt a coldness creep through her body and she pulled her dressing gown tighter around her slim body. What news were they talking about? Had he been arrested?

After another short silence, Cath responded, her tone less abrasive than before. 'Well, OK, then. But just into the kitchen, mind. It's through there.'

Scarlet heard two sets of footsteps move into the house and down the hallway, before the front door closed and her mother hurried after them. Worried now, she moved to the stairs and crept down the first few treads, then sat and strained her ears to listen.

'Can I just ask, Mrs Drew, when was the last time you saw your husband?'

'It was this morning, before he went off to work,' she replied. 'At the *factory*,' she continued pointedly. 'His place of work. You can confirm that's where he went with our daughter who works there with him, or my sister-in-law, who's his business partner.'

'And that would be a Ms Lily Drew, is that correct?'

'Yes, it is. Listen 'ere, why are you asking me all these questions? I ain't answering any more until I've spoken to my husband. I thought you had some news for me? What's going on?' Cath began to sound agitated.

'Did anyone get hold of Lily Drew yet?' the male officer asked quietly.

'Let me check with dispatch, hang on.' The female officer's voice tailed off until Scarlet couldn't hear what was being said.

'You're trying to trip me up here, ain't ya?' Cath asked. 'I've had enough of this. Get to the point now, mate, or otherwise get out. I don't appreciate being woken up in the middle of the night for a trip around the houses, I'll tell you that much.'

'They've spoken to Lily Drew already,' the female officer piped up. 'Apparently, she's on her way over here now.'

'Lil?' Cath asked, confused. 'Why is Lil coming over? What's going on?'

'I'm so sorry, Mrs Drew,' the male officer said gently, 'but we have some bad news. A body was found earlier this evening and we've confirmed through the ID in his wallet that it's your husband.'

Scarlet gasped and she put her hand up to cover her mouth. The cold worry that had flooded her body before now turned her to ice. She shook her head. Surely that wasn't right. They must have made a mistake. Her dad was fit and healthy for his age and he was always careful. They had to be wrong. It had to be a case of mistaken identity, she reasoned, as her thoughts all began to race and melt into each other.

The silence stretched on in the kitchen, and Scarlet nearly stood to go down, but then her mother finally spoke.

'No,' she said, her voice strong with certainty. 'You've got it wrong.'

'That's right,' Scarlet whispered, tears beginning to form in her eyes as the officer's words resounded in her head. 'You tell 'em, Mum.' Her mum would know the truth, she was sure of it.

'It can't be my husband,' Cath continued. 'It just can't be.'

'I'm so sorry, Mrs Drew. I know you don't want to believe it, but it's true,' the female officer said gently. 'We ran every check to be sure before we came over.'

'No. You're lying.' A wobble appeared in her tone now, and at the sound of her resolve breaking, Scarlet's heart dropped. 'It can't be.' A sob cracked through her last word.

'We're so sorry,' the male officer repeated.

'Not my Ronan. No,' she wailed. 'No. No, no, no.'

Scarlet tried to stand up, but for some reason she couldn't. Panic began to overwhelm her, and her breathing started to spike. Her dad wasn't dead. Was he? They'd only gone for lunch a few hours ago. He'd been right there opposite her.

Her chest began to heave as huge silent sobs took over. She bent down and put her head between her legs, fighting for breath as the whole situation overwhelmed her.

'He can't be dead,' Cath cried, her heart breaking for all to hear. 'He – he can't leave us. We need him. We need him here, at home.' All strength was gone from her words now, replaced only with sorrow and fear. 'He can't leave us. We love him. We love him,' she repeated. Her voice trailed off into a heart-wrenching sob.

The sound of her crying filled the air for a few moments, and Scarlet's tears fell between her knees to the floor unchecked as she tried to gain a grip on her breathing. The world seemed to be spinning and she couldn't slow it down, because every time she held on to a clear thought, it told her that her dad was gone forever. And that didn't make sense. No matter how she tried, she couldn't seem to get her head around this piece of information. It was all too surreal. It was like some sort of nightmare. Perhaps it *was* a nightmare. It had to be, surely?

'How can he be gone?' she heard Cath ask, through her tears. When no one answered, Cath began to shout in anger. 'I said, how can he be gone?' Her sobs grew louder as she grabbed on to this anger like a lifeboat. 'I just don't understand. What happened?' she screamed at the officers.

'We're still investigating what exactly happened, but it appears that someone cut through his oesophagus with a blade of some sort—'

'They slit his throat? They *slit* my Ronan's throat? That's what you're saying to me?' Cath screeched, her sobs becoming hysterical.

'Please, Mrs Drew, I know this is a very big shock but please try to stay calm.'

'Stay calm? Stay *calm*?' she cried. 'I've just heard that someone slit my husband's throat, the man I love, have loved forever…' She began to wail, once more overtaken by the grief.

Scarlet heard the front door open and looked up. Lily walked in, her face whiter than Scarlet had ever seen it before and with a look of shock and pain etched into it. She paused in the hallway as she caught sight of her niece on the stairs to her right and her sister-in-law ahead of her in the kitchen, debating who to go to first.

Cath, roused by seeing Lily, began to shout in anger again, this time aiming her vitriol towards her. 'This is your fault,' she hurled. '*You* did this to him. You did this to him; you killed him. You fucking killed him, Lily,' she screamed, her voice getting louder and more hysterical with every word.

Scarlet heard a scuffling sound.

'Get out of my way. Let me through, for God's sake! This is on *you*, Lily Drew. His blood is on *your* hands. Get *off* me I said! You killed him, Lil. This is on *you*. This is all on you…'

CHAPTER SEVENTEEN

Lily pulled an extra blanket out of her airing cupboard and walked down the hallway to her daughter Ruby's old room where she had left Scarlet. As she entered, Scarlet tried to rub the falling tears off her cheeks. She was sitting on the bed, her knees pulled up to her chest and her arms wrapped around them. Lily looked down on her with a wave of pity. She looked so vulnerable in that moment, just a little girl who'd lost her father, no sign of the strong young woman underneath.

She placed the blanket on the bed and sank down in the chair next to it, reaching across and laying her hand on Scarlet's arm. She'd had to take the girl out of that house, away from the scene Cath had made. In her pain and panic, Cath had completely lost it. She'd screamed and fought the police officers, trying to get to Lily. She'd poured all her terror into anger and aimed that all at her sister-in-law, getting more and more incensed the more they held her back.

Lily had wanted to tell them to let her go so that she could try and calm Cath down, but stuck in her own shock, she couldn't work out how and had just stood there, mute and numb. In the end, the officers had called for medical assistance and Cath had been sedated and taken off to a local mental health institution for observation and assessment.

Cath had spent time there, many years before while recovering from a breakdown following the loss of two babies close together. It had been early on in their marriage. All she'd ever wanted was to have a family with Ronan, and so when the doctors had told her that her chances of carrying full term were slim, she hadn't been able to cope. Scarlet had been their miracle baby a few years later, and she'd never shown signs of declining mental health since. But with all this on her record, the officers had decided to take no chances on leaving her alone in the state she'd worked herself up to. In any other circumstance Lily would have fought to keep her out of a place like that, but right now she couldn't help but think it was the best place for her. Just until they could get a grip on things and work out what was going on.

They were all in shock, all devastated by the news. If she was being honest, it still hadn't truly sunk in. She half expected someone to knock at the door and tell them they'd made a mistake. But that hadn't happened yet, and she was beginning to realise it never would. Once the ambulance had driven away with Cath, Lily had guided Scarlet out to her car without a word and driven them both to her house. Now here they were together, confused, in pain and in shock.

Lily noticed Scarlet was shaking and opened up the blanket, laying it around the girl's shoulders.

'I'm not cold,' Scarlet said in barely more than a whisper. 'I'm warm; I just can't seem to stop the shaking.'

'That's the shock setting in then,' Lily replied quietly. 'I'll get you a whisky; it will take the edge off.'

'No,' Scarlet said quickly, her hand shooting out to grasp Lily's arm as she began to rise. 'Please don't leave me,' she begged, her tone trembling with uncertainty.

Lily lowered herself back down in the chair and grasped her niece's hand. 'Of course,' she said softly. 'I won't go anywhere. I'm here, little doll.' Tears filled her eyes and she blinked them away.

'Little doll...' A brief nostalgic smile flitted across Scarlet's haunted face. 'You haven't called me that in years.'

Lily nodded and swallowed the lump in her throat. 'I haven't needed to,' she replied. It was something they'd called her as a child and as she'd grown whenever she'd sought comfort.

Scarlet laid her head back against the wall and stared off into the distance, tears still running unchecked down her face. Lily watched her in the soft glow from the lamp that was lighting the room. Somehow the pain had aged her young face by years.

'You called me little doll and what was it you called Ruby?' Her forehead puckered into a small frown as she tried to remember. 'Little angel, was it?'

'That's right,' Lily replied, her broken heart sinking even lower at the mention of her daughter. She pulled a sad smirk at the irony of the name. These days Ruby was as far from an angel as she could possibly get. 'When she was born, with her curly red hair and her pale skin, she looked like this angel we used to put at the top of the Christmas tree. Don't know what happened to it over the years; I think it got lost. But yeah, we started calling her little angel. Then when you were born, with your big grey-blue eyes and little puckered mouth, you looked like a porcelain doll. So that's how that all came about.' She closed her eyes as grief began to set in. 'Your dad, he was the one who coined those.'

Scarlet sniffed again, her tears falling faster. She squeezed her eyes shut for a moment. 'I just don't understand,' she said through a sob. 'Was it a robbery?' She looked at her aunt, her eyes pleading for answers that Lily didn't have. 'Were they mugging him? Why was he even out there?' Ronan had been found in a small village outside London that none of them had heard of before today. 'Was that where his meeting was? Who was he there with?'

'I don't know,' Lily admitted.

'What, where the meeting was or who he was with?' Scarlet asked.

'Any of it,' she replied unhappily. 'Ronan didn't tell me what he was doing today. Yesterday, I guess now,' she added, looking at the clock. It was 4 a.m. 'He just said he had a meeting. I figured he'd just update me later…' She tailed off and shook her head. 'We don't always keep up with each other's schedules – we just tell each other what we need to know.'

'Where would he keep the details – a diary?' Scarlet pressed, trying to cling to anything that could give them an answer.

Lily shook her head once more. 'Ronan doesn't keep anything written down that's not strictly factory business. Neither of us does. It's the easiest way to get caught out. There will be no trail related to this meeting.'

'There has to be something,' Scarlet cried, the pain shining through her eyes.

Lily stood up and joined Scarlet on the bed, seeing how close her niece was to completely falling apart. She scooted up next to her and pulled her into her arm.

'I promise you, I will do everything I can to find out what's happened. I won't rest until we know. But with how careful your dad was, it's going to take time,' she said.

They sat in silence for a while, the only sound Scarlet's sobs as she cried into her aunt's shoulder. Lily stroked her hair, blinking away the tears that threatened to fall from her own shock and grief. She still couldn't believe they were having this conversation at all. The idea that Ronan was no longer on this earth, that he wasn't going to walk back into the factory tomorrow still didn't feel real. But somehow it was, and the whole world as they knew it was crashing down.

Scarlet's sobs finally subsided and she grew calm. Lily continued to stroke her until she sat up and leaned back against the wall beside her once more.

'It's down to us now, Scarlet,' she said quietly. 'This family has been broken. A huge chunk of it has been ripped away from us.' She swallowed. 'So it's up to us to keep it together. You and me.' She squeezed Scarlet's hand and turned to look at her. 'We need to keep everything together, for him.'

Fresh tears fell from Scarlet's eyes and she shut them in grief. 'Yes,' she breathed. 'We do.'

Lily exhaled and rubbed her forehead. 'You'll stay here for as long as you need,' she said resolutely. 'Your mum just needs a rest and a little help processing things, then she'll be back home. But until then, you can stay with me. If you want to, that is,' she added, remembering that Scarlet was a grown woman, even if she was vulnerable right now.

'Thanks. I'll stay until she comes home, then I'd better go back. She'll need me.' She sniffed and wiped her eyes with her sleeve.

Lily nodded. Scarlet was right – Cath would need her. Cath had lived her whole life centred around Ronan. Now she would be completely lost, and Lily wasn't sure how she was going to cope.

'What about Ruby?' Scarlet suddenly asked.

'What about her?' Lily replied.

'What if she comes back to visit?'

Lily looked around the room sadly. This had been Ruby's room for so many years. She had kept it exactly how she'd left it when she was sixteen, hoping against hope that she would come back for good one day. From her teenage years, Ruby had been rebellious, running away whenever the mood or some boy took her. Lily had spent years pulling her hair out with worry, scouring the streets at nights for her. Sometimes she found her and would take her home; mostly Ruby would turn up days later with a bad hangover and a foul attitude. Lily had lost count of the nights she'd sobbed and fretted, praying to God to deliver her precious daughter home safely.

As Ruby had grown, so had her bad taste. Naughty boys made way for dangerous men and alcohol escalated to drugs. Lily had continued fighting to get back the lovely girl she'd known and loved. She'd cleaned her up and taken her to rehab countless times, only for Ruby to run away at the first opportunity. When Ruby refused to move home for good, she'd set her up in a new flat for a fresh start, helped her find a job, given her money and

clothes and everything she needed to find her feet again. She
set her up this way time and time again. But every time Ruby
ended up turning on her. Every job she found her, Ruby would
walk out, or stop turning up or even steal from them. Lily had
had to pay out to smooth things over with Ruby's angry victims
numerous times.

One day Ruby had started stealing from Lily too. At first she'd
ignored it, pushing more and more funds Ruby's way in the hope
it would be enough to stop her treating her own family like this.
But it was never enough, and the more Lily gave her, the worse
Ruby became. Every penny went on booze and drugs or into the
pocket of some low life who was sleeping with her at the time.
Every offer of help to get clean was met with aggression and strife.

Eventually, Lily had come to the painful realisation that by
giving Ruby money, all she was doing was enabling her to access
more of the bad things she craved. It had almost killed her to do it,
but she'd stood up to her daughter and told her that, whilst she'd
help her out now and then and whilst she was always welcome
to come home, she wouldn't be funding her life anymore. Ruby
had kicked and screamed and threatened all sorts, but Lily had
stood firm despite the fact it had broken her heart.

Ruby had barely been seen since. She turned up once in a
while when she had nothing better to do and was hungry. She'd
stay for dinner, perhaps stay a day or two, insult them all and
then leave again, usually with some cash in her pocket to see her
through a few days.

She still held on to the hope that one day Ruby would wake
up and want to change. Quietly she dreamed of it all coming
together, of being able to save her only daughter from herself.
She knew realistically the chances of it happening at this point
were slim, but she just couldn't bear to think of the alternative.

'I doubt we'll be seeing her in the next couple of days,' she
replied.

She saw the quickly veiled look of relief on Scarlet's face and felt sad. Ruby and Scarlet should have been close. They were cousins, Drews, two shades of the same colour. But instead they despised one another. She could understand Scarlet's feelings to an extent. Ruby was a live wire, caused trouble and destruction wherever she could. It was natural for Scarlet to be wary of her. She just wished it didn't have to be this way.

With a sigh she pushed her thoughts of Ruby away. Ruby would always be a worry but nothing had changed there tonight. What had changed was that Ronan was gone and everyone else was now falling apart. He was gone and he wasn't coming back. As the thought re-registered in her mind, a gaping hole opened up in her chest and she suddenly felt as though she couldn't breathe. Not wanting to alarm Scarlet and having a natural aversion to showing weakness in front of anyone, even family, she pulled herself forward and stood up.

'One minute,' she managed to mutter as she walked out of the room with a casualness that belied her inner turmoil.

Once in the hallway she sped up, almost running into her own room and through to the walk-in dressing room. Quietly closing the door, she went to the back of the closet and deep, heaving sobs finally made their way out of her chest. She squeezed her eyes shut and tried to control them, but they wouldn't be controlled. Her brother was gone. It was real. It had really happened.

As the realisation finally hit her properly, she fell to the floor and bent over, putting her forehead to the ground as the pain flowed out through her tears. It had all been for nothing. Raising him, loving him, protecting him, carving out a life for him to raise his own family in had all been pointless. Because he was gone.

She, his big sister, Lily Drew, had failed.

CHAPTER EIGHTEEN

Cath sat on the edge of her bed and stared at the picture on the wall in front of her. It was of their wedding day, of her and Ronan about to start their big life adventure together. That's what he'd always said to her, that life was the biggest adventure of all. Except now his adventure was over. And he'd left her all alone to carry on with hers. She wiped a stray tear that ran down her face.

It had been just over a week since the night they'd found out he'd been killed. Just over a week since their whole world had come crashing down. The first few days were a bit hazy in Cath's memory now. She'd screamed and shouted and then completely lost the plot once Lily had turned up, she remembered that. Seeing her there standing in the hallway had been like a red flag, salt in the freshly carved wound in her heart. In the end, the police had called an ambulance and she'd been taken to some sort of hospital where she'd been sedated. They'd kept her in for a couple of days until she'd calmed down and all their tests concluded that she wasn't an actual risk to anyone.

She'd felt so guilty then, when Scarlet had come to collect her. Her beautiful daughter was so young, yet she'd left her alone to cope with the news of her father's death with no one but Lily to help her through it. And the boys, of course, but they were no substitute for her own mother.

She looked down to the ring she was slowly twisting in her hands. It was a simple band – platinum, thick and strong. It was the only thing of Ronan's she'd been able to get back so far.

The coroner was refusing to release his body until they'd worked out exactly what had happened. And so she hadn't been able to arrange a funeral, or sort anything out, because they were all just stuck in this strange limbo. She wiped another tear from her cheek.

A soft tapping sounded at the door and then Scarlet's head appeared as she leaned round it. 'Hey,' she said. 'Are you coming down? I've made us a cuppa.'

'Yeah, alright, love,' she replied, her voice barely stronger than a whisper. 'I'll be right there.' She tried a smile but could feel it barely made it halfway up her face.

Scarlet tried smiling back, but Cath could see the same strain she felt echoed in her daughter's face.

'Great. Um… You remember Aunt Lil is coming over today, don't you?' Scarlet asked tentatively.

Cath exhaled heavily. Lily had tactfully kept her distance since the night they'd been given the news, but now that the dust had settled Cath knew the issue needed to be addressed. She had lashed out at her terribly and said things that could never be unsaid. But they were family, and right now, for better or worse, they all needed to stick together and get through the storm they found themselves in. Because that's just what they did. And it's what Ronan would have wanted them to do.

'I remember,' she said quietly.

As if on cue, a car pulled up outside and two doors opened and slammed before footsteps sounded on their way up to the house. There was a pause and then the doorbell rang. Lily had obviously decided against just walking in on this occasion. Cath closed her eyes for a moment.

'I'll go let them in…' Scarlet started.

'No, don't.' Cath stopped her. 'I'll go. It should be me.'

'Oh, OK. I'll give you a minute then.'

'Thanks.' She shot Scarlet a brave smile and stood up, slipping Ronan's ring back onto her necklace and fastening it around her neck.

She opened the front door and stepped aside, gesturing for Lily and Cillian to come in. Lily glanced at her warily as she entered, and Cath stalled her with a hand on her arm.

'You don't have to stop using your key, Lily,' she said. 'We're still sisters by marriage. This is still a family home.'

Lily stared at her for a long moment. 'Thank you, Cathleen,' she said. 'That's good to know.' She walked through to the kitchen, her black heels tapping loudly on the hard floor and her stance unusually rigid as the elephant in the room grew more prominent. 'Is Scarlet around?' she asked eventually.

'She is,' Cath replied. 'Look, Lil…' She sighed and looked away, her fingers fiddling with a loose button on her top. 'I was in a state the other night…'

'There's no need to explain,' Lily said. 'It was a hard shock for all of us. We all say things we don't mean in times of stress.'

'But that's just it, Lil.' Cath turned to look at her, raw sadness in her eyes. 'I'm not going to pretend I didn't mean it, because I did. I've made no secret of my distaste for the darker side of this family's business over the years. And we all know it was you who drove it from the beginning.'

Cillian stepped back and leaned against the counter with a silent whistle, bowing out of the exchange. Whilst he would defend his mother to the end, he obviously knew this wasn't his battle to fight. This was too personal.

Cath swallowed as Lily stood stock-still, her expression unreadable. When Lily still didn't say anything, she continued. It was now or never, to tell Lily the things she needed to say.

'I was just speaking my mind, when I said those things. So I can't apologise for that. But what I am sorry for is the way I attacked you with it.' She nodded. 'I am sorry for that. Because we *are* family and there's love here, and I know that you would never have wished harm on Ronan. You've tried to protect him your whole life.' She gave her a sad smile. 'I know you have, more than anyone. But your lifestyle, the choices you made… they're the reason it's come to this. That's just a simple truth. And I can't pretend it's not.' She sniffed and wiped under her eye as a tear threatened to fall. 'But it is what it is, and there's no changing it. So there's no point discussing it further; we just need to stick together now. More than ever. That's all I wanted to say.'

Lily stared out of the window, into the garden, folding her arms across her chest. Cath watched as she stood there, saw the wobble in her bottom lip and the tears form in her eyes. She saw, too, the strength with which she clenched her jaw, and the rapid blinking to dispel these signs of what Lily would see only as weakness. After a few moments she cleared her throat.

'Well, I'm glad that's all you wanted to say, Cath,' she said, her tone flat and as unreadable as her expression. 'Now we can put that entire conversation to bed. Because, like you say, we need to just stick together now.'

Cath opened her mouth, but then closed it again, unsure how to react to that statement. She wasn't sure what she'd expected Lily to say. What was there *to* say? Lily could have taken offence and argued, but that wouldn't have got them anywhere. And what was the alternative? She stood awkwardly for a moment. As she dithered, Lily abruptly changed the subject.

'Cillian, I see there's a pot of tea on the table. Please would you pour everyone a cup,' she ordered.

'Sure,' Cillian replied, clearly relieved to be given something to do.

Lily caught the swiftly veiled look of surprise at her lack of reaction as he turned to the task. Cath had invited a row more blatantly than a neon sign, but although every wounded atom in her body ached to respond, she didn't. The family was already fractured. The last thing any of them needed was another fall out. Her phone pinged in her pocket and she pulled it out with a deep calming breath.

'Bugger,' she muttered.

'What's up?' Cillian asked with a frown.

'We've got an issue at the factory.' She gave him a meaningful look, then turned her attention to Cath. 'I'm so sorry, Cath, but we can't stop after all.'

'Oh. Don't worry, I understand,' Cath replied.

In truth she didn't understand how Lily could still be working as though nothing had happened. She could barely drag herself out of bed at the moment, consumed with grief over losing Ronan. And yet Lily was still going into the factory and running the business like always. *Did Ronan mean so little to her?* She mentally swatted away the question as it crept into her mind. Of course Lily cared. But she certainly did have a strange way of showing it. She turned and sat in one of the chairs, exhausted by their exchange. Everything exhausted her at the moment.

Scarlet walked in, and Cath turned to her daughter with a frown, looking her up and down. 'Why are you dressed all smart?' she asked.

'I'm going into the office,' Scarlet said, glancing at her aunt. 'If that's OK with you?'

'Of course,' Lily replied. If she was surprised, she didn't show it.

Cath's eyebrows, on the other hand, shot up into her hairline. 'What?' she asked, aghast. 'You can't be serious? Your father has just *died*, Scarlet.'

'I'm well aware of that,' Scarlet replied. 'And that's exactly why I'm going.' She turned to Lily. 'I know you said there won't be a trail, but I have to look. I have to search his office and go through everything. There might be something he overlooked, some crumb trail we can follow. I can't just sit here, not knowing what happened. I can't do nothing.' Emotion coloured her tone. 'We need to find out who the hell did this and why.'

Lily nodded her understanding.

'No, Scarlet you need to be at home. Leave this to the police,' Cath argued. 'They're looking into it.'

'But they aren't, Mum,' Scarlet replied. 'At least not in the right places.' She took a deep breath. 'They aren't looking at the side of Dad's world that he hid.'

'And neither should you,' Cath shot back, alarmed. 'It's dangerous.'

'And no one knows just *how* dangerous, Mum,' Scarlet argued. She rubbed her forehead, stressed. 'For all we know this could just be the beginning – we could all be in danger. We need to figure it out.'

'Well, then let your aunt and cousins handle it.' Cath looked to Lily for support but found none. 'Lily?'

'I need to keep busy, Mum.' Scarlet's voice wobbled. 'I can't just keep sitting here waiting. It's driving me insane. I need to keep busy or I'm going to break,' she admitted. 'I need to find out what happened to Dad. And I need to help Aunt Lil out at the factory too, because despite the fact our world has stopped, the rest of it keeps on turning.' She made to leave before her mother could argue further. 'I'm still here for you, Mum, and I'm not going to do anything dangerous, I promise you. I'm just going to the office. I'll be home in a few hours.'

Cath stared after her, a look of horror on her face, then turned her gaze to Lily. 'Lil, I don't want her going into all that – you know I don't.'

'She's part of this family, Cath; she has every right to look into this. And she's also a grown woman,' she added. 'I know you don't want to hear this, but she has to make her own choices. You can't keep her wrapped up in cotton wool forever.'

Cath opened her mouth to reply, but then shut it again, turning away as tears formed in her eyes. She didn't want Scarlet anywhere near that factory, anywhere near *any* of it. But clearly she wasn't going to find an ally in Lily, even after what had happened to Ronan.

Cillian made to move after his cousin and Lily quickly followed suit before further conversations were forced. She wasn't going to argue with Scarlet. She wanted the girl there. 'I'll see you Sunday, Cath,' she said. 'The family dinner at my house, like always.'

'Except it ain't *like always*, is it, Lil?' Cath responded sadly. 'Because Ronan's gone. It will never be the same again.'

The two women stared at each other for a long, heavy moment. 'No,' Lily said eventually. 'It won't.'

CHAPTER NINETEEN

Cillian split off to take a call and Lily followed Scarlet up the metal stairs towards the offices, watching her carefully. The girl had been silent on the car ride over and she hadn't pushed her. Scarlet would talk in her own time. They reached the door to her office and Lily reached out and touched her arm.

'Listen, this isn't really factory business, what's going on inside there. Why don't you sit in your' – she hesitated – 'in the other office, until we're done. It shouldn't take long.'

Scarlet glanced at the door to Ronan's office and a fleeting look of fear passed over her face. She didn't want to be alone in there just yet, Lily guessed. Her gaze moved towards Lily's door and her clear grey-blue eyes hardened.

'No,' she said resolutely. 'I want to join you.' She looked at her aunt and lifted her chin. 'I need to find out what happened to my dad and I'm probably not going to figure it out on my own in the office. If you'll let me, I'd like to sit in.'

Lily nodded. 'If you're sure, then of course you can. But be aware, Scarlet' – she gave her a hard stare – 'the more people who see you at meetings like these, the more word will spread that you've joined the firm.'

'Except I haven't,' Scarlet replied quickly.

'No. You haven't.' Lily's gaze travelled across her niece's face critically. 'I won't lie to you and pretend I don't want you here – I do. More than ever now. You know your father did too,' she pressed. 'And it is still your decision, but be warned…' Her level gaze intensified. 'This isn't the corporate world. You can't dip in and out as you please. Once you start playing this game, you're in. And once you're in, there is no escape clause. You can't just hand your notice in. Once you're in, you're in for life. So you can come in to this meeting with me today, but you need to make a decision, and quickly. Are you part of this firm, this life? Or are you not? Because if not then you need to tie up whatever business you feel you still have here and start packing your things for Scotland. Because going there and leaving all this behind… That's the only way you can truly separate yourself for good.'

Scarlet swallowed, clearly at a loss as to how to answer. Giving her one more hard look, Lily turned and walked into the office.

'Lily Drew, it's so good to see you,' came an overly enthusiastic voice from one of the chairs by the coffee table at the side of the room. The voice belonged to a tall, awkward-looking man who watched Lily, but whose eyes constantly flickered away as if looking directly at her pained him somehow. His companion didn't seem to have the same affliction, watching Lily with dead eyes and an uninterested expression.

'Harry Snow. I would say the same but we'd both know I was lying.' Lily didn't bother to fake a smile as she crossed the room and took the seat behind the desk that Connor had just vacated. He stepped back and stood behind her, a menacing look in his dark brown eyes. They flicked momentarily to his cousin with curiosity, but then rested back on the newcomers in the room.

Harry chuckled, the sound a strained mixture of amusement and stress. 'You always were direct, weren't you? So very direct.'

'What do you want, Harry?' Lily asked, folding her hands in her lap and narrowing her gaze.

Harry Snow had extorted them so many times when they'd had no other options that they were way beyond fake pleasantries.

'To offer my condolences,' Harry replied, his head snapping to the side with a nervous tic as he forced himself to look at her.

Lily resisted the urge to curl her lip in disgust. He reminded her of a snake. A broken, dysfunctional snake that was always ready to strike even when it looked weak. She looked down to the silver cigarette box on the desk and opened it, lighting one up. She purposely didn't offer one to her guest, despite knowing he smoked.

'That's interesting, Harry,' she said. 'That you would come all this way to offer us your condolences. Did they run out of cards at the corner shop?' Her quiet tone was laced with subtle sarcasm.

Harry chuckled once more and pulled his own cigarettes out of his inner pocket. He lit up and Lily watched him carefully.

'The thing is, Harry,' she continued, her casual tone hardened by a dangerous edge, 'a little birdy told me that you've been talking about causing problems over here with our firm. And then not a heartbeat later Ronan is found dead in an alley.' Her dark eyes grew colder, never leaving his face. 'And then suddenly out of the blue I find you here in my office. Now...' She took a drag on her cigarette and blew out the smoke slowly. 'What should I make of that, do you think?'

'Let me guess,' Harry replied, a humourless half-smile pulling up one side of his weathered face. 'That little birdy of yours was none other than good old Raymondo,' he mocked. 'Am I right?'

'I wouldn't let him hear you call him that. He might think you're taking the piss, Harry,' Lily replied drily.

Harry's twitching gaze locked with hers for a few seconds before he pulled it away. 'That's the reason I'm here. To stop that little mind of yours barking up trees that ain't right. I am looking to expand some businesses that might concern you at some point in the future, yes.' He nodded. 'But I didn't have anything to do with Ronan. I had no reason to want him dead. He was a good customer. I'll be sad to see that income go, to be honest.'

'*We* are good customers, Harry,' Lily corrected. 'And your income from this firm won't be changing any time soon. Assuming, of course, that I *don't* find out that you were responsible for my brother's death.'

Harry's eyebrows rose and he glanced at her with interest. Lily wasn't surprised by this reaction. In the past, especially at the beginning, they had fought for their position in a very biased world; a man's world where women were seen as weaker beings. It had served them well to use Ronan as the face of the business. But times had changed, and although there would always be some bias remaining, it was time to make the true situation known. Lily was the hard rod of steel behind everything they did. And those who assumed she was just hanging off Ronan's shirt tails were about to be in for a rude awakening.

'I see,' Harry said, his tone calculating. 'You feel confident you can take over from your brother, now that he's gone?'

'Let's clear something up, shall we?' Lily proposed, the cold smile on her face not reaching her eyes. 'I'm not taking over from Ronan, because we were equal business partners from the start. My brother and I crawled up from the gutters of life to everything we have now *together*.' She lifted her chin proudly. 'We've known every level of desperation and every victory on our way up the ladder as a team. To be completely clear, there has been no bridge crossed, no dirty deed that Ronan has ever done that I haven't done right alongside him. And would do again on my own with no qualms whatsoever.' It was veiled, but a clear threat just the same.

After a few long seconds Harry held his hands up in defeat with a smile. 'I meant no offence to you. I am of course aware of your standing, I meant only to refer to the additional workload on your shoulders now that there is only one of you where once there were two.'

Lily swallowed the lump of grief that sat in her throat, not willing to let Harry Snow see her pain. He was lying about what he had meant by his question. His expression had betrayed him.

This was a backtrack. But it mattered little. What mattered the most right now was finding out what had happened to Ronan. It had been a week and the police had come up with nothing. Which meant it was down to her to find out which underworld low life had decided to take her brother out. And it had to be someone from the underworld. A rookie or chancer wouldn't be able to get away so cleanly without leaving evidence, she was sure of it. Her enquiries had got her nowhere so far, but they would eventually. No one could hide forever.

'I'm not alone in running this company, nor was it just myself and Ronan before he was killed. This is a family firm, and I have many extra pairs of hands to make sure nothing interferes with the smooth running of our businesses. So you need not concern yourself.'

'Ah yes, your sons are indeed fine men.' Harry's mouth curled up into a smile of amusement once more. 'And this...' He turned his sly gaze towards Scarlet. 'This must be the heir apparent.' His flickering gaze moved up and down as he studied her curiously. 'You'll certainly be an interesting one to watch.'

Lily didn't respond to this probe. He was looking for confirmation, but as yet she had none to give. She watched Scarlet's jaw clench and her gaze cool as she stared back at Harry. She didn't look away as many did when he turned his attention to them. *Good girl*, she thought. *Stand your ground.*

'Anyway.' Harry stood up, stiffly. 'Like I said, I had nothing to do with Ronan's death. My men and I were over near Bristol with your beloved Ray, setting up a new transport stop. Feel free to check with him to validate my alibi. I'm sure you'll trust his word more than mine.'

'By miles,' she replied drily. 'But I'm actually already aware of that.' She stubbed out her cigarette in the ashtray on the desk with neat precision. 'You were the first person I asked about.' Her tone sharpened, along with her gaze. 'If I hadn't already discovered your watertight alibi, you certainly would have seen me long before today. And it would not have been such a civil meeting.'

'Ooh.' He smirked. 'Promises, promises, Lily.' He smiled, the action strange on his naturally pained face. 'I will be sure to ask around about Ronan and let you know should any information come my way, of course. We must stick together in times such as these.' He left the office, his companion following behind. 'I'll be seeing you,' he called over his shoulder.

'I'll bet,' Lily growled under her breath as the door closed.

'Sorry to call you back here,' Connor said, moving forward from his position behind her and sitting down in the seat Harry had vacated. 'He just turned up.'

'It's fine – you did the right thing.'

'What was he looking for just now?' Connor mused, staring at the office door with a thoughtful expression.

'Weakness,' Lily replied.

She looked over towards Scarlet, who was taking it all in with interest. 'You're looking for clues, Scar,' she said. 'So here's the first thing you should know. Family are the only ones you can ever freely trust. Other than us, no matter what situation you're in, no matter who's in front of you, you don't show weakness at any time. Not ever. Because the day you show them there's a crack…' Her gaze bore into Scarlet's. 'That's the day they will break you.'

CHAPTER TWENTY

Harry Snow sat in the back of the car and stared out of the window, mostly still for once as he turned the meeting over in his mind. He hadn't expected it to go quite the way it had, and it had given him food for thought.

'What do you make of that then, boss?' came the question from the front of the car. Dave, one of his most trusted men and companion in the meeting they'd just left, looked at him in the rear-view mirror.

Almost immediately the nervous tic started up and Harry sighed. He didn't like having to speak to people, even his own men, for this very reason. He couldn't seem to control the jerky movements of his body, or the placement of his gaze when he was forced into conversation. But annoyingly, conversation was a part of life, and so, as always, he forced himself to make the effort.

'I'm not quite sure yet,' he answered.

'Do you think there's going to be issue with the market roll-out?' Dave asked.

'Most definitely,' he responded, with a nod.

He was surprised that Lily had heard about his new business plans. He'd been careful to keep them quiet and away from Ray Renshaw especially, knowing he would always have Lily's best interests at heart. But it appeared he hadn't been quite careful enough. Now that she knew, she would have her guard up. And she'd brought some fight to the table too, which he hadn't expected.

It had been a mistake to assume she was the lesser of the duo. Ronan had always been the front man, the one who conducted their meetings and agreed their terms. He'd been a formidable man with a temper no one in their right mind would want to get on the wrong side of. He had assumed that it was he who had put their little firm on the map. Not the petite, quiet sister sitting in the shadows of every meeting, ever watching and listening. He'd made a colossal error in judgement there.

He'd hoped that with Ronan's death the firm would now be vulnerable. He'd envisioned Lily walking in with red-rimmed eyes and a defeated stoop, accepting his condolences as a broken woman, scared and worried about the future now that their leader had passed. It would have been ideal. He could have swooped in and offered to buy her out of the market stalls, offer to take a load off her shoulders and give her finances a cushion for a while. He'd imagined how grateful she would have been as he offered what would have appeared to be a generous amount to the unsavvy sister of the deceased crime boss.

But that hadn't been an unsavvy tagalong, and there had been nothing broken about the woman at all. The person who'd walked into that office today was as hard as steel. It had been a real surprise. She had never revealed that side of herself in front of him before. She'd had Ronan do all the heavy talking, when they'd found it necessary. It was a clever move really. He had to give her that. Because now it was *he* who was wrong-footed and Lily was well in control.

This was why he'd gracefully retreated before any real talk of the markets came up. His idea of swooping in as some sort of business-minded saviour in her time of need wasn't going to cut it with *this* Lily Drew. Certainly not at the price he'd been thinking of offering. He'd have to revise his strategy.

'What are you thinking now then?' Dave asked.

'I'm not sure yet,' Harry replied. 'We could still go in with an offer. If she turns it down, we'll just take what we need anyway,' he mused. 'Then again, maybe we should skip the pleasantries, save the money and take it straight away.' He stared out of the window at the passing cars with a slight frown. 'But then if we haven't at least tried to be reasonable, we'll upset Ray quite significantly, and of course Ray is a very valued customer.' He pursed his lips. 'We shall have to think about it.'

Harry had fallen into a life of crime partly by accident, many years before. His father had passed down an oddly mismatched handful of successful businesses that were dotted around the country. Among other things Harry had inherited a haulage company, a small shipping fleet, several toy stores, an industrial bakery and a finance company. He'd quickly seen the potential for extra money and had built up a network of men who assisted him in making all the right connections with all the wrong people. He'd tripled his income almost overnight and now many of the smaller firms in big cities, such as the Drews, counted on his services to allow them to smoothly run their jobs.

Now, Harry was looking to expand across London, by taking over some of the busier markets. Clients often needed a fluid, fast-moving sales outlet, and whilst he was able to help them with all sorts of transportation, laundering and loans, he wasn't currently able to offer any sort of decent sales channel. It irked him to have to say no when there was so much more money to be made. And now that his son had made a potentially very lucrative new deal, dependent on having this sort of outlet, it was time to change this.

'Things are changing in London, Dave,' he said as he continued to stare at the passing cars, unseeing. 'Power is not a static entity. It's not something you're born with or can hold on to indefinitely. It's ever-moving, accorded to those with the right mindset and the right tools at the right time.' He sat back in the chair. 'I may have underestimated Lily Drew, but they're still vulnerable now that Ronan has gone. And their power was never that far-reaching anyway. However we decide to proceed, we *will* get what we want.' His gaze darkened determinedly. 'And the Drews will fade further and further until they're nothing but a memory of a firm that was a player in the big game, once upon a time.'

CHAPTER TWENTY-ONE

Scarlet sat at the small desk at the side of her room where once she had sat to do her homework, but which now doubled as a dressing table. She stared into the mirror and serious grey-blue eyes stared back. These eyes held no answers to the questions in her mind, but still she kept on staring as though some might magically appear. The room was almost in darkness as the evening swiftly fell, but she barely noticed. When it became so dark she could no longer see, she switched on the desk lamp.

As the small circle of warm light fell across the desk, her eyes were drawn down to the prospectus for St Andrews.

She felt the familiar pull as she opened the first page and looked down at the list of facilities. It looked like such a wonderful place. Somewhere she yearned to call her own, a place she dreamed of being part of. And that dream was about to become a reality. Her course was set, her room in halls had been allocated and her list of books had been emailed over to her. The future she'd worked so hard for, had studied through so many long nights for, was finally about to happen. It was all she'd thought about since the day she'd received her acceptance letter.

But how was she supposed to leave now? How could she abandon her mother? How could she leave London without knowing who killed her father and why? And on top of all of that, how on earth was she supposed to turn her back on the family business now?

Raised voices wafted up the stairs and through her bedroom door, and Scarlet tilted her head to the side with a small frown. It sounded like her aunt, though she hadn't realised she was even here. She must have come to visit her mother. As another sharp retort sounded, she opened the door and made her way downstairs to find out what was going on.

As she descended, she caught sight of her mother and Aunt Lily standing in the lounge, facing each other. Her mother had her hands on her hips and Lily stood ramrod straight with her chin held high in defiance. Neither of these were a good sign.

'I don't care what you say about it, Lily Drew,' Cath snarled, 'it ain't happening. I ain't losing her the way I've lost Ronan, so she's going to bloody Scotland and that's the end of it!'

'You want to ship your only daughter off to *Scotland* just weeks after her father's died? Is that what you're telling me?' Lily shouted back. 'You want to split this family even more than it has been already?'

'Yes, I do,' Cath retorted strongly. 'Ronan is dead; I don't want the same for her. So if that means getting her as far away from this family as possible, then so be it!'

'You can't mean that,' Lily replied with a small growl of frustration. 'I know you don't mean that. You don't want to lose her too. And you don't want her to be alone up there, to struggle through her loss without the very people around who love her, who raised her—'

'You did not raise her!' Cath cut her off with an angry roar. '*I* raised her. Me and Ronan.'

Scarlet ran forward, breaking free of the shock which had caused her to pause. 'Jesus, stop this, both of you!' she exclaimed. Neither seemed to hear her, each locked in their own side of the battle.

'I may not be her mother but we've all raised our children together,' Lily replied, her words full of emotion. 'We all picked them up when they cried, cleaned their scraped knees, taught them to be who they are. It takes a village, Cath, and *we're her* village. You can't just cut her off from that. And you can't take away the fact that the firm is the beating heart of this family. It provides our life blood, the money we need to live, to survive.'

'Guys…' Scarlet begged. She couldn't bear to see them at each other's throats like this. Not now, not when they needed to stick together.

'That's not true,' Cath argued, turning away and putting her hands to her face.

'It *is* true and you know it.' Lily drove it home, seeing the crack in Cath's argument. 'Everything you have is down to that business, whether you like it or not.'

'Stop this!' Scarlet tried to step in between them, but Cath pushed her out of the way with a sweep of her arm and stuck her finger in Lily's face in fury.

'She is *not* joining you in the fucking underworld,' Cath shot back, rounding on Lily once more with a face full of thunder. 'I am not sending her off with you towards the dangers that killed my husband. I *will* send her off to university; I *will* get her away from *you!*'

'I said *stop it!*' Scarlet suddenly roared, her temper snapping.

Both of them turned to look at her, finally taking note that she was there. She glared at each of them in turn. 'I'm sick of this! You need to stop tearing into each other like you're enemies. We're *family*,' she stressed. 'And right now we need each other more than ever.'

'*Exactly*,' Lily cried, turning back towards Cath. 'We need to stay together.'

'She is *going*,' Cath replied, incensed.

'*She* can talk for herself,' snapped Scarlet, 'and *she* is not going anywhere.'

They both turned back to her, their attentions caught.

'Scarlet...' Cath began.

'No, Mum. I'm done. The decision is mine and it's been made.' The last hope in her heart of going to St Andrews died as she realised she couldn't leave. Not now. Not ever. This was her life. This was her destiny and her duty and there was no point trying to ignore it any longer. 'I'm not going anywhere. I'm joining the firm,' she confirmed, her tone resolute. 'And there is nothing more to be said about it.'

CHAPTER TWENTY-TWO

Connor rolled over and collapsed next to Chastity with a sound of contentment. His bare chest was slick with sweat, and he took a few moments to catch his breath. Chastity curled up into his arm and he half-heartedly pulled her close. She ran a long-manicured nail down his torso.

'Well, well, tiger,' she purred. 'It seems you did miss me after all.'

'Apparently so,' he replied. He guessed he had in a way. Her body anyway. He wasn't so sure about the rest of her – she was getting on his wick if he was being honest. But she had this way about her when it came to sex which just seemed to mesmerise him. He'd never been with a woman with such skill in the bedroom, so he endured the whining and the high-maintenance ways for now.

'We still really do need to talk about your mum though,' she pushed.

Ah yes, he remembered. *That's what she'd been trying to do.* He sat up and gently pushed her off, reaching over to grab his T-shirt and pulling it over his head.

She shuffled up onto her elbow and watched him, her long blonde locks falling down over her pert breasts as she angled herself attractively. 'If we're going to make this work, we need to warm her up to me somehow. Surely you want your mum to like me?' she asked.

Connor had his back to her now and rolled his eyes. She had no idea where she really sat in the grand scheme of things. She had no idea that he – and Lily – knew exactly what game she was playing. 'Look, don't worry yourself about all that,' he said in a placating tone. 'It ain't my mum you're seeing, is it?'

'No, but she's a huge part of your everyday life; I'd like to be able to get on with your family,' Chastity replied with a stubborn pout.

'You get on with Cillian,' Connor countered.

'Yes, but if we're ever going to level up in this relationship—'

'Level up?' he cut her off with a laugh. 'Jesus, this ain't *Mario Kart*, love; we're just having some fun, ain't we?' He turned to her and lifted an eyebrow.

Chastity's pleasant mask slipped at this comment, but she quickly worked to hide her irritation. 'Yeah, of course,' she replied with a bright smile. 'But all this fun we've been having has been the most fun I've ever had with anyone.' She leaned forward, pushing her breasts against him as she pulled him back down. 'Isn't it the same for you?'

Connor grinned as she began kissing his neck, teasing his skin with her teeth. 'It certainly has been fun,' he answered before gently pulling away. 'But right now I need to stop having fun and get dressed. Cillian will be here in a second and I need to go. Can you see yourself out, yeah?'

'Yeah, sure,' she replied, her disappointment obvious.

Connor stood up and hid his irritation. She'd been hinting for a while that she wanted to get serious and maybe even move in, but that was never going to happen. Yes, she was a lot of fun, but that was all it was ever going to be. He couldn't take someone like her seriously. She played the part but they both knew why she was really there. She used him for his money, so he used her for her body. It was no more than a business transaction when it really came down to it. He didn't feel bad about this. He'd never pretended to her that it was anything more than that. It wasn't his fault if she chose not to listen. He reached for his deodorant and sprayed liberally under his arms, then quickly smoothed his dark hair in the mirror. It was time to set her loose really, but her ample assets kept him from pressing the release button.

Pulling his trousers on, he shot her a brief smile as the knock at the door sounded. 'That will be my brother. I'll catch you later.'

'OK, so when are you thinking? Are you free tonight?'

'Not tonight. I'll text you,' he called back over his shoulder as he opened the door. Cillian chuckled with amusement and Connor rolled his eyes once more. 'Bye.'

He shoved his feet into his shoes, grabbed his jacket from the peg by the door and walked out quickly before she could reply.

*

'How's the missus?' Cillian asked, tongue in cheek.

'Shut up,' Connor shot back.

'She's getting rather attached, that one.'

'Yeah, she's been on about trying to win Mum over this morning,' Connor admitted.

Cillian laughed. 'Good luck with that,' he replied.

'Nah, it ain't happening,' Connor said firmly.

'What, the dazzling Chastity ain't the love of your life, brother?' Cillian mocked.

'Oh please,' Connor replied with a frown. 'It'd take a few more brain cells and a few less sticky fingers to fit that description. When I do settle down, it will be with someone who's got a bit of something about them. Not a pair of tits on legs who only fancies my wallet.'

'Well, I'd be happy to take her off your hands if she's that much of a problem,' Cillian said with a jokey wink.

'Gross!' Connor exclaimed, swatting at his brother. 'And you ain't her type anyway.'

'How can I not be her type?' Cillian scoffed. 'I'm literally *you* but funnier.' He puffed out his chest with a swagger.

'You ain't as funny as you think,' Connor replied. He dodged the side swipe Cillian aimed at him. 'What's the word today then?' he asked, changing the subject.

'Dunno. Mum said to meet at the factory. She didn't say any more than that.'

'Did you collect the wedge from the backroom sales?' Connor asked.

'Yeah, grabbed it last night. We'll need to do the rounds with it. It's more than usual, which is great, but not sure where she'll expect us to launder it all,' he added with a frown.

'No, me neither,' Connor agreed.

He knew his mother had been pushing his uncle to figure out a better way to launder more illicit income for a while now, but he'd been pushing back. Now that his uncle had passed, he couldn't help but see the opportunity for growth. As his uncle reclaimed the space at the very front of his mind, his heart dropped and his frown deepened.

'What's up?' Cillian asked, noting the change.

'Just thinking about Uncle Ro. Can't believe there's still nothing to go on.'

Lily had got hold of the police report from a friend at the local station, but there had been nothing there that could help them figure out who'd killed him. Ronan had been found in an alleyway in a sleepy village in Essex, somewhere none of them had any reason to go. Him being all the way out there made no sense at all to any of them.

His throat had been cut with a sharp knife, but that was all they'd managed to surmise so far. There didn't appear to be any sign of a struggle; all his personal items were still on him – his wallet, his car keys, even his Rolex – and the killer had left no clues behind. The village itself was small and had no cameras nearby which could have picked them up. The nearest main road had an ANPR camera, but the report showed that Ronan hadn't been caught on it coming into the village. If anything, it was as if Ronan had been trying to stay off the radar entirely. It was all a great mystery, and one that was frustrating all of them.

'I wish he was here to tell us what to do,' Cillian admitted quietly.

'Me too,' Connor replied. He tightened his jaw as a wave of sadness and then anger overtook him for a moment. 'Whoever did this is going to fucking pay.'

'When we find them,' Cillian added.

'When we find them,' Connor agreed. 'And we need to find them. Because right now we don't know what's going on. No one had any reason to top Uncle Ronan.' He pulled a grim expression. 'So what are we going to do if they ain't done?'

They exchanged a look. 'I've been wondering the same thing,' Cillian admitted. 'That's why I've been sticking close to Mum. If they're gunning for the firm, she'd be the next in line.'

Connor exhaled heavily. 'There has to be something we've missed, some clue. We'll take another drive up there tonight, see if we can get in with any more of the locals.' They had already tried once with no luck, but it was worth another attempt. You never know who might remember something. His gaze darkened. 'Whoever it was is going to rue the day they ever decided to fuck with this family.'

'Do you think Mum's OK?' Cillian asked suddenly.

'What do you mean?'

'Well, she's just… Aunt Cath has had a breakdown. Scarlet's completely broken. You and I miss him like hell. But Mum just seems to carry on, you know? She seems a bit more stressed and that, but…' He frowned, a confused expression covering his face. 'I'm just a bit surprised she ain't more upset.'

'She is upset,' Connor responded with certainty. 'She's just as cut up as the rest of us. More so probably. But that's just her way. That's how she copes. You know that,' he added.

'Yeah, I know. I just thought this would be the thing that really broke her, seeing Uncle Ro gone. They've done everything together their whole lives.'

'And that's why she'll work even harder at hiding it than ever. That's how she's holding it all together.' He looked at his watch. 'Come on – we'd better get a move on. She'll have our balls for earrings if we keep her waiting too long.'

As they walked out into the daylight, he made a beeline for his brother's car.

Connor knew his mum was hurting. She was as warm and loving and loyal as they came on the inside. But she had a shell made of pure steel. And the deeper the hurt, the harder that shell became. It was the way she'd survived all these years, and it was the way she would keep on surviving all that was still to come.

CHAPTER TWENTY-THREE

Connor and Cillian walked into Lily's office and closed the door behind them. Lily was on a phone call and Scarlet sat opposite her at the desk. Connor sat beside his cousin with a wink of greeting and Cillian leaned against the sideboard as they waited for their mother to get off the phone.

'… see to it you bloody well do.' She slammed the receiver down with an irritated tut and glared at her sons. 'What time do you call this?' she asked, raising one pencil-thin eyebrow.

'Blame Connor,' Cillian piped up. 'I had to drag him out of Chastity's loving arms.'

'Eugh.' Lily pursed her lips. 'Does that girl not understand the concept of working hours?'

Connor shot Cillian a scathing look and ignored the talk of Chastity entirely. 'What's um…' He glanced at Scarlet. 'What's on the agenda today then?'

'It's OK,' Lily said, picking up on his hesitancy. She took a deep breath in and gave them a look. 'As of now, Scarlet is part of the firm.'

'Oh,' replied Connor with a tone of surprise. He turned to his cousin and looked her up and down thoughtfully. 'Really?' he asked with a small frown.

'Yes, really,' Scarlet replied in a hard tone. She raised one eyebrow at him in question.

'I didn't mean… I just meant…' Connor started.

'He meant welcome to the family, love,' Cillian swooped in smoothly. 'The *real* family.'

'I've always been part of the family, Cillian,' Scarlet replied quietly. 'But now I'm coming to work too.'

Cillian nodded and gave her a welcoming smile, but Connor just turned to look at Lily. She stared back at him with the same serious expression he knew mirrored his own. Scarlet had always been protected from this side of their life on Cath's demand. Whilst she knew who they were, she had no idea the extent of what went on in the dark hours of the night when she slept. Lily subtly shrugged, and he looked away, shaking his head. He didn't agree with Scarlet joining them. Not right now, at least, with things as they were, but it was apparently already decided. Scarlet was being taken into the fold. And that meant that not only would they be working together, but she was now another person he would have to defend and protect with his life. More responsibility, more weight on his shoulders.

'Welcome to the firm,' he said with a smile that didn't quite reach his eyes.

'Thanks,' she replied with a smile that didn't quite reach hers.

'With that in mind, I need you to take Scarlet out with you today on the laundry rounds, Connor,' Lily said. 'I have to sort out a supplier issue. The eejits who supply our rubber fucked up the last delivery at a colossal level. Which is the third time this year. I need to find someone more reliable and figure something out for the orders due to be fulfilled today, so that's going to tie me up for a few hours.'

'Don't you want to teach Scar about the factory first?' Connor asked.

'She's going to pick that up as she goes,' Lily replied with a dismissive wave. 'It's a smooth enough operation here. But there's a lot for her to learn on the outside. So we need to get her education moving.'

'OK,' Connor conceded.

'Cillian, I need you elsewhere,' Lily continued. 'You know Dan, the one with the kebab place who tried to lighten his bag a few weeks back?'

'Yeah?'

'Go to the estate, find some youths looking to make a bit of money and gain some brownie points with us. Get them to smash the place up a bit. Nothing that will shut him down for more than a day or so, but enough to shit him up,' she ordered. 'Make sure they deliver the reminder that we're watching him and we haven't forgotten his little indiscretion.'

Connor glanced at Scarlet. If she was shocked, she didn't let on. Her expression was as smooth as if they were discussing the weather.

'Sure thing.' Cillian saluted his mother and stood up.

'Take what cash you need from the day safe,' Lily added.

'OK.' He buttoned up his jacket and smoothed it down, shooting a charming smile at his young cousin. 'Enjoy your first trip out on the rounds,' he said cheerfully. 'Catch you later.'

Cillian left the room and Lily turned to Connor. 'Right, off you go then. Crack on.'

'Right.' Connor exhaled reluctantly. 'Let's go then,' he said to Scarlet brightly. He followed her out with a lump of concern settling into his stomach.

Was Scarlet jumping into the criminal side of their firm really what she wanted, or was it just a knee-jerk reaction to losing her dad? He locked his jaw and his face darkened. He prayed she was here for the right reasons and that she was strong enough to take what was coming, because if she wasn't, the girl was as good as dead. And there would be nothing but trouble ahead for all of them.

CHAPTER TWENTY-FOUR

Scarlet slid her gaze sideways towards Connor as he drove. 'Where are we heading first?' she asked.

'The Eric and Treby,' he answered, slowing down and turning left at the junction.

Scarlet raised her eyebrows then quickly smoothed her expression, not wanting to let Connor see that she'd reacted. Luckily he didn't seem to notice. The Eric and Treby estate was an area she'd always been warned to stay away from. It was rife with crime, and small-time gangs warred there regularly.

'What interest do we hold in the Eric and Treby?' she asked.

'We provide protection to some small businesses there, and a lot of the people who work for us live there,' he replied.

'But what about the gangs?' She looked over at him, concern and curiosity in her eyes.

'They work for us,' he replied. 'Not exclusively, of course. They have their own things going on. They collect work from firms such as ours wherever they can, and in return we have an understanding. They show us respect and don't touch any of the businesses under our protection.'

'OK.' She twisted her lip thoughtfully. 'So they're our street-level soldiers then?'

Connor looked sideways at her and nodded approvingly. 'You're getting it.'

'So just to clarify, we're safe in there?' she questioned warily.

'To a degree,' he replied. 'We need to introduce you, spread the word you're one of us. Expect some pushback at first – they'll test you to see if you're going to hide behind us or whether you can hold your own.'

Scarlet nodded. 'That's fair enough,' she said reasonably.

'You think you're ready for that?' Connor asked.

The look in his dark eyes told her that he didn't, but she ignored it. 'Any time,' she replied.

As they continued down the road, she turned this new information over in her mind. Knowing she was about to come face to face with people from an estate gang initially filled her with dread. Of course it did. It would fill anyone with dread, she reasoned. But she had chosen to step up in the firm, and that meant she needed to harden up and show the underworld that she was her father's daughter. She was no wallflower. She had never been a wallflower, no matter what she'd faced before. She had never had to face anything like this, of course, but she needed to start somewhere.

Lifting her chin a little higher, she narrowed her eyes and looked straight ahead. She'd spent her whole life looking up to her father, and now he was gone. She felt her bottom lip wobble as the thought of him sent a spear of grief through her heart and bit down on it hard, clamping her jaw tightly. The wound was still raw. She doubted it would ever not be, so she had to try and work out how to live with it. He'd been her favourite person in the world and she felt truly lost without him. Life hadn't turned out the way she'd thought it would, and that was hard. But jumping into the firm, taking her place in the machine he'd lovingly built over the years was already helping her to feel closer to him and that helped a little.

She knew that nothing she could do would bring him back or take away the hollow void his death had left in her heart. And there was another pain, a secondary pain, that came from not knowing what had happened to him. This was the one she was trying to focus on for now. She knew she wasn't the only one who felt it. Everyone wanted to find his murderer and take their revenge. And unlike most families who went through this sort of thing, their family would actually *take* that revenge. Knowing that felt strangely comforting, but there was still a barrier of frustration that they needed to get through. They still needed to actually find out who it was.

Scarlet had methodically searched her father's office drawer by drawer and file by file, but as Lily had predicted, she'd found nothing relating to the meeting he'd been murdered at. She and Lily had visited several allies in the underworld asking questions, searching for any piece of information that could help them work out what had happened, but so far no one seemed to know a thing.

With nothing to go on, Lily had sat down with Scarlet and shared her list of potential subjects. Harry Snow had been at the very top but had been scribbled out after finding out he'd been miles away with Ray that day. The rest of the names on the list had been scribbled out too, all dead ends. Her aunt had frustratedly admitted she was no closer to finding the murderer, and now that left them with the hard task of taking a closer look at their allies. They'd spent all this time looking at foes, but could it have been a friend?

'Here we are.' Connor's voice cut through her thoughts.

'Great, let's go.' She was glad to be busy at the moment, to be throwing herself in the way she was. Anything that could distract her from her pain was welcome right now.

Scarlet took in the tall, brown-brick buildings around them as she stepped out of the car. A couple of older women stood talking on the walkway outside their front door a few floors up on the building in front, but they stopped to stare down at the newcomers. A few kids kicked around an old football on the small patch of grass, and a group of young men stood together in an alleyway outside the window of one of the flats where music boomed out loudly.

As they caught sight of Connor, one of these men tapped another on the shoulder and whispered something in his ear. He immediately disappeared down the dark alley, leaving Scarlet to wonder what had been said.

Taking his time, Connor straightened his jacket, looked around and lit a cigarette before ambling over to the group. Scarlet followed, staying a couple of steps behind.

'Damo,' Connor acknowledged the man who'd whispered in the other's ear. He grasped his hand and briefly patted his shoulder in a familiar way before letting go and stepping back. 'How's it hanging?'

'So-so, Drew, so-so,' he replied. 'What's the word on the next shipment?'

'There's one coming in in a couple of weeks. Good load from the sound of it, all high street. Plenty to go around,' Connor said.

The young man who'd disappeared returned and gave Damo a nod. With this, Damo stepped aside with a smile. 'Chain's in the shop. He's expecting you.'

Scarlet followed Connor down the alleyway, keeping a careful eye on the young men as she passed them. They were all staring at her now, sizing her up with no subtlety at all. They carried on past another block of flats and through to a small row of shops.

'Who's Chain?' she asked quietly.

'He runs a shop selling second-hand tech goods. It's mainly a front. He launders money for us, and his guys back there shift a lot of our goods,' Connor replied.

'OK. Why do they call him Chain?'

'It's his choice of weapon.' Connor glanced at her. 'There's a lot you can do with a chain.'

'I see.' Scarlet fell silent as they reached the shops.

Connor pushed open a door and they entered the tiny cramped space. Shelves from floor to ceiling were overflowing, and Scarlet had to grab a pack of lightning chargers to stop them falling to the floor when her elbow knocked them. Wiping the dust from the long-untouched item from her fingers, she was careful not to knock anything else as they made their way to the back of the shop.

A broad man with a brooding expression on his face sat back in the chair behind the counter. He wore a dark tracksuit with a white tank top beneath. A thick gold chain which Scarlet presumed was one of his choice weapons hung around his neck. He stood up as Connor stopped and towered over the pair of them. His expression lifted into a smile.

'Wah gwan, my friend?' he said, his thick East End accent still holding a trace of his Caribbean roots.

'What's up, Chain? Good to see you,' Connor replied with a brief grin.

'You got something for me?' Chain asked. He looked Scarlet up and down while Connor reached into his inner jacket pocket. He kissed his teeth and pulled back, looking at her at arm's length. 'What we got 'ere then, bruv? This your bird? This ain't no place for a date, Connor man. Geez... At least take her to a Nando's or something, get some meat in her. She's a bit skinny, innit?'

'*She* is Connor's cousin, not his date,' Scarlet shot back sharply. 'And *she* is also perfectly fine as she is, thank you.' She glared at him with a cold hard expression. Connor had told her she needed to hold her ground, so that was exactly what she was going to do.

Connor chuckled as he pulled out the wedge of money wrapped in brown paper. Chain pulled back even further and his eyebrows shot up so far they almost disappeared into his hairline. He stared at her for a moment. Eventually, his eyes flickered up and down her body.

'I don't like your skirt,' he said in a low deliberate tone, narrowing his dark brown eyes. 'Too long for my liking. I like 'em short and sweet – easy access.'

'That's OK,' she retorted, her level gaze unfaltering. 'I don't like your chain. Too blunt a weapon for my liking. I like them sharp and to the point. Much more efficient.'

There was a short silence and then suddenly Chain burst out laughing, throwing his head back in mirth. 'Ah… You're alright, you are.' He turned to Connor. 'She's working with you now, is she?'

'Yeah, she is,' Connor replied. 'This is Scarlet. Scarlet, Chain.' He gave the introduction and then turned his attention back to the money in his hand.

Scarlet relaxed now that the initial tension had been broken. 'Good to meet you,' she said.

'Likewise.' Chain looked at her critically. 'You're Ronan's girl, that right?'

Scarlet felt her muscles tighten at the mention of her father. 'That's right,' she said levelly.

'I'm sorry about your dad,' Chain said. 'He was a good man.'

'He was the best,' she replied in a low voice, the emotion she was trying to hide sneaking in on the last word. She clamped her mouth shut and turned away, pretending to look at the goods on the shelves.

Connor cleared his throat. 'Right, so there's twenty grand here. Can you clear that in two?'

'Weeks? Sure.'

'Good. I just spoke to Damo out front – we've got a big high-street shipment coming in a couple of weeks so I'll bring some down to you.'

'How much?' Chain asked, putting the wedge of money away under the counter.

'Hard to say. It's a medium truckload, but it will be full. Details are a little vague, but it'll be too much to shift through just the stalls, so I'll have a good amount for you.'

Chain gave another shrug along with a nod of consent. 'Two weeks? OK, I'll have the crew waiting.'

'Catch you then.' Connor put two fingers to his head in a casual salute and walked back out of the shop.

Scarlet nodded goodbye and followed, staying silent as they walked back through the estate and past the group of men to the car. She waited until Connor had started the engine and pulled away before she began asking questions.

'Why are you bringing goods here? I thought all the high-street stuff went through the markets?'

Connor settled back in his seat, leaned his arm on the car door and rubbed his dark stubble with his hand. 'When we get a lot of stuff in, there's sometimes too much for the markets to handle. Safely, I mean,' he added. 'We'd love to push more through, but it has to be a small enough amount that it can be hidden when the pigs or the market inspectors come sniffing round.'

'I thought you'd have the inspectors on payroll,' Scarlet responded, surprised.

'Some of them we do, but not all of them. And we can't control the police presence – it's too wide for us to handle,' he admitted.

'Fair enough.' She looked out of the window. 'Chain seems alright,' she said, changing the subject. 'I mean, obviously after you push back a bit,' she added.

Connor's head immediately swivelled round and his dark eyes locked onto hers. 'Don't ever be fooled by his friendly face, Scarlet,' he warned, his tone serious. 'Don't ever let your guard down or assume he's your friend because he isn't. He's a cold hard thug who would hurt you in an instant if it meant coming out on top. That playful banter he afforded you back there was because you were with me.' He eyed her hard. 'You were safe in there because you're a Drew. No other reason. And even though you're a Drew, until you show them otherwise, they will have in the back of their mind that you're the weak link if they ever need one to break. You need to remember that and take it seriously.'

Scarlet pulled a grim expression and looked away. She had clearly been naïve in thinking that that conversation was as hard as it would be to get in with the local gangs. She was going to have to do a lot better, she realised. But only time would allow her to do that.

Connor looked at her and saw the flush of embarrassment creep up her face. 'Look, it's fine, you wouldn't have known that. But that's why I'm telling you now. Just keep your guard up.' He turned to focus on the road ahead with a small sigh. 'This world is full of dangers, Scar,' he said, his tone grim. 'Ones you're going to have to pick up on fast if you want to survive it.'

CHAPTER TWENTY-FIVE

Ruby pulled her hood over her frizzy ginger hair and ducked down slightly as she dashed past the wall that ran along the front of the building she was trying to avoid. She looked down to the ground and pushed her hands deeper into her pockets as she slowed to a fast walk, jumping slightly as the sirens on a passing police car came on. The blue lights flashed and passed her before disappearing around the next corner. She shook her head, feeling stupid for jumping. It wasn't like police sirens going off was an uncommon occurrence around here. The part of the Polthorne estate where she currently resided was a squalid area rife with drugs and thefts and all sorts of other small crimes.

Passing the front of her old building, she stared up at the window to her old lounge wistfully. The light was on, which meant someone was in there waiting for her. But she wasn't stupid enough to go home, not now. She owed too many people too much money. Bad people.

Another wave of pain rippled through her thin body and she clamped her jaw against it. The need for her next hit was becoming very real, but she was out of cash and none of her dealers would give her anything without payment up front anymore.

Hurrying through the estate, she headed to the place she was staying. Perhaps Sandy had some cash she could wheedle out of her again. Sandy was one of the local whores, one of the few who worked alone without a pimp. She'd taken pity on Ruby and was currently allowing her to camp out on her sofa until the heat died down. It was a shithole of a place, and Ruby had to listen to her service customers at all hours of the day and night, but it was far safer than sleeping on the streets. And as far as Ruby was concerned, there was no alternative.

Like a lot of addicts, she had a home and a family to go back to if she wanted, but she didn't want to give up the drugs or the level of freedom she so fiercely clung to. She couldn't bear to be around her mother, who would beg and plead with her to get clean, or see the look of disapproval on her brothers' faces. So this was her only option, if she wanted to stay off the streets. For now, at least.

Reaching Sandy's flat, she let herself in and headed to the lounge. As she walked in, she paused, almost turning around. Sandy was stark naked on the sofa, her legs splayed, showing the world her wares, and a man of around fifty, Ruby guessed, was pumping away at her, grunting with pleasure as he thrust into her again and again. Ruby's presence didn't seem to bother him in the slightest – nor Sandy, who shot her a quick smile of greeting.

Ruby debated leaving again, as she'd have to pass the bucking pair to get to the kitchen where she could sit and close the door, but it was getting cold outside, and the longer she was out in the open, the more chance there was of being seen by the wrong people. She gritted her teeth and passed them as swiftly as she could, narrowly avoiding the man's hairy backside as she skirted around him to the kitchen.

She closed the door and sat down, placing her elbow on the small table and resting her heavy head in her hand. She closed her eyes as she felt the coolness of her touch on her forehead. She was burning up. Another sign she needed a hit, and soon if she was to avoid going into full withdrawal. She stayed this way with her eyes closed until the groans reached a crescendo and the man finished what he'd come here to do. There was some mumbled conversation by the front door as he left and then finally it closed.

She lifted her head, about to go through to the lounge to speak to Sandy when she heard another voice. She groaned internally. Sandy's next client was here already, it seemed. She settled back into the chair and debated making a cup of tea when the kitchen door opened and Sandy came in, closing it behind her.

Dressed in nothing but a threadbare dressing gown, which she pulled tight around her ample bosom, she took the seat next to Ruby, lit a cigarette and took a deep drag. She was in her late thirties but looked almost ten years older and wasn't in the best physical condition. But she kept her prices and her standards low, and so she was never short of customers from around the local estates.

'You alright?' she asked, looking at Ruby critically as she smoked.

'Not really,' Ruby admitted. 'I need to get some gear but I'm out of cash.' Ruby looked back at her with a small smile of apologetic hope. 'I don't suppose I could borrow some off you, could I? I'll pay it back soon as I can. I just need to get myself straight.'

Sandy sighed. 'I wish I could, but the rent's due this week and the bills are coming out too. I need all I've got.' She took another drag and twisted her mouth to one side. 'I do have another option for you though,' she added.

Ruby looked up at her warily. 'What option's that then?' she asked.

'My regular out there just turned up with his mate in tow, asked if I could fit them both in. I have another appointment after him, so I was going to say no. If you want to sort him out then the cash is yours.'

'No – no way,' Ruby said immediately with a strong shake of the head. 'I ain't doing that.'

Sandy shrugged. 'Suit yourself,' she said, taking another drag. 'Just thought I'd give you the option. It ain't that bad really. A few minutes work then it's over and you've got cash in your hand.'

Ruby felt another wave of pain wash over her and she squeezed her eyes shut for a moment. She really was getting desperate. But was she really *that* desperate? As she tensed her muscles against the complaining ache that was settling in, she realised she was. She knew with disappointment that she was getting to the stage where she would do anything at all to avoid withdrawal.

'What would I have to do?' she asked in an uncertain tone.

'He asked for a suck and a fuck,' she stated bluntly. 'You insist he puts the cash down first – that's important; don't forget. Then strip down so he's got something to look at, suck him off for thirty seconds or so then let him do his business. They never take very long. Job done, forty quid in your pocket.' She shrugged as if it were the most normal thing in the world.

Ruby swallowed. She couldn't believe she was even considering selling herself for a measly forty quid, but what choice did she have? The pain was getting more intense by the minute and she knew she wouldn't last without her heroin much longer.

'Alright,' she said in a small voice.

'Good girl,' Sandy said approvingly. 'You never know, you might find you even like it. I don't mind it meself.' She stubbed the cigarette out in the overflowing ashtray on the table and stood up. 'Come on then – time's money. You can use the bedroom; I'll stay in the lounge.'

Ruby rose on wobbly legs, feeling her stomach jump up into her throat at the thought of what she was about to do. She could still back out, she told herself. But she knew she couldn't. She needed that money to stop the pain. There was nothing else for it.

She followed Sandy back into the lounge and stared at the two men waiting there. One she recognised – she'd seen him there the week before. He had to be the regular Sandy said she'd expected. Her gaze flicked across to the other, a man of around forty with salt-and-pepper stubble around his jaw, small dark eyes and a rounded beer belly popping out of an otherwise slight frame. His T-shirt had a stain on it, she noticed abstractly.

'Ruby, this is Wes; Wes, Ruby.' Sandy made the introductions. 'She'll take care of you today.'

Ruby saw his little eyes light up as they raked over her body and she suppressed a shudder. Sandy gave her a nudge and she stumbled forward, the increasing ache in her body reminding her why she was doing this.

'Er, this way,' she said awkwardly, walking into the only bedroom in the small flat. She heard the door close behind her and she took a deep breath before turning round. As she turned, she realised he was already undoing the belt on his trousers and was watching her with a feral hunger in his eyes.

'Money first,' she snapped, making him pause.

'Alright, how much?' he asked in a gruff tone.

'Forty. On the table.' She gestured towards the small wooden bedside table and waited as he pulled the money out of his wallet and placed it down.

'There. OK?' he asked.

She nodded. 'OK.'

He pulled his T-shirt over his head, revealing a hairy torso beneath, then continued with the belt buckle and began to pull down his trousers. Ruby averted her gaze and reluctantly began stripping off her own clothes. As she got down to her underwear, every instinct was to cover up, but she forced herself to carry on. She felt her cheeks burn, but even as they did, she felt the wail of the monster inside her even more prominently, begging her to get its medicine. She looked up at him with determination. Nothing mattered but getting those drugs. Nothing mattered but getting his money.

Her gaze lowered to his hand, which was now casually massaging his erect penis. It was larger than she'd expected, but not the largest she'd ever seen. It would be fine, she reasoned. It was a business transaction. Her body for his money.

Wes reached over and grabbed one of her breasts, squeezing it a little hard, and she made a small sound of shock. She wasn't sure why she hadn't been expecting it, but as he made a sound of approval, she felt the bile rise in her throat and swallowed it down with difficulty. She forced herself not to recoil as his hand wandered down to the area between her legs and he roughly pushed his fingers into her most private parts.

'Oh yeah,' he moaned under his breath. 'Sit down then,' he ordered.

Ruby did as she'd been asked, knowing what was coming. He wanted to be in her mouth; he wanted to get what he'd come for. She perched on the bed and braced herself as he came towards her. Her small brown eyes widened as he pushed himself towards her face and grabbed the back of her neck. She automatically opened her mouth to protest and as she did, he thrust himself in there with a loud groan of pleasure.

Ruby felt him fill her mouth and almost gagged as he began to move back and forth. She closed her eyes and reminded herself over and over that this was what she had to do – it was what she'd *chosen* to do – to get what she needed. But after a few thrusts, she couldn't stop the wave of nausea and pulled back, gasping for breath in order to stop herself from throwing up.

Wes paused for a moment then shrugged. 'Alright then, straight to it.' He pushed her back on the bed and lifted her knees up in one swift movement, spreading them apart and positioning himself between her legs. He stared down over his protruding belly at her vagina and licked his lips in anticipation as he lined himself up.

Still gulping in air, Ruby blinked, not mentally ready for this next stage yet. But before she had a moment to process it, he pressed forward and pushed roughly inside. She gasped as she felt him thrust as deep as he could get.

Taking her gasp as a sign of pleasure rather than a sign of shock, Wes was spurred on and began to pull back and forth, quickly getting into a fast rhythm and working himself into a frenzy. He groaned and moaned as the friction began to push him towards the brink of explosion. His mouth gaped open and his breaths became almost laboured as he bucked into her again and again.

As she stared up at him, at the stranger she'd just met who was old enough to be her dad, she was suddenly filled with revulsion. She felt him inside her, filling her, using her, and her whole body suddenly felt tainted. She tried to push him off.

'Stop,' she said. He either didn't hear her or ignored her, but either way he continued having sex with her, his panting intensifying. 'I said *stop*,' she said louder.

This time he looked down at her quizzically but still didn't stop, dismissing her words as he focused on reaching the finish line. Ruby started to panic, sex with him now feeling more wrong than anything ever had before.

'I said *stop*,' she yelled, pushing him off her with force.

He looked down on her, anger colouring his face. 'What the fuck are you playing at?' he growled. He reached forward and grabbed her legs again, forcing her back into position, this time with a strength she hadn't realised he possessed. He shoved her legs apart easily, despite her resistance, and pushed himself back inside her, thrusting harder this time, pushing painfully far in.

'I said *fucking stop*,' she yelled again, her own anger coming to the fore.

He was momentarily taken off guard by the change in her tone, and she used the opportunity to push back off him once more. This time she didn't just stop there, knowing he would only continue to rape her if she gave him the chance. Putting all her strength behind it, she kicked out at his groin hard and felt momentary elation as her foot hit its mark.

Wes cried out in shock and pain and fell to the floor, rolling around in agony as he held his privates. As quick as lightning Ruby shot off the bed and shoved on her trousers. Stepping into her trainers and throwing her top over her head as she moved, she grabbed the money off the side. Whether he agreed or not, she'd more than earned it. Pausing for a split second as she eyed his trousers on the floor, she then bent down and snatched his wallet out of the pocket. She'd seen the wedge he'd had in there when he'd pulled out her payment earlier and it was a damn sight more than forty quid.

'Hey, what the fuck!'

She realised Wes had caught on and swiftly turned and ran out of the small bedroom before he could try and grab the wallet back.

Sandy was walking towards her on the other side of the door, pulling her gown around her waist. 'Ruby?' she asked, confused. 'What's going on?'

Ruby didn't stop to answer – instead she ran out through the front door and down the street until she was well away from the small flat and its sordid inhabitants. She ran and ran until what little strength she had left was spent.

Once she felt confident enough that she wasn't being followed, she slowed to a walk and pulled her hood up over her hair.

With the initial danger now behind her, tears began to fall down her cheeks, unchecked. She wrapped her arms around herself, trying to walk off the dirty feeling all over her body from what she'd just done. Why had she done that? But even as she asked herself, she knew the answer.

She needed to find a more permanent solution to her money issues, because she knew now that she could never bring herself to do that again. And she didn't ever want to be in a position where she had no other choice again.

She shivered and her hand tightened around the wallet she'd just stolen. She needed to get to her dealer and buy enough to see her through the next few days. Once she'd had a hit, she'd be able to think clearly and work out what she was going to do. Because she couldn't go back there, not after what she'd just done. Sandy wouldn't welcome her back now.

With a shake of her head she put Sandy out of her mind. Right now she just needed to get some heroin in her system. But as she changed direction, she clocked the man staring at her from just a few yards away and froze. Turning back the way she'd come, she bolted, running as fast as her aching legs would carry her.

CHAPTER TWENTY-SIX

Scarlet locked the car and walked up the front path towards the house, glad to be home. It had been a long day.

After doing the laundry rounds with Connor and learning as much as she could about the people they worked with, she'd put in a few hours on the paperwork at the factory. It was a simple enough operation: she'd figured out the general way of things already, but she wanted to make sure she understood everything inside out.

It had only been once she'd reached the bottom of a pile of paperwork that had been waiting to be sorted for a while that she realised it was already dark outside and much later than she'd thought. Lily had left a few hours before – off to sort out some other issues that weren't to do with the factory – and the production line had long turned quiet. She'd packed up for the day, grabbed her bag and headed on home, ready to take a long soak in the bath and go to bed.

For the first time since her father had died, she was actually looking forward to going to bed. Every night so far she'd lain awake, locked in her grief, crying herself into an uneasy sleep. But today she was so tired that although she had no doubt that she'd still end up having a cry, she'd most likely fall asleep pretty quickly from exhaustion. It was a welcome thought in the darkness they were all currently trapped in.

She let herself in and walked through to the kitchen, where a plate sat on the side wrapped in clingfilm. It was a simple meal, chicken salad with some coleslaw, but the fact that Cath had dragged herself out of her grief-induced trance long enough to make it for her lifted Scarlet's hopes. She'd been looking after her mother since it all happened, making her food, putting her to bed, trying to get her to get up and move around in the day. So to find Cath had been in the kitchen putting food together for her was a good sign.

Wearily, Scarlet dumped her bag on the kitchen island and pulled back the clingfilm. She picked at a stray piece of coleslaw with her fingers, popping it in her mouth before reaching into the drawer for a fork.

'You're back.'

Cath's voice surprised her slightly. She hadn't heard her approach. 'Oh hey,' she said with a tired smile. 'Yeah, sorry, I was engrossed in paperwork; I didn't realise the time.'

'Paperwork?' Cath asked with a sceptically raised eyebrow.

'Yeah, there was some stuff that had been piling up – it needed sorting. Took some time,' Scarlet answered.

'Sure…' Cath slurred the word slightly and sauntered in from the hallway. 'If *paperwork* is what we're calling it now.'

Scarlet paused and her gaze dropped to the glass of wine in her mother's hand. 'How many of those have you had?' she asked.

'What, wines?' Cath asked, sitting down heavily in one of the dining chairs. 'A few.' She took another sip.

Scarlet pursed her lips and balled the clingfilm up in her hand before dropping it in the bin. She took a mouthful of her dinner and leaned forward onto her elbows as she chewed. Cath often had a few drinks with family or friends but never enough to get drunk like this. And considering the fact she hadn't, to Scarlet's knowledge, touched a drop since the night of Ronan's murder, this was a little concerning.

'So what have you really been up to?' Cath asked.

'I just told you,' Scarlet replied between mouthfuls. 'Paper-work.'

'Right.' Cath made a snorting sound of disbelief. 'You know you might as well just be honest with me, Scarlet.'

Scarlet frowned, irritated, and stood upright, putting down her fork. 'I'm not lying to you, Mum. I've been sat in the office all afternoon doing paperwork. I'm trying to learn the business. And yes, both sides,' she added. 'You know that.'

Cath's eyes flashed with anger. 'Well, there we go. He's not cold in his grave – well, not even in his grave at all yet, and here you are in that viper's clutches already. I'm—'

'That's enough,' Scarlet snapped, turning to her mother. She took a deep breath and tried to calm her tone. 'Aunt Lil has done nothing wrong. And I was always going to end up choosing this path, whether Dad was alive or not,' she lied. There was no point riling Cath more by revealing just how close she'd been to leaving. Not now. She closed her eyes and exhaled. 'I don't want to hurt you,' she said, 'but I've joined the firm and that's all there is to it.' She lifted her chin a little higher. 'I'm not discussing it again.'

Cath's cheeks filled with colour. 'Well then,' she said bitterly. 'You're heading down the same fucking path that killed your father.' Suddenly a deep rage seemed to overpower her and she hurled her wine glass across the dining room. It smashed against the wall and fell to the floor in tiny pieces.

'What the hell!' Scarlet exclaimed in shock. Cath had always had some fight in her, but she'd never seen her lash out like this before Ronan's death. Wine dripped down into the puddle below, but Cath didn't seem to care.

'What are you doing, Scarlet?' Cath continued, her words turning into a loud wail.

'What am *I* doing?' Scarlet retorted. 'I'm *working*, Mum. I'm picking up where Dad left off – I'm joining the rest of my family and trying to carry on his legacy.'

'His legacy!' Cath barked out a bitter laugh. 'That ain't his legacy, Scarlet, *you* are. Not that foul, dirty world he and Lily worked in. He didn't want you there, not really,' she shouted, standing up and pointing at her daughter. 'He wanted you to be clean and safe, not dragged down by that sister of his.'

'What he wanted was for me to join him, and you know it,' Scarlet shot back, anger bubbling away inside her. 'You just don't want to admit that to yourself.' She eyed her hard, trying to keep on top of her emotions. 'Now you need to stop slagging Lily off. Just because you're drunk, it ain't an excuse. We *all* miss Dad. *All* of us. But we have to carry on as best we can, and for me that's by carrying on with my life as best I can.'

'That ain't a life, Scarlet,' she spat. 'You have a chance, a *real* chance to make a *good* life for yourself at that university. The way neither of us did. And you're chucking it away, for what? He'd be ashamed of you, Scarlet, if he could see you now. If he could see you throwing yourself away into that criminal world of hers.'

'For fuck's sake,' Scarlet roared.

Cath blinked and swayed slightly, shocked by the unusual outburst.

Scarlet took a deep shaky breath to control her anger and placed her hands on her hips for a moment before continuing. 'I'll tell you something now, Mum,' she said through gritted teeth. 'He'd be damn proud of me if he were here and don't you *ever* tell me otherwise again.' Her voice rose and wobbled slightly. She swallowed. 'And Dad did what he did because it was in his blood, it was who he was. It's who we *all* are. I'm not throwing St Andrews away for nothing; I'm choosing another path. I'm going into the family business that Dad built with all his heart and soul. A business he chose and loved, not one he was forced into. *Neither of us* have been forced, not by Lil or anyone. And the sooner you realise that, the better.'

Without waiting for her mother's response, Scarlet grabbed her bag and walked back out the front door, slamming it behind her.

CHAPTER TWENTY-SEVEN

Lily walked to the door with a slight frown. She hadn't been expecting anyone tonight. She peered through the peephole, and her frown turned into a look of surprised recognition. She opened it and stepped back, giving Scarlet room to walk in.

'What's wrong?' she asked, noticing the red rims around her niece's eyes straight away.

'Oh, it's just…' Scarlet put her hands to her face for a moment and shook her head. 'It's just Mum. Can I please stay with you tonight?'

'Of course you can,' Lily replied, closing the door. Her frown reappeared, though this time in concern. 'What happened?'

Scarlet put her bag on the stairs and headed for the study, where her aunt liked to sit in the evenings. 'She's had a few too many and started mouthing off about Dad and about me working in the firm.' She sat down in one of the armchairs.

Lily raised her eyebrows. 'I see.' She had an inkling there had probably been a few choice comments about her too, but if so Scarlet was tactfully keeping these to herself.

'She threw her glass at the wall,' Scarlet said, shooting her aunt a look. 'I don't think I've ever seen her do anything like that. There was wine and glass all over the place and she just didn't care. But it wasn't that – it was the comments she made about Dad. I just saw red. I needed to get out.' She rubbed her eyes tiredly.

Lily pulled a grim expression. It was only natural that Scarlet had made her way here. The two of them had always had a close connection, even when she'd been small. Lily was the one Scarlet turned to, and they understood each other better than the rest of the family did. But although she felt for her niece and wanted to support her, she knew Cath was suffering and her inbuilt need to protect everyone forced her to speak neutrally.

'Your mum only has you now, you know,' she said, resting her head back on the chair and staring through the wall. 'She's lost your dad and she's scared she'll lose you too. And she doesn't know how to process everything.' She sighed. 'I'm surprised she's drinking though. That was never her style.'

'No, me too,' Scarlet replied.

Lily glanced at her. Her niece looked tired and drawn, her pale face was whiter than usual and her bright grey-blue eyes looked heavy and dull for once. 'You need a drink yourself,' she said. 'What do you fancy?'

'Have you got vodka?'

'Of course,' Lily replied and walked over to her loaded drinks trolley. 'With?'

'Whatever you've got, I don't mind.'

Lily busied herself with pouring Scarlet a vodka with soda and lime and added a couple of cubes of ice from the small bucket she'd brought in earlier for her own drinks. It wasn't surprising that the two were arguing. Cath seemed to be arguing with everyone at the moment.

She handed Scarlet the glass. Scarlet smiled back gratefully. Picking up her gin and tonic from where she'd left it earlier, she sat back down.

'You can sleep in Ruby's room – the bed's made up,' she said.

'Thanks,' Scarlet replied. She took a deep drink from her glass and rested her head back in the seat. As her shoulders finally dropped, so did her brave front, and her misery began to show in her face.

'I really miss him, Aunt Lil,' she said quietly, emotion colouring her words.

Lily turned to see two silent tears slowly running down her niece's cheeks. She felt her own eyes prickle at this and swiftly blinked them away, swallowing hard. She missed him too, more than anyone could imagine.

'I know you do,' she said, once she'd gained outward control of herself. 'I know it must feel as though a chunk of your heart has been ripped out.' She reached across and squeezed Scarlet's hand as the girl bent her head and finally gave in to the flood of tears. 'And that's OK. All that means is that you loved him and that he mattered. And that's how it should be.' She nodded and clamped her mouth shut as her own emotions threatened to spill over once more.

Scarlet squeezed Lily's hand back and took a deep breath, wiping her tears with her other hand. 'I just never expected him to be gone. That's stupid, I know. We all end up saying goodbye one day. But I just didn't think it would be now. Not yet. He was still so young.'

Lily nodded and struggled to maintain her composure. 'Yep,' she managed tightly, before biting down on her lip. She sniffed and straightened up, clearing her throat.

She looked down at the glass in her hand and focused on the clear liquid within, watching the chunks of ice make their slow journey around the rising bubbles. Mentally she gathered up all of her pain and balled it into a sphere of angry energy. As she allowed her thoughts to circulate around it, she felt the pain dull to a more controllable fury and she took a deep breath, releasing it and allowing the tension in her shoulders to drop. Anger she could cope with. Anger she welcomed.

'Whoever did this has a lot to answer for, Scarlet. And I promise you, they will pay, when we find out who they are.' She nodded slowly, staring through the study wall into a future only she could see. 'An eye for an eye, the Bible says. Because even God agrees that when someone does you wrong, you have no choice but to pay them back in kind.'

CHAPTER TWENTY-EIGHT

Scarlet woke slowly, the hazy comfort of sleep still lingering as she gathered her thoughts. The pillow her head rested upon was fluffy, and the sheets were warm and soft on her skin as she lay embraced in comfort. It wasn't her bed, however, and it was as she remembered the previous evening that the memory of Ronan's death came crashing back into her mind too, like a boulder of pain. Her heart sank back down into the rut it had been caught in for the last couple of weeks, and she squeezed her eyes shut hard for a second, bracing herself against the grief, before pulling herself up into a half-upright position.

As she sat up, she realised she wasn't alone. Someone was sitting in the chair across the room, watching her, and as her head swivelled and she focused on who it was, she almost let out a small groan. The frizzy red hair, sharp nose and naturally downturned mouth could belong to no one but her least favourite cousin.

'I turn my back for five minutes and there you are, jumping in my grave,' Ruby said in a low, dangerous voice.

Scarlet sighed and sat up with a withering look at her older cousin. 'Hello, Ruby,' she said resignedly. 'It's been a while.'

'It clearly has, Goldilocks,' Ruby replied with a sneer. 'Now get out of my fucking bed or this little bear's going to eat you for breakfast.'

*

Scarlet padded downstairs and pulled the long, warm cardigan her aunt had lent her the night before around her waist. Ruby followed, her feet thumping loudly on each step behind.

'Scarlet?' Lily called from the kitchen.

Scarlet turned towards her voice, thankful that she'd be able to palm her cousin off on her aunt. Lily would deal with her. She was the only one who could. She entered the kitchen to find Lily pouring out two cups of coffee.

'Was that you on the stairs just now? I thought I heard…' Lily's frown turned from one of confusion to one of surprise. 'Ah. Hello, Ruby,' she said cautiously. 'Coffee?' She lifted one eyebrow in question and reached for a third cup.

Scarlet sat down at the end of the breakfast bar, purposely away from her cousin, and grabbed one of the already-filled cups.

'So you assume the thumping had to be me then?' Ruby asked petulantly. 'Does *Princess Scarlet* not make noise when she moves? She floats above the fucking carpet, does she, in all her glory?'

'No, no floating,' Lily replied, eyeing her daughter with a mixture of hope and wariness. 'And I never assume anything.'

'Oh, whatever,' Ruby spat back sarcastically.

Lily sighed and softened her tone. 'It's nice to see you, Ruby. If this is a social call,' she added carefully.

'Well, of course it's a social call – what else would it be?'

Scarlet turned her face away so that Ruby wouldn't see the blatant look of disbelief upon it. Lily did, however, she realised, as she caught her eye briefly by mistake. But her aunt didn't react.

Ruby was a livewire, a loose cannon in the Drew family. Lily had given up trying to keep her close a long time ago, because the more she tried to keep her in check, the worse her behaviour seemed to become. Ruby would turn up from time to time though like a bad penny, always when she wanted something. In fact, Scarlet couldn't remember a time that Ruby had come to visit her mother just for the sake of seeing her. She doubted Lily could either.

'So how are things?' Lily asked brightly. 'What have you been up to?'

Scarlet saw the wistful expression her aunt so quickly hid and felt a spark of pity for her. It had killed her, the way Ruby chose to live her life, and the fact that she had no control over her daughter's self-destruction. Lily always wanted to save everyone in the family. But some people were just beyond saving.

Ruby sat down at the other end of the breakfast bar warily, taking the cup of coffee that Lily offered. 'Things are alright,' she said gruffly. 'Or they were until I came home to visit and found someone else had taken my place, in me own house, in me own bed.' She shot a scathing look at Scarlet, who purposely ignored it.

'Scarlet was just staying the night, Ruby,' Lily replied. 'Your bed was made up and I had no idea you were planning to visit. You didn't let me know you were coming, as usual.'

'I couldn't let you know I was coming, because… Um. Well, because my phone was stolen.' She nodded, as if agreeing with her own story, and Scarlet resisted the urge to shake her head. Her cousin had never been very good at lying, for someone who so often depended on lies to get what she wanted.

'I was attacked and mugged – they took everything I had. My phone, my bag… every penny I had to me name was in that bag. They took everything.' Her tone was heavy with self-pity, but neither Scarlet or Lily reacted with shock. Instead, they shared a glance over Ruby's hung head, before Lily addressed the statement.

'How terrible that must have been for you, Ruby,' she replied evenly. 'What did the police say?'

'Well, I didn't go to the police. Drews don't go to the police. What if they started looking into the family? I had to protect you all, didn't I?' Ruby blustered.

'But you aren't part of the firm, Ruby,' Lily responded. 'There's no need to keep something as terrible as an attack to yourself.'

'Well, I did, all the same,' Ruby said with a sour face. 'To protect you. We have to look out for our own, don't we?'

Scarlet pursed her lips and stared out of the window. The only person Ruby Drew had ever looked out for was herself.

'Well, that's very valiant of you, Ruby,' Lily replied, her tone neutral. 'And if that's really the case then thank you.'

Ruby ignored the inference and took up a look of superior martyrdom. 'You're welcome,' she said. 'So that's why I couldn't call ahead. I have no phone now.' She quickly dropped her face, glancing up briefly at Lily to see if it was having any effect.

Lily sighed. Clearly Ruby wanted to lead her somewhere, so got right to it. 'Well, when did the attack happen?' she asked, her gaze piercing Ruby's intently.

'Oh, um… It was a couple of days ago,' she replied.

'So, what… Tuesday?'

'Um, yeah. Tuesday,' she confirmed.

'Where?'

'What?'

'Where did it happen? Where were you attacked?' Lily continued, her gaze never leaving Ruby's face.

'In this alleyway I was walking through,' she responded, a tinge of red beginning to colour her pale cheeks.

'Where was the alley?'

'Jesus, what is this, twenty questions?' Ruby cried, rolling her eyes.

'No, I just want to know, Ruby. Where was the alley?' Lily pressed.

'Down near Mile End, off Alfred Street somewhere, alright? Christ, it's like telling a bleedin' Nazi rather than me own mum,' she complained.

'Alfred Street. OK, no problem.' Lily stood up and took a sip of her coffee. 'I'll have one of your brothers check it out, see if there were any shops with CCTV nearby that might have picked it up.'

'What? Why?' Ruby asked, sitting up straighter sharply.

'To see if we can find out who mugged you, of course,' Lily replied. 'Maybe we can get your phone back, but if not, at least your brothers can give whoever hurt you a good kicking. Like you say' – she took another sip – 'we have to look after our own.'

'Well…' Ruby's mouth flapped open and shut a few times. 'There weren't no cameras where I was – I checked.'

'You checked?'

'I checked, yeah.' Ruby's gaze flicked away as she shifted uncomfortably.

'Which end did you say it was on Alfred Street?' Lily pushed.

'I didn't!' Ruby shot back, beginning to lose her temper. 'Oh, forget it, you don't believe me. You never fucking believe me. Here I am after being attacked, beaten half to death I was, and you couldn't give a shit. I didn't even report it because all I could think of was protecting you, and now I'm broke with nothing because of it. And what do I get? Nothing, that's what I get.'

Scarlet rolled her eyes and turned towards her cousin. 'Oh please… Beaten half to death?' she repeated. 'There's not a bruise on you.' She looked pointedly down at her cousin's bare arms and at the pale unblemished skin above her low-cut top.

'And what do you fucking know?' Ruby rounded on her cousin, enraged by the fact she'd called her out. 'Why are you even here anyway? Ain't you got somewhere to be?'

'Alright, that's enough,' Lily interjected. 'Stop it, both of you.'

Scarlet exhaled heavily and stood up, deciding to leave the conversation. It wasn't her argument anyway. 'Actually, I do have somewhere to be,' she said. 'I'm going to grab a shower if that's OK, Lil?'

'Of course. Grab a towel from the airing cupboard,' Lily replied, her placid expression unchanged during the course of the conversation.

'*Lil?*' Ruby repeated, her eyebrows shooting up indignantly. 'She's your aunt, you know, you cheeky cow. Turn eighteen and think you can suddenly waltz around talking to my mum like she's an equal, do ya?'

Scarlet took one last sip of her coffee and walked through the kitchen past her cousin. 'She's also my boss and we decided to drop the title for the sake of professionalism. Not all of us grow up to be work-shy, Ruby,' she shot over her shoulder as she made her way up the stairs.

'Who the fuck does she think she is?' Scarlet heard Ruby exclaim as she nipped up the stairs towards the bathroom.

'Oh Ruby, she doesn't think anything. Leave her alone,' she heard Lily reply as she picked out a towel. 'Now let's get down to what you're actually here for, shall we? I was hoping it might have been to see me, but clearly not by the sounds of things…'

Scarlet closed the bathroom door and turned on the shower, grateful for the water blocking out the sound of her cousin's response.

Half an hour later she came down the stairs, combing her fingers through her long, wet hair and listening warily in case Ruby was still carrying on. When she reached the bottom without hearing any further arguments, she paused, unsure why the house was so silent. Lily's tight blonde curls bounced around the side of the lounge door as she stuck her head out.

'I'm in here,' she said.

Scarlet walked in and sat opposite her aunt on one of the plush beige sofas, curling her legs up beneath her. She was slightly constricted in the tight black knee-length dress of Lily's she'd borrowed, but she managed to get comfortable enough in the end. She looked around.

'Where's Ruby?' she asked.

'Gone.' Lily looked down and Scarlet caught the sorrow that flitted across her features.

She nodded her understanding. 'What was she after?' she asked.

'Money, as usual,' Lily replied with a sad smile.

'I'm sorry,' Scarlet said.

'Don't be. It's not the first time, and it won't be the last. I gave her enough to sort herself out for a while, but we'll see what happens.'

Scarlet nodded and looked away out of the window at the cloudy skies beyond. She knew what that meant. They all did. Ruby Drew was down on her luck, so this was most likely only the first of several visits until she rinsed all she could from them and outstayed her welcome. Her jaw formed a hard line. This was a bad time for her cousin to be distracting Lily with emotional drama. Because right now Lily was the only real strength they had holding off the appearance of vulnerability within the firm. With Ronan gone, the vultures were circling. But whether they liked it or not, it seemed they would be seeing more of her problematic cousin yet.

CHAPTER TWENTY-NINE

Ian Walker watched the clock in the outer hallway of his work-place as the second hand moved ever closer to the top. As it finally clicked over 5 p.m., he pushed his ID card down in the clocking-out slot with a satisfied smile. It was Friday, the pub was calling him and he had absolutely no intention of keeping it waiting by spending a moment more than he had to at work. He wasn't one of these crazy people who lived to work. Oh no, not Ian. He worked to live. He did what he had to each day to get the salary it warranted paid into his account at the end of each month and that was it.

He whistled cheerfully and swung his jacket over one shoulder as he pushed through the door back into the outside world. He drew the air into his lungs with gusto, already mentally forming his excuses as to why he couldn't get home to watch the soaps and eat Chinese with his wife Theresa. He tipped his head towards another couple of guys he knew as they came in to start their shifts and turned the corner towards the rear car park.

His jaunty, energetic pace slowed to a stroll as he caught sight of the two men standing by his car. One of them had his back to him, staring out towards the busy main road behind and the other was half sitting on the bonnet, smoking a cigarette. Both were smartly dressed in black suits and shiny shoes, both had neatly cropped black hair, chiselled jaws and dark brown eyes and he still – despite the years he'd known them – couldn't tell them apart until they started talking. The only difference he could make out between the Drew brothers was that Connor was routinely more serious.

Glancing back over his shoulder to make sure no one was watching, he made his way over. 'Alright, lads?' he said cheerily. He glanced back again, feeling uncomfortable at how exposed their meeting was. They didn't usually come to the depot. 'Wasn't expecting to see you here – everything OK?'

The one leaning against his car just smiled as he drew in another inhalation of smoke, and the one who was standing turned around and walked over, hands shoved into his pockets.

'We were in the area,' he said, cutting straight to the point. 'I need the route for that truck full of high-street stuff coming in next weekend. You got it for us?'

Ah, thought Ian. *This one's Connor.*

'Not on me, but I can go back and get it,' he said, half hoping they'd let him deliver it the following day as initially planned instead.

'Good,' Connor replied. He glanced at Cillian and his brother stood up, flicking the cigarette away and blowing out the last of the smoke from his lungs. 'We'll wait for you in The Old Frog. Don't be too long.'

''Course, I'll meet you there,' Ian replied to their retreating backs. 'Fuck's sake,' he muttered under his breath, making sure it was too quiet to sneak into their hearing. There went the early start to his Friday night after all.

*

Cillian twirled the beer mat around on the table in front of him, watching the door. Connor faced him, looking at some point in the distance behind him. He had seemed annoyed and distracted all day.

'What's up?' Cillian finally asked.

'Hm?' Connor's attention slowly wandered back to the table.

'What's up with you? You seem off. Everything alright?'

'Yeah, I'm fine,' Connor replied with a dismissive shake of the head. He sat up straighter and took a sip of his pint. 'Just thinking about Scar.'

'What about her?' Cillian asked, twirling the beer mat again. He'd been surprised too at the sudden turnaround with Scarlet. One day she was just their kid cousin, the next day she was all grown up and one of them. It was a big change. But then life was full of change, and they'd all had to jump in the deep end at one point.

'She's so young, that's all. I'm not sure she's ready for all of this.'

Cillian gave a small shrug. 'We were younger than her when we jumped in,' he reminded him.

'But we were always set to join the firm. We knew what was what from the start – Mum never shielded us from it. There was no big shock when it came to it,' Connor replied. 'Plus, she's a girl…'

'And? What about it?' Cillian said with a frown. 'Mum's a girl. I'd like to see you repeat that to her.' He chuckled.

Connor rolled his eyes. 'OK, maybe that's unfair. But she's still green. She ain't as hard as us.'

Cillian's gaze shot up towards his brother's face and he studied his double thoughtfully. Connor was a smart man, but sometimes he didn't see everything that he and Lily did. Scarlet wasn't some delicate little butterfly – her mind was razor sharp, and she had a strength in her that would serve her well in their way of life. It was raw and unharnessed, yes. But she had her father's head on her shoulders. Lily was throwing her in at the deep end on purpose. There was no point pussyfooting into this world. They resided in deep, dark waters, and anyone who came to join them either had to sink or swim. But Scarlet would swim; he knew she would. Lily knew that too. Connor just needed to have a little more faith.

'I think you underestimate her, Connor,' he said. 'Give her time. Let her win a few challenges. I think she'll surprise you.'

'Maybe so,' Connor conceded. 'But in the meantime, we have to make protecting her a priority. Not so that she knows, of course. But we need to keep her safe.'

'Of course,' Cillian agreed. 'That's why we're here, ain't it?' He gave his brother a wry smile. 'Mum might run things, but we protect this family – *all* the family – through thick and thin. To the last breath.'

'To the last breath,' Connor repeated, chinking his pint glass against his brother's.

Cillian's gaze flickered up to the door and back as it opened. 'Heads up,' he said quietly.

Connor cleared his throat and set his face into a hardened expression as Ian sat down on the chair between the two brothers.

'OK, I've got the route details,' he said, looking around and shifting in his seat uncomfortably.

Ian was a shift manager at one of the largest truck depots in the east of England, and the man they paid to feed them the highly protected routes for the trucks they hijacked. The depot had hundreds of trucks coming and going or passing through in any one day. So many companies used the depot that the brothers were able to hit one every now and then without coming under any serious suspicion.

Ian was lazy though, and the brothers purposely kept him on his toes to make sure he delivered everything they needed. Whilst the lure of the money he made off them was more than enough motivation to get involved, he was a middle-aged man who had no real ambition and who had settled into the comfortable rut of routine over time. He was all for the easy options in life.

'About time,' Connor said curtly, his dark gaze boring into the older man's. 'Let me see what we're dealing with.'

Ian swallowed and reached into his pocket, pulling out a folded and crumpled set of papers. He lay them out on the table and tried, rather unsuccessfully, to un-crease them with the heel of his hand. 'Here we go.' He pointed at the trail marked on the map and then to the second sheet with the timings. 'This route's a bit more direct than what you usually like to hit, but there is a leg here...' He leaned over and squinted at the map, finding the point he was looking for with his finger. 'This is where they come off the main roads through the country for a bit. It's a small window, but it's pretty rural there for a few miles.'

Cillian pulled the paper closer towards them, eyed the section Ian had indicated and twisted his face in uncertainty. It wasn't a big area – no room for mistakes or delays if other people happened to be on the road. He followed the route back, looking for another option, but there wasn't one.

'You don't like it,' Connor stated, reading his face.

'I don't,' Cillian agreed. 'Do you?'

'No, not really. It's not in the best area for transporting it either.'

'You want to take the whole truck?' Cillian asked, surprised.

'I don't think we'd have time for an offload here,' Connor said reluctantly. 'It's too close to civilisation. We'd have to hit fast and get in and out quick.'

'It's more risky than usual,' Cillian added.

'But it's a big haul,' Connor countered. 'We could leave a longer break before the next one if we wanted.'

The brothers stared at each other for a few moments, each mulling it over.

'We could stage a block behind, divert any potential traffic,' Cillian mused. They'd done it before, when the window of opportunity had been tight. They'd had some of the men who worked for them pose as road workers to make sure they were undisturbed.

'We'll have to take the driver too – this isn't rural enough to hide him in the woods. Plus, after last time...' Connor pulled a face.

'What happened last time?' Ian asked, curiosity written all over his features.

The brothers glared at him and he immediately dropped his gaze to the table, his cheeks colouring. They turned back to the route.

'It's doable,' Cillian said eventually. 'Let's pull some of the boys in and work it out properly.'

'OK.' Connor turned to Ian. 'Are these photocopies?'

'Of course,' he replied as the brothers stood up either side of him.

'Good. We were never here; you never saw us,' Connor said with a warning glance.

'Yep, yep, no problem,' Ian stuttered.

Without another word the twins turned and walked out of the pub, the photocopies of the route safely tucked in Connor's pocket.

CHAPTER THIRTY

Harry Snow walked through the busy Roman Road market slowly, his knuckles white with stress as he gripped the top of his cane. He didn't really need the cane to walk – he wasn't that old and had no debilitating condition in his legs – but he found that it helped to focus some of the involuntary jerks his body made when he was in a crowded area. His neck twitched his head to the side, and the muscles stayed taut as a loud group of children ran past. He gritted his teeth and forced his head back into a straighter position.

Dave stood by his side, matching his boss's slow pace and not commenting on his clear discomfort out of respect. Two more men walked a few paces behind, there for their muscle and nothing more.

Harry Snow was a shrewd businessman but wasn't blind to his own weaknesses. His business crossed over into the underworld and he found he had the stomach for the more violent side of it from a distance, but he wasn't physically violent himself. And so he made sure to keep a selection of men at hand to carry out that side of things for him, and to protect him from anyone who wished to do him harm.

They reached a fruit stall and he paused, reaching for a punnet of cherries. 'How much?' he asked, his gaze flickering between the woman selling the fruit and the punnet in his hand.

'Two pound, love,' she called back.

He reached into his pocket and pulled out some change, handing it over as she put the cherries in a brown paper bag. His gaze moved across the busy market and settled on a large clothing stall a few metres away. A woman shouted out the deals available and sorted some change from the money bag around her waist when a customer walked over with a couple of T-shirts.

'Here you are.' The woman handed over the paper bag and he passed it to one of the men behind to hold for him.

'The lad, three o'clock, leaning against the wall,' Dave said quietly.

Harry slid his gaze to the side and homed in on the young man Dave was referring to. He looked around eighteen, maybe twenty, dressed in a loud tracksuit with an equally loud cap, smoking a cigarette. He was also surveying the area – subtly – but not so subtly that they couldn't clock who he was. He was the watcher. It was his job to check the area for police and market inspectors. As they watched, his hand holding the cigarette paused on the way up to his mouth. He quickly dropped it and tapped something out on the phone in his other hand. Finishing his text, he looked up at the clothing stall and then to two or three others.

Harry followed his gaze. The woman on the clothes stall put her hand to her pocket, where he guessed she must have felt her phone buzz. Without bothering to look at it, and after asking the customer she was with to wait for a moment, she turned, reached up above one of the walls of clothes and dropped a sheet. Harry lifted his eyebrows, impressed. The sheet looked as though it was the outer wall of the stall and had prices and offers pinned to it. It was as though the clothes hidden behind had never been there.

'Note those stalls down. That bag stall and the homeware one down there.' He pointed it out.

'The other clothes one down this side just reacted too,' Dave added.

'Good. That's four. I know there are more – we'll just need to keep scoping them out.'

It pained Harry to have to figure out the Drews' market stalls this way. It took too much time and manpower. They were highly secretive about which stalls they ran, for obvious reasons. But figure them out he would. And then he would take them over. One way or another. He'd come himself today just to see the lie of the land, but from tomorrow he would send his men instead. At least now they had a better idea of the set-up and a way to spot what they were looking for.

'No muscle by the looks of it,' Dave said.

'No, there would be no need,' Harry answered. 'They've got watchers – that's enough for this sort of hustle unless there's trouble.'

'Which there will be,' Dave replied.

'Which there will be,' Harry agreed. 'But they don't know that yet.'

As they spoke, a young man walked over with a jaunty stride and a coffee in his hand. His floppy brown hair fell over his forehead and he flicked it back, smoothing it into place with his free hand.

'Hello, Jasper,' Harry said, touching the man's arm briefly in greeting.

'Hello, Dad,' he replied, looking around with interest. 'How's it going?'

'We've clocked a few,' Harry replied, careful to keep his voice down. 'Walk with me,' he said, realising that the lad leaning against the wall was watching them with mild curiosity. 'Look at the stalls.'

'Not my kinda stuff, thanks,' Jasper replied with a smirk.

'Nor mine, but why would we be wandering through a market like this if we weren't interested in any of the stalls?' Harry replied, the patience in his tone wearing thin.

'Fair point,' Jasper conceded. He turned towards the nearest stall and began looking through the old records they sold there with faked interest. Harry stood beside him and nodded to Dave, who melted into the crowd with his other two men.

'Have you spoken to your contact about the delay?' Harry asked, pausing on an old Beatles album with a smidgen of genuine interest.

'I have, but he's not happy,' Jasper replied with an edge of annoyance. 'I need things to start moving with these stalls. I don't want him going elsewhere.'

'I'm more than aware of that.' Harry pursed his lips and dropped the album back into the box. 'But we aren't on the playing field we thought we were.'

'Well, how much is she likely to want? Maybe we just pay it out, take that initial hit.' Jasper turned and they slowly made their way out to the edges of the market.

'I'm not sure. It would be well above what they're worth though, even if she could be persuaded. They're lucrative outlets for the Drews, and Lily knows it.'

'Why did you ever think she didn't?' Jasper ran his hands back through his hair, exasperated. 'I wish you'd figured that out before I told my contact we could pull this off.'

'Because I made a wrong assumption. A very wrong assumption,' Harry replied grimly. 'Let my failing here be a lesson to you,' he added. 'But we still can pull it off. We're just going to have to use brute force. I'd been hoping to avoid that, but it seems we have little choice.'

The more he'd thought about it, the more he realised his best shot was just to take what he needed from under them. There would be comeback from it, sure. But so long as he took them unawares, he would hold the upper hand. He could make sure that there was so much protection around them that they couldn't strike back with any real force. It could anger some of his clients,

Ray Renshaw for certain, but at the end of the day they still needed him. And business was business. It would all settle down eventually, no matter how disgruntled they were – he was sure of it. And perhaps to appease clients like Ray after the fact, he could offer Lily a small payment for what he'd taken, out of the goodness of his heart. Or perhaps not. He'd see how things went and how he felt at the time.

'Well, however we do it, we need to get the ball rolling,' Jasper said grudgingly. 'It's a very lucrative contract and I don't want to lose it.'

'I know, I know,' Harry replied, putting his hand up to stop his son from continuing. 'We will. Very soon.'

They carried on in silence and made their way out of the market where Dave and his men were waiting for them.

Jasper had been working for Harry for the last few years since leaving school, and although he'd slotted into the business well enough, he'd been itching for his own project to run. Harry had offered him several opportunities to take over one of the arms of the company, but that hadn't been enough. He wanted to be a pioneer, start something up on his own.

It was something Harry admired in him greatly, but it also left him in a predicament. New business opportunities didn't just turn up every day. However, after going over to France one weekend, Jasper had come home with a sparkle in his eyes. He'd been introduced to a new gentleman, who had access to several large warehouses used to store excess stock by big-name brands. He'd worked out a way to fiddle the electronic system to lose twenty per cent of the stock without a trace. It worked all the way back to the client, whose books would be altered without any alert. It was practically foolproof. All the guy needed was a channel to sell the goods on through.

Jasper had quickly told the man that with his shipping contacts, he could get it over without suspicion so that it could be sold on in the UK, far from its original source. But it couldn't go through normal shops – that would put the product codes back onto the radar. So it had to be the markets. Quick sales, lots of cash and, most importantly, no paper trail.

When Jasper had come to Harry with the venture and asked for his assistance in setting up a market chain, Harry had been more than happy to oblige his only son. It was the perfect set-up – other than the small fact that the markets were already run throughout London by several local firms. He'd taken over a couple of set-ups already, by paying them out and making deals, but some of them were too big to mess with. And then there was Lily. Her chain was just big enough to cover what they needed, her firm just small enough to override. They'd thought after Ronan's death this would be easy. It was now clear that this wasn't the case, but they were still weakened without him, and that was all Harry needed to work things to his advantage.

'We'll sort this out, son,' Harry said as they reached the cars. 'This is your time, and your business is a good one. So don't you worry about the obstacles still in our way. One way or another, we'll take the Drews' stall chain. And we'll make sure they never see it coming.'

CHAPTER THIRTY-ONE

The next couple of weeks passed in a cloud of uneventful yet busy days for all, as Scarlet became more deeply immersed in the business. She'd returned home the night after staying at Lily's to a grudging apology from her mother. They weren't on the best terms, and things were still strained, but they'd settled into a slightly better routine at least, from what she'd told Lily.

In the search for her father's killer, Scarlet and Lily had begun quietly looking into their allies. With no suspects left in their pool of enemies, they'd had to start looking closer to home, but they didn't want this to become common knowledge. If it *did* turn out to be a friend then they didn't want to alert them to their probes too early, and if it wasn't, then they didn't want to offend them. They were making slow to no progress. They were partly glad of this. No ally had been uncovered to be a secret enemy just yet. But they were also frustrated at being no closer to finding Ronan's killer.

In the factory, Scarlet had now taken over most of the paperwork, under Lily's watchful eye, and had begun suggesting improvements to make things more efficient. She'd met with a couple of their suppliers and had spent more time on the factory floor, learning how everything worked from delivery to output.

Lily was impressed by how quickly she'd taken everything in, and although she wouldn't want to test her theory so early in Scarlet's career, she privately believed that should she ever need to leave it under the girl's control for a period of time, at the very least it wouldn't all go to pot.

On the other hand, Scarlet still had a long way to go with the rest of the business. She'd picked up the general gist of how they did things with the protection clients, the heists and the stalls, but she still had a lot to prove to the people watching, and there were still a couple of other moneymakers they had in the background that she had yet to learn about.

Lily leaned in through the open door of Ronan's office – she still couldn't think of it as Scarlet's yet – and knocked on the door frame to get her niece's attention. 'Hey, have you got a minute?' she asked.

'Of course,' Scarlet replied, closing the lid of her laptop. 'What's up?'

Lily sat down in the chair on the opposite side of the desk to Scarlet and crossed her slim legs, settling back comfortably and studying her niece with a half-smile.

'How's your mother?' she asked, lacing her fingers together in her lap and resting her elbows on the arms of the chair.

'She's OK,' Scarlet responded, a slight frown marring her usually smooth forehead.

'She's still drinking a lot?' Lily enquired.

'Yeah.' Scarlet sighed. 'But if I bring it up, the conversation twists into one about personal choices, and me working here…' She tailed off, shaking her head.

'I noticed she put a lot away last Sunday,' Lily mused. 'But I guess no one can blame her.' She looked over to the picture of her brother smiling with his wife and daughter on the wall. As the familiar ache of loss and guilt tugged at her chest, she refocused on what she'd come in to talk to Scarlet about. 'Listen, there are a few things you're still not aware of, in our business.'

'Oh?' Scarlet's frown deepened and her gaze sharpened. 'What things?'

'You know our main businesses, but there are a couple of smaller things we run on the side that are quite lucrative too. Things your mother was never made aware of.'

'Oh. OK.' Intrigue settled into Scarlet's expression and she leaned forward on the desk. 'What things? How come she never knew?'

'Your mother knew about our main income and turned a blind eye, as you know. But when we started venturing into certain other areas, we decided to keep it just between those of us who were working them. Your mother wouldn't have understood. It would likely have been the final straw for her, and your father knew this. But' – she held her hands out to the sides – 'the money was too good to ignore. And the opportunities were there. We would have been stupid not to take them up.'

'What opportunities are we talking?' Scarlet asked.

'Well, for starters we run an illegal gambling club.'

'A gambling club?' Scarlet asked, surprised.

'Yes. Here in the factory. In the basement. Once a month we hold a high-stakes poker game – no paper trail, no register. People like us come to play. They can use their cash with no questions asked, it's private and what happens in there stays in there. It's a great money-spinner,' Lily said with a twinkle in her eye.

She loved their poker nights. It was one of the few times she felt she could truly have fun and relax, whilst the boys kept a close eye on things and made sure everyone behaved as expected. It was rare that any trouble occurred, as all the crooks who came to these nights didn't want to be taken off the guest list. So even those who had beef with each other tended to keep it to themselves until they were elsewhere.

'OK. But why would that be an issue with my mum?' Scarlet asked, confused.

Lily leaned to the side in her chair and switched her crossed legs around. 'Around the time that we were thinking about setting this up, I think Father Dan caught wind of it.'

Father Dan was the priest at the church they'd attended every Sunday since they were children. An ex-boxer and solid part of the local Irish community, Father Dan had been fresh in the game back then and had stayed on ever since, delivering sermons with a passionate tone and the flush of secret pre-service whisky in his cheeks. They all respected Father Dan, but no one more so than Cath. She hung off his every word.

'The week before we were going to trial the first game out, Father Dan delivered a very strong sermon on gambling and how it was a sin and would send the immortal soul straight to the devil.'

'Oh wow,' Scarlet said, her eyebrows rising up.

'Yes.' Lily gave a small smile of amusement. 'Well, that was it, you see. The second we got home, all Cath could talk about was this sermon. She made everyone swear not to gamble and even stopped your dad doing the lottery.'

Scarlet laughed. 'The lottery?'

'Oh yes, she took it very seriously. Perhaps it took her mind off the other things we were doing, I don't know. But as time went on, she just seemed more and more set on this belief. And so we never told her.'

'So you don't believe poker will send you to hell?' Scarlet asked with a laugh.

'No,' Lily replied. 'Not gambling.' Her gaze wandered back to the picture of her brother again. What would he be thinking as he looked down at them all now?

The question of where her soul would end up when she said goodbye to this world had taken up a lot of her head space over the years. She was faithfully religious and believed wholeheartedly that God would judge them all one day, but she wasn't convinced on the rigidity of their priest's take on things. In the end, after many years of mental debate, she'd decided that although they may be on the wrong side of the law, and although a lot of the things they did were bad, they weren't evil at heart. The things she and her family did were for the good of the people they loved, not because they took pleasure in dark deeds. And when her day came, God would know that, she'd decided.

'What else?' Scarlet asked.

'Hm?' Lily focused in on Scarlet.

'You said there were some other things?'

'Yes.' She sat up a bit straighter and cleared her throat. 'We also run an escort service. Your mother wouldn't be pleased about that for obvious reasons. It was easier for Ronan for us all to just keep that private.'

'Oh. Yes, I doubt she'd have been very happy. So how does that all work then?'

'Well, it's only a small business – we keep high-end girls for high-paying clients. They're not as easy to find as you think; most escorts aren't up to the sort of standards our clients enjoy. Plus we don't have the manpower to be running more than a handful. They need housing, protection and negotiators for their clients.'

'So, we're pimps...' Scarlet said slowly.

'So crass,' Lily admonished with a tut of disapproval. 'No. The ladies we supply are for company only. They get taken to dinners, parties, conferences; all sorts really. They dress well, make good conversation and as far as anything else goes, that's their business.' Lily pulled her slimline cigarettes out of her pocket and lit up. 'We're aware that they do solicit further services, but that money is their own. We only make money from the front on that one.'

'It's legal then?' Scarlet asked.

'Actually, yes,' Lily replied, blowing out her smoke. 'We put that through the books. And launder a little through there too. Not too much though, as that gets looked at from time to time.'

'To be expected, I suppose,' Scarlet mused.

'Indeed.'

'So what input will I be having on these two ventures?' Scarlet asked keenly.

'On the escort side it's really just the accounts at the moment, which I'll do with you, and management of the website. From time to time one of the girls might need assistance with something, but nothing major.' She took another drag on her cigarette, savouring the hit, then blew it out slowly. 'As for the gambling, I want you to start coming along, getting to know people.' Her deep brown eyes locked onto Scarlet's. 'You need to show these people who you are, your strength, the reasons you're going to be a strong leader one day.'

'Leader?'

Lily realised a second too late that she'd slipped. She bit the inside of her lip, annoyed. She hadn't wanted to discuss that yet, not for a long time, but surely the girl understood where all of this would one day lead?

'Well, I won't be around forever, Scarlet,' she said. 'You're the next generation. People will be watching to see whether or not you're strong enough to carry this firm.'

'But what about the boys?' Scarlet asked with a frown.

Lily took another drag on her cigarette, taking her time to exhale in silence. Her boys had been in the business from a very young age and had grown into hard, smart, capable men. They were respected and feared in all the right places and had carved out their positions in this world with style. But however good they were at their jobs, they weren't natural leaders. They needed guidance. They needed someone who would assess a situation and take a tactical path, who would plan out the route they needed to take. Left to their own devices, they often made wrong or reckless decisions.

Scarlet, on the other hand, was strategic and cautious. She was young and had a lot to learn, which was something Lily would have to cure over time. But there was a natural steeliness about her, a detachment from the world, as if she was observing life from a distance. She assessed every situation with sharp intelligence and then approached it with a shrewd strategic confidence. She had backbone, and she had a temper that wasn't easily riled, though when it was, it was glorious in its ice-cold fieriness. That fire Scarlet had inherited from Ronan, and Lily could see much of herself in the younger woman too. She was a Drew, through and through.

Ignoring the question, Lily stood up and stubbed the cigarette out on the ashtray her niece had kept in there for her. Scarlet needed to form her own opinions on how the boys worked within the firm. 'The next poker night is tomorrow night.' She looked her up and down. 'Come to my house in the afternoon. I'll have an outfit waiting.'

'OK.' Scarlet nodded.

'You need to be on top form,' Lily added as she made her way out of the door. 'Because you'll be walking into the middle of a pack of wolves. And they'll be looking for any chink of weakness in your armour.' She looked back at her niece. 'It's your job to make sure they don't find one.'

CHAPTER THIRTY-TWO

Connor drove down the deserted country road and pulled to a stop beside a small cluster of trees.

'Come on then – grab the seat,' he ordered as they both jumped out of the car. He reached into the back for the jack. There wasn't a lot of time to spare; the truck they were about to hit was only two or three minutes behind them.

Cillian opened the back door of the old banger they'd borrowed from the scrapyard. He pulled out a baby car seat and tugged the hood forward so that no one would be able to tell it was empty.

They'd discovered a few years back that when they caused a distraction to try and lure drivers out from their cabs, they were often too wary to do so, suspecting – correctly – that they were being targeted for their haul. However, when the distraction was what appeared to be a vulnerable baby on the side of the road, their concern for the infant tended to override any deep suspicion and they quickly offered assistance.

Cillian placed it down near the back wheel facing forward and then jogged off to kneel behind one of the nearby bushes, pulling his balaclava down as he melted out of sight.

Connor checked his balaclava was still folded up on his head like a hat, then kneeled by the back wheel, securing the jack to the underside of the car. He began working the jack, slowly lifting the groaning old car as the sound of an engine became louder and louder behind him. The roar of the truck diminished as it slowed down. The road was too narrow for the truck to pass, now that he was blocking the way. He continued pumping the jack slowly, then after a few seconds the truck door opened and he heard the driver step down.

'Oi, mate, you alright there?'

Connor didn't turn, made no indication that he'd heard the man's words. There was a pause and then the sound of the man taking a few steps towards him. Connor calculated that Cillian should be creeping around the back of the van about now and closing the gap between himself and the driver.

'Oi, I said are you OK? Do you need a hand?'

Come on, Cillian, he thought irritably. He turned his head slightly, careful to hide the majority of his face behind his shoulder. 'Oh, hiya,' he called in what he hoped came across as an Eastern European accent. Anything to throw the man away from the truth. 'Ya, I could… could use…' He slowed to a stop as he heard the driver cry out in surprise and fear.

'What the fuck!'

Quick as lightning, Connor pulled the balaclava down then turned and jogged over to where Cillian had the driver on the ground. Their years of experience and skill coming to the fore, they twisted the man onto his front, movements in sync, and quickly bound his wrists and ankles with zip ties.

'Ouch! Jesus, what are you doing?' the man roared, outraged. He struggled but it was to no avail – he was trussed up like a turkey.

'One, two…' Cillian counted and as he reached 'three', they hoisted him up between them by his arms and legs.

'Oh God, oh God,' the man began to wail in a panic. 'Please let me go. Take it, take whatever you want, just let me go. I don't give a crap – it ain't my stuff. I won't tell them anything, I swear.'

They reached the back of the truck and after a short pause so that Cillian could open the back door, they threw him in. Connor jumped up, swiftly followed by Cillian, and the pair dragged the now-screaming driver as far back as they could. They ignored his pleas as they secured him to the back of the cab with another zip tie, and then Connor pulled a thick roll of gaffer tape from his pocket.

'Hey, listen,' he said in the same accent as before, slapping the driver's cheek to get him to focus. 'This is going on your mouth. Calm down or you'll block your nose. You'll be let go soon; no harm will come to you. But you need to stay calm and quiet till then for your own sake. You got it?'

The driver looked up at him, terror in his eyes, and nodded shakily.

'Good man. Now close your mouth and breathe.' He placed the tape over the man's mouth and tapped his shoulder in what he hoped came across as a reassuring gesture.

Cillian was waiting at the door, urgency clear in his stance. They tried to talk as little as possible on jobs, so that nothing was given away, but Connor got the silent message. He jumped down and they closed the truck back up again.

'We need to get moving,' Cillian mumbled quietly. 'You want the car or the truck?'

'I'll take the truck.' Connor passed his brother the keys to the car.

Cillian opened the boot and pulled out two fake number plates. He handed them to Connor, who quickly fixed them over the real ones and then jumped up into the cab.

He took a second to get his bearings then moved the truck forward, following his brother as he continued on down the road. They would move in convoy to the barn and then back again. He took a deep breath and thought over what was ahead of them. Unlike most of the routes they took, today they had to cut through South London. From where they'd taken the truck, it was unavoidable unless they wanted to drive straight through a known catchment for police spot checks. This wasn't welcome at the best of times, but especially not when they had a man tied up in the back. So the only way was through.

He gripped the steering wheel tighter and clamped his jaw grimly. The risk on this one was higher than they usually liked. But they were all in now, whether they liked the look of things or not. Connor just prayed they got through without being stopped.

CHAPTER THIRTY-THREE

Cillian took one last look at the frightened man in the back of the truck and then slammed the door. He was terrified, naturally, but he was taking the situation well. He'd stayed calm and hadn't tried anything stupid whilst they'd unloaded.

It had been a good haul. Everything they'd hoped for, in fact. The truck had been packed to capacity with clothes, shoes, handbags and accessories, all from big high-street names. These were the best catches, in his opinion. The high-end stuff might be more expensive, but the clients haggled the price down, and it was slower and harder to shift. This lot would keep the markets full, and there would be enough left over to feed through the gang in the estate. When they were put to the task, they were actually pretty good salesmen, and whatever they took was sold at a decent profit in no time.

Cillian brushed his gloved hands together to dislodge some dust they'd picked up unloading all the crates. 'OK, you ready to head back?' he asked.

Connor placed the lid back on the box he had been looking in. 'Yeah, let's go.' He jumped up in the cab and started the engine, while Cillian got in the car and was soon leading the way back out. It wasn't too long a drive to take this one back, not like some of them. There were times they had to travel for two or three hours to hijack a truck, to make sure that their pattern of hits was well scattered around the country. They could easily have stuck to the routes around London, but it would have allowed the police to close in on their rough location over time, so they were careful to keep it random. This was a short trip though, which Cillian was grateful for. He needed time to get showered and dressed for the poker game.

He checked the clock on the dashboard. There was plenty of time for that still. Hours in fact, before they needed to show their faces.

They drove for a while, back the way they'd come, until the environment around them became busier and more built-up. The traffic started to get heavier, and Cillian moved into the slow lane in an attempt to keep Connor closer behind him. But cars kept cutting in, and the distance between them started to grow.

Just as he was wondering if he should find somewhere to pull over, his phone rang. He pulled it out of his pocket, put it on speaker and laid it in the centre console.

'Hey, what's up?'

'This is getting too busy.' It was Connor's voice. 'Why don't we cut through Dennett Road and jump over that side?'

'You're joking, right?' Cillian asked in surprise.

'Nah, it's fine.'

'Not if we get seen it ain't,' Cillian replied, raising his eyebrows.

Most of Croydon was ruled by a particularly violent Jamaican firm who made a point of being friends with no one. They ran all the weed in South London and their holding house for all that weed was bang smack in the middle of Dennett Road. The house was guarded at all times, and it was well known that members of other firms weren't welcome to come too close.

'Why would they see us? We're in an old banger and a truck – they won't look our way twice,' Connor replied. 'Come on, I just want to get this done with. I don't like being here, and there's a traffic jam ahead.'

Cillian looked forward and saw that his brother was right. He pulled a face. He was fast approaching Dennett Road. It was now or never.

'Fuck's sake, Connor,' he swore under his breath.

'It's for the best. Let's just get out of here,' came the reply. 'Keep the comms open, yeah?'

'Yeah, 'course,' Cillian responded.

As the truck turned in behind him, the sound of sirens blasted through the air from the main road they'd just left.

'Jesus,' Cillian heard Connor say. 'Not before time, us getting out of there. That was lucky.'

The sirens grew louder and louder, more than just one car, and Cillian felt his heart rate quicken. He took a deep breath and swallowed. They couldn't be after them, could they? Surely not. He tried to count how many sirens were mingling with each other but it was difficult. If he had to guess he'd say three, but he couldn't be sure. He watched the end of the road in the rear-view mirror, cursing the fact that Dennett Road was so long and straight. They would shoot past any second now, and then they could breathe again. He noticed his brother had gone very quiet, most likely feeling the same anxiety he was.

Blue lights flickered and to his horror two police cars screeched into the street behind them.

'Fucking lucky, are we?' he shouted, furious with Connor for sending them down this path.

'Shit!' Connor exclaimed.

'What now, genius?' Cillian yelled. He ran one hand back through his hair in stress.

'Go down that next left,' Connor ordered.

'It's a dead end!'

'Just do it!'

Cillian swore under his breath once more, his heart thumping so hard against his chest he was sure it was about to break through his ribs. They had always had to be mentally prepared for being caught and arrested, but now that there were police cars hot on their tail, he couldn't think straight.

'They ain't here for us,' Connor said as if he could read his brother's thoughts. 'Just turn and park up, like we're normal people.'

'Normal,' Cillian snorted. But he did as Connor asked and turned, making sure to indicate properly.

As the truck followed him in, the two police cars shot past down the road. Cillian immediately felt a weight lift off his shoulders and breathed a sigh of relief.

'See?' Connor said, parking up on the side of the road. 'Told you.'

'Yeah, alright, Einstein,' Cillian shot back sarcastically, 'now what?' The sirens weren't disappearing into the distance as he'd hoped, which meant that they'd likely reached their destination. And knowing what they did about this particular road, it didn't take a genius to figure out what was happening. The Jamaicans were being raided.

'We wait it out. Just switch the engine off, keep your head down and we'll get out of here as soon as they're gone.'

Cillian twisted his mouth to one side as his curiosity began to override his previous fear. He tapped the steering wheel for a moment and stared into the rear-view mirror.

'Cillian?' Connor asked when his brother didn't respond, his tone wary.

'Yeah, I'm gonna go see what's happening.'

'No, wait!'

'I'll call you back.' Cutting off his brother's protests, Cillian ended the call and stepped out of the car. He grabbed his long, grey wool coat from the back seat and shrugged it on, immediately transforming his black heist outfit into something that looked more normal and sophisticated.

He pushed his hands down into his pocket and walked back towards Dennett Road. He had no choice but to pass his brother in the truck, and as he approached Connor wound down the window.

'What are you doing?' he hissed.

'I'll be careful, relax.'

Cillian carried on towards the end of the road, pulling his phone out and pretending to be writing a text. He lingered on the corner for a moment, peering down the road out of the corner of his eye. There were actually four patrol cars outside the Jamaicans' weed house just a few yards up, two of which had obviously come from the other direction. As he watched the front door opened and half a dozen officers in full body protection came back out dragging four heavily protesting men.

He pulled back and hid behind an overgrown bush poking awkwardly out of the garden of the corner house. He could see everything clearly enough through the leaves, but they wouldn't be able to spot him unless they came right up close.

'Da fuck you think you're doing, man?' he heard one of the men being dragged exclaim. 'Don't you know whose house this is? You're gonna regret this.'

The police officer didn't respond. *Wise*, Cillian thought. If they gave any clue as to who they were, there would be retribution for this.

He watched from the bush as they arrested each man, brought out several bagged-up weapons and conducted a thorough search of the property. As the last officer came out, a woman – who Cillian assumed was the detective in charge – waved all but one of the cars away to process their latest detainees. Two officers lingered on the road and Cillian strained to hear the conversation between them and the detective.

'Keep watch and start taping the place up,' he thought he heard her say. 'There's so much product in there I'm going to have to outsource, get a crew in to load it out. Start securing the place while I make a call.'

The officers hurried off, and the detective crossed the road and began ambling towards him as she placed her call. Cillian held his breath as she drew closer. If she continued a few more steps, she'd see him. He pulled back out of the bush and busied himself on his own phone, trying to look natural.

'Julie, hi, it's DC Marsons. I'm in need of a crew to pick up a load of weed from a house raid on Dennett Road, Croydon. It's a lot – the whole house is full. Trees, bags, lamps, it's a huge set-up. We'll need a large van. Have you got anyone in the area?'

There was a pause and Cillian carefully pressed forward to have a look. The detective was just a few feet away but she'd stopped and was staring back towards the house.

'An hour and a half? Can no one make it sooner?' She turned and paced a few steps the other way then came back to the same spot. 'No? OK. Book them in then. I'll ping you the address. I've got to shoot but tell them to ask for PC Dougherty or Fisher. They're who I'm leaving to watch over the place. OK, great. Thanks, Julie.'

She clicked off the call and walked back across the road. Cillian listened as she told them the news and then disappeared in the remaining police car. His mind started to whir as the two officers exchanged glances.

'Come on,' he heard one of them say. 'Let's tape up the back first, then we can stay out front.'

The pair of them disappeared and mischief began to dance in Cillian's dark brown eyes. He bit his lip and turned back to the truck. Connor wound the window back down as he reached the door and he grinned up at his brother with barely concealed excitement.

'I've had a brilliant idea...'

CHAPTER THIRTY-FOUR

'This is a terrible idea,' Connor said to Cillian. 'A fucking terrible idea.' The brothers were sitting together in the cab of the truck and moving back down Dennett Road towards the weed house.

They'd quickly driven both vehicles out whilst the officers had been busy taping up the back of the house and had hidden the car a few roads away. They'd then raced to the fancy dress emporium on the high street and the charity shop next to it and had done all they could to change the way they looked without appearing completely suspicious.

They both still wore their plain black outfits, but Cillian now wore a cap and a fake moustache, and Connor had added a bobble hat to hide most of the blond wig he wore underneath it. He made sure to keep some tufts showing at the front and sides, and his eyes looked strangely bright with the blue contacts he'd inserted. To top the look off, they each wore a pair of white gloves, originally part of a magician's outfit but which looked close enough to evidence-handling gloves to get by. They weren't the best disguises in the world, but they looked different enough that the officers shouldn't remember them as twins.

'It's not a terrible idea,' Cillian argued. 'It's a *ballsy* idea, but that's exactly the reason why we're going to pull this off.'

'Yeah?' Connor turned to look at him. 'And what if they come round the back of the truck as we're loading and find the full-grown *man* tied up there?'

'I told you, we'll bring the trees down first and hide him behind that. And I'm pretty sure your threat was enough to keep him quiet.'

Connor had jumped in the back and explained briefly that they were going to pick up some product before he was able to drop the driver back to safety. He'd added a few lies into the mix, telling the frightened man that they were in enemy territory and if he drew attention to them at all, a man called Carlo would not only murder them all but he'd do it slowly and whilst taking great pleasure in their pain. The driver had almost cried and had quickly agreed to stay silent with a nod. He wasn't the fighting-back sort; he just wanted to get dropped off in one piece. The brothers had been in the business long enough to recognise that.

They pulled up on the side of the road and Connor felt his heart drop. Something was bound to go wrong. This was the most stupid thing they'd ever done. But at the same time, he couldn't help but admire Cillian's plan. If they pulled it off, they would make so much money it was unreal. He took a swift deep breath in and opened the door.

'Right. Here goes nothing.'

Stepping out onto the pavement, he swallowed and hoped that the sound of his racing heart wasn't as loud to everyone else as it was in his own ears. Cillian joined him, stepping forward towards the officer standing at the front door. The other must have stayed to keep watch at the back, Connor realised.

'Hello,' Cillian said in a cheery tone, dropping the East End out of his accent as best he could for the occasion. Connor stayed a step behind. 'You PC Dougherty?' The officer opened his mouth to speak, but Cillian was quick to pick up on the small shake of the head. 'Sorry, Fisher, isn't it?'

'Yes, that's me, and you are?' the officer checked his watch with a frown.

'Here to load up the evidence,' Cillian replied, not missing a beat. 'We managed to get away from the last job earlier than we'd thought.' It had been barely more than half an hour since he'd overheard DC Marson's phone call. They'd rushed as quickly as they could, knowing that time was of the essence before the real crew turned up.

'Oh, great,' he said. 'You come straight here then?'

'Yeah, think they're still sorting the paperwork,' Cillian replied, pulling a face. 'But I was hoping to get a head start. It's my youngest's birthday today.'

Connor glanced up at the officer, gauging his reaction. He seemed to be buying that they were who they said they were so far.

'Ah, how old?' Fisher's face broke out into a smile.

Cillian mirrored the smile. 'She's four. My little princess,' he said lovingly. 'Wanted a pony, so I'm hoping the rocking horse we got her won't be too much of a disappointment.' He added a chuckle and shook his head.

'Oh, I remember those days,' Fisher replied. 'Mine's fifteen now though. And I'll tell you what, when they hit the teens, you'll wish you could go back to the days they cried over not getting a pony.' He laughed and then sighed as he stared off into the distance.

Connor's gaze flickered to his brother and back to the officer. They needed to get into the building quickly. If he was going to stick to the book and make them wait until they had the correct paperwork, they were screwed. The best they could hope to do was slip away quickly. But it would be a shame, after coming this far.

'So, are we good to get in…?' Cillian prompted.

'Oh, yeah, sure. Go ahead.' Fisher moved to the side and allowed them past. 'I think you might have to make more than one trip with that truck though. You won't believe what's in there.'

'Cheers,' Cillian called back.

Connor followed his brother in, keeping his head tilted just low enough to avoid being looked at too closely but not enough that he would appear suspicious.

The smell was the first thing that hit them. It was overwhelming, almost to the point it made their eyes water. Cillian paused and peered up the stairwell, and Connor carried on down the hallway into the first room, which would once have been the main living room. As his gaze travelled around the room, his jaw slowly dropped and his eyes widened. Bags upon bags of ready-to-go green were stacked in tall piles all around the room, and several rows of mature trees ready to be harvested took up what little space there was left. It was only the first room, but already there was enough to fill the entire truck. He sensed Cillian walk down the hall and come to a stop behind him.

'Holy mother of God,' he uttered, a look of pure glee creeping up on his face. 'We've hit the fucking jackpot!'

CHAPTER THIRTY-FIVE

Lily looked at her watch with barely concealed annoyance. The boys were supposed to have been at the factory over an hour ago. It was game night. People would be arriving at any moment, and they weren't around to play their parts.

The poker games made the Drews a lot of money, every time. Back in the day, the crooks who attended these nights used legitimate casinos to launder money. They'd hand over ten grand at a time for chips, play a hundred pounds or so and cash out, directing the money into their bank account. The money then had a clear paper trail and no one could prove it was anything other than luck. It was the perfect scam. The government had got wise to this though, and now every chip came with an ID sensor which logged whether or not it had been played. Suspicious transitions were flagged, and criminals could no longer launder their money so easily. Client accounts became mandatory too, which meant even bets made for pleasure were closely watched. It was no longer so safe to flash large amounts of cash. So when Lily opened up her underground ring, a lot of the underworld's big players flocked straight to it. Here they could play as much as they wanted with no fear.

Lily turned in a circle, her high heels tapping sharply on the hard floor as she tried to breathe through her irritation. The boys knew they needed to be here before the first guest arrived. It wasn't like they had to do much – they just needed to show their faces and keep an eye on the tables, make sure there were no problems. Everything else was taken care of. Two of the men on her payroll had already brought over the tables and chairs and numerous ornate lamps from storage that they used for these events. Everything had been set up, and the bar was currently being stocked. One would mind the room and take jackets, and the other would mind the bar and bring orders to the tables. In a moment Lily would start playing smooth jazz in the background, the final touch in creating the warm, welcoming space her clients knew and enjoyed, and then they would be ready to go. It was a well-oiled operation. But that didn't mean the boys could suddenly just not turn up.

She checked her watch again and tutted. They were cutting it fine. She knew the heist had gone OK – they'd called her to confirm that earlier on. But she hadn't heard a peep since. A picture of Chastity sitting half naked in her son's home with a smug smile on her face crept into her mind and her eyes narrowed. If they were late again because of that good-for-nothing gold-digger, she'd have more than a few choice words to share with her son. Huffing, she moved across the room to the sound system and pressed the play button.

Scarlet walked into the room, shrugged off her jacket and handed it to George, the man Lily had watching the room. She held up a bottle of Scotch with a questioning expression. 'Is this the right one?'

Lily glanced at the label. 'That's the one. Andy...' She turned and called to the man stocking the bar. 'Keep this cold, will you? It's Mr Cleaver's favourite.' Mr Cleaver was a very big spender and had the worst luck with cards of anyone she'd ever seen, so having a good stock of his favourite Scotch was just good business sense.

'No probs, Lil,' Andy called back.

Brooding and burly, both George and Andy looked exactly like what they were – Lily's muscle. George and Andy had worked for Lily and Ronan since the twins had been just children and were an integral part of the firm. They knew all of the ins and outs of the firm's business and were two men she trusted with her life. In their world, trust was more valuable than gold – and certainly rarer.

Scarlet handed over the bottle to Andy and turned back to Lily, biting her bottom lip with a thoughtful expression.

'Don't do that – you'll ruin your lipstick,' Lily chided.

Scarlet immediately stopped and rubbed her red lips together to smooth the colour over. 'I've been through all I can find on Mr Asha, by the way. There's nothing there we can use,' she said.

'That's OK,' Lily replied, 'I think I've found our man.' Her eyes glinted with hope as her gaze met Scarlet's.

'Really?' Scarlet asked, lowering her voice to an excited whisper.

Lily nodded. Aside from having no clear suspects for Ronan's murder, they were also lacking the finer details. The police had been stubbornly unhelpful, refusing to give them any real information and refusing her access to the full file as it was still an open case. But she was certain that there had to be something there she could use. Something the police didn't understand. So Lily had turned her attentions towards the staff at the morgue. After rummaging through her contacts for information, she'd finally obtained a list of their names. She and Scarlet had been methodically researching them one at a time to see if they could find any weaknesses they could manipulate, a reason they might be open to a bribe.

'What it is? A mistress? Debt?' Scarlet questioned.

'No, a child,' Lily replied. 'He has an ex-wife withholding access to his daughter. It's an expensive business going through court for access, and he's struggling to find the money.'

Scarlet shook her head. 'That's a shitty situation,' she said quietly.

'It is. But one we might be able to use to our advantage.'

'God, I hope so.' Scarlet's tone was heavy. 'I just want to get him home, Lil. I just want us to be able to lay him to rest.' She closed her eyes for a moment.

'We all do, Scarlet,' Lily replied. 'But that's not going to happen just yet.' She locked her jaw with a grim expression. The fact they wouldn't release Ronan's body ate away at her like a sore, but until the case was solved, that wasn't going to change. 'The pigs have no intention of hurrying this up. Ronan is just another dead criminal to them. One less to have to catch.' A wave of anger washed over her and she swallowed it down. 'We need to solve this ourselves. And once that's done and we get his body back, then we need to dole out retribution ourselves. Whoever did this isn't going to be allowed the luxury of relaxing in prison. Not after what they've done. So the sooner we can get that file the better.'

'Well, then we have to make damn sure we get it,' Scarlet replied, her tone hard and determined. She met her aunt's gaze. 'Whatever it takes.'

Lily nodded. 'Whatever it takes.'

There was a long silence as they each thought it over.

'So, what shall I do now?' Scarlet asked, changing the subject.

'Nothing,' Lily answered. 'Now we wait for our clients to arrive and greet them at the door, where I shall introduce you. I'll give you an in for conversation wherever I can and then you spend the rest of the evening networking. This is a good setting; you can join tables to watch the game – feign interest, even if you couldn't care less. You can take part in conversations, check people are OK for drinks, et cetera, et cetera…' She waved her hand in small circles. 'Just get things going and leave a good impression. You're a smart girl; you can hold your own. Just remember' – she met Scarlet's gaze – 'cool, confident, switched on. That's what they need to see. How you show that is your concern.'

Scarlet nodded. 'Got it.'

Lily looked her up and down subtly and gave a small, satisfied nod. She was a natural beauty, with her father's full lips, and at five foot eight, she was tall for her slender frame. Her posture was confident, and her elegant black dress made her look more sophisticated than ever. She would turn more than a few heads tonight, of that Lily was certain. And this wouldn't hurt, to help leave a lasting impression. Her gaze moved up to Scarlet's face. Her expression was calm, but Lily could see the troubles behind her eyes.

'You made the right decision, you know,' she said quietly.

Scarlet glanced at her and flashed her a tight smile. 'Of course.'

Lily nodded slowly. 'I know it was… difficult for you, making the decision to stay.' It was something Scarlet had never talked about, yet Lily knew she still thought about St Andrews. She also knew that if Ronan had still been here, Scarlet would most likely have gone. She could tell the girl had been working up the courage to tell him before he'd died. But things had changed. For everyone. And she'd done the correct thing in taking her rightful place.

Scarlet raised her chin a little higher and swallowed. 'It was never difficult to stay,' she said slowly. 'This is my family – the business is as much as part of me as of any of us. But it *was* difficult not to leave. If that makes sense.' She fell quiet for a few moments. 'But that's redundant now. There was no real question about it,' she continued. 'With Dad gone, I need to be here.' She clamped her jaw shut as a wistfulness crept into her tone, then she swiftly changed the subject. 'Anyway.' She snapped on a smile. 'Andy looks like he could do with a hand.' She walked away to the bar.

Allowing Scarlet her respectful exit from the conversation, Lily wandered over to the extra table they'd set up at the side of the room. She looked down at the display they'd created and felt the familiar sadness run through her. Ronan's smiling eyes looked up at her from the pictures that usually hung upstairs in the office. In the largest one, he looked as though he was mid laugh. The more she stared at it, the more it appeared as though he was about to carry on laughing. But he didn't. He never did, no matter how many times she looked at it. And he never would again.

Tonight was the first poker night they'd run since his death. And as they hadn't yet been able to hold a funeral, she knew there would be a lot of people coming tonight to pay their respects.

'Lily Drew…' The familiar voice momentarily cut through her pain and anger like a balm, and she turned towards Ray with a smile as he joined her at the display. He leaned down and kissed her passionately, looking her up and down with approval. 'You look as beautiful as ever,' he said, shrugging off his smartest jacket and handing it to George.

Lily straightened the front of his crisp white shirt and breathed in the warm musky scent of his aftershave. He couldn't take away the pain of losing her brother – nothing ever would. But having him close seemed to help take the edge off.

'You're not looking so bad yourself,' she said.

He glanced down at the display, noticing it suddenly, and his expression turned grave. 'I'm sorry, Lil; tonight must be hard for you.'

Lily pulled away with a tight smile and headed for the door, swallowing hard. 'Tonight is business,' she replied. 'But yes, I imagine some of our clients will want to pay their respects. I thought that was fitting.' She gestured to the display.

Ray looked down and nodded. He squeezed her arm. 'He'd have liked it.'

One side of Lily's mouth pulled upwards into a smirk. 'He'd have hated it. He always thought he looked fat in that photo of him and me together. But I liked it, so he kept it in the office. He was like that.' She felt her lip begin to wobble and clenched her jaw. 'Always putting the rest of our feelings before his own.' She sniffed and blinked hard. 'Bloody softie,' she added with a forced laugh, trying to lighten the mood.

'Yeah, don't go telling too many people that,' Ray replied, catching on to her need to laugh things off. 'You'll ruin his reputation, and I don't think he'd like that very much, wherever he's watching from now. And you can bet your last Rolo he's watching ya. Cursing and swearing as you put that photo out, that's for sure.'

Lily's smile relaxed as it became more genuine. 'I hope so.'

Scarlet came to join them, and Ray leaned in to kiss her cheek in greeting as she gave him a quick one-armed hug. 'Hey, Ray, good to see you.'

'Wow, look at you,' he said, raising his eyebrows to Lily. 'Christ, it seems like only yesterday you were running around in nappies.' He laughed, his deep voice rumbling throughout the room.

'I can assure you it was much longer ago than that,' Scarlet replied.

Lily's head turned as she heard their next guests arrive. 'Ray, do get yourself a drink and make yourself comfortable. We need to greet everyone.' She steered Scarlet off to meet the man at the door, one of the most notorious villains in North London. 'Come, Scarlet.'

Cos Cristou was a very powerful man. An invaluable ally or a dangerous enemy. If Scarlet played this right, she would be glad of his friendship one day. Because hard paths lay ahead. And she was going to need all the allies she could make.

CHAPTER THIRTY-SIX

Lily laughed as she blew her smoke out across the poker table. She was sitting back in her chair next to Ray, her legs crossed and a drink in her hand. To anyone else she looked as though she was off the clock, enjoying herself as she tended to do on game nights. But in reality she was anything but tonight.

The tables were in full swing, and Scarlet was holding her own on the next table, in animated conversation with Bill Hanlon, an old friend and respected face in the business. Lily kept watch on her in her peripheral vision, whilst also keeping an eye on the door. The twins had still not arrived and she was fuming.

She'd texted both of them when neither had answered their phones and had only twenty minutes earlier finally received a brief response, telling her they were on their way. She kept a fixed smile on her face as the dealer dealt once more and pretended to be interested in Ray's hand.

'Oh, I forgot to mention when I came in,' Ray said, leaning towards her, careful not to take his eyes off the cards. 'I had to meet Harry Snow the other day about a transportation deal.' He kept his voice low, so no one else at the table would overhear. 'His son, Jasper, was there. Showed interest in coming tonight. I said he could come along with me, meet me here. I figured that would be OK?'

Lily's brows lifted in surprise. Ray glanced at her briefly and caught the expression.

'Oh,' he said, misreading her face. 'Sorry, I know you aren't much a fan of Harry, but I thought the games were open to everyone in our line of work. He's not due to meet me quite yet; I can cancel...'

'No, no,' Lily reassured him. 'He's part of the underworld; he's as welcome as anyone else.' She shrugged. 'If I pushed out everyone I didn't like, it would be a short guest list.' She looked around at all the people here tonight. 'Business is business. Personal feeling doesn't come into it.' She took another drag of her cigarette and blew out the smoke slowly. 'Plus,' she added, 'the less I like them personally, the more I enjoy taking their money.'

She looked at him with a glint in her eye and they both laughed.

'You're as ruthless as they come, Lily Drew,' Ray said with a low chuckle.

Two figures appeared at the door and Lily quickly stood up. 'Finally,' she muttered, shooting them a glare. 'Ray, I just need to pop upstairs. I won't be long.' She glanced at Scarlet and subtly indicated for her to join them. The girl had networked flawlessly all evening so far, but she still didn't want to leave her alone in a room full of high-level crooks without supervision just yet.

The two women joined in the walkway between the tables and marched out of the room to where the twins stood waiting.

'My office – now,' she snapped with a murderous expression. 'And you two had better have a bloody good explanation.'

*

'You did what!' Lily roared. She glowered at them, her eyes filled with even more fury than before.

Scarlet dropped her jaw, aghast, and leaned back heavily on the sideboard against the wall of Lily's office. Her breath constricted and a chill ran down her spine. Even she knew what a colossal fuck-up this was. No one messed with the Jamaicans. That firm was well known as one of the most violent in the city. They were as good as dead, she realised with horror. All of them. They didn't take lightly to anyone so much as going near their businesses, let alone mugging them off for all they had. She put her hand to her face and ran it down over her mouth in stress.

'Look, chill out. We saw an opportunity and we took it,' Cillian said, standing up for their actions. 'Mum, you don't understand, it was literally just sat there, all tied up neatly in a bow right in front of us. It couldn't have been an easier lift.'

'You stole from the fucking *Jamaicans*, you stupid boy!' Lily yelled. 'Gift-wrapped or not, you *never* steal from people like them. Don't you understand? You've sealed all our death warrants!' She shook her head in disbelief. 'When they find out you took it – and they will,' she stressed, 'they'll come in the night with fucking machetes and make you wish you'd never been born. Make *all of us* wish we'd never been born. There will be no way out of it, no talks or negotiations – they don't mess about. Oh Jesus Christ...' She ran her hands through her curls and looked up to the heavens in despair.

Scarlet's gaze flicked between Lily and the boys and back again. She'd never in all her years seen Lily look this flustered. Not even when she'd had to deal with the man in the house who'd tried to kill her father. Lily never lost her cool, even when committing murder. Which meant this was very, very bad indeed.

'Mum, calm down,' Cillian said, exchanging worried looks with his brother. 'It was a risk, yes, but not as much as you think. The police had taken all of them – they were gone; the place was empty. We wore disguises; we didn't even look like us. Or each other,' he added, walking cautiously closer to her. 'It was as safe as it could possibly have been. We were gloved up, careful to leave no trace, and we used the truck to transport it all before we dumped it. There's no way anyone can connect us back to that. Honestly.'

Lily squeezed her eyes closed and shook her head, putting her fingers together and to her mouth.

Connor glanced at Scarlet, who just shook her head at him slowly with a look of utter disbelief. She was beginning to understand what reckless livewires her cousins really were. Who in their right mind would do something like this?

'Look, Mum…' Connor stepped forward. 'I get why you're worried, but you don't need to be. There's nothing to link us to it. Even if they had someone watching – which is unlikely or they'd have tipped off their guys inside to run out the back before they were caught – there's no way we could have been recognised.' He took his mother's hands in his and pulled them down away from her face. 'All we need to do is sell this shit on as quick as we can, and—'

'What?' Lily snapped, looking at him as though he'd suddenly grown two heads. 'What the hell are you talking about?' She pulled her hands away and ran them through her hair again, pacing with a bark of bitter amusement. 'What is *wrong* with you? We can't *sell* it. We can't do *anything* with it! Think about it. We've never sold weed before. Suddenly we start selling a shit ton through a brand-new set-up, which, I'm assuming, involves the estate gangs, yeah?'

'Well, yeah…' Connor's tone faltered into one of uncertainty.

'Right. So the gangs suddenly get hit with a ton of weed from a local firm who've never dealt in green, *exactly at the same time* the Jamaicans are scouring the city for a truckload of green which was stolen from them.'

'So we sell it somewhere else,' Cillian replied.

'It doesn't matter where we sell it, it will be an obvious anomaly in the weed market,' Lily snapped back. She closed her eyes and exhaled heavily. 'It will get back to them, they'll follow the trail and the trail leads back to us. There's absolutely no way on earth that we can sell this on without giving ourselves away.'

Scarlet bit her lip and thought back over the people she'd met throughout the evening. Was there another way?

Cillian sighed irritably and frowned. 'There has to be some way to sell it on, Mum, because we didn't do all that for nothing. Clearly you don't like that we did, and I get that, but it's happened. Alright? And I'll be damned if I'm gonna flush that much money down the kaiser. It's worth a fucking fortune.'

There was a long silence as Lily glared at him. 'Where is it? In the barn?' she finally asked.

'Yeah, stacked and covered in the back,' Connor answered.

'Right.' She reached for the slim cigarette case on the desk and pulled one out. 'I'll figure something out. But right now you need to get out of my sight,' she ordered. She lit the cigarette and took a deep drag. 'Get downstairs and do your fucking jobs. And not one word of this to anybody,' she warned. 'I mean it. Not one soul.'

Cillian huffed once more and marched out, Connor swift on his heel. The door closed behind them and Lily exhaled smoke into the room, rubbing her forehead.

Scarlet waited until her aunt had taken a couple of deep breaths before she spoke. 'Does Ray sell weed?' she asked.

'No,' Lily replied quietly, her stress still evident but the fury gone from her tone now the twins had left the room.

Scarlet bit her lip. 'Who do we have as an ally that does?'

Lily looked up at her and held her gaze thoughtfully for a few long moments. 'I'll have a think on that.' She looked up at the clock. 'We need to get back down there or we'll be missed.' She straightened up and took one last deep drag before stubbing the cigarette out. She straightened her dress and fluffed back her hair. 'Like I said to the boys—'

'Not a word to anyone,' Scarlet said, cutting her off. 'I know. You can trust me.'

'I know I can,' Lily replied.

The two women walked down the factory floor and made their way back to the basement. George held the door open for them as they entered, and Ray immediately called them over. Scarlet plastered on a smile as they headed to the table.

'Here they are,' Ray said with gusto. 'Lily, you remember Jasper, Harry's son?'

'I do indeed,' Lily replied pleasantly, holding out her hand to shake his.

Harry? Scarlet's ears pricked up. *Surely not Harry Snow?*

'And Jasper, this is Scarlet Drew. Scarlet, Jasper Snow.' Ray made the introductions and Scarlet was careful not to let her smile drop.

'Lovely to meet you,' she said, shaking his hand as her aunt had done.

'Likewise,' he said, shooting her a winning smile.

Scarlet studied him subtly. He looked nothing like his father, though maybe she just thought that because of his father's nervous tic. It had clearly not been inherited, for Jasper stood there as confidently as anyone else in the room. His hazel eyes twinkled as he smiled, and she found she quite liked the look of his slightly too long chestnut hair. He'd combed it neatly back, but the natural wave in it sent a lock down over his forehead, which he kept trying to push back into place.

'Everything alright?' Ray asked Lily.

She didn't respond, and Scarlet turned to look at her. Lily hadn't appeared to have heard. She was staring across the room at Bill Hanlon, the man Scarlet had been talking to earlier, with a thoughtful expression.

'Lil?' Ray prompted.

'Hm?' Lily turned back to him with a questioning expression.

'I said, is everything OK?'

'Oh, yeah, 'course.' She smiled brightly. A little too brightly, Scarlet thought, as Ray's eyes narrowed with suspicion. 'Listen, I just have to talk to Bill about something. I'll catch you in a bit.'

Lily floated off across the room towards Bill, and Ray turned his gaze towards Scarlet. 'She alright? She seems distracted.'

'Oh, yeah.' Scarlet flapped her hand dismissively. 'She's just pissed off at Connor for being late because of his girlfriend again.'

'Ah, I see.' Ray chuckled, but his expression told Scarlet he didn't fully buy the story.

She turned her attention to Jasper. 'You haven't got a drink. That won't do now, will it? Let's go to the bar.' She touched his arm and began walking away from Ray, drawing him to join her. 'What's your poison?'

'I'll go for a brandy, thank you.' He paused as they reached the bar and studied her face with a curious half-smile. As she caught his eye, she felt a small shiver of interest make its way up her spine.

'I, er… Right, yes.' She swallowed and turned to Andy. 'Can I have a brandy for my guest? And I think I'll have a white wine myself.' She pushed her dark hair back behind her ear and composed herself before turning back to Jasper.

'Er, where were we…'

He really was very good-looking. And she couldn't help but notice the pleasant smell of his aftershave. But what was she doing, going all girly like this over some guy when they had problems to deal with? Life-and-death-type problems at that. She mentally shook herself and Jasper gave a small laugh of amusement.

'Are you always this distracted, Miss Drew?' he asked.

'Sorry,' she said with a sudden grin. 'It's just been a bit of a crazy day. I don't know where my mind is at the moment.'

'Well…' Jasper reached over for the drinks and handed over hers. 'Then it seems you need this. Come – let's go play a few rounds together, shall we? I must say, it's a nice change to be in a place where one can talk freely and not have to hide certain less legal aspects of life in conversation. Don't you agree?'

Scarlet found herself nodding as Jasper led her away to a table. 'Actually, yes,' she agreed. She looked up into his hazel eyes and felt another flutter. What was it about Jasper Snow that had her so enamoured already? Perhaps it was what he'd just said. With him, there was no need to hide who she was or what her family did. He already knew. And she needn't fear that he was only interested due to their notoriety either, because it seemed he was already one of them.

'Blackjack?' he asked, pausing at a table and placing his hand lightly on her lower back. The warmth from his hand sent a spark up her spine, and she caught her breath as she smiled at him.

'Sure, why not,' she answered as casually as she could manage.

As she took her seat, she glanced back at Ray and saw his hawk-like gaze settle back on Lily. The feeling of warmth faded. She'd have to tell Lily about the lie she'd just told him. And the twins. The story would need to be maintained. Because no matter how loyal he was to their family, Ray couldn't know. Lily had said that no one could know. Not now, not ever. Their safety depended on it.

CHAPTER THIRTY-SEVEN

Scarlet pulled her earrings off and placed them back into her jewellery box on the chest of drawers, staring off into the distance as she replayed parts of the night in her mind. The twins had landed them all in a colossal mess, that was for sure. What could possibly have possessed them to do something so utterly stupid?

She loved her cousins dearly, had grown up with a close connection to them – had looked up to them even, over the years – but she was beginning to see now why her aunt kept them under such an iron rule. They were good at their jobs – hard, respected, smart men – and their hearts were in the right place. But despite all this, left to their own devices, they seemed to be absolute liabilities.

She breathed out heavily and stared into the mirror. Her aunt had mentioned yesterday that she was the next generation. So were the boys. And that meant that one day down the line, they three would be the ones at the top of the tree. What then? Her eyes clouded over as she stared back at herself. Without Lily to steer them down the right paths, would things like this become a common occurrence? Was *she* supposed to be the one to stop them destroying all their parents had built?

She reached over her shoulder and unzipped the black dress Lily had lent her, shimmying her hips from side to side until it dropped to the floor. She laid it out neatly on the chair and then shrugged on her nightie.

A pinging sound echoed through the room and she padded over to her phone. As she opened the text and began to read, she couldn't help the smile that crept up on her face, despite all that was going on. It was Jasper, telling her what a pleasure it had been to meet her tonight.

It had felt liberating discussing their similar entries into the world, and as their conversation had developed, so had her interest in the charming young man. He was maybe a few years older than her, not many, and his strong confidence had drawn her attention more and more as the night went on. When they'd parted ways, they'd swapped numbers, and he'd casually invited her to meet him for dinner sometime.

She'd accepted, surprised by how eager she was to see him again. For the first time she could remember, she was actually genuinely interested in someone. It was a new feeling and one that wrapped around her like a warm hug in the bitter existence she was struggling through right now.

A sound made her pause, and she tilted her head to listen. It came again, like something being knocked over downstairs. She frowned. It was nearly three in the morning. She crept to her door and pulled it open, straining her ears. A few moments passed and then she heard a shuffling coming from the floor below. She glanced to her mother's bedroom door and her heart rate began to quicken. Cath's door was firmly closed. Biting her lip, she looked back into her room for something to take with her. There weren't many options that seemed strong enough to defend herself with if needed, so in the end, she settled for a wireless curler. She weighed it up in her hand. It wasn't much, but it was better than nothing.

Creeping down the stairs she kept close to the wall in the shadows and skipped over the step she knew would creak. The house was silent now, no more sounds of any kind reaching her ears. She paused as she reached the bottom. Why was it now so silent? Had whoever was there heard her coming? Who was it? Could the Jamaicans have figured everything out already? Or was it whoever had killed her father? Her throat constricted for a moment as this possibility registered.

She swallowed, her heart pumping hard against her chest now. Whoever it was, they weren't here on a social call. No good ever came from someone creeping around your house in the middle of the night.

The shuffling sound came again, and this time she could tell it was coming from the utility room at the back of the house. She exhaled slowly. The back door to the garden was in there. Her fingers tightened around the curling iron.

Tiptoeing to the understairs cupboard, she pulled the door open and reached in to where her dad had always kept the baseball bat. She grasped it with a feeling of relief and discarded the curling iron. Wrapping both hands around it, she held it up in the air.

With the bat in her hand, she suddenly felt stronger and less afraid. For one fleeting moment, she felt her father there beside her. *That's it*, she heard him say. *Hold it up high and remember, the bigger they are, the harder they go down if you smash 'em in the face with a bat.* That's what he'd taught her. A sad smile flickered across her lips, and then they formed a firm line as she made her way determinedly through the dark hallway.

Whoever it was, they were about to get a hard welcome. Her dad might be gone, but that didn't mean this house was vulnerable. It would never be vulnerable with her around. She would protect her home and her mother just as he had. With every bit of fight she had left.

Taking a deep breath, Scarlet tensed, tightened her hold on the bat and then pushed through into the utility room, ready to face whoever was in there. But as she registered the scene before her, she stopped dead and let the bat drop down to her side, her eyes widening in horror.

Cath lay slumped in a heap on the floor, two empty bottles of wine next to her and an empty glass. The wash basket and the box of washing tablets and fabric conditioner that had been in it were sprawled across the floor. She quickly surmised that Cath must have grabbed hold of them on the side in an attempt to get up and knocked them over.

'What the hell are you doing?' she breathed.

At the sound of her daughter's voice, Cath opened one eye and looked up at her. 'Oh. You're home,' she said, slurring her words. ''Ere, help me up.'

'What are you doing?' Scarlet repeated, bending down to help support her mother as she struggled to find her balance. 'Have you been down here all night?' She glanced at the empty bottles as Cath's foot sent one flying.

'Whoops.' Cath swayed slightly, clearly still the worse for wear. 'I need to go to bed,' she said suddenly, almost falling back over.

Scarlet steadied her and took her weight, wrapping her arm around Cath's waist. 'Yeah, you do,' she agreed. 'Come on – I'll help you up.'

'Nah, just get your dad to…' Cath trailed off as she remembered, then her face crumpled and she began to cry pitifully. 'He ain't here,' she said brokenly. 'He's gone; my Ronan's gone.' As her soft cries turned into loud sobs, she turned into her daughter's shoulder.

Scarlet held her, tears smarting as she stood there in the dark, holding her mother while she drunkenly broke down. She closed her eyes and hugged her mother close, her heart breaking all over again for them both.

CHAPTER THIRTY-EIGHT

Lily stared up at the building in front of her with trepidation and took another drag on her cigarette. She hadn't told anyone where she was going tonight, or what she had planned. There was too much riding on it. Every second that ticked past was another second that weed sat there in her barn, and she didn't know how long it was going to be until the Jamaicans started to look in their direction. She needed to get it out – and fast. And after wracking her brains and thinking about every angle, she'd narrowed her chances of getting out of this down to just one. The man she was about to see was the only person in the world who could help her. And there was no guarantee that he would. If he wanted nothing to do with it – and she couldn't really blame him if he didn't – they were out of options.

She took one more deep drag on her cigarette and flicked it away before determinedly setting forward.

The dull thumps from the music became louder and clearer as she walked through the doors into the modern, expensive-looking club in West London. She looked around with appreciation. It was a sophisticated place, with beautiful people lounging around drinking cocktails in the booths and at the tables. The lighting gave off a more chilled vibe than she imagined it would on a heavy weekend night, the footfall tonight more those who just wanted to enjoy a few relaxed drinks with friends as they prepared for the week ahead.

She immediately clocked Bill, who was waiting for her at the bar. He greeted her warmly. 'You found it OK then?'

'I did, thanks,' she replied. Despite having known the owner for most of her life, she hadn't seen him in person for many years and had never set foot in one of his clubs before today. 'Is he in?' she asked, her hopes teetering on the edge of a very dark abyss.

'He is. He knows you're coming. I'll take you up.'

Lily breathed out in silent relief and followed Bill through the club to a doorway that led to a set of stairs. Bill signalled to the man behind the bar that she was OK to be let through, and she clocked Dean and Simon watching her from another table, both of whom she knew worked for the man she was visiting off the books.

They ascended the stairs and Bill stood aside, gesturing towards the only door in the hallway. She nodded her thanks and he melted away, leaving her to go on alone. The pump of the music seemed to echo her heart as it beat inside her chest. So much was riding on this meeting. She just prayed that it would go the way she needed it to. A vision of her sons being hacked to death with machetes flashed across her mind and she shook her head to dispel it.

She raised her hand and knocked sharply, lifting her head and straightening up.

'Come in,' came the invitation.

She opened the door to a large, opulent office, stepped inside and allowed it to close behind her. Staring at her from the large mahogany desk across the room was a handsome man in his late thirties, sharply dressed and with a curious expression in his hazel-green eyes.

'Well, Lily Drew, to what do I owe this unexpected pleasure?' he asked.

Lily's face broke out into a broad smile. 'Freddie Tyler. Well, didn't you go and grow up when I wasn't looking?'

He threw his head back and laughed as she joined him at the desk. He gestured to the seat opposite him and poured two glasses of whisky.

'You still drink whisky, I take it?' he asked, handing her one.

'I do, though not as often now. It's all about the gin these days, don't you know?' she replied.

Freddie pulled a face. 'Can't stand the stuff. But I remember you were partial to a good Scotch.'

'Still am.' She took a sip and let the warm liquid burn down the back of her throat.

'I was so sorry to hear about Ronan.'

The gentleness in Freddie's words caught Lily off guard and for a moment her eyes began to mist. She blinked rapidly, turning her face so that he wouldn't see.

'I know how hard it is, losing a sibling, especially one that close.'

She heard Freddie pause and swallow his own pain. She nodded sadly, turning back to him. 'I bet it still feels like Thea's going to walk through the door, doesn't it?' she replied. Thea was Freddie's sister. She'd been murdered three years before – a senseless murder which had shocked them all. Lily still remembered the funeral. Not that anyone who'd attended would ever forget it. It had been a very eventful day.

'He'll be missed by everyone. I don't think I ever met a person who didn't like Ronan,' Freddie continued. 'I wish I could tell you I had a clue who did it, but as I told Bill at the time—'

'I know,' Lily cut him off with a sad smile. 'Bill told me you'd put feelers out and nothing had come back. I appreciate that.'

There was a long silence as they both sipped their whiskies. Freddie watched her from across the table. 'So,' he said. 'You never answered my question. What brings you here to visit me?' He lifted the glass to his mouth again, not taking his eyes off her face.

Lily took a deep breath and exhaled. Freddie had always liked to cut to the chase, even as a kid. 'Could I not just be here to see an old friend?' she asked with a laugh, half relieved by and half dreading the change of subject.

'You could be, and you'd be welcome here for that reason at any time. You know that,' Freddie replied. He tilted his head to one side, his expression neutral. 'But we both know that ain't why you're here today.'

Lily lowered her gaze and nodded, reaching into her pocket for her cigarettes.

'Please, have one,' Freddie offered, holding out his own packet to her.

She smiled and accepted, letting him light it for her before sitting back and taking a deep drag. She blew the smoke out upwards, rolling her neck before straightening back up.

'I'm in a fix,' she stated simply. 'A bad one.' There was no point pussyfooting around it. She and Freddie had known each other long enough to speak plainly.

Freddie frowned. 'What's going on?'

Lily sighed and met his gaze. 'This can't go any further than this room. No one can ever know, other than those who absolutely have to,' she said gravely.

'Of course,' Freddie replied. 'You know you can trust me.'

Lily smiled – a genuine smile. 'I do. That's why I'm here. You're one of the few people in this world I can hand on heart say I genuinely do trust.'

Lily was eight years older than Freddie. They'd grown up in the same area and their mothers had been friends. After her parents' deaths, she'd stayed close to the family and often babysat Freddie and his siblings so that his mother could go out and do extra work in the evenings. They'd grown up knowing each other's hardships first hand and had both ended up becoming part of the underworld, though they'd taken different routes.

Freddie had joined a well-established firm, climbing a lot higher than she had, and after taking over from the retiring bosses a few years back, he was now practically the top of the tree. Underworld royalty. No one messed with the Tylers if they wanted to survive in London. Lily had built her own smaller, independent firm from scratch – between their busy schedules and family commitments, they saw each other less and less over the years, but their deeply bonded roots still remained.

'Have you heard about the Jamaicans' weed store down on Dennett?' Lily asked.

'That they got raided yesterday, then before they could remove the weed, someone stole a load from right underneath the pigs' noses?' Freddie laughed hard and shook his head. 'Yes, I did. Funniest thing I've heard all year.'

'It was my boys,' Lily replied, not joining in on the laughter.

'Oh.' The amusement on Freddie's face dropped immediately into a more sober expression.

'Not so funny now, right?'

'Not in the fucking slightest,' Freddie replied. He sat back and blew a long breath out through his cheeks, running his hand back through his dark hair. 'Why? What were they thinking, messing with the Jamaicans?' he asked.

'They weren't thinking,' Lily replied, taking another drag on her cigarette. 'That's the problem.' She shook her head. 'They were dropping a truck back after a lift. It was all fine, everything had gone smoothly, but they had to cut through Croydon to avoid a police trap. God only knows why they decided to go down Dennett of all fucking roads…' She closed her eyes and clenched her jaw, still furious at her sons. 'But they did,' she said, tapping her ash into the crystal ashtray on the desk. 'Only, as they were driving down, the pigs turned up and they had to wait it out. They then saw what they interpreted as an opportunity…'

'They did that off the cuff?' Freddie butted in, surprised. 'It wasn't planned?'

'Totally off the cuff,' she confirmed.

'Jesus.' Freddie's frown deepened and he took a long drag on his own cigarette, staring off to the side as he processed what she was telling him.

'And the rest is history, I guess,' Lily concluded. 'They apparently sorted disguises, blagged their way in and made off with a full truckload. With the driver tied up in the bloody back, nonetheless!'

Freddie's eyebrows shot up towards his hairline. 'I mean…' He shook his head in disbelief. 'There's ballsy and then there's jumping on a fucking death wish. And this is definitely the latter.'

The reminder sent a chill up Lily's spine, and she shifted in her seat, crossing the other leg. 'Yes, well.' She pursed her lip for a moment and watched the smoke rise from the end of her lit cigarette. Where there was smoke, there was fire. And she needed to extinguish that fire before it burned them all to the bone. Her serious gaze lowered to meet Freddie's. 'That's why I'm here.'

CHAPTER THIRTY-NINE

Connor pulled up outside the grey block of flats and idled the engine, checking his texts whilst he waited for Chastity. In usual form, she kept him waiting for a good ten minutes before putting in an appearance, and he was about to call her to hurry her up when she opened the passenger door.

'Finally,' he said, irritation clear in his tone.

She didn't seem to notice this, however, and slipped her pert backside across the leather before pulling her slender legs in and shutting the door with a smile. 'Well, it takes time to look this good, you know,' she purred.

Connor looked at her properly. She was made up to the nines, her long blonde hair full of thickening extensions, a flawlessly finished Barbie doll face and a pink miniskirt barely covering the top of her bronzed legs. 'Wow, what's the occasion?' he asked.

Chastity blinked, her thick fake lashes reminding Connor of a couple of moths he'd once seen at a butterfly farm as a kid. 'Well, I thought we was going out,' she said. 'You said to be ready.'

'No, I asked you if you were home and if you could meet me at the car if I came over,' he corrected.

'Right. And usually when you pick me up it's because we're going somewhere,' she replied, her tone unsure now. 'Somewhere nice, I'd been hoping.'

Connor pulled an apologetic face and watched the hope fall from her expression. 'Sorry, not tonight. Things are a bit crazy at the moment – I need to work.'

'You're always working,' Chastity complained with a petulant pout. 'Why have you come over if we ain't going to do anything?'

'Because I need to talk to you about something.' He shifted in his seat so that he was facing her.

'Yeah?' Her face lifted slightly. 'What do you want to talk about?' She ran one long pink fingernail up his thigh.

Connor stilled her hand and held it tight. 'Last night, what were you doing?' he asked, his dark brown eyes locking onto hers, a serious expression on his face.

'Last night? Nothing,' she said, a small frown wrinkling her bronzed forehead. 'I had a bit too much on Friday, so I was hanging. Just watched a film and crashed out early. Why?'

'OK. Was your mum in? Did you tell anyone you were in on your own?' Connor pressed. Chastity lived with her mother, a gossipy old hag who Connor detested. If she'd been in then there was no hope.

'Nah, Mum went out early with some mates for drinks and then bingo. I didn't even hear her come in so it must have been a late one. What's all this about, Connor?' Chastity looked at him, thoroughly confused.

'Right. Good. Listen, you need to tell people I was with you last night. Can you do that for me?' he asked, lifting one dark eyebrow. She nodded. 'Great. I need you to let it slip out naturally in conversation, OK? To your mates and your mum and that, so it's a known fact already if anyone were to come asking.'

'Sure, OK,' Chastity replied, sitting up a little straighter and nodding. She seemed quite pleased to be asked.

'Great. So, this is our story… I came over to you early – you can't remember what time – and we chilled out on the sofa and watched…?' He waited to find out what she'd watched.

'Oh, *Bridesmaids*,' she replied.

'Really?' He lifted an eyebrow. *Of course it was a chick flick.*

'Well, we can say something else if you like.' She shrugged.

'Nah, best to keep as close to the truth as possible, less to remember,' he said. 'OK.' He moved on, rubbing the dark stubble on his chiselled chin as he played the evening out in his mind. 'We watched *Bridesmaids* and just chilled as we were both hungover…'

'I bought pizza,' Chastity suddenly declared. 'And a big bottle of Diet Coke. From Ray's. Got it delivered. It was ham and pineapple.'

Connor closed his eyes and shook his head in disappointment but decided not to waste time opening the argument that no one in their right mind should ever order pineapple on a pizza. 'Right. Ham and pineapple pizza. Anything else?'

'Nah, that's it,' she said. 'I hit the sack before ten and crashed out till morning. I was up before Mum, so you can say you stopped over if you like.'

'No, I left before nine to meet my mum. Remember that bit – that's important,' he stressed.

'Sure, whatever,' she replied. 'So what did you really do?'

'That don't matter,' he said, brushing the question off dismissively.

'Well, it does if I'm lying to cover your arse,' she retorted.

Connor's gaze hardened as she looked at him and he could have pinned the exact moment she remembered who she was talking to from the contorting expressions on her face. 'That don't matter,' he repeated in a low growl. 'What matters is whether or not I can trust you to do as I've asked.'

'Of course you can,' she said quickly. 'I'm your girl.'

And don't I know it, he thought moodily. She was getting more and more of a strain to keep around by the minute, and her charms were dulling fast now. But as Scarlet had set up the story, it had to be followed through. So for now he still needed her.

'Good,' he said. 'Because all I'll say is that the consequences of that story falling down are brutal. For everyone involved. Do you understand me?'

Chastity stared at him, her previously playful expression fading into a more serious one. 'I do, yes.' She squeezed his hand. 'You do know, though, that you can tell me anything, right?' She gave him a tentative smile. 'I mean, I know who you are, Connor. And I'm in this for the long haul. So you can trust me. With this and with anything else.'

Connor gave her a tight smile. 'I need to go,' he said. 'But have a good night, yeah? Here…' He reached into his pocket and pulled out a wedge of notes. He peeled several off and handed them to her. 'Treat yourself and some mates to drinks. Or dinner, or whatever, seeing as you're all dressed up. OK?'

Chastity's smile broadened at the sight of the money and she preened, sticking her ample chest out towards him. 'Thanks, babe,' she purred. 'You're a great boyfriend.' She leaned in and gave him a long, lingering kiss before opening the door and stepping back out. 'See you tomorrow maybe, yeah?'

Connor just smiled and waved her off, glad when the car door shut. He exhaled heavily. *Boyfriend.* He wasn't her or anybody else's boyfriend. Unbeknown to her, she'd sealed her own fate with the use of that word. As soon as all this had blown over, Chastity was history.

CHAPTER FORTY

Scarlet toyed with the granola in her breakfast bowl and stared out of the kitchen window into the neatly tended garden beyond. For how much longer it would be neatly tended she wasn't sure. The gardener had approached her the day before and told her his invoices had been unpaid since her father's death and needed sorting if he was to continue working for them. She'd promised to sort it all out by the end of the week, but the discovery had made her wonder how many other bills and services had been left unpaid. It had also cemented in her mind the fact she'd made the right choice in staying. She couldn't have left this house and her mother and swanned off to St Andrews. Who would have looked after them?

It had been a month since Ronan had been found, and life just seemed to be stuck in a horrible heavy limbo. They couldn't focus on the funeral and saying their final goodbyes, because there had still been no headway with the case, so the police were in no hurry to release his body.

She'd buried herself in work to get through, just as Lily had. But Cath had nothing to bury herself in. Her husband had been her life. Supporting him, looking after him, loving him, that's what she'd lived for. And now he was gone.

Scarlet forced another mouthful of granola into her mouth and began to chew robotically, going through the motions but not really tasting it. Most things had lost their taste since she'd lost her father. She figured she was probably still in shock. Her feelings were raw and unbearable when they surfaced, but somehow as long as she focused on pretending she was OK and on mundane everyday tasks, she seemed better able to function and ignore them. Somehow it made her even better at her job. And that was something.

Cath shuffled into the kitchen still wrapped in Ronan's big bathrobe, which seemed to be her constant companion around the house these days. Her hair was a dull mess, sticking up all over the place, as though she'd tossed and turned all night, and there were dark circles around her red-rimmed eyes.

'Do you want a coffee, Mum?' Scarlet asked, standing up and wiping a couple of crumbs from the front of the cigarette trousers she'd paired with a black silk blouse for work today.

Cath looked her up and down and smiled sadly. 'You're looking more and more like Lil every day with those suits,' she said. Scarlet turned away and she put her hands up quickly. 'Oh no, I didn't mean that badly. Whatever issues I may have with Lily, I've always admired her style. You look nice.'

'Thanks, Mum. So, coffee?' Scarlet walked over to the coffee machine.

Cath put her hand to her head. 'Yes, and a couple of paracetamol please. I have a bit of a headache.'

'You have a bit of a *hangover*, you mean,' Scarlet retorted, immediately biting her lip in regret.

She didn't want to upset her mother – she was already going through enough. But Cath's drinking was getting worse, and it was worrying her greatly. Which, added to her growing list of other worries, was something she could really do without.

She sighed and closed her eyes for a second, wishing that at eighteen she hadn't already had to become the parent in their relationship. 'I'm sorry,' she said, pouring coffee into a fresh mug. 'That was uncalled for.'

There was a short silence as she finished pouring and placed the jug back under the machine. As she turned, she saw the defeated slump in her mother's shoulders droop a little more.

'No need to apologise for telling the truth,' Cath said tiredly.

Scarlet raised her eyebrows. At least Cath was admitting it today. That was an improvement. She placed the coffee in front of her mother at the breakfast bar. 'I'm just worried about you, Mum,' she said. 'I know you're not coping with Dad's death.' She watched her mother wince as she said the words. 'And that's understandable. We're all heartbroken. I feel like...' She stared back out of the window unhappily. 'I feel like I've been hit by a bus and I'm in mid-air, winded' – she moved her hand to her chest – 'shocked, trying to understand what's happening. And I'm just suspended in that moment before I hit the ground, where everything has all just happened and none of it makes sense and it all hurts.' She swallowed hard as the monster of raw pain inside tried to rear back up. 'I'm stuck there, unable to move.' She took a deep shaky breath in. 'And that's how it feels for me, every day. Every second.'

She turned and found her mother watching her with tears in her eyes. 'So, I get it,' she said. 'This feeling, Dad being gone, how he went, all of it is just constant hell. And all we can do is try to focus on something to help pull us through. But focusing on the dullness that drink brings you every day...' She shook her head and mashed her lips together as her gaze settled on the latest empty bottle by the bin. 'Mum, I don't want to have to see you go to an early grave too.' She heard Cath gasp. 'Drinking yourself into nothingness will only lead to *actual* nothingness. And then I'll be all alone.' She looked up at her mother and saw that her words were beginning to hit home. 'And I know you don't want that.' Her voice wobbled and rose an octave as a hot tear escaped her eye. It rolled down her cheek and she wiped it away with a sniff.

'So.' She cleared her throat. 'I need you to stop drinking the way you have been. And I need you to start being my mum again,' she said, her voice clear and strong. She looked her mother in the eye, levelly. 'I need to know you're OK, and if you can manage it, I need you to start making sure our castle is running smoothly again.'

It was something her father always used to say, in his usual jokey fashion. He was the hunter who brought home the meat and Cath was the queen who ran the castle. But now Ronan was gone and *she* was the hunter. And she needed her mum to step up and do her part.

Cath wiped away her own tears. 'Scarlet…' she exhaled heavily. 'I can't promise you I can do that just yet. The simple things just seem very hard right now.' She closed her eyes and more tears ran down her cheeks. 'But I will try. I promise.'

'And that's all I ask,' Scarlet replied, walking around the breakfast bar and pulling her mother into a hug.

They stayed that way in silence for a long few minutes until Scarlet gently broke away. 'I need to get going,' she said. 'But if you can manage it, the gardener's invoices need paying. You still have the company cards – if you could pay that it would take something off my plate.' Hopefully giving her that one small task might encourage her to start functioning again, even just a little. She gave her a smile and waved goodbye as she walked out into the hallway.

She reached for the keys to her little car but then paused, her hand hovering over the key hooks as her eyes rested on the other set that belonged to Ronan's Mercedes. She abandoned her own and picked up those instead. Whether she'd wanted to be or not, she was the head of this household now. So she might as well start acting like it.

CHAPTER FORTY-ONE

'So what did you make of the prodigal daughter?' Harry asked, sitting back in the chair in his office above the toy shop. The buzz of retail chatter could be heard through the walls, which irritated him some, but so long as his office door remained firmly shut, he could live with it. His hand twitched and he squeezed his pen tighter in an effort to stop the movement.

'Charming, attractive, confident...' Jasper reeled the words off in a bored tone. 'But green, of course. Not much of a replacement for the bear of a man her father was.'

'No, well, she wouldn't be yet,' Harry replied.

'I've been texting her, invited her out.'

'Oh?' Harry raised an eyebrow in interest. 'That could definitely be used to our advantage at some point,' he mused. 'It's a good time to make a move, with the current dynamics. Lily may be strong, but she's still only half the force she and her brother were together,' he mused. 'And if she's distracted with teaching the girl how to play with the big boys then she'll never see it coming.'

'So you want to move soon,' Jasper stated, reaching into a box of Red Vines and pulling one out. He chewed one end of it, twiddling the other absentmindedly. 'And we're going with the more direct option?' he asked, arching an eyebrow.

'I think it's the wisest course of action,' Harry replied. He leaned forward and unrolled a map of East London on the desk between them. 'They have two main market hubs. There are a few stalls elsewhere, but if we gain control of the ones in Roman Road in one swoop, the others will follow. Here...' He outlined an area on the map with a pen. 'Here's Roman Road, then this smaller one where they have the others is merely a few streets away, here. A ten-, fifteen-minute walk at most. They have four scouts on duty at any one time, then the stallholders themselves. On a busy Saturday they have one or two more on hand in case they need to create a distraction. At twelve o'clock, half the stallholders go for a break whilst the other half watch their stalls and the scouts move in a little closer. They take fifteen minutes then swap over with the others. *That's* when we'll hit.'

'The ones on break won't go far,' Jasper pointed out, flicking his hair back off his forehead.

'Of course not, and perhaps the noise will bring them running back, but the point is they'll be taken off guard and the people left watching will be spread thin. They won't realise it's happening until it happens.'

'So you'll send the men in tooled up, I imagine?'

'No, if there's a dispute, we don't want them getting arrested over carrying a weapon,' Harry said, shaking his head.

'Well, there definitely will be a dispute,' Jasper said, raising his eyebrows with a laugh. 'They aren't just going to roll over and accept this.'

'They'll have no real choice in the matter,' Harry replied with certainty.

'Go on.' Jasper sat back in his chair, listening with open curiosity.

'The stalls will be taken by force. The illegal goods the Drews have been peddling will be swiftly rounded up and thrown into a truck which will be waiting in the wings. When the inspector or police are called to the scene the stallholders will no doubt be creating, our new stallholders will calmly explain that they're only taking back what's theirs. They'll then produce their full trading licences outlining the stalls which belong to them – meaning us, of course.'

'Except those will be fake and all it takes is a system check…'

'And when they do that, they'll find our paperwork is in pristine order and that there's no record of the previous stallholders having renewed their licences from the previous year. By legal right the stalls will belong to us.'

'And how on earth did you pull that off?' Jasper asked, impressed.

'It didn't take that much, to be honest,' Harry replied with a crooked smile. 'Often the simpler plans turn out to be the best. I had a hacker go into the local council system, scrub the last known licences and replace them with my fake ones. For all anyone can tell, they're legitimate. And the ones they have are fakes. No record that they ever existed.'

Jasper chuckled. 'That's genius.' He reached for another Red Vine and bit into it.

'There will be a few scuffles, perhaps some arrests, but we'll give them an hour to remove their products and get out, otherwise we'll burn it. After that the stalls are ours. We'll have to pay out for extensive security for a while, but once they stop kicking and screaming, they'll realise there's no way of taking it all back. They'd have to rebuild again from scratch.'

Jasper nodded. 'They won't just walk away though – you know that.'

'Which is why we keep hold of their stolen goods.' Harry shifted in his seat. 'When they start pushing too hard, we threaten them. If they don't back off, we'll take it to the police with details of where we found it all. If they do back off, we'll keep the goods hidden out of the goodness of our hearts.' He grinned nastily.

'That should do it,' Jasper replied with a look of approval. 'When do we move?'

Harry reached forward and took one of the Red Vines for himself. 'This Thursday,' he said. 'We move Thursday. And they won't have a clue what's hit them.'

CHAPTER FORTY-TWO

It was the middle of the day, so The Black Bear pub wasn't particularly busy, but there were a few tables of people sat in conversation over drinks. Lily recognised a couple of them and nodded in acknowledgement. It had been a while since she'd last been here, but it was a well-used hotspot for those in the underworld and a safe place to conduct meetings without cameras or gossips. What happened in here stayed in here; it was an unspoken rule. Her gaze moved across the space, scanning the tables until she found who she was looking for.

She hadn't met the man she was here to see before in person, as it had been Connor who'd made the arrangements, but he wasn't hard to spot. Sitting on a chair in the far corner, his back was ramrod straight and to the wall as he warily eyed her. His Adam's apple bobbed up and down as he swallowed nervously and his fingers whitened as he clutched a file a little tighter. She suppressed a smile as she walked over. It was perhaps daunting, coming here, if you weren't from this world, she supposed. It was well known for what it was.

Reaching the table, she sat down and smiled at him. 'Hello,' she said, her tone as smooth as velvet.

'You're Lily?' he asked, nervously glancing at the door.

'I am,' she confirmed. 'And you're Mr Regan, is that correct?'

'Yes,' he said. 'That's me.'

'Good.' Lily smiled again, her eyes dropping to the file. 'I believe that's for me?' She raised an eyebrow and held her hand out.

He clutched it tighter. 'Maybe.' He licked his lips. 'Do you have something for me?'

'Of course.' Lily reached into her handbag and pulled out a brown envelope holding a wedge of twenty-pound notes. She put it on the table between them. 'It's all there. Feel free to count it, though I personally wouldn't want to advertise that I had that much cash on me in here.'

No one in here would touch the money she'd given him, having seen the hand-over. No one would interrupt another firm's business in that way. But she couldn't help herself – she had to have a little fun with the man. She watched his cheeks pale and pulled a face to pile it on.

'Best pop that away in your pocket,' she whispered conspiratorially.

He quickly picked it up and jammed it into his inner pocket after a quick glance at the contents. 'OK, well…' He handed over the file a little resentfully. 'Photocopies of the whole file. These can never be found, OK?' Worry flitted across his face and Lily could see the internal battle wavering his resolve.

She leaned in and put a hand on his arm. 'These will never see the light of day, I promise you,' she said sincerely. 'As soon as I'm done, they'll go on the fire. They don't exist.'

He stared at her for a moment, biting his bottom lip. Finally, he broke his gaze away. 'OK, well… Good luck with it all.' Standing up, he brushed himself down and walked out of the pub, holding his jacket to himself securely and watching everyone closely. Lily watched as he almost jogged away past the window. She shook her head with a small smirk of amusement and turned her attention to the file.

She flicked the cover open and began to read through the notes on the first page carefully. The photocopies were of the file from the coroner's office dealing with Ronan's case. It had taken some doing to get hold of these. Connor had approached him and offered him enough money to fight the ex-wife for access in return for the simple favour of providing copies of the file. But Mr Regan hadn't given in to their request easily. He'd resisted at first, trying to stay on the right side of the law. But after yet another failed attempt to see his daughter, he'd given in.

The notes on the first page didn't tell Lily anything she didn't already know, but she paused before turning the page. She knew what was coming next. The pictures of Ronan, dead on the ground. She swallowed and took a deep breath, then flicked the page over before she could talk herself out of it.

Sure enough, there he was. Her breath caught in her throat, and she closed her eyes in grief for a moment. Although she'd imagined the scene so many times in her head, and she hadn't spared herself any details, seeing it for real still hit her like a ton of bricks. She felt sick, a dull ache settling into her diaphragm. She forced herself to look at the pictures again, searching for clues, anything that might point her in the direction of his killer.

Ronan lay face down on the ground in a pool of blood in the first few crime scene pictures. The next shots were of him laid out on a slab, cleaned up, with close-ups on the wound. She swallowed the bile that rose to her throat and moved on to the particulars on the next page. Details of his blood type, a few strands of generic lint found on his chest that didn't come from his clothes and the probable size and detail of the knife used were listed, but nothing much else. The notes claimed all the local establishments had been visited, people questioned, but no one remembered seeing him. The area had no street cameras, and the only CCTV – which had been at a newsagent's nearby – had been pointing in the other direction.

The only thing that was of interest was a button that had been found a few feet away. It had come away from a shirt, and there was a potential link to the lint. The notes claimed they were currently tracing the shops that used the button in the hope they could narrow a search within a customer base, but it sounded like a long shot to Lily. She sighed and rubbed her forehead tiredly. No one seemed to be getting anywhere. She'd hoped that by looking at the file, she might have noticed something the police hadn't, or were unwilling to look into. Everyone she'd questioned herself – or asked to keep an ear out – didn't seem to know a thing. The underworld was unusually devoid of information.

Perhaps it really had been a case of wrong place, wrong time. But it just seemed so unlikely. Ronan was a seasoned criminal, a force to be reckoned with. How could someone like that end up dead in an alley with his throat cut? And if it was a chance robbery, why hadn't they taken anything?

The door to the pub opened, and Lily shifted in her seat so that she could check out who was coming in out of the corner of her eye. As she focused in on the newcomer, she froze. Forcing herself to breathe, she subtly shifted back to face the wall again and buried her head back in the file. She stared right through the paper, unseeing, as she strained to listen to the conversation at the bar behind her.

'Alright, Ty? What can I get you?' Keith, the barman asked.

Ty Rainer was one of the heads of the Jamaican firm whose weed the twins had taken. He was well known as a powerful, dangerous and incredibly volatile man, and was someone Lily had always been more than happy to avoid, even before the boys had stolen from him. She knew from Cillian that he'd been arrested in the raid. He must have been let out on bail.

'I ain't stopping for a drink,' Ty's deep voice rumbled low.

'OK,' Keith said warily. 'What can I do for you?'

'You'll have heard about the thieves that raided our green,' he stated.

'Only that it happened,' Keith quickly replied. 'Nothing more than that.'

'No whisper in the bar of who might have done it?' Ty pushed.

'No, nothing. Not yet anyway,' Keith replied.

There was a long silence, and Lily felt her heartbeat quicken. Why was he so silent? Did he not believe Keith? Was he staring out everyone in there, searching for anyone who might look guilty? She quickly turned the page she was staring at, trying to look as absorbed in what she was doing as possible.

Ty finally spoke again. 'You put the word out that I'm looking, and I ain't going to stop until I find the cunt who took it. Make it known that there's a ten-grand reward to anyone who tells us who it was.' His tone dropped to a menacing growl. 'And that whoever did take it is in for a very special reward of their own.'

'Of course – no problem,' Keith replied. Lily thought she could detect a note of relief in his tone.

'Good.' Ty turned and raised his voice to a shout, making Lily jump. 'And that goes for all of you,' he roared. 'I know you're all fucking listening,' he continued.

Lily quietly twisted in her seat so that she could see him. He stood in the middle of the room, his six-foot frame looking more menacing than ever as he flexed his muscles. His long dreads hung down his back, tied neatly together above his dark T-shirt, and Lily's sharp eyes caught the outline of the knife hidden down the side of his trousers.

'Ten grand to the man who tells me who it was. Another five if you bring the fucker to me and save me the hassle.' There was a short silence. 'Now back to your fucking drinks.'

With anger bubbling in his dark stare, Ty looked around at everyone once more. Lily gave him a polite nod as his gaze reached her, trying to make sure she acted as she usually would. Then as suddenly as he'd arrived, he left, glaring at everyone he passed to get to the door.

Lily glanced at Keith and saw his shoulders slump in relief. He didn't catch her eye, instead stared thoughtfully at the door Ty had just left by. She looked around and saw the conversations start up, people speculating on who it might be. The ball of worry that had lain in her stomach since the twins had told her what they'd done grew and turned to ice.

She needed to get that weed out of their storage barn. And fast.

CHAPTER FORTY-THREE

Pouring herself a gin and tonic, Lily almost put the gin down before lifting the bottle again and adding a little extra. It had been a long, stressful day, and the following conversation wasn't going to be much more relaxing.

The front door opened and closed, and she waited for Connor to join her, Cillian and Scarlet in her study.

'Well, thank you for finally gracing us with your presence,' she said with sharp sarcasm as he took a seat beside Scarlet.

'I was running errands,' he replied.

'That's not an errand, that's a whore,' Lily replied in a bored tone. 'Please try to learn the difference.'

Connor's cheeks flushed as he realised his mother had seen straight through the lie. He pulled a grimace at Cillian and rose from the seat to get himself a drink from the open cabinet.

'Right.' Lily sat down and rubbed her face. 'I have a way to get rid of the weed, but it has to be tomorrow night.'

'What do you mean, get rid of it?' Cillian asked.

'I mean I've managed to sell it as a job lot to someone who already deals in high quantities of green. They'll trickle it into their own loads, sending it down the chain and off into the market without raising any flags.'

'Who?' Connor asked with a small frown as he sat back down with his drink.

'The Tylers,' Lily replied.

'What!' Cillian exclaimed. 'How much for?'

'About a third of its value,' Lily replied. 'I had to make it an attractive deal – the risk of touching it at all is already high for any potential buyer.'

'Fuck's sake, Mum,' Cillian complained.

A flash of anger shot across Lily's eyes and she leaned forward towards him. 'We're lucky anyone is interested in buying it at all, you foolish boy,' she snapped. 'If the Jamaicans ever get wind of this, it's a death sentence for everyone involved.'

There was a long silence. Cillian sighed and looked out of the window, Connor took a deep drink from his glass and Scarlet stared at her aunt with a look of grave worry.

'How do we know they won't find the risk too high anyway and shop us all in?' Scarlet asked quietly.

'They won't,' Lily replied, shaking her head with certainty. 'Freddie Tyler is one of the most honourable people I know. And one of my oldest friends. We can trust them.'

Scarlet nodded. 'Well, you know what you're doing so that's good enough for me,' she said resolutely. 'What's the plan?'

'The plan is this…' Lily repositioned herself and waited for the twins to give her their attention. 'We have to drive the weed into Soho—'

'Soho?' Connor asked, exchanging a surprised look with Cillian.

'Soho,' Lily repeated. She looked at each of them in turn. 'I'm aware of the risk that poses in itself, but it's the only way we can make the deal.'

'Where exactly are we talking?' Connor asked.

'You've heard of Club Anya, the burlesque club in Dean Street?' Lily asked.

'Yeah, I know it,' he answered.

'That's part owned by Anna Davis, Freddie Tyler's significant other.' She picked up her packet of cigarettes and tapped one out. 'She and her business partner also run a whorehouse down the side street right by it. It's discreet but secure. They'll hold it there and quietly feed it down through their dealer tree. Their dealers won't know, of course,' she added. 'As far as they're aware, it will be the same weed they always get.'

'That's still a lot of people who do know though,' Scarlet replied with a frown of concern. 'What's the deal with the business partner?'

'Part of the firm too,' Lily replied. 'Freddie knows the severity of the situation.' She paused to light the cigarette still in her hand. 'He's spoken only to those who are in his inner circle.'

Connor nodded. 'Well, I guess that's that then,' he said. Cillian gave him a look and he shrugged. 'What?' he asked. 'Some money's better than no money.'

'And anything is better than a machete to the limbs,' Scarlet added, with feeling.

'Exactly,' Lily replied.

She blew her smoke into the air and watched Scarlet stare Cillian out. Cillian broke eye contact first, looking away bored, as she knew he would. Scarlet was getting more and more confident by the day. It just strengthened Lily's belief that the girl was born for this life. Her strength and her hunger for it all was growing, the same way it had for her and Ronan when they were starting out. It would get harder – much harder. And there were some gruelling times to come, but she knew Scarlet would take them head-on. She had already committed herself. There was no going back now.

'How are we getting it there?' Connor asked.

'We're borrowing an old laundry truck chop-shop-Steve has in the yard. It's legal, so no need to worry about the plates flagging up. Then we're going to buy a load of sheets and towels to wrap the product in.'

'Sheet's won't hide the smell if we're pulled,' Cillian pointed out.

'If we're pulled, we're screwed,' Lily stated in a matter-of-fact tone. 'So we need to make sure there's absolutely no reason we would be. The sheets are for appearances the other end. It's central Soho. It doesn't matter what time of the day or night we do this, there will be people around. We can get close to the door, but the back will be wide open for all to see whilst we move it in. If it's a laundry truck full of sheets then it will raise no suspicion.'

'And if the law comes along?' Connor asked.

'They own all the flat foots in the area. If any do appear, when they see where we're delivering to, they'll just walk the other way,' Lily replied. 'The Tylers are well set up once we hit Soho. *Very* well set up. It's the journey where we have to be careful.'

There was a long silence as everyone thought the plan over. Lily studied each one of them in turn. These three were the future of the firm. The future of the family. The boys were hard and smart, well cut out for the life. And Scarlet had been born for this. But she was so young and time moved fast. Could she get Scarlet up to the sort of level she needed to be fast enough? Ronan's death had thrown Lily's own vincibility into harsh light. Now, more than ever, she needed to make sure that if something happened to her, the firm would still thrive.

'Let's get this done,' she said, reaching for her gin and tonic. She took a deep drink from the glass and put it back down. 'Let's get this done and then never speak of it again. This was the most stupid thing you boys have ever done, but it's done, and soon it will be dealt with. We need to move on and never look back. Because we have more than enough to focus on here.' Her gaze landed on a picture of the family all together. 'We have a murder to solve and justice to dole out. There will be no comfortable prison for the man who killed Ronan. An eye for an eye – that's what the Bible says is fair justice in this world.' Her expression darkened. 'And whoever took my brother's last breath from him will draw his own sooner than he thinks.'

CHAPTER FORTY-FOUR

Scarlet held on tight to one of the straps on the side of the truck. She assumed it was to secure the laundry baskets and could understand why. She'd never been bumped around so much in her life. As they went over yet another bump, she slid sideways and nearly fell off her makeshift seat entirely, saving herself with the strap once more. She pulled herself back into position and planted her feet further apart in the hope this might steady her more.

She glanced over to her aunt, who sat in similar fashion opposite her. The big difference between them was that her aunt didn't seem to be having half the trouble staying upright that she was. In fact, Lily looked perfectly at ease, her body swaying with the movement of the truck rather than jerking violently against it the way Scarlet's was. As she watched, Lily reached a hand up and pushed a lock of her tight curls back off her forehead. It reminded Scarlet of something she'd been meaning to speak to her about.

'Hey, so I've been thinking,' she started, getting Lily's attention.

'Hm?'

'About our money-laundering issues and what we can do about that.'

'OK?' Lily's neutral expression turned to one of mild interest.

'We're maxing out all our current avenues and there's no backup if one falls, as we both know, so right now we need one more decent business. Ideally a cash-flow business, which can take the pressure off elsewhere, right?' Scarlet leaned forward, almost letting go of the strap but remembering she still needed it just in time for the next bump.

'So what are you thinking?' Lily asked.

'I know you had your sights set on bringing up a false line in the factory, but I think we could go one better.' Scarlet's grey-blue eyes gleamed brightly in the dull light of the back of the truck. 'You want the business to be ours, under our control rather than an external party. Our stalls are being used for something else already, we can't waste those, but what if instead of milking the factory we opened a hairdresser's?' She watched Lily's face but her aunt wasn't giving away her feelings on the matter just yet.

'Think about it – it's actually better than the other options on a few fronts. The price point, for starters. At a takeaway, one person might spend ten or twenty quid maybe, but one woman at the hairdresser's can easily do fifty to two hundred in one visit. It's mainly a cash business, or can be anyway,' she added. 'The stock is almost impossible to keep track of, because they order in bulk but don't log who used what or where. I mean, colouring – the hairdressers take a bit of this colour, mix it with a dollop of that bleach and add a squirt of whatever is in another bottle to get what they need for a colour. So stock count is vague at best in a straight salon. Then you have the chairs. Salons rent chairs out to stylists and then negotiate a percentage of their earnings per customer, which of course is so variable and untrackable it's a joke.' She smirked. 'We could open one up, genuinely hire out half the chairs to look legit and then hire the others to fake stylists who have a full diary of non-existent customers who mainly pay cash.' She sat back and waited.

For a few long moments, Lily didn't say anything, and a sliver of doubt began to creep into Scarlet's mind. She'd been so sure it was a good idea, she'd gone over and over it from every angle and couldn't see a fault in her plan. But perhaps she was wrong.

'That's actually not a bad idea,' Lily said eventually. 'It certainly would be, as you point out, very easy to hide the money, and we'd be able to push good volume through without being obvious about it. The issue that springs to mind though is who would run it?' She continued, 'Money fronts under our control are always the ideal, but you have to have someone you trust running the place. Someone who will work with you to hide the money. You can't hide laundered money from a general manager who has access to the accounts.'

'I've thought about that too,' Scarlet replied. 'I have a friend, a close friend. She knows who we are and what we do – to an extent anyway. She's working in a salon over in Barking as a stylist and has been standing in recently as the assistant manager. She loves what she does but she hates it there – the owner's an arsehole. It was actually her moaning about it on the phone last week that gave me the idea.'

Lily's expression remained unconvinced.

'She's trustworthy,' Scarlet pressed. 'She's just looking for somewhere she can be happy and make her own mark. I think if we approached her, she'd be more than up for this. And we could teach her to do things our way from the start.'

Lily pulled a face. 'This would be a pretty big venture, Scarlet. It's not exactly something we can bring someone new in for.'

'But she's not new,' Scarlet replied. 'Mum and Dad know her well, or… well, he did…' She swallowed the pain that rose up at the thought of her father and pressed on. 'She's trustworthy, knows how to keep her mouth shut. You know her actually. You met her a few times – Natalie?'

'Natalie Baker?' Lily asked, a glimmer of recognition in her eyes. 'Ronnie Baker's daughter?'

'Yeah, that's her.' She'd forgotten Lily knew Natalie's dad. They went back years, though they weren't close anymore.

Lily thought it through as Scarlet waited in silence. It hadn't been an outright no, which was promising.

The truck turned a corner, and Scarlet put her free hand out to steady herself, cursing under her breath. They slowed to a stop and the rumble of the engine died away. Lily tilted her head to the side, listening to the sounds coming from outside.

'We're here,' she said.

Scarlet let go of the strap, thankful to not have to be cramped up swinging around in the back any longer. She made up her mind to insist the boys traded places on the return journey.

Lily moved towards the back door as Connor pulled it open and offered her his hand. She turned back as she jumped down. 'We'll discuss it further later, alright?' she said.

'OK, sure,' Scarlet replied. She smiled as she let Connor help her out, pleased that Lily liked the idea.

As she straightened up, a door opened. The door had no sign on it, no advertisement of business. She guessed that it must be the place they were looking for. A woman of average height with long dark hair, deep blue eyes and bright red lipstick walked out and stared at them all in turn. As her gaze met Scarlet's, she felt it pierce straight through her, powerful and authoritative. She stifled the urge to look away, holding her ground. The woman seemed to notice this and the corner of her mouth turned upwards into a half-smile.

'Please, come in,' came the smooth voice. 'If you make a chain, it will be quicker to move. Bill has disconnected that camera for now' – she pointed to a CCTV camera across the road – 'but they'll notice soon enough so you'll need to get moving.'

'Thank you,' Lily said, stepping forward. 'I'm Lily.' She extended her hand.

The woman shook it politely. 'The famous Lily Drew,' she said, open curiosity in her tone. 'A pleasure to meet you. I'm Anna. Anna Davis.'

CHAPTER FORTY-FIVE

Lily watched the way Anna's sharp gaze studied them all. She was smiling, but her jaw was set hard and her stance was strong and unyielding. Her beauty was staggering, but somehow she reminded Lily of an ice queen she'd once read about in a book. From first glance, Anna Davis seemed every inch the woman Lily had heard about.

'OK then. Come on, boys – let's get this moving,' Lily said, turning back to the truck.

'Why don't you bring it into the hallway here first, then we can close the door and move it all upstairs in private,' Anna suggested, holding the door open and stepping back as Connor and Cillian came through with the first two bags of what on the outside looked like sheets.

'I'll help – we'll get them in quicker,' Scarlet said, before disappearing around the back of the van.

'Shall I show you where we're taking them?' Anna asked, one perfectly arched eyebrow raised in question.

'Yes, that would be good,' Lily replied.

She followed Anna into the building and up the steep stairs to the first floor. The door at the top was closed and Lily could hear the dull thud of background music behind the murmur of voices. A flirtatious giggle made its way through, followed by a deep throaty male laugh.

'The lounge and bar area,' Anna remarked, passing the door towards the next set of stairs. 'It's an after-hours anything-goes area where the clients can unwind with their lady of choice.'

Lily nodded, understanding the concept. It was more of a high-end whorehouse, not one of the quick rub-and-tug conveyer belts that were so easily accessible elsewhere throughout the city.

Anna ascended the next set of stairs, her high stilettos tapping sharply on each step as she went. Lily followed, taking note of her surroundings. There wasn't much in the hall, but there were more doors on the upper floor. She wondered where each of them led. Anna continued to the end of the hallway and walked through the last door. Lily joined her and looked around with interest at the assortment of junk that lay around the edges.

'Where should we stack it?' she asked, wondering if she should perhaps move some of the odds and ends against the wall out of the way.

'Oh, it's not going here.' Anna smiled, her blue eyes sparkling suddenly. 'Come, let me show you our hidden room.'

Anna pulled one of the shelves on an old bookcase. The entire bookcase swung forward, the hinges that were holding it to the wall behind not visible from the angle at which Lily was watching. Behind that was a smaller half-size door. Anna unlocked it and gestured for Lily to look inside.

She bent down and peered into the space beyond. It was a large area, long and thin, leading off to the sides, the ceiling sloping sharply downwards towards the edge of the building. A small window had been sealed off, black paper taped over it securely and a small camera was attached to the wall, pointed at the doorway. She nodded and pulled back out, standing up.

'That's some decent security,' Lily commented.

'Bill sorted it out. He's so good at that kind of thing,' Anna replied.

'He is,' Lily agreed. 'He's been our go-to man on a few things like that in the past.'

It was well known that Bill worked mainly for Freddie, but although his loyalties lay with the Tylers, he was more of a free agent than most people in the life. He possessed some very specialist skills, which any of his friends in the underworld were welcome to hire him for.

Anna closed the door and they began walking back the way they'd entered. 'You've known Bill a long time?' she asked.

'Oh yes, almost as long as I've known Freddie.' Lily smiled.

'Yes, Freddie said you used to babysit when they were young.' Anna placed her hand on the stair rail and began descending.

'Well, I'm not sure how much babysitting I actually did with him. Little bugger used to slip out from under my nose whenever he saw an opportunity,' Lily said with a laugh. 'Paul would go with him sometimes too. I'd be frantic trying to figure out where they were and get them back in before Mollie came home.'

Anna threw her head back and laughed. 'I don't think I've ever heard Freddie referred to as a little bugger before,' she said.

'Well, he definitely was one, back in the day,' Lily replied fondly. 'The others were a lot younger – they used to be easy enough. You'd put them to bed and not hear a peep. But Freddie...' She shook her head. 'He couldn't sit still, that boy. Always looking for an opportunity to make money, even at ten years old. He'd sneak out when I had my back turned, looking to make a few quid to help his mum. And Paul just wanted to be wherever Freddie was, of course. If he hadn't fallen asleep before Freddie escaped, he'd follow along like a little shadow. I'll never forget the time I found them down on the train track, because Freddie had heard a rumour that the bridge above it was where scorned spouses would throw their rings from.' She rolled her eyes. 'Scouring the stones, he was. In the pitch black in winter, Paul standing guard in case a train came. I could have lynched the pair of them. Luckily Mollie never found out.'

Anna's face softened momentarily as she relayed the memory and for a second she saw the naked love the woman felt for Freddie. It warmed her to know that the ice-cold businesswoman had a genuine space in her heart for him. He deserved that.

'He'd still do anything for Mollie now,' Anna said as she started down the second set of stairs. 'For any of the family.'

Lily nodded. 'He's as loyal and as genuine as they come, that one. It's why I knew I could come to him.' She met Anna's gaze. 'You're a lucky woman, catching his heart,' she said plainly.

'Well, that's something we can agree on,' Anna replied with a controlled smile. She paused on the stairs and surveyed the scene below.

Connor was just shutting the door, the last of the bags clearly stacked up on the hallway. There was no room for them to leave the stairs so Lily waited and caught Cillian's eye.

'Are we heading up?' he asked, looking to her in question.

'We are. Start moving – I'll lead the way.'

Lily waited as the boys and Scarlet all grabbed as much as they could carry, then turned and beckoned for them to follow. As she left Anna behind, she locked her jaw and her lips pursed into a grim line. Freddie trusted Anna and Lily trusted Freddie. So as far as storing the weed here went, everything was in order.

But it was still a worry. Because now Anna was one of the few people who held the information the Jamaicans wanted. She knew everything about the situation. And the weed was sitting under her roof. If the Jamaicans ever caught wind of their green being here, how far would Anna really go to protect the identity of a complete stranger? Would she really stay quiet as they cut into her flesh and stripped her arms from her body? Of course she wouldn't. No one would die for a complete stranger. And so until Freddie had fed this green down through his chain and it was completely gone, they were still in just as much danger as ever.

CHAPTER FORTY-SIX

Chastity stared at her phone screen once more with a pout. Connor still hadn't replied to her and it was grating on her nerves. She was bored and wanted to see him, go out shopping with him maybe, see what she could wheedle out of him this week. But he'd been too busy to see her again. She sighed and tapped her long pink nails on the kitchen table, then ran her fingers across her forehead. Was she getting a wrinkle? She hoped not. She relied on her flawless looks to get what she wanted out of life. Age was her enemy. That's why she needed to tie her cash cow down and soon. But no matter what angle she tried to work it from, getting Connor to commit to her was like trying to draw blood from a stone. She scowled as she thought about his mother once more.

That mean old bitch was the only major thing in the way of her end goal. For some reason Connor hung off her every word, as though she was some sort of oracle. But it should be *her* every word he was hanging off, not his mother's. She should have been raking it in by now, spending whatever she wanted from his overflowing pot of gold and playing queen bee in his plush flat, instead of sitting here, broke and bored, in this cramped two-bed hovel she still shared with her mother on the Eric and Treby estate.

Was she wasting her time with Connor? She'd taken quite a liking to him. On top of his thick wallet, he was one of the best-looking guys she'd ever met. He had a hard reputation too, which gave her a reputation by association, and she'd found this to be quite enjoyable. He'd have made a nice long-term catch. But there were other fish in the sea – perhaps she should accept her failure to seal this deal and move on.

As she pondered her options, she unfolded her arms and grabbed her breasts, squeezing them, testing them to see if they'd dropped at all. She needed breast implants. It was something she'd decided a while ago. Hers were nice enough but clearly didn't hold enough wow factor to secure the sort of position she craved. But where was she going to get five grand from? That's how much the surgeon had told her it was going to cost, when she went for a consultation. Connor wasn't going to give her the money – she'd already tried that and he'd laughed her off. And she didn't fancy working like all the plain Janes around her had to. Hard graft was beneath her, in her opinion.

The door opened behind her and her mother entered the small kitchen, a lit cigarette in her hand.

'Oh fuck's sake, Mum,' Chastity complained, wafting the smoke with her hand. 'I just washed me hair.'

'And?' her mother asked, in a raspy voice.

'*And* I don't fancy stinking like a bleedin' ashtray for the rest of the day,' she said.

'Well, fuck off out then, love,' her mother replied, blowing out another lungful of smoke. ''Cause I need me fag and a cuppa to set me up for the day, and I ain't giving that up because you're feeling precious about your barnet.'

Chastity scowled and glared at her as she stomped past into the lounge. She picked up her handbag and shoved her feet into her shoes.

'Get some milk before you come home. And bread actually. We're out and I'm skint,' her mother called after her.

Chastity left the house with a glum expression. Her mother was always skint. They were both always skint. This was why she needed her boobs done. Then she could land a rich bloke blinded enough by her assets to put a ring on her finger and be out of this shithole for good.

She marched down the three sets of stairs to the ground floor and out of the building, heading to the local pub where she knew at least a couple of her friends would be drinking their problems away. Friends was a loose term. They were girls around her age she'd grown up with and hung out with when she had nothing better to do. But they depressed her really. They'd given in to their fate a long time ago, accepting that life on the estate was all they were going to know.

She walked in and looked around the rundown pub, then headed over to the table where two young women sat drinking what looked like glasses of Coke. She sat down with a big fake smile, acting as though she was pleased to be there.

'Ooh, well, if it isn't Lady Muck come to join us,' one of them joked.

Chastity's smile tightened. 'Nice to see you too, Katie,' she replied drily.

'I'm only joking. How's things?' Katie replied.

'Oh, you know,' Chastity said breezily. 'They're great. I've just popped back for a bit to see me mum, spend some time back home, you know.' She liked to keep up the pretence that she spent most of her time at Connor's, though this wasn't really the case.

'Like your handbag,' the other one said. 'That real or a knock-off?'

'Real,' Chastity said smugly. 'Connor bought me it. Said he didn't want his girl going round with any of that crappy fake shit. That I deserve the best,' she lied. He hadn't said that at all. She'd pestered him for days to buy her this.

'Ahh, that's nice,' the girl said warmly with a smile.

Chastity smiled back. She liked Janine more than Katie. She might be a bit of a loser, but she was a really nice girl at heart. 'What you guys drinking, Cokes?'

Katie leaned in and showed her the bottle of vodka they were hiding under the table. 'Yeah, we're buying Cokes, but then we're slipping this in when he ain't looking.' She gestured towards the bartender. 'Too skint to buy them by the shot today.'

Chastity pulled a face. It was so tacky, bringing your own booze into a pub like that. Did they have no self-respect? It was also still pretty early, not even twelve o'clock.

'Why don't you get yourself a Coke – you can have some of this,' Janine offered. 'It's a lot cheaper,' she added, seeing Chastity was about to decline.

Chastity paused and thought about the last few notes sitting in her wallet. She was running out of cash and her benefits weren't coming in for another week. She mentally shrugged and gave in to the situation.

'Fuck it, go on then.'

As she waited at the bar while the barman served a customer, the door opened and a large, muscular man walked in. She eyed him with interest, wondering what he was doing here. She knew who he was. Everyone knew who Ty Rainer was. But he was rarely seen up in this neck of the woods.

He came and stood almost next to her, so she turned her body towards him and studied him closer. He was an attractive man, his hard muscles clearly defined through his tight T-shirt, dreads that hung to his shoulder blades and a chiselled jaw framing his face. His eyes were deep and dark, and he had a dangerous look about him that sent a small thrill through Chastity. Her eyes dropped to his watch. It was a Rolex. Her interest grew, and the cogs in her brain began to turn. He was a big fish in the underworld. Even bigger than Connor.

He suddenly turned and stared at her, his look so intense she wasn't sure whether to feel alarmed or turned on. His gaze flickered up and down her body, then back to the barman who was now coming over. Chastity exhaled, aware she'd stopped breathing for a moment.

'Hey, Ty, how's it going?' the barman said warily. Chastity vaguely registered that he probably expected trouble, seeing Ty arrive like this.

'You've heard my weed got stolen a few days ago, yes?' he asked, his deep voice rumbling through the small room.

'Yeah, I did hear about that,' the barman replied.

'You spread the word that anyone who comes to me with the name of who did it gets ten grand. Another five if they bring the thieving fuck to me themselves,' he said loudly, ensuring everyone in the room could hear. 'You got that?' he asked.

'Yeah, absolutely.'

Chastity's eyes narrowed as something began to niggle. 'What day did you say it was taken?' she asked, breaking the silence in the room.

He turned and leaned over her menacingly and she cowered, slightly alarmed by the closeness of his body. 'I didn't,' he said in a low, dangerous voice, his face close to hers.

She breathed in his musky aftershave and found she rather liked it. She straightened up and looked him in the eye, showing him she wasn't afraid.

'Saturday,' he said, straightening up and backing off.

Chastity's mind flew back to the conversation she'd had with Connor. That had been on Sunday. He'd been adamant that should anyone come asking, she tell them he'd been with her the night before. This had been why. It had to be. Connor had been the one who'd stolen Ty Rainer's weed. As it all clicked into place, she suddenly realised what it all meant. The options before her began lighting up, as did the gleam in her eye.

Ty made to walk out, and she touched his arm to stop him. He rounded on her and she blinked, aware that she probably shouldn't have done that.

'Ten grand, you say?' she asked. 'To whoever tells you who took it?'

'Ten grand. Another five if they bring the thief to me,' he repeated.

Chastity smiled. 'That's a lot of money to some people,' she said. 'A lot of money indeed.'

CHAPTER FORTY-SEVEN

Lily woke slowly, the sound of her phone pinging rousing her from sleep. She frowned, wishing she'd put the damn thing on silent. It had been a long night, what with picking up the weed, taking it to Soho, delivering the truck back to the scrapyard and then finally sorting out the everyday tasks that came with the running of their businesses. When she'd finally reached home and crawled into bed, her head had barely hit the pillow before she'd fallen into a deep, dreamless sleep.

She groaned and pushed her wild curls back off her face, reaching for the offending phone. Blinking as the light from the screen momentarily blinded her, she focused on the messages and frowned. She'd missed several calls and now the texts were coming through at a rate of knots from Jack, one of her watchers at the Roman Road market. She touched through to the texts and began to read. As the words registered, her eyes widened in shock.

'Jesus Christ,' she hissed, throwing the phone to the side and jumping out of bed. She flew to the wardrobe and grabbed the first clothes her hands touched.

She pulled on her black knee-length leather skirt and quickly zipped it up, throwing on the black long-sleeved T-shirt that was next to it. Pushing her hair back off her face once more and ignoring the fact it just bounced straight back out of place, she grabbed the phone and made a call as she ran down the stairs. It rang and rang, her frustration growing with every ring.

'Pick up, pick up,' she muttered, grabbing her keys and stepping into her shoes. The call connected as she opened the front door. 'Finally!' she exclaimed. 'You need to get down to the Roman right now. I'm on my way but you're closer. We're being fucking taken over.'

Lily marched down the middle of the market, Connor by her side, heading straight for the cluster of people loudly arguing with each other and the market inspector. He was attempting to get them to calm down but not having much luck. Lily wasn't surprised. She was as enraged as they were.

'What the fuck is going on?' she demanded, her anger exploding as she reached the crowd. Half of them turned to her in relief, all glad to see their boss appear, all trying to talk over each other to explain. The other half stared her out with thinly veiled looks of menace. She glared at these, stepping forward right in front of them.

'Who are you?' asked the flustered market inspector.

'I represent the people that these imposters are trying to oust from their stalls,' Lily replied in an angry tone, turning to him. 'Why the hell have they not been told to leave?'

'That's just the issue though, madam,' he replied. 'Technically these aren't their stalls.'

'What do you mean these aren't their stalls?' she asked, her tone rising with indignation. 'These have been their stalls for years – ask anyone on the strip.' She gestured up and down. Several of the stallholders who didn't work for her shouted out in support of her statement.

'That may be true, but they still don't technically have the right to the stalls,' the market inspector replied unhappily. He clearly didn't want to be here today. He'd only picked the shift up to help out a colleague and was greatly regretting that decision now, as he stared into the angry mob in front of him.

Lily stepped forward. 'You're going to need to elaborate,' she said strongly. 'Because what you're saying to me makes no sense whatsoever. These people are nobodies.' She pointed at the newcomers. 'They ain't even from round here, and they've turned up out of the blue and disturbed a whole load of hard-working locals for no reason, trying to take their stalls by force. *That's* the issue here.'

One of the men in the opposing crowd gave her a mean sneer, and she saw Connor step towards him and ball his fist. She subtly touched his arm, warning him not to start anything. Not yet at least.

The inspector sighed heavily. 'These stallholders do not have the correct licences to be trading on these stalls. They used to,' he quickly continued, seeing Lily open her mouth to argue, 'but the licences were not renewed when they ran out six months ago. Whatever the situation was that brought it about, I don't know, but that's what happened. And these gentlemen here have since purchased those licences, which means legally, they now belong to them.' He held his hands out helplessly.

Lily pulled back in surprise. 'What do you mean they weren't renewed? I renewed them myself, and then I delivered them *here* myself. Joel? Where's Joel?' She swivelled until she clocked him. 'Where's your licence – have you got it?' He handed it to her. 'Here, see?' She glanced at it and then held it up in front of the inspector's face. 'It says right here, look at that. Look at the dates.'

'I'm sorry but these are not on the system. And the ones these gentlemen hold are.'

'How can that be possible?' Lily glanced at the papers the other men were holding. She couldn't see the details from a distance, but she could see they were laid out in the same format as her own licences. She frowned and shook her head. 'You've made a mistake. Look these up again,' she demanded.

'I have,' the inspector said, sighing once more. 'I've checked the system three times, but the results remain the same. The licence numbers on your people's papers don't exist, whereas these other ones do. I don't know what to tell you. If you want to take it up with someone more senior you will have to call into the office, but as of right now these men want their stalls, and I have no choice but to ask the previous stallholders to remove their goods and leave. I can give you one hour, due to the strange nature of today's situation.' He held his hands up and stepped back.

Lily stared at him, stumped. Eventually, her gaze moved around to study the faces of the newcomers. She didn't recognise any of them – they were complete strangers. Each face was equally as hostile, but none of them said a word. They didn't need to, she realised. They had already won. She shook her head and rubbed her temple.

'I can't believe this is happening,' she muttered. 'What happens if I tell you to do one and tell all my stallholders here to completely ignore you?' she asked.

'Then I call the police, have them forcefully removed and all the goods will be seized. Technically I should already *be* seizing the goods as they've been trading illegally for six months, but as this seems to be a complete surprise for everyone, I'll turn a blind eye if you all just get out quietly,' he said, trying to put some force into his words. It was obvious he really couldn't be bothered with the amount of paperwork seizing the goods of so many stalls would create.

Lily closed her mouth, her mind whirling and her anger bubbling. With difficulty she swallowed the anger down and turned to her group of stallholders, shaking her head. 'I can't believe I'm saying this but you'll have to pack up for now.' She held a hand up to silence the protests. 'I will deal with this and sort it out, but until I can do that, I need you to hang back and wait. It's not going to do anyone any favours if they seize your goods.' She gave them a meaningful look and they all became quiet.

There was a huge stash of illegal items in each and every one of those stalls. They needed to get them out before the inspector began looking too closely. She turned back to him, pointedly ignoring the smirks on the faces of the men taking over.

'We'll go – for now. But this is a mistake.' She pointed at him with a glare as her people began their retreat. '*You've* made a mistake here. And I'm going to get to the bottom of it.' She swung her gaze over to the newcomers. 'I wouldn't get too comfortable if I were you. This will bite you in the arse. And that's a promise.'

She felt Connor gently pull her away, and she let him turn her around.

'What now?' he asked, looking back over his shoulder as they walked away.

'I'm not sure yet. I need to get down to the council office, work out what's happened. It has to be a glitch or something in the system.'

'What, that specifically fucked over our stallholders and no one else?' Connor asked, disbelief on his face.

'Hey! Lil!' A shout came from the nearest stall and they both turned as Carrie, the stallholder, ran over with a look of worry on her face. 'It's all gone,' she whispered. 'The hot goods – they've been cleared out, the lot.'

'What the fuck!' A complaint sounded from the next stall and they looked up into the horrified eyes of another of their stallholders. He pointed at where they knew he hid the illicit goods they gave him and shook his head.

Lily watched as one by one each stallholder confirmed the same thing. Whilst they'd been busy arguing their case, someone had been burrowing through each stall, taking their stash of illegal goods. Suddenly, with stark, heart-sinking clarity, Lily knew exactly who was behind the shit show they'd all been sucked into.

CHAPTER FORTY-EIGHT

Harry's grin widened as he watched the scene unfold on the street below. He and Jasper were looking down from the top window of a two-level teahouse on the side of the market. It was the perfect spot. From here they could see everything, but they wouldn't be spotted themselves. Whilst Harry enjoyed putting plans like this into action, he wasn't one for joining in or putting himself into a dangerous position. He might have to deal with gangsters, and he was happy to work at their level in order to get ahead, but he wasn't one himself. He knew he could never claim that.

Gangsters were hardened people, prepared to do whatever they needed to, to survive and thrive in the underworld. Harry didn't have the balls to do most of the things he ordered himself. He was a coward through and through, and he knew it. He was also completely OK with it. Some people wanted to be heroes, some people wanted to be infamous villains. Harry just wanted to be rich. And there were no scruples blocking his path.

He chuckled as he saw the realisation dawn on Lily's face. 'Call the men,' he instructed Jasper. 'Tell them to come get us. When we get home, we'll need to double up on our personal guard rota. They'll need to be on us twenty-four-seven for the foreseeable future.'

'You think she'll figure it out?' Jasper asked, mild curiosity lurking at the back of his bored tone.

'She already has,' Harry replied with certainty. 'We may not have approached her about the markets outright, but we've not been subtle in our discussions surrounding our need of good market stalls, or our interest in theirs. Even if no one else has, Renshaw will have tipped her off for certain. It doesn't take a genius to add it all up.'

'So what will you do when she comes knocking, as she inevitably will?' Jasper asked.

'Nothing,' Harry replied. His head twitched to the side as the waitress passed by, and he clutched the top of his cane tighter. 'We have the situation sewn up. She can stamp and shout all she likes – it'll get her nowhere. Plus,' he added, his mouth curling up in one corner. 'We now have all their illegal goods headed over to the shed. All we have to do is threaten to expose it to the police and they'll soon retreat with their tails between their legs.'

'It's a dirty move,' Jasper said. 'Threatening the law is a definite no-no in the underworld rule book.'

'*Their* rule book,' Harry responded. 'We may cross some lines here, but we're not officially part of their world and therefore their rules do not apply to us. We're better than them, Jasper, and don't forget that.' He lifted his chin and narrowed his eyes as he looked down on the people below. 'They have their uses, but once we've taken advantage of those, they are of no consequence. So don't get hung up on their apparent standards.'

*

Harry was so engrossed that he didn't notice the woman two tables away listening keenly, nor that her brows rose high in disbelief at his last statement. And neither did he notice her slip away, with one last long look at the pair of them as she memorised all that she could.

*

Lily marched into the house and angrily threw her bag on the side table in the hall. Connor followed, slamming the door shut behind him, not hiding his own feelings any better.

'Where is your brother?' Lily asked irritably. 'I thought he'd be here by now.'

'Always so fixated on the whereabouts of your precious boys, aren't you, Mother?' Ruby said in a bitter tone from her place on the sofa facing the hallway. 'Do you worry about me this much?' She smirked humourlessly.

Lily stopped and turned, leaning backwards to see into the lounge. She clocked Ruby and exchanged a look with Connor. With a sigh she changed direction and made her way into the room.

'I'm not worrying about Cillian; I was just expecting to see him here,' she replied.

'So that's a *no* then,' Ruby said with a laugh.

'Oh, Ruby…' Lily tutted, annoyed. 'Of course I worry about you. More than anyone actually. But right now I've got a lot of other things going on. Absolute fucking nightmares actually.' She rubbed her forehead. 'What are you doing here anyway? You've run out of money again, I take it?'

The resigned tone shot a stab of annoyance through Ruby's stomach. If it had been either of her brothers asking for money, Lily would have jumped at the chance to rain cash on them. She lived for the opportunities to shower the twins with her wealth, yet whenever *she* came asking for a few crumbs of the family pie, she was treated like some sort of leper.

'Yes, I have as it happens,' she said, sticking her sharp chin out. 'But that ain't why I'm here.'

Lily pursed her mouth and waited for her to continue.

'I was actually dealing with my money problems myself,' she said, giving her mother a defiant look. 'Or was in the process of doing so anyway.'

It wasn't a lie; she'd been on the lookout at the market for any easy wallets to steal. When she'd spotted Harry, with his richly tailored clothes, big pockets and slow, anxious demeanour, she'd thought she'd hit the jackpot. She hadn't known who he was at the time, only that he was clearly out of place and appeared to be an easy target. He hadn't been that easy though, keeping a watchful eye over his shoulder, his younger companion doing the same. She'd followed them both to the teahouse, hoping for an opportunity to arise there. What she hadn't expected was quite such a big opportunity – the chance to gift her family with information on the men who'd just done them over. It should be exactly what she needed to milk some extra cash out of them.

She drew herself up to full height and her small brown eyes shone with self-importance. 'But something bigger came up. Something that affected my *family*.' She gave them both a look. 'And I, of course, always look out for my family.'

''Course you do,' Lily muttered.

Ruby exhaled and ignored her mother's jibe. 'Aren't you interested in what I have to say?' she asked.

'Look, Ruby, I'm more than happy to sit down and talk about whatever you want to talk about later, if you'll stay. But right now I really need to talk to your brothers. We're a little busy right now with some work issues,' she responded.

'I'm aware.' Ruby stood up and walked over to her mother. 'Your markets have just been taken over and all your illegal goods have been seized.'

Lily's eyebrows shot up in surprise. 'Well, well,' she mused. 'Good news travels fast.'

'It's not common knowledge yet; I just happened to be there. I saw what happened. And I overheard the men behind the move talking about it.' She paused for dramatic effect. 'Two men, one old, one young. The younger one was tall, quite attractive for an arsehole. The older one had a weird twitch and a cane, and—'

'And goes by the name of Harry Snow. Yes, we know,' Lily finished, cutting her off. 'The younger one would likely be his son, Jasper. They conduct most of their business together.'

'Oh.' Ruby was taken aback, but she swiftly recovered. 'Well, Harry Snow did say you'd likely have figured it out. He reckons Ray told you he was sniffing about.'

'Well, he reckoned right.' Lily shrugged off her jacket and looked at her watch. 'So thank you for coming to tell us all that, Ruby.' Her tone was softer now, more genuine. 'But we're OK. Don't worry about it. We'll sort it out soon.' She turned her attention back to Connor. 'Can you call Cillian, find out how far away he is? We need to make a plan and quickly, tackle this head-on.'

Ruby felt her heart sink as she watched the opportunity to get into Lily's good graces melt away. She needed money, and she needed it fast. Her stash had all but run out, and she still owed her dealers more than she could repay. Her body had already begun aching all over again. It was only going to get worse if she didn't get another hit soon.

'Well, how are you going to do that?' she asked, moving into Lily's line of sight once more.

'That's our concern, Ruby. Don't worry yourself about it.'

'Well, do you know how you're going to find where he's hidden your goods yet?' she pressed.

'No. Not yet,' Lily admitted. 'Why?'

'Because I overheard him talking about it. He said the goods were on their way to *the shed*, whatever that means.'

Her mother's gaze travelled critically up and down her body, and Ruby pulled her sleeves down over her track marks quickly.

'Thank you, Ruby, that's actually very useful.' She touched her arm. 'Listen, there's some leftover lasagne in the fridge – why don't you warm yourself some up, put some salad with it?' she offered.

Ruby almost laughed but caught herself in time. It wasn't food her body needed. 'Nah, I'm good. I'm going to need to get back out there, see if I can find myself some cash. Half the day has already got away from me, after coming here to warn you guys.' She left the hint lingering in the air and saw her mother register it.

Lily sighed, and disappointment crossed her expression. 'So you *are* only here for money then,' she said.

Ruby's eyebrows shot upwards. 'Wow. I come here to help you and that's what you still think?' she asked indignantly.

'How much do you want?' Lily asked.

Ruby fought the urge to fight her mother further. What was the point in pretending? She did need money, and it seemed like her mother was in such a distracted place she was happy to hand some over without giving her too much of a hard time. 'How much have you got on you?' she asked.

Lily sighed and reached into her purse, counting out what cash she had there.

Connor sighed and shook his head in disagreement. She ignored him. His opinion of the situation didn't matter. Her mother was the one who made the decisions in this house.

Lily handed over the notes and Ruby quickly took them. 'You know, you could always try holding down an actual job, Ruby,' Lily said. 'Then you'd have your own money.'

'Well, maybe you should *give me* an actual job, pay me the same way you do the boys,' she replied sharply. 'Treat all your children the same for once.'

'The boys earn the money they make, ten times over,' Lily replied, placing her hands on her hips. 'There are no free rides here, Ruby, whatever you may think. And I don't have the time or space in this firm for someone who expects a regular payment for sod all in return. That ain't how it works.'

'Oh really?' Ruby sneered. 'And you expect me to believe that, when you've got my kid cousin on the payroll? Earning her keep, is she? Doing what, her fucking schoolwork?'

'Ruby, you have no idea what goes on in this company. But I can assure you, Scarlet earns her keep too. She may be young, but she's a damn hard worker and has a good head on her shoulders. Maybe if you stepped away from the poison you pump into yourself for a while and tried working out what actually matters in life, you could show those sort of qualities too.'

'Huh!' Ruby snorted. 'If I stopped having any sort of happiness in my life, I could decide working myself to the bone is what it's all about, yeah? No thanks.' She glared at her mother, but Lily's expression remained unchanged. She glanced down at the money in her hand. It wasn't much, a hundred quid perhaps. It wouldn't last very long. 'So you're not going to give me anything else then, no?'

'To shoot straight into your arm?' Lily asked. 'Do you really think I didn't see those?' She pointed at Ruby's covered arms. 'No, Ruby. There's enough there for you to do a decent food shop. Though even if your fridge is empty, I doubt that's where you'll bother spending it.' Her face finally fell into an expression of sadness, and her shoulders slumped. 'Ruby, why do you do this to yourself?' she asked. 'You're not stupid – you know that stuff doesn't lead anywhere good.'

'Well, that's where you're wrong,' Ruby replied, stepping back, away from her mother. 'Because that shit is the only thing that brings any fucking happiness to my life. Without that I ain't got anything.'

'You have us,' Lily pressed. 'We're your family. And we might not always see eye to eye but we love you very much.'

'Not enough to help me with any decent amount of money though, eh, Mum?' Ruby snapped, tired of the turn the conversation had taken. Her mother couldn't care less about her. All she really cared about were her precious boys and her precious business.

'I won't give you unlimited amounts of money to kill yourself with, no,' Lily replied, her tone resolute. 'But I will pay for the best rehab clinic in the country. If you'd just give it a try and get clean, we can look at setting you up somewhere for a fresh start…' she pleaded.

'Oh, would you give it a rest!' Ruby shouted, cutting her off. They'd had this conversation time and again, and she'd already made her feelings on the subject more than clear. 'I ain't going to fucking rehab.'

Lily held her hands up in surrender. 'I'm not trying to fight with you, Ruby. I'm just giving you the option. I can't force you to take it, but it's there, and as your mother I would really like to see you at least try.'

Ruby's thin lips curled up into a spiteful smile. 'It drives you crazy, don't it?' she asked. 'That there's no way you can legally make me go there. That it's something the great Lily Drew can't control or force.' She spat out a hateful laugh. 'You can control your boys and the firm and little Scarlet, but you'll never be able to control me, will you?' She picked up her bag from where she'd dumped it on a chair and slung it over her shoulder. 'Well, you can't do fuck all about my life choices. I like doing what I do and I'm going to do it as long as I damn well please. And one way or another, *you* are going to pay for it, Mum. Because you owe me.'

She barged her shoulder into her mother's as she marched past her and out of the house, then slammed the door behind her.

'Ruby!' Cillian lifted a hand and smiled in greeting as they crossed paths on the drive.

'Oh, go fuck yourself,' Ruby spat, furious that the conversation had yet again ended up all about how bad her life choices were.

'Charming,' she heard him mutter as she stalked off.

Part of her felt bad for being so rude to her brother for no reason. It wasn't like he'd done anything or that she disliked him – she loved her brothers to bits. But her worries were swiftly turning into a full-on panic. She needed to get her hands on some more money and soon. Because whilst what Lily had given her would get her another few hits, she owed a lot of people – a lot of bad people – for the drugs she lived on. And if she didn't pay up soon, things were going to get very bad very quickly.

CHAPTER FORTY-NINE

Scarlet got out of her car and walked up the road towards her aunt's house, annoyed that there were no nearer spaces. She yawned and clutched the two coffees she'd grabbed on the way over a little tighter. It had been a long, late night and although she'd slept all morning, she really could've used another few hours in bed. But it seemed that there really was no rest for the wicked after all. Bedlam was occurring, and her aunt wanted them all at the house to sort it out.

Hearing Cillian's voice ahead, she looked up in time to see her cousin Ruby storm past him rudely. He shook his head and carried on into the house, and Ruby continued marching angrily down the road towards her. She suppressed the groan of annoyance that threatened. Ruby was the last person she wanted to see today. As her cousin neared and clocked her, she forced a tight smile.

'Hi, Rubes,' she called out, trying to sound friendly.

'Oh, of course you're here,' Ruby spat back. 'Of course you are. Princess fucking Scarlet here to shine, as usual.'

Scarlet frowned in annoyance. 'Excuse me?' she demanded as Ruby finally reached her.

'No, actually. I won't.' Passing her without stopping, Ruby reached across and tipped one of the coffees Scarlet was holding up from the bottom, hard, causing it to spill out all over the front of her beige outfit.

'Oh, you fucking *bitch*!' Scarlet exclaimed as the burning hot liquid scalded her skin. She rounded on her cousin with a low growl but then held herself back as Ruby hurried off.

She closed her eyes and mentally counted to ten as she slowly exhaled her fury. In pain and enraged by Ruby's actions, she wanted nothing more than to run down the road after her and pour the second coffee over her spiteful little head, and if it had been anyone else she would have, without pause. But knowing how the situation would escalate with Ruby, and not wanting to add any more to her aunt's troubles, Scarlet decided it was wiser all round to move on without retaliation.

She swore again under her breath and stalked up the path towards her aunt's front door, starkly aware of how drenched she now was with each uncomfortable step. She'd figure out a way to get even with that cousin of hers another time. In a way that the red-headed little viper wouldn't see coming.

She walked into the large hallway to find her aunt and twin cousins already in a heated conversation.

'But why would you even give her that?' Cillian asked Lily, his tone annoyed.

'Give who what?' Scarlet asked, closing the door behind her.

'Mum gave Ruby some money,' Connor explained, glancing down at her dress with a frown.

'Because she needed it,' Lily replied, putting her hands on her hips.

'For *drugs*,' Cillian replied exasperatedly. 'For fuck's sake, that's all she ever spends it on. You *know* this.'

'I do know that, yes,' Lily snapped, her cheeks colouring as her temper came to the fore. 'But what am I supposed to do when she's got nothing? She's skin and bones; she's literally starving. If she has some money in her pocket, at least she might actually spare some to buy herself something to eat.'

'And the rest on drugs,' Cillian shot back. He turned in a circle and ran his hands down his face. 'You're not thinking straight. It's the worst thing you can do, giving an addict money. If they have no money, they can't get drugs – it's that simple.'

'If she's got no money, she'll get them another way,' Lily yelled back, tears beginning to form in her eyes. She turned away for a moment, blinking them out, and Cillian fell silent. 'For Christ's sake.' She took a couple of deep breaths before turning back around. 'You're right, I'm not thinking straight. I'm thinking like a mother. I *know* she's an addict, I *know* what she's out there doing right now. It kills me every fucking day.' She glared at both the twins. 'I would give me left lung to get the girl off that shit and clean and healthy again. Lord knows, I've tried *everything*. But she will not be helped. So all I can do is try and manage the balance as best I can. I don't give her too much, not enough to allow her to enjoy herself straight into the grave, but enough to keep her going, to keep her breathing. And I wish to God that my money didn't go on enabling her damn addiction, but I don't know what else to do. She's my daughter. What am I supposed to do?' She held her arms out to the sides and then dropped them with a defeated slump. 'I can't cut her off completely, and I can't help her, so what else can I do, Cillian? What would you do?'

Cillian looked down and nodded. 'I know, Mum.'

'No, you don't,' Lily replied with a shake of her head. 'And I pray to God that you never will. I pray that one day when He blesses you with children that He never allows them to stray down the path our Ruby has. Because I don't want you to know even one of the sleepless nights of worry and pain I've suffered these last few years.'

Connor frowned. 'There has to be a way of forcing her to—'

'There's not,' Lily cut him off, rubbing her temple. 'Legally there's nothing you can force on an addict. And she won't come home and let us help her, so we're out of options.'

Lily sighed heavily and turned to Scarlet as if just realising she was there. She looked her up and down with a small frown. 'What happened to you?'

'Oh.' Scarlet looked down at her beige dress and matching jacket, now half covered in a dark brown coffee stain. 'I um, I tripped on the road outside.' She held up the empty coffee cup with a grimace. 'The lid was loose, so...' Seeing how upset the conversation about Ruby had made her aunt, she decided to keep the truth to herself. Catching Cillian's shrewd gaze, she looked away. He'd probably guessed the truth, having seen Ruby walk in her direction, but if he had, he kept quiet.

'Oh. Well, come on upstairs. I've got something you can change into.' Lily pulled herself up to her full height. 'We have a lot to work on. Harry Snow has taken the markets.'

Scarlet gasped. 'Taken them? What?' She felt her insides go cold. If Harry had taken the markets, stolen some of their business from under them, did that mean Jasper was in on it too? She suddenly felt sick. They'd been texting for days – she'd been getting excited about him, had begun to really like him. Had he been playing her all along?

'Yes. And he's also taken our hot goods, no doubt as something to hold over our heads. Which puts us in a predicament.' She stared them all out in turn, her gaze landing lastly on Scarlet. 'He believes that will keep us at bay, that we'll have no choice but to retreat. But he doesn't know us as well as he thinks he does.' Her gaze darkened. 'Because we don't take things lying down. We're not mice, and this is not a game – this is our business, our life.' She walked towards them, her heels tapping loudly on the hard floor. 'So we're going to get our shit back, we're going to reclaim the stalls and we're going to pay that bastard back in ways that will make him wish he had *never* set his sights on anything that belonged to this family.'

CHAPTER FIFTY

'Jesus,' Ray exclaimed, sitting back in his chair. 'I knew he was sniffing around – like I told you – but I didn't know he was planning something like this.'

'Yes, well, he wouldn't exactly go telling you that, would he?' Lily leaned forward and let him light her cigarette. 'He knows you'd come straight to me.'

'When's Bill getting here?' Ray looked at the clock above the bar.

They were sitting in the St Heliers Tavern, Ray's pub. She'd chosen to meet Bill here so she could kill two birds with one stone and find out any information Ray might have whilst he was around to listen.

'Now,' she replied. 'Here he is, bang on time as always.'

The area Ray had cordoned off for his own use was slightly raised with two steps leading up to it, so they could see across the busy pub without having to move. Bill weaved his way through the crowd, and one of Ray's men stepped aside to let him through. Everyone here knew who Bill was – he needed no announcement.

'Lily, Ray.' Bill nodded to them each in greeting and sat down on one of the comfortable chairs between them. 'How you both doing?'

'Surviving,' Ray replied.

'Thank you so much for coming, Bill. I know you've got other things on,' Lily said.

'It's a busy time, but it sounded like it was urgent. What's up?'

Lily took a deep breath and prayed he would take on the job. She didn't know anyone else she could trust to do something like this, let alone who had his sort of skill set. It wasn't as though people like Bill were easy to come by.

'Our markets were taken over this morning, by Harry Snow.' She dived straight in and saw a look of surprise cross his face. 'Somehow he hacked the council's system and replaced all our licences with new fake ones under his men's names. Or I think that's how he did it anyway. I can't think of any other way it could be done.'

'So you want me to hack in and change them back?' Bill asked, nodding. He shifted his weight and leaned forward. 'That can be done, no problem. I have no love for Harry Snow,' he continued in his deep craggy voice. 'He's a fucking leech, feeding off the gains of the real grafters.'

'I'm with you on that one. And yes, but that ain't all I'm after.' She pushed her curls back off her face and took a deep drag on her cigarette, glancing at Ray and then Bill. 'Do either of you know of a place he calls *the shed*?'

'The shed?' Ray frowned and looked off into the distance as he thought about it. 'I feel like I've heard it said, but I can't think when.'

'Well, I need to know, because that's where he's holding my stuff.'

'What stuff?' Bill asked.

'All the hot goods we push through the markets. He took the lot. Didn't touch anything else, just that. Ruby overheard them talking about it. If I push back at them, they're going to blackmail me with it, threaten to hand it over to the filth. So.' She held her hands out and sat back in her chair, her expression serious.

'So you want me to track it down and get it back for you?' Bill asked.

Lily shook her head. 'I can get it back myself; I just need you to find out where he's holding it and, if you can, what sort of security he's got on the place.'

Bill nodded. 'That much I can do.' He sighed, a look of disgust on his face. 'It's a lowdown fucker who plays the game and then threatens others with the police. That ain't on. It just ain't done.'

'No, it ain't,' Ray agreed with a deep frown.

'Well…' Lily leaned back and pursed her red lips. 'Clearly Mr Snow thinks he's above such things as honour among thieves.' She crossed her slim legs and cast her eyes across the room, checking once more that there was no one else within hearing range.

'I could have some of my men tail him,' Ray offered.

'No, he's too smart for that. The goods will already be wherever he planned to keep them by now, and he won't go near them again for fear of being followed. He has no need to – he already has the power over me just by holding it. So that's not how we're going to solve this,' Lily replied.

'I'll find it, Lil,' Bill said. 'Don't worry.' He looked up at her, his eyes hard under his heavy brow. 'Right now he spends his evenings at a new transport hub he's in the process of setting up. He approached Freddie about it,' he explained, 'so I checked it all out. He's busy there after his normal working day ends for two or three hours every night. That son of his too,' he added. He glanced at his watch. 'It's too late tonight; he'll be home already, but tomorrow I'll go to his place while he's out and search there. If there's anything written down related to this shed place, it'll be in his home office. I'd bet my last pound on it.'

'Thank you, Bill,' Lily said with feeling. 'For taking this on. I really appreciate it. I'll compensate you well for it.'

'I know you will, Lil,' he replied, standing up. 'I have to go – there's a lot going down up West at the moment. But I'll be in touch in a couple of days and let you know what I've found.'

Lily nodded and shot him a smile of gratitude, then settled back into her seat as Bill left, feeling more hopeful than she had all day.

Ray studied her for a moment. 'He's a clever cunt, I'll give him that,' he said, reaching for his whisky. 'Harry, that is. But he underestimates you.'

'And that will be his downfall,' Lily replied.

Ray nodded slowly. Lily watched the muscles in his face work as he warred with himself. He wanted to say more, to get involved and take over the situation for her. It was a natural reaction for a man as powerful as Ray when it came to someone he loved. But she'd made it clear many times over the years that she liked to deal with her own issues and if she needed or wanted assistance that she'd ask.

'Well,' he said, changing the subject. 'Now that's set up, there's not much to do right now other than wait for Bill. So what do you say we try to forget your troubles, have a few drinks and relax?' he asked.

Lily tapped her cigarette ash into the ashtray. Usually this was a place she *could* relax, but not tonight. 'I wish that was all there was going on right now,' she said with a sigh. 'But there are other things I can't just forget about at the moment.'

'What things?' Ray asked, topping her wine up from the bottle chilling in a bucket on the table between them.

'Ruby turned up this morning,' she replied with a sigh. 'She's back on the brown.'

'Fuck's sake,' Ray muttered with a shake of his head. 'I'll never understand what the kids see in that shit. Cocaine, sure; weed, not my bag but I get it,' he said. 'Heroin though… That stuff's just nasty.'

'It was that dirtbag ex of hers, the one that stuck around like a bad smell because he thought she had access to the family money. He got her onto it. Showed her the needle-lit path to hell.' Lily picked up her wine and drank deeply from the glass. 'She's been on and off it ever since. If I could just get her to agree to rehab, get her cleaned up properly and set her up again fresh then I'm sure she'd leave it behind. But she's never fully off it, and she won't listen to me.'

'Since when did you ever just roll over and take no for an answer?' Ray asked. 'So what if she don't agree? Get the boys to grab her, take her to one of those places where they'll lock her up and get her clean. Sign her in yourself.'

Lily laughed bitterly. 'If only it were that simple. Gone are the days when you could lock addicts up without their permission. The law changed a long time ago. Now they have to go in voluntarily and can leave at any time.'

'What?' Ray looked shocked. 'What a stupid law.'

'Well, it all goes back to the human rights argument, I guess,' Lily said with a shrug.

Ray shook his head. 'What about you?'

'What about me?' Lily asked, confused.

'Why don't you go old school? Grab her, board up a window in a room somewhere, get some heavy locks on the door, bring food and water and everything she needs and force her to go cold turkey.'

'Believe me, I've considered it,' Lily said heavily. 'But if I were to do that or order that to happen, she would never forgive me.' She took another sip of her wine. 'Ruby holds grudges. I'm already far from her favourite person, but if I physically forced that, she would never talk to me again. And as much as she is the biggest pain my backside has ever known, she's still my daughter. I love her. I couldn't bear for her to turn against me forever.'

'So what are you going to do?' Ray asked.

'I don't know. I really don't,' Lily replied. She stared off into the busy pub, her eyes glazing over unhappily. 'But I need to figure something out soon. Because I've never seen someone aim so clearly towards an early grave. And no mother should ever have to bury their child.'

CHAPTER FIFTY-ONE

Lily woke almost as tired as she'd been when she finally fell into bed the night before. She'd tossed and turned well into the early hours as all the things she needed to figure out kept chasing each other around her head. Ronan's death, where Harry was holding her goods, how she was going to get those back, Ruby's addiction. No one else was going to solve the issues – it all rested with her. She checked her phone to see if Bill had called, but he hadn't. She'd hoped he might have been in touch with some information by now, but it had only been a couple of days. These things could take time, she reminded herself.

She washed and dressed quickly, then went downstairs and brewed herself a pot of coffee. As the familiar, smoky smell of the beans filled the air, she began to file her thoughts into some sort of order, ready to face the day with a proactive attitude. Things may be dismal, but the only way that was going to change was if she dealt with them head-on, like always.

The doorbell rang as she was pouring her second cup, and she frowned, glancing at her watch. It was too early to be the boys; they'd both worked late, and Scarlet was already on her way to the office – she'd texted to say so. Ruby wouldn't bother knocking – and neither would Ray for that matter, she thought, as she mentally dismissed each person in turn. So who could be at her door?

She walked through to the hallway with a frown which swiftly turned into a look of surprised distaste as she caught sight of her uninvited visitor through the side window.

For a moment, she considered just turning around and rudely ignoring the girl, but wary curiosity won out. She opened the door and looked Chastity up and down pointedly. The girl was dressed like whorehouse Barbie with a fluffy pink jacket over a white boob tube that barely covered the essentials and a matching miniskirt.

'Are you lost?' she asked drily.

Chastity immediately widened her smile, but Lily didn't miss the sly, calculating glance at the inside of the hallway.

'Oh far from it,' she replied, far too confidently for Lily's liking. 'Can I come in?'

Without waiting for a response, Chastity marched past Lily and into the hallway. Raising her eyebrows, Lily closed the door and twisted round to face the younger woman. She rested her hands on her hips and waited as Chastity explored the hallway in a slow circle, peering nosily through each open door.

'Nice house,' Chastity said. 'Must be lonely though, all this space to yourself.'

Lily's cold gaze cooled even further. 'Loneliness is for idiots who have no idea how to fill their time and who do not appreciate the benefits of their own company. What do you want, Chastity?'

'I thought we could maybe start over,' Chastity said with what was clearly meant to be a winning smile. 'I mean, I think we started off on the wrong foot, you and me.' She took a step closer to Lily. 'But the thing is, I'm dating Connor now. Have been for a while, and I ain't planning on going anywhere.' A glint of challenge flashed through her eyes, behind the big fake smile. 'So I think it would be best for all of us if we got on, don't you?'

Lily suppressed a smirk. 'You're dating, are you?' she asked. 'Is that what they're calling what he uses you for these days?'

Chastity's cheeks flushed with annoyance. 'He ain't *using* me for anything, thank you very much. He ain't using me any more than I'm using him.'

'Oh, come on now, Chastity,' Lily chided. 'Let's be honest, shall we?' She stalked towards the girl. 'He's using you for the cheap wares you're so eager to display.' She gestured to her skimpy outfit with a curl of the lip. 'And you use him for his money and his status. It's not exactly a new arrangement – there have been many before you, and there will be many after. You're all the same.' She looked her up and down in disdain. 'You're a time-filler to Connor, nothing more.' She saw the flush in Chastity's cheeks grow redder and anger begin to flare behind her big blue eyes. 'I'm sorry if that's news to you, but it's the truth. So do us all a favour and stop wasting my time.' She walked back towards the door and opened it again. 'Go on, out you go.'

Chastity glared at her for a moment, and then slowly the smile reappeared and the red in her cheeks began to fade. 'Perhaps that's all girls have been in the past,' she said, 'but this time things are different. Connor trusts me, you see – even used me as an alibi for the night he stole the weed from the Jamaicans.'

Lily drew a sharp breath in and felt her throat constrict. She swiftly recovered, not allowing her surprise to register on her face. How on earth did Chastity know about that? Surely Connor wouldn't have told her? He wouldn't be that stupid – she knew he wouldn't.

'What on earth are you talking about?' she asked with a frown.

Chastity narrowed her gaze. 'You know exactly what I'm talking about. When Connor asked me to be his alibi that night, I of course just agreed. That's what good girlfriends do, after all.' She smiled sweetly. 'It was only later when the Jamaicans sent men round the estate to ask around for information that I put two and two together.'

Lily's insides turned cold at the mention of the Jamaicans. She'd thought this business had been dealt with, that it was in the past. But here it was, rearing its ugly head again in the worst place possible.

Chastity paused at the open front door. 'Of course I kept to our alibi. I have to protect *my man*, don't I, Lily?' she asked. The fake sweetness of her smile dropped to reveal the ugly smirk underneath. 'But hell hath no fury like a woman scorned. I don't like to be scorned, Lily. But I do like money.' Her true colours began to shine out in an ugly fashion as she dropped the act. 'I like it very much. I've come to enjoy life with your son and all that it brings me, and I don't plan on letting that go any time soon. I wouldn't want to suddenly be without the benefits being with Connor brings. I mean…' She turned to face Lily square on. 'If I suddenly found myself in a less happy situation, I'd probably be rather tempted by the Jamaicans' reward. Ten grand is a lot of money. And all for the simple action of telling the truth.'

Lily resisted the urge to scratch Chastity's face off right there and then in her hallway.

'So,' Chastity continued, looking down on her in contempt. 'If you want to keep your precious son safe, here's how things are going to go. You're going to change your tune and start supporting me, because for some reason my dear Connor holds your opinions in very high regard.'

Lily's hand balled into a fist at her side.

Chastity stepped out of the door and turned back to Lily, looking her up and down in the same way Lily had done to her when she walked in. 'Because I'm going to be a much more permanent fixture around the place now, *mother dearest*. And with this in mind,' she added, 'I believe it's time I started integrating into the family properly.'

She waited to see if Lily would respond, but she was met with a stony silence. 'I'll begin with the weekly family lunch tomorrow,' she continued, getting into her stride with more confidence now that Lily seemed to have no comeback. 'It would be nice of you to extend an invite for me to join you, but if you're not quite up to that we can start with your acceptance when Connor brings me along.'

She grinned nastily. 'I'm here to stay whether you like it or not, and *you're* going to start welcoming me with open arms.' Turning on her heel, she walked slowly back down the path. 'For Connor's sake,' she called over her shoulder with a cold stare. 'And yours.'

CHAPTER FIFTY-TWO

The laptop screen glowed brightly in the darkness of the car as Bill tapped away on the keyboard. He paused and glanced up at the wall surrounding the large, detached house he was parked up outside. With one last flurry of his fingers, he pressed enter and the small red light on the nearest visible CCTV camera dulled to nothing. He clapped the lid of the laptop shut and slid it back into the black rucksack on the passenger seat. Pulling on his leather gloves, he got out of the car, locked it and approached the side gate, tapping in the entrance code he'd pulled from the system and walking through. No one was in, of this he was certain. Harry was keeping all his men close since he'd taken the markets and clearly had enough faith in his home protection system not to worry about leaving anyone here to keep watch. People were far too reliant on technology in Bill's opinion. He'd made a very good career out of undermining it.

He crossed the garden and jimmied the lock on the kitchen door within seconds, entering without making any sound. Once inside, he pulled a small handheld torch from his pocket and switched it on, shining the light around. The kitchen was solid oak, sturdy and large, though messy and cluttered.

Bill moved on into the hallway. After peeping in through a couple of doors, he found the office and got to work searching methodically through the desk. Boxes of various sweets littered the top of the desk and took up most of the space in the drawers.

Harry clearly had a sweet tooth. Or perhaps Jasper, Bill considered. They both lived here – the office was likely used by both of them.

He moved the mouse and the monitor came to life. After a quick search, he found the password written on a Post-it note underneath the second drawer. He trawled through the few files on the desktop, but there was nothing on there of interest. His legal books, a few family photos and plans for a small extension off the back of the house, but no details on his various holdings or anything that could be linked to his more nefarious businesses. Logging back off, Bill leaned back in the chair and rubbed his chin as he looked around. He tapped his finger on the desk, trying to think where he would hide information in a room like this.

A set of drawers sat to the side of the room, and he crossed over to it, checking through the contents. As he reached the bottom drawer, he pulled it out and paused, tightening his gaze. To the untrained eye, the bottom drawer was just another drawer, but Bill was no stranger to hidden compartments. The bottom was shallower on the inside than it should have been. He pulled out the folded shirt that sat in there alone, then felt around the edges until he found what he was looking for and lifted the false bottom up.

'Bingo,' he muttered, shining the light on the diary underneath. He pulled it out and took it back over to the table, settling in to read through it.

The diary contained a few codes linked to the Snow's illegal sites and kept track of their plans and meetings. It was colour-coded – red pen used for Jasper's entries and blue for Harry's. Standard stuff, as far as a second diary went. He flipped through the pages, searching for anything that could relate to the shed and where it might be located. He noted one or two potentially useful bits of information and filed them away for later, but still the details he was looking for eluded him.

He continued on through the weeks and months, searching carefully through every single entry until his gaze came to a stop on one in particular. He frowned and read it through again, more slowly. He checked the date and read it through a third time, his frown deepening with every second. Pulling back from the diary, his hands hovered in the air for a moment as he processed what he'd just found.

Reaching into his pocket, he pulled out his phone and took a photo of the entry, then closed the diary and stashed it back where he'd found it, careful to leave the drawer as it had been. He hadn't found anything on the shed, but what he had found was an awful lot more concerning. His lips formed a hard line as he left the house. He needed to show Lily. Because right now she was completely in the dark about how deep the game Harry was playing ran. And that it was more dangerous than any of them had imagined.

CHAPTER FIFTY-THREE

Lily typed in the code to the building with her free hand, holding the phone to her ear with the other. 'Yes, I've told you, I need it done tonight. Now, in fact… No, your brother can't go. I don't give a shit how late it is, it needs doing, so just get on with it,' she said.

It was nearly one in the morning and she'd had Connor running errands all night. He was tired, she could tell, but she needed him occupied for just a little while longer.

'Look,' she said, placatingly, 'it's Sunday tomorrow – you can have a day off, get some rest, have a few drinks and then come in late on Monday. OK? OK, thank you. Text me when you're done.' She ended the call and entered the lift, pressing the floor she needed and checking through her emails whilst she was transported up.

It had been a long day all round, especially for a Saturday. She and Scarlet had been tied up with problems at the factory half of the day, and then there'd still been a lot to do for the rest of the businesses. That was the trouble with running an empire such as theirs – it took sacrifice. And more often than not, that sacrifice was their time and sanity. She had to hand it to Scarlet though – not once during the late nights, early mornings and weekends had the girl complained. She was fully committed to making the business work. It was a good sign. She sighed tiredly and walked out of the lift, pulling the key and a small sharp knife out of her handbag.

She paused outside the door and put her ear to it, listening for any sounds of life within, before silently unlocking it and entering the flat. The place was in darkness, as she'd hoped it would be at this hour. She moved like a panther through the pitch-black hallway to where she knew the door to the bedroom was. It was slightly ajar, so she pushed it gently, allowing the room to come into view. As her eyes adjusted to the darkness, and with the aid of the moonlight coming through the open curtains, she made out the form of the sleeping figure in the bed.

With narrowed eyes and cold hatred in her expression, she crossed the room. For a moment she looked down at the sleeping girl. Without so much make-up and the ridiculous Playboy bunny outfits Chastity looked younger than she'd initially thought. And without the ugly, calculating personality shining through her fake expressions, her face almost looked soft and sweet.

Silly girl, she thought. *Bad choices lead to bad consequences.*

Reaching forward, she grabbed a handful of long blonde hair and twisted it in her fist, yanking the girl up by it with all her strength. As Chastity flew up into the air and screamed, Lily wrapped her free arm around her chest and pushed the sharp blade up against her exposed neck. She put her mouth to the screaming girl's ear.

'Not another sound,' she said in a quiet, deadly voice. 'Or I'll slice right through to shut you up myself.'

Chastity's screams immediately dulled to panicked sobs as she tried to contain her fear, and she froze, still half kneeling on the bed as Lily held her tight.

'That's better,' Lily said, making sure the hold she had on the girl's hair was as painful as possible without inciting further screams. 'Now, we're going to have a little chat. And by chat I mean I'm going to talk and you're going to listen. I thought I'd turn up unannounced for this chat, a bit like you did this morning, when you came to *my* house and threatened my son.

Do you remember that?' She waited and then yanked hard on her hair again when the girl didn't answer.

Chastity squealed in fright. 'Y-Yes, yes,' she cried.

'I don't like people threatening my sons. It makes me feel rather murderous actually. And I also don't much like people turning up at my home unannounced,' Lily continued, her calm tone a stark contrast to the aggressive hold she kept on the girl. 'It irritates me, you know? I like to plan for people's visits. And I like the option to decline anyone I don't want to waste my time entertaining. The way I would have declined you.' She pressed the knife a little harder and Chastity let out another sob. 'Because, you see, I don't like you, Chastity. I never have, even before your stupid decision to go up against me today. But of course you know that.' Her eyes hardened in the dark room. 'And it ain't because of the way you look or that I don't want to accept Connor having someone else in his life. I would,' she continued, 'if he found someone decent who wanted to be with him for the right reasons. But you don't. You're a gold-digging nobody with nothing to offer him but strife and potentially death, it now seems. And I did not spend twenty-seven hours labouring to bring my son into this world or work myself to death all these years to bring him up to be the man he is today for some greedy little gutter rat like you to bleed him dry or put him six feet under.' She yanked Chastity's head back and twisted it round slightly so that she could look her in the eye. 'Not a fucking chance,' she spat.

'L-Lily, please, you're hurting me…' Chastity sobbed. Lily pressed the knife harder once more and Chastity stopped, whimpering in pain.

'The thing is though…' she continued, pushing Chastity's head back to face forward again. 'I would have left him to it before today. As a mother, all you want to do is protect your children from the things that are bad for them. But you also have to let them make their own mistakes. It's a thin line. So I was content enough to sit back and let him make this mistake. He'd have got bored soon enough and cut you loose. But then' – her voice lowered to a deadly hiss – 'you upped your game, didn't you, Chastity? You thought you'd come play with the big girls. Blackmail him into staying with you, blackmail *me* into accepting you. And that was your big mistake. Because this ain't a game, the life we lead. We ain't plastic gangsters – we are fucking dangerous people. You see the nice suits and flash cars, the social status, but you ain't got a clue the dirty work that goes on to get all that. It seems exciting to you, don't it? A little bit dangerous, but you don't really understand why…' Her tone was pure mockery. 'Well, like I said, this ain't a game. And I don't take my boys' safety being threatened lightly.'

'I – I didn't mean it. I – I wouldn't…' Chastity stuttered, tears of real fear rolling down her cheeks.

'Damn right you wouldn't,' Lily hissed in her ear. 'Because I warn you now, if the Jamaicans or anyone else for that matter ever catch wind that Connor wasn't with you that night, I'll be back again one night with this knife at your neck. And it won't be for a nice little chat like this. There won't be *any* chat at all. All there will be is the sound of air gargling through blood as you fight for breath with a cut throat. Have you ever heard someone trying to breathe when their throat's been cut, Chastity?' she asked.

'Wh-What?' Chastity asked in horror.

'I have,' Lily continued. 'They don't die straight away, you see. They fight for breath as their lungs fill up, and they slowly drown in their own blood. It's a sight to behold,' she whispered darkly. 'And *that* is the terrible, painful way *you* will die, if you ever threaten the safety of one of my family ever again. Do you understand me?'

'Y-Yes,' Chastity uttered, terror clear in her tone.

Lily smiled coldly into the darkness. The girl had waded into waters far too deep to swim in. She wasn't hard, she wasn't meant for their world. She was just a stupid, shallow girl out to get what she could. The fear and regret she was now feeling was so strong Lily could almost taste it in the air. She wouldn't be a problem again, not after this.

Pulling the knife away from her throat, Lily yanked her backwards off the bed by her hair. She fell to the floor with a thump and a cry, and raised her hands to her head. In one swift movement, Lily ripped the knife through a section of Chastity's precious long blonde hair and then held the severed locks up in front of her face. The look of horror on the girl's face intensified as she realised what Lily had done.

Lily leaned forward with a hard glare and pointed the knife in her face, and Chastity quickly crawled back away from the blade until her back was against the wall and she could go no further.

'*That* is for coming to my house and making threats this morning. A reminder that next time it will be your throat. No one threatens my son's life and gets away with it. Now, you've got two choices. You can either get dressed and get out of this flat,' she said calmly. 'Cut your hair into a nice, neat bob to even it out, and move on with your life after telling Connor you can't see him anymore. Or,' she said, tilting her head to one side, 'you can stay with him and try your luck with patching things up. I'll tell him what you did today, of course – the fact you were going to hand him in to the Jamaicans to be slaughtered if you didn't get your way, and then we can wait and see what he has in store for you himself. It's not the choice I'd take,' she added. 'Because I'll tell you something' – she leaned in with a conspiratorial whisper – 'if you think my rage is bad, you've not seen a thing. I wouldn't like to tell you the things my son has done to people who've dared cross him before. Let alone what he's done to people who've tried to cross me too.' A cold smile raised the corners of her mouth and she lifted her head, looking down at the girl in contempt. 'I think even you realise how badly he would take the news of someone trying to blackmail his mother. But it's up to you.' She leaned back. 'Those are your choices. I suggest you have a long, hard think on it.'

Shaking, tears still wet on her cheeks and her eyes wide with fear and resentment, Chastity slowly stood up. She righted her skimpy nighty, where it had fallen off one shoulder in the chaos, and backed away from Lily, keeping one fearful eye on her and the knife.

'Take your time with your decision,' Lily continued, when Chastity didn't immediately speak. 'The choice is yours, and to be honest I don't much care which option you take, so long as your mouth stays shut about the rest. Oh, and by the way,' she said, pausing to look back as she made to leave. 'You were never going to be welcome at the family lunch you tried to invite yourself to tomorrow.'

She looked her up and down one last time before walking back out of the flat. 'Because like I told you before,' she called over her shoulder, 'Sundays are for family – fucking – only.'

CHAPTER FIFTY-FOUR

Cath pulled the large pork joint out of the oven and smelled it with a tentative feeling of pride. It was coming along nicely. It had taken her too long to see what she was doing to Scarlet, and although she still wasn't quite out of the dark place Ronan's death had plunged her into, she was definitely in a better place than she had been. It had been hard to stop heading straight for the bottle in the mornings. What had so swiftly become a habit was surprisingly hard to kick.

Every morning she woke up and in the brief half second that her consciousness lingered between the land of dreams and reality, she would turn towards Ronan's side of the bed, expecting him to be there. But of course he wasn't, and the crash into the dark reality they all now resided in hurt just as badly now as it had a month ago. That pain would swell into a gaping hollowness, and the only way she knew how to ease it was with wine. But although every instinct screamed at her to hide in the alcoholic hug she'd grown accustomed to, she fought against it with what little strength she had. For Scarlet's sake.

She popped the pork back in the oven then turned back to the vegetables all set out on the counter waiting to be chopped. This was the first Sunday she was hosting the family meal since Ronan's death. She'd had several cries about it already, knowing his absence was going to be more prominent than ever. Usually at this point he'd be helping her get everything ready and opening up a bottle of wine for them to share over the preparation. But not today. Today she had to hold things down on her own. Well, not totally alone, she mentally corrected as Scarlet walked in. She still had Scarlet.

'Did you find the napkins?' she asked.

'Yep, they were in the understairs cupboard,' Scarlet replied, brandishing the pack.

'Ah, of course they were,' Cath replied. 'I remember putting them there now.'

Ronan had been telling her a joke at the time, so she'd been distracted. He had always been so good at making her laugh. It was one of the things she loved most about him. She took a deep breath as the pain in her chest intensified and tried to focus on her preparations.

'I, um...' She swallowed. 'I didn't have what I needed to make dessert from scratch this time, so I defrosted a cheesecake,' she said. 'I took it out the packet and put in on a serving dish.' She glanced at Scarlet with a small smile. 'Don't tell your aunt it ain't fresh.'

Scarlet laughed. 'I won't. It will be our little secret.'

Cath's smile widened. She liked that. Their little secret. She'd felt so distant from Scarlet of late, ever since she'd started working with Lily. But now she was trying to get better and be there in the ways a mother should, she and Scarlet seemed to be getting closer again.

The sound of a car pulling up on the drive caught their attention, and Scarlet's face rose and fell in a shrug-like expression. 'Huh,' she said. 'Guess they must be coming early today.'

Lily walked in, followed by the twins, who each went and gave their aunt a kiss on the cheek. Cillian handed Cath a bunch of pink roses. 'Thought you might like these,' he said awkwardly.

'Oh,' Cath exclaimed with a smile, her cheeks flushing pink at the thoughtful gesture. 'They're lovely, Cillian. Thank you.' She took the pretty bouquet over to the sink to sit in water until she had time to properly trim and arrange it. Neither of the twins had brought her flowers before. She knew they were making an effort to cheer her up. It was sweet. They were lovely young men, underneath their hard exterior.

Lily went straight to the kitchen cupboard she knew housed tea towels and the like and pulled on a spare apron. 'I thought you might need a hand,' she said, joining Cath at the breakfast bar.

'I'm OK,' Cath replied. 'Really. Why don't you grab yourself a glass of wine and relax? You've been hosting every week for, well… for a while,' she said, looking down.

'Nah, I'm OK,' Lily said with a dismissive wave of the hand. 'I don't really feel like drinking today, to be honest. I need a detox. And as for these vegetables, you know what they say – many hands make light work.' She picked up the bag of carrots and a knife and began chopping them into rough chunks.

Cath glanced sideways as they began chopping together in companionable silence and felt a wave of fondness towards her sister-in-law of so many years. They may have their differences – and lord knows they did – but the one thing that could always be said of Lily was that she was there for her family. *All* of her family. Even her. Lily had never turned down a glass of wine. The woman drank like a fish. But Scarlet would have been updating her on everything that was going on at home, so her sister-in-law had clearly chosen not to drink in front of her for the time being. And although she didn't actually need the help, having her here and having the hustle and bustle of the kids together temporarily filled a small part of the aching gap in her heart.

She pursed her lips, all the things she wanted to say to Lily running through her mind. The gratitude she felt towards her right now, the sadness she felt at the way they couldn't work out the issues between them, the grief she knew they both shared. There was so very much she wanted to say and share. She cleared her throat.

'I was thinking I'd glaze the carrots in honey today, and throw the parsnips in with them too,' she said instead.

'Lovely,' Lily replied. 'I am partial to a honey glaze on a parsnip.'

The two women exchanged a look and then continued chopping. Yes, there was so much Cath wanted to say. Probably so much that Lily wanted to say too. But neither of them would.

Connor wandered back into the room, frowning at the screen of his phone. 'Hey, Aunt Cath, can I grab a beer from the fridge?'

''Course you can – you know where it is,' she replied. 'You alright?' He looked confused at whatever he was staring at.

'Yeah,' he said slowly. 'It's just this bird I'm seeing…'

'Yes?' Lily asked. Cath noticed the sharpness in her tone and glanced at her. Connor didn't seem to pick up on it though, so she cast her gaze back down and waited to find out what was happening.

He shrugged and locked his phone. 'Nothing. Just appears she's had enough of me. She's ended things.'

'Oh right,' Cath said, watching Lily's face slyly out of the corner of her eye. It was subtle, but she thought she could detect a hint of triumph in her expression. 'Fond of her, were you?'

'Not particularly,' Connor replied. 'Just a bit surprised, that's all. I never get dumped.' He sounded so put out by the concept that Cath couldn't help but laugh.

'Well, never mind. At least you didn't really like her.'

'Yeah, saved me a job, I guess,' he said. 'She was getting a bit too attached for my liking. Or so I thought,' he added.

'What a shame,' Lily said sarcastically. 'Oh well, maybe you'll stop being late for work for a while.'

'Till the next one at least,' Cillian piped up, coming into the room behind his brother.

Connor handed him a beer and they both wandered back into the lounge to sit with Scarlet. Cath turned her stare towards Lily, but Lily kept her gaze trained steadfastly on the carrots.

'You had something to do with that,' Cath murmured quietly with an amused smile. 'I know you did.'

'I don't know what you're talking about, Cathleen,' Lily replied innocently.

Cath chuckled. 'No, 'course you don't.'

There was a loud knock on the front door and they both glanced at each other. Lily frowned. 'You expecting someone?' she asked.

'No, 'course not,' Cath replied, wiping her hands on her apron. 'It's Sunday.' Sundays were for family. They all knew that. And all the family was here bar Ruby, who they weren't expecting to join them.

She walked around the breakfast bar, out into the hallway and opened the door, peering round it with a frown. Her frown turned to a look of surprise and she opened the door wide.

'Bill!' She gave him a wide smile. 'Christ, it's been years since I last saw you – come on in. What are you doing here?' The frown reappeared as she tried to work out what his visit could mean.

'Sorry to disturb you on a Sunday, Cath,' he said politely in his deep rumbling voice. 'I just really need to speak to Lily. It couldn't wait.'

'Bill.' Lily had joined them as soon as she'd realised who it was. 'Everything alright?'

'No, not really,' he replied. His gaze flickered between the two women, landing back on Lily. 'It's about that job. I found some things I wasn't expecting to find. Some things you really ought to know.' His gaze flicked over to Cath again and she stepped back, looking away.

'Sorry, I'll leave you to talk,' she said. 'If you want to use Ronan's office…' She trailed off with a sad smile but gestured towards it.

'Actually.' Bill held his hand out to stop her walking away. 'I think it's something you should know too.'

'Really?' Cath felt a flutter of unease in her stomach and looked at Lily. She didn't get involved with the business. She never had and she had no wish to start doing so now.

'Bill?' Lily questioned with a look of warning. 'I'm not sure that—'

'It's about Ronan,' he said, cutting her off. 'Not about the other, Lil. This…' He shook his head and his jaw formed a hard line before looking at them both in turn. 'I know who killed Ronan.'

CHAPTER FIFTY-FIVE

Lily stared at the picture on Bill's phone and her mind began working overtime. 'It can't be,' she said slowly. 'He was with Ray that day – it was the first thing I checked out.'

'They colour-coded their diary. Blue for Harry's meetings, red for Jasper's,' Bill replied.

She stared down at the picture, the red writing glaring up at her defiantly.

Meeting with R Drew. Location tbc. No trail.

Everything started slowly clicking into place, and she kicked herself for not thinking of this possibility sooner. Harry hadn't killed Ronan. He'd even made sure he had a watertight alibi with someone Lily trusted completely to throw her off the scent. And whilst he'd been busy playing the game with Ray, staying in full view miles away from the crime, Jasper had met with Ronan and killed him.

But why? And why all the secrecy? Why had Ronan not told her about the meeting? Why had there even been a meeting in the first place? Lily couldn't imagine what business Ronan could have possibly had with the younger man. The questions began to swim around her mind, and she had no idea which one to try and address first. She shook her head, trying to make sense of it all.

Cath spoke first, her tone harder than Lily had ever heard it before. 'This is for definite?' she asked. 'This person killed my husband?'

Bill nodded. 'It definitely looks that way. This diary was hidden, the meeting was in there for the day he was killed.'

Cath nodded slowly, hurt and anger in her eyes. 'Then he needs to pay,' she said.

Lily looked over to her and Cath's jaw clenched in a hard line.

'I want him to pay, Lily. You've always said an eye for an eye – well, here you go. Here's your eye. And this time I'm fully behind you.' Her bottom lip wobbled. 'He took everything from me. From all of us,' she said vehemently, her voice cracking with emotion. 'He took Ronan's life. He was a husband, a father, a brother. He was a friend.' Tears began to fall unchecked down her face. 'He had so many years ahead of him. So this... whoever he is' – she gestured towards the phone – 'he needs to fucking pay.'

'What?' Scarlet's tone was filled with confusion as she walked into the hallway with her cousins. 'What's going on?'

Lily looked at them all in turn, her expression grave. 'We've found out who killed Ronan,' she said heavily. 'It was Jasper.'

'No,' Scarlet breathed, her expression filling with horror. 'No, oh God...' She sat down on the bottom stair heavily, bending over and holding her hands to her face.

Lily's heart went out to her niece, knowing how sick to her stomach she must feel after exchanging all those messages with him. She'd liked the man, had even been excited that he'd asked her out, and she'd been hurt and embarrassed when she'd discovered the Snows had taken the markets from them. To find out he was the one who'd killed her father would be the heaviest blow of all.

Cath stepped forward, her face contorting as she tried to contain all the emotions she was feeling. Lily put her hand on her arm to still her and nodded.

'He will pay for this, Cath. I promise you here and now that I will *make* him pay. That snake will be dead before this week is through.'

CHAPTER FIFTY-SIX

Scarlet stared out of the window in a daze, watching the rundown buildings and cars pass by. She still couldn't get her head around it all. How could he have stood there that night, laughing and joking with her, *flirting* with her, all the while knowing he'd killed her father? How could he have even looked her in the eye? She rubbed her head in agitation. They pulled up on a side road near the high street and she undid her seat belt, reaching into the glove compartment for the two packages full of money. She stuffed one of them into her handbag and passed the other to Cillian. He looked at her questioningly.

'It'll be quicker if you do one and I do the other,' she said. 'Instead of doing both together.'

He pulled a face of agreement. 'You're sure?' he asked.

'Yeah,' she said with a dismissive frown. 'It's fine; it's just a drop. Besides…' She shut her door and looked at him over the top of the car. 'You can't babysit me forever. I need to start doing things like this on my own. I'm a Drew, for God's sake, not some melt that was bought up wrapped in cotton wool and fed on fairy dust.'

Cillian raised his eyebrows with a surprised but approving smile. 'There you are,' he said. 'Finally. Good. I told Connor he was wrong.'

'What?' she asked, frowning.

'Nothing.' He straightened his suit jacket and checked his sleek dark hair in the car window. 'Crack on – I'll meet you back here when you're done.'

Scarlet turned and pushed her shoulders back, a determined glint in her big blue-grey eyes. Her red lips formed a hard line and she set off towards the Indian takeaway. Her heels clipped out a rhythm on the pavement, and her long black hair swung out behind her as she went. A passing young man gave her an appreciative smile and she rewarded him with an icy glare. She was trying to carry on as normal, though inside she felt anything but. She felt angry and agitated, and she couldn't shake it off.

The question of why Jasper had done it swam around in her mind, unanswered. It made no sense. And it likely wouldn't until he actually answered the question himself. She went over the moment she'd met him again in her mind for the hundredth time. In his early twenties, he was suave and attractive, he'd been smartly dressed and held interesting conversation. It was the first time she'd been genuinely taken with someone. She'd never been interested in the foolish boys at school or in the bland oafs Natalie was always pushing in her face. But Jasper had been different. He'd had no need to try and gain favour with her family; he was already part of their world. It had been a refreshing change. He'd been charming, he'd made her laugh. She'd been looking forward to seeing him again, no idea she was being charmed by her father's murderer.

She drew a deep breath in and exhaled heavily, trying to dispel some of the fury bubbling underneath the surface. As expected, it did nothing to help.

Reaching the takeaway, she pushed the door open and walked in, approaching the young man who was playing with his phone behind the counter. The place was empty. It wasn't particularly popular with the locals, as the food was atrocious. But of course this was exactly the reason they used it. They could push more money through a failing takeaway than a successful one.

The man glanced up and then put his phone down when he saw who it was. He looked her up and down, his expression uninterested. 'Alright?' he said in a lazy drawl. 'Where's your cousin?' He stared at her rudely, not moving from his seat.

Scarlet narrowed her eyes, her icy expression growing even colder. 'Elsewhere,' she said in a clipped tone. She lifted the counter and pushed past him, walking into the back where they usually conducted their business. He followed her through with a frown.

Looking around the filthy, unkempt kitchen with ill-concealed disgust, she addressed the man who stood smoking by the back door. 'Take a break.'

He looked at her and then at the man who had followed her in. 'Vas?'

Vas nodded and waved him out, and the smoker disappeared.

Reaching into her bag, Scarlet pulled out the packet of cash and threw it onto the nearest clear side. 'There's the usual ten in there and an extra five. You need to filter it through with the rest,' she ordered.

'Whoa, hang on a minute, little girl,' he started with a tone of annoyance. 'My agreement is for ten. I ain't sticking my neck out for another five, especially for you.' He looked her up and down. 'If this is for real, send the big boys over and then we'll talk.' He began to turn away, but Scarlet moved into his path, blocking his retreat.

Her gaze hardened and bored into his. 'Vas Khan,' she said, looking him up and down in return. 'Failed restauranteur, small-time drug dealer and big-time nobody. The only reason this place is still open and you still have enough money to live on is because of the money *we* feed through here.' She stepped closer, drawing herself up to full height. With her heels she was slightly taller than the man and used this to her advantage now. 'Remind me, who was it that offered you this little arrangement and agreed those terms?'

'Cheeky bitch,' he muttered, though with much less confidence now she was glowering down at him. 'Ronan,' he said. 'He was who set this all up with me. And I ain't a—'

'Ronan Drew,' Scarlet said, cutting him off. 'You ever try to cross him?' she asked, her tone menacing.

'Cross Ronan?' Vas pulled a face. 'Fuck no. You mad? I ain't on a death wish.'

'Right.' She leaned over him, forcing him to pull back. 'Well, that was my dad. And I take my position in the firm just as seriously. And whether you like it or not, you work for me now. My cousins, yes,' she added. 'But also me. And I'll tell you something now. You *ever* call me *little girl* or treat me with disrespect again,' she warned in a low, dangerous tone, 'and I'll show you exactly why it's a mistake to cross me too.'

She stared him down for a few moments, to make sure he'd received the message loud and clear. By his expression, he clearly didn't enjoy being spoken to the way she just had, but he also seemed to accept defeat.

She pointed at the package. '*Fifteen,*' she reiterated. 'Get that through the books in the next two weeks. *All of it.*' She turned and left the way she'd entered. 'Or you can kiss our contract and the likelihood of this shithole's survival goodbye.'

Walking out into the fresh air, Scarlet breathed in deeply, and this time when she exhaled, she felt slightly better. She may not be in control of the Jasper situation, but she sure as hell was here. Here *she* decided how things went. And that made her feel powerful. Holding her head high, she started back towards the car.

CHAPTER FIFTY-SEVEN

Connor and Cillian stood quietly in the shadows at the back of the industrial unit. Cillian leaned back on a nearby railing and chewed on a toothpick, eying the circle of light over the back door. Connor glanced over at him.

'Why the fuck have you started chewing toothpicks? You look like some sort of Twenties mafia boss,' he said irritably.

'What's it to you?' Cillian replied with a frown. 'I'm trying to give up smoking – it helps keep my mouth busy.'

'Your mouth don't need no help with that,' Connor responded wryly. 'And why are you trying to give up smoking?'

'Bad for your health, innit?' he said.

Connor raised one eyebrow, unimpressed, then slowly and deliberately lit a cigarette. He stared his brother out as he took a long deep drag.

'Arsehole,' Cillian muttered. He stood up and walked a few paces away, settling back on the railing there and crossing his arms.

Connor sighed, took another couple of deep drags and then stubbed it out, chucking over the railing into the abyss beyond. He joined his brother further down the railings and faced the doorway once more.

'*I* ain't giving up smoking,' he said quietly in a stubborn tone.

'No one asked you to give up smoking,' Cillian replied, equally quietly.

'Well, I'm just saying, I ain't going to. You're giving up smoking, and usually when you do something that means *we* do something, and I ain't giving up smoking,' Connor continued.

'No one asked you to give up smoking,' Cillian repeated, his arms still crossed as he chewed the toothpick and stared at the door.

'Good, that's fine then,' Connor replied. 'Because if this is one of those times when you tell me that you're—'

'Shhh.' Cillian cut him off sharply and raised a hand in warning. Connor immediately fell silent. 'Here he comes.'

The back door opened and Jasper walked out, looking down at something on his phone. The twins silently flew across the empty car park between them and the door and split up, coming at him from both sides.

Connor accidentally knocked a bottle top across the tarmac and the sound caused Jasper to look up. He squinted into the darkness and caught sight of Connor hurtling towards him. As he registered who it was, he turned as fast as lightning and ran back into the building.

'Fuck,' Connor swore. 'Quick, get the bastard!'

They sped up and crossed the rest of the distance in seconds, running in through the back door after him.

'He's up there,' Cillian shouted, hearing the sound of running feet reaching the floor above. 'He's heading for the office.'

They took the stairs two at a time and followed him. It wasn't ideal that they hadn't managed to catch him outside, but it wasn't entirely unexpected. They had accounted for a situation like this. The CCTV outside the back door had been covered with tape, they had covered up and worn gloves, and now they were inside they'd pulled down the ski masks that had been folded up on their heads. Jasper knew who they were now, but no one else would, should there be cameras on the inside.

They reached the office door and ran in, clocking Jasper kneeling down behind the desk.

'Get the fuck up,' Cillian roared, running round one side whilst Connor headed over the other.

Jasper was fumbling in the bottom drawer of the desk, and Cillian pushed him back away from it with force. He looked down into it and saw the false bottom that had been raised. Inside was a box, and he was pretty sure he knew what was inside but he needed to check to be sure.

'Grab him,' he said to Connor.

Connor did as he'd been asked, roughly pulling the other man to his feet. Jasper struggled and tried to punch his way out, but Connor was too fast and ducked out of the way, twisting the other man round and wrapping an arm around his neck.

'Get the fuck off me,' Jasper yelled. 'You'll pay for this.' He kicked out backwards but got nowhere. Connor was bigger and stronger than he was by a lot. 'There will be comeback from this – you can't take me. You can't fucking touch me.'

'I can and it looks like I already fucking am,' Connor growled in his ear. 'So shut up.'

Cillian opened the box. The small handgun he'd rightly suspected was inside sat in its holder still. He held it up. 'Gonna take us out with this, were you?'

'Fucking right,' Jasper spat with murder in his eyes.

He took it out of the box and held it up in the light. 'Pretty little piece, I'll give you that,' he said. Placing the empty box back into the bottom of the drawer, he closed it all back up as though it had never been opened. 'Think I'll keep it as a souvenir.'

Connor started dragging Jasper back out of the office, and after slipping the gun into his waistband, Cillian twisted Jasper's arm back and began helping to move him along.

'Ouch, fuck's sake!' Jasper roared as Cillian tightened the twist. 'Where the hell do you think you're taking me, eh?' he asked. His hazel eyes flicked back and forth between the brothers, and he licked his lips, fear beginning to seep through the bravado.

'Come on, where? Let me guess – you're going to hold me ransom until my dad releases your market stalls,' he said mockingly. 'How well thought out – or rather how *not* well thought out. We've got your stolen goods, you idiots,' he hissed through gritted teeth. 'And your prints are all over the stuff. There are only so many places you can take me, and the minute my dad hands your shit over to the police and tells him you've got me, it's only a matter of time before they locate me and you're behind bars. Don't you get that? This is checkmate,' he declared defiantly. 'You want to let me go now and walk the *fuck* away, if you have any idea what's good for you.'

They reached the back door and Connor kicked it open. Then they pushed Jasper out and marched him across the dark car park to their car, ignoring the string of threats that were still falling out of his mouth. He didn't waste time screaming for help, as they'd predicted. There was no point. No one else would be anywhere near the remote deserted unit at this time of night, and he knew it.

They reached the car and Connor swung him round, shoving him against it hard. He lifted the ski mask and pushed his face into Jasper's with a menacing look. 'This ain't anything to do with the markets. You're right – that would be a very stupid plan indeed. And we weren't born yesterday.' He watched as Jasper blinked in confusion and as a wary expression fell over his pale face. 'Nah, this is about my uncle. You remember him, don't ya?' Connor's dark brown eyes glittered dangerously in the moonlight. 'Big guy, dark hair, the one whose throat you slit in that alley that night.'

'Wh-What?' Jasper stuttered, taken aback. 'I don't know what you're talking about.'

'Oh, but you do, Jasper,' Cillian chimed in, opening the back door and pulling out a roll of gaffer tape. 'You know exactly what we're talking about.' He pulled a length of tape and pressed it over the complaining man's mouth, silencing him.

'And as for your dad,' Connor said, 'he won't be sending police round our way any time soon. Because we're not going to let him know we have you.' He watched as Jasper's eyes began to fill with real fear. 'There's no point holding you ransom, because we don't want nothing from him. We want something from *you*. An eye for an eye, the Bible says,' he quoted his mother and pushed the man down into the back of the car. 'And it's time for you to pay your debts.'

CHAPTER FIFTY-EIGHT

Lily pulled up outside the house and waited with the engine running in the darkness. She had texted ahead to tell Scarlet to be ready. It had been a long day, but it was about to get longer still. They had a hard night in front of them and none of it was going to be pleasant. She wondered once more if she should have just dealt with it herself, kept Scarlet out of it, but it was too late now. Plus, the girl needed to understand how the world she'd jumped into really worked. If she wanted to walk away then maybe she still could.

If tonight was too much for her, Lily would give her an out. But they were at a crossroads now where Scarlet only had two choices. She was either in and prepared to delve into the darkest parts of this life, in which case she stood a chance of becoming a successful force down the line. Or this would be the line she couldn't cross, and it was time to change direction whilst she was still young and unestablished enough to do so. The period of easing in was over.

She took a deep breath and reached for her cigarettes, lighting one up and opening the window. Light flooded the driveway for a moment as the front door opened and then shut behind her niece. A movement in one of the windows upstairs drew Lily's eyes upwards and she found herself staring at her sister-in-law. They held each other's gaze for a few long moments. Lily saw the struggle in Cath's eyes, the anger and pain mixed with fear and uncertainty, and finally the question as to what Scarlet was doing leaving with her at this time of night. Lily cast her gaze back down and pulled the car back off the drive as Scarlet shut the door. She couldn't answer that question. Because it was an answer Cath wouldn't understand or be able to deal with. They drove off down the street.

'You know what's happening tonight, don't you?' Lily asked.

'You have Jasper?' Scarlet questioned.

Lily nodded. 'We do.'

There was a short silence. 'Then yes, I guess I do know.'

Lily turned the corner towards the factory. 'You understand this is part of our life, don't you?' she asked. 'This life we lead is a dark one. We're old school because staying ahead means we have to be. That's the way the underworld works. Your dad was murdered in cold blood, and if we don't answer in the same fashion once it becomes clear we know who did it, we show ourselves as weak. And if we appear weak, the wolves descend.' She turned another corner. 'They show no mercy. They take and demolish everything your father and I built up in this life, so that they can rise above us. And we cannot let that happen. The firm must be protected at all costs. And all those who are part of the firm are its protectors.' She glanced at her niece. 'If *you* are part of this firm, that makes it your responsibility too.'

'There is no *if*,' Scarlet responded. 'I already am part of this firm, and I'm prepared to do whatever I have to.' She stuck her chin out and held her head higher in the darkness. 'My father is dead, but he lives on through me, and I'll be damned if I fail him now. No.' She shook her head. 'I won't ever fail him. That bastard tried to take everything from us and made a complete mockery of me in the process.' Her cheeks flushed an angry shade of red. 'I…' She exhaled heavily and pursed her lips, too angry to continue.

Lily glanced at her and then back at the road, her expression grim. She knew the young man had been texting Scarlet and that the two had been flirting. She'd even been secretly pleased at how well they'd been getting on, before the Snows had revealed their true colours. It was hard, the life they chose to lead. It was a life half-lived in the dark, full of secrets that could never be shared with outsiders. So to find romance within their own circles was ideal, when it was possible. But he'd just been leading her on, playing with her this whole time. And she knew how deeply embarrassed, hurt and angry her niece must be feeling. It wouldn't be an easy discovery for anyone, but Scarlet was fiercely proud and strong. It would be an even harder blow for her.

'Well, he won't be laughing much longer,' Scarlet continued, her anger lowered to a more controllable simmer. 'He's treated me like a fool and that was a big mistake. Because however long I've been part of this firm, I'm just as big a part of it as anyone else. And I'm just as prepared to do what it takes. He shouldn't have underestimated that.'

Lily nodded. 'OK then,' she said. She glanced sideways again as they passed a street light. Scarlet's expression was determined and angry, but there was still an element of fear in her eyes.

Good, she thought. If the girl wasn't scared, she would be more worried. She fell silent and left Scarlet with her thoughts for the rest of the journey. She hoped the girl was mentally preparing herself. Because saying it and actually going ahead with it were two different things. And although she hoped Scarlet was strong enough to see this through, none of them would know how she would cope when faced with Jasper in person until they were in the moment.

They stepped out of the car and walked into the darkened factory together, the only sound their heels clipping loudly on the factory floor. The moonlight shone through the large windows, throwing eerie shapes around the machinery, and a coldness crept through their clothes to their skin now that the heating was turned off for the night. Scarlet shivered but quickly covered it with the action of pushing her hair back over her shoulders.

They descended the stairs to the basement and entered the room where the twins were waiting with Jasper. The lights were on in here. With no windows or other access to the outside world, there was no threat of anyone seeing and questioning what was going on in a factory in the middle of the night. There was no chance of anyone hearing screams either, being so deep into the building.

Connor and Cillian sat waiting at the edge of the room, watching the man in the chair struggle fruitlessly. They'd taped his mouth and wrapped the same tape around his wrists at the back of the chair several times to keep him secure. He kicked out as they approached, trying and failing to move the heavy wooden chair he was attached to across the room. It was a decorative chair Ronan had once had sitting in his office – a large, throne-like piece that was as heavy as it was ugly. Lily had never liked it. Ronan had grown bored of it too eventually, annoyed by the amount of space it had taken up, so it had been relegated to the basement. Lily had wanted to throw it out, but now it appeared it had come in useful after all.

Leaving Scarlet on the sidelines, Lily stepped forward and leaned down into the face of their captive. She studied him openly for a few moments, before standing back up.

'Take the tape off,' she said. Connor stepped forward and ripped the tape from Jasper's mouth roughly, causing him to cry out in pain. 'Why?' Lily asked him simply. 'Why did you do it?'

'I don't know what you're *fucking* talking about,' Jasper yelled, spittle flying from his mouth and his floppy hair falling forward over his eye. He flicked it back and glared at Lily. 'Let me out of here – *now*,' he demanded.

'No,' she said curtly. 'I'll ask you again – why?' She lifted an eyebrow and waited.

'I've already told you, I don't know what you're talking about, you stupid bint.' He cried out once more as Cillian punched him hard on the side of his head.

'Insult my mum again,' he warned, 'and I'll cut your fucking tongue out.' With a hard look, he turned and walked back to sit with Connor.

Lily waited calmly as Jasper rolled his head and groaned, her expression cold and unmoving. Pulling out her phone, she found the picture of the diary Bill had taken and held it up so he could see it. As he registered what he was looking at, the colour drained from his face. Lily locked the phone and slipped it back into her pocket.

'Now, I'll ask you one last time. Why?' she said, tilting her head to one side.

Jasper stared at her, fear and fury warring in his eyes. He clamped his mouth shut and locked his jaw, clearly not willing to answer her question.

Lily nodded slowly. 'OK,' she said. 'Well, then I guess there's nothing left to say.' She gave a discreet hand signal to the twins and without a word they stood up and left the room. Walking over to the table they'd just vacated, she picked up the gun that lay there and the bullets that sat beside it.

'From what I understand,' she said, pulling out the magazine and loading the bullets in one by one, 'this is your father's gun.' She paused and looked back at him over her shoulder. 'Is that right?'

He looked at the gun, the fear intensifying in his face, and back up at her.

'Well, that's perfect really. Means we can stage it as a suicide.'

'Why on earth would I commit suicide?' he blurted out, his tone panicked. 'I have a great life – I have no reason to kill myself, so that wouldn't add up.' He licked his lips. 'They'd see how fishy that is straight off. You really think you can get away with murder?' He forced out a laugh. 'Not likely. They'd catch you. Then you'd be put away for life. You really want that?'

'They'd catch me?' Lily turned with a small smile of amusement. 'Well, they never have in the past, so I'm not sure why that would suddenly change now.' She stared at him, her deep brown eyes mocking him coldly across the room. 'And actually, you have a very good reason for topping yourself.' She finished loading the bullets and pushed the magazine back in with a click, then turned to face him. 'You see, the note you're going to leave will contain a full confession to the murder of my brother, and the explanation that you just couldn't live with yourself any longer. It will be cut and dried, and the police will celebrate. Two closed cases for the price of one.'

Jasper's gaze danced around the room, between Lily and Scarlet. He licked his lips again. 'Look, what do you want? I'll give you anything. You want your markets back? They're yours. Done. You want financial compensation, you can have it. Whatever you want. You know how many businesses my father owns – you name your price and it's yours.'

He saw the glare on Scarlet's livid face intensify and focused his efforts on Lily. 'Please,' he begged. 'This is an opportunity for you. One you'll never get again. You're right, I'm in your debt and I'm willing to pay it. No price is too big. Think of what you can achieve with that. Think of how far you can boost your firm. You can step up miles beyond any level you'd be able to reach yourselves. This situation can be turned around. For all of us.' He pleaded with his eyes, wishing Lily was easier to read.

Lily approached him slowly. 'Our firm can step up, you say? Higher than we could reach ourselves?'

'Yes,' he said, grasping what he saw as a lifeline with both hands. 'Your firm can become *great*. Your firm can go down in history as one of the biggest success stories in the underworld. All you have to do is let me pay my debt financially, rather than with blood. I mean, what will blood really achieve here? Think about that for a moment.' His eyes widened in hope as a small smile played out on her face.

'What will blood achieve…' she repeated. 'You don't really belong in this world, Jasper. Nor does your father. Because neither of you actually understand what being here means.'

She crossed her arms and began to pace slowly across the room, the gun still in her hand. '*Blood* is what made this firm in the first place. Our blood. Mine and my brother's. We built everything we have today from nothing, with *blood*, sweat and tears. We *drew blood* for the first time, many years ago, protecting this firm. We established ourselves in the hardest ways possible and it took a great toll. We made great sacrifices. And this firm' – she turned in a circle, gesturing to everything around her – 'this firm is exactly where we want it to be – and that's at the level *we* can reach ourselves. The level *our blood* works so hard to reach. We don't want handouts, we don't need to take from people like you to step up the ladder a bit further – what would be the point in that? It would mean nothing if we didn't get there ourselves. That wouldn't be an achievement at all.' She narrowed her gaze at him in disgust. 'We weren't raised like you, to sit back and expect everything to be handed to us, thinking that having something we didn't even work for makes us something special. And we don't go around killing people for no good reason. The only time we do kill is when it's in retribution. As we will today.' She stopped her pacing and gave him one last long look.

'Please, Lily, wait…'

Ignoring his pleas, Lily walked over to Scarlet. The girl was almost frothing with anger at the way Jasper had tried to buy his way out of the situation. At the way he'd tried to compensate them for murdering Ronan with cold meaningless money. She stepped into her line of sight until she had her full attention.

'I'm going to leave this here, Scarlet.' She held the gun up and then slowly lowered it to the table beside them. 'And I'm going to the office.'

Surprise registered in Scarlet's eyes, then uncertainty and finally understanding. Lily grasped her niece's arm and stared her down hard. 'Come and join me when you're done.'

Without another word, she left the room and closed the door behind her.

CHAPTER FIFTY-NINE

Jasper watched Lily leave the room with surprise and then turned his gaze back to Scarlet. Her almost translucent cheeks were tinged with a shade of hot red, and the fury in her eyes left him in no doubt of her feelings towards him. This was something he could use to his advantage, if he was smart. Scarlet alone was a situation much easier to manipulate his way out of. He'd been waiting for an opportunity and this was it.

He twisted his wrists around as much as he could, easing the pins and needles that were threatening to set in. Gently he curled his hands down to the gap in the chair just behind his lower back. If he could reach what he'd stashed there earlier, he would be OK.

'Scarlet,' he said, his tone soft.

'Don't,' she snapped. She ran her hands over her face, the stress she was feeling clear in her expression.

He used the brief moment unwatched to push his hands down further. His fingers touched his waistband just as she opened her eyes.

'Do you really think I wanted to do it?' he asked, making his voice as soft and pitiful as he could. He stared into her eyes beseechingly.

'I don't know what to think,' Scarlet replied. 'But whether you wanted to or not doesn't really matter. You killed my father.'

'Because I had to,' he pressed. 'You know what it's like when you join your family in this game. My father made me do it. Exactly the way your aunt is going to make you do the same thing to me.'

Scarlet scoffed and turned in a circle, her hands on her hips. 'Don't compare me to you,' she said.

'But it's true, isn't it? We're the same, you and I.' He pushed his hands further and felt the hard handle of the small blade he'd hidden in the back of his trousers.

When he'd seen the twins, he'd known immediately that he wasn't going to get out of being taken. There was nowhere to escape to and there had been no one around to call on for help. He'd had precious little time, so he'd run to the office where he knew there were several weapons. He'd just had time to stash the small blade before they'd caught up. His attempt at reaching for the gun was mainly to throw them off wondering if he had anything else on him, and it had worked. Now that blade was going to help him get out of the tape he was bound with. If he could just get his hand around it.

He eyed the gun on the table by the door and then focused back on Scarlet. 'We've both been thrown into this life, into families who expect us to do things we don't want to do, things we're not comfortable doing.'

'*You* might have been thrown into it, but I chose to join my family,' Scarlet replied, lifting her chin.

This threw Jasper off slightly. He hadn't pegged her for one who would be so eager to jump in. 'That might be the case, but are you honestly telling me you want to end my life?' he asked. 'You want to be responsible for killing someone?' He shook his head sadly. 'I'll tell you now, it doesn't feel good.' He hung his head for effect and to hide the look of triumph as he finally got a good grasp on the blade. 'The guilt, the feeling of doing something so wrong to another human being.'

'The feeling of paying back the person who murdered the man I loved and respected most in the world?' Scarlet added. She swallowed and began pacing up and down the room.

Jasper eyed the gun again. She was slowly walking further and further away from it. 'I hated doing that to him,' he lied in a sorrowful voice. 'I've had to live with that heavy burden every day since. And I hate myself for it. Especially after I met you,' he added softly. 'We had such a connection that night.' He looked around the room pointedly. 'In this very room. Though it looked very different back then – do you remember?'

'Stop it,' Scarlet snapped angrily. 'You stood there that night talking to me, *flirting* with me, being all friendly to me when the whole time you *knew* who I was. You *knew* you'd killed my father in cold blood. You paid your goddamn respects to the shrine my aunt had set up!' She pushed her fingers up into her hair as the audacity of it all became too unbelievable to process.

'I know,' he lamented as he began sawing through the tape as fast as his bound fingers would allow. 'And I hated myself for it. The whole time I was stood there wishing I could just tell you, wishing I could take it back, but I couldn't.'

'Stop lying,' Scarlet demanded. Her eyes flashed with anger and he bowed his head, trying to look as sorry as he could.

'It's not a lie; it's the truth,' he said quietly. 'And I know your aunt wants you to kill me, one life in payment for another. But do you really want to end up being just like me?' He looked up at her and saw the fire in her eyes waver. 'Do you want to be looking my father in the eye, pretending everything is OK when you know you took the life of his only son?'

He sawed a little faster, his fingers becoming more nimble as he passed the halfway mark. It wouldn't be much longer now until he was through his binds and he needed to get her as far away from the gun as possible. He glanced at the opposite side of the basement and eyed the sink in the corner.

'Look, I get it. You have to do what you have to do. And… And I want you to know I forgive you that.'

'Shut up,' she snapped, shaking her head as if trying to get him out of it.

'I'm sorry,' he said more softly. 'That's all I'm going to say.' He coughed and licked his lips. 'Can I ask for some water? Please?' He gave her a tentative smile of hope. 'I know it makes no difference now, but… I would just really like a drink if you could spare me that.'

Scarlet stared back at him, the anger warring with her inner goodness and he waited with anticipation to see if she would accept.

CHAPTER SIXTY

Lily didn't notice the person sitting in the dark behind her desk until she'd closed the door. She jumped and her hand flew to her chest as she turned on the light and they came into view.

'Jesus, Mary and Joseph, Cath, you gave me the fright of my bloody life!' she exclaimed, sagging as the shock faded away. 'What are you doing here?'

'What are *you* doing here, Lily, in the middle of the night?' Cath demanded. 'And where's Scarlet?'

Lily exhaled slowly and walked over to her desk. As Cath was in her seat, she took the one opposite and reached into her cigarette box from there. She lit it and took a deep drag before she spoke. 'Scarlet is otherwise engaged at the moment with things that you don't want to be concerned with,' she said carefully.

'With your illegal businesses,' Cath stated, pursing her lips. Her face twitched as her gaze bored into Lily's. Lily looked down to her cigarette, tapping it lightly on the edge of the ashtray before taking another drag.

She could tell Cath wanted to know what Scarlet was up to, and if she outright asked again then she wouldn't lie. But she knew Cath also wanted to keep her mental distance from the parts of the business she'd steadfastly ignored her entire life. And this was the war being waged in her head right now. She hoped the latter won out, because if she had to tell Cath what was going on, it would kill her. And most likely be the straw that broke the camel's back, as far as their already strained relationship went.

'Did you follow us here?' she asked.

'Yes, I followed you,' Cath replied with a scowl. 'I've been following Scarlet all day, trying to keep an eye on her. But it's harder than I thought.'

Lily's eyebrows rose up to meet her curls and she blew out the smoke she'd just inhaled. This was news she hadn't expected to hear. 'Why have you been following her?'

'Because of Jasper,' Cath said, standing up suddenly in irritation and folding her arms. 'That little shit took my husband's life for no apparent reason,' she said, her lip wobbling. 'And so how do I know he ain't after Scarlet now, eh?' She shot an accusatory glare at Lily. 'You've been throwing her out there, all about town, letting it be known she's the new heir to the bloody throne. Well, what if she's the next target, huh? Did you ever stop to think about that?'

'Actually, yes. I did. And she isn't,' Lily replied, tapping her ash away once more and leaning back into her chair.

'And how do you know that then?' Cath asked.

'Because it was never about Ronan specifically – it was about weakening the firm. Scarlet wouldn't have been the next target; she's not strong enough to worry them yet. The next target was going to be me.'

She eyed the decanter of brandy she kept on the desk wistfully but refrained from pouring one. She needed a strong drink more than ever, but she'd made the decision not to drink in front of Cath until her sister-in-law had regained control over the unhealthy relationship she'd developed with alcohol.

Cath frowned and her arms dropped down to her sides. 'What do you mean? Why would they go after you?'

Lily pulled a face. 'They might not have, but it would be my next move if I were them. They were after the markets. When Harry came to offer his condolences after Ronan died, they were surprised to see me in a position of strength. It caught him off guard, and I could tell there was something underlying it all at the time, I just didn't know exactly what. Ronan was always the face of things. You remember how it was when we were starting up, Cath,' she said. 'It was a backwards world – women had their place and it wasn't in the higher ranks of the underworld. It was easier to work things out behind closed doors between us and then present Ronan as the main face. Our friends and close allies over the years knew better, but not everyone. Not Harry,' she added.

Cath frowned and rubbed her forehead with a nod. 'Yeah, I remember,' she said.

'I think Harry intended to try and take the markets from me quietly, expecting me to see it as a relief. One less thing to take on from my charismatic successful brother. Because I was just the sister that had always sat in the background riding his coat tails.'

'Huh!' Cath exclaimed with a humourless snort.

'Exactly,' Lily replied. She stubbed the cigarette out and watched the last curls of smoke rise and disappear in the air. 'And so he was surprised. He ordered the hit on Ronan to weaken us and take the stalls, so when he found the firm still standing, he took them by force and with blackmail as a backup instead.' She looked up at Cath. 'So you see, if they were going to go after anyone else in this family, it would have been me. You really needn't have worried about Scarlet.'

'I will always worry about Scarlet,' Cath replied sharply. 'I'm her mother, and she's gone and thrown her future away, jumping straight into the death sentence of a life that took her father. And *you're* the one who let her,' she added, angry tears forming in her eyes.

'Cath, I never forced Scarlet to do anything,' she said. 'She chose her path of her own free will.' She held Cath's gaze levelly and eventually Cath looked down. 'I won't lie to you,' she said in a calmer tone. 'I'm glad she did. She has such fire in her, Cath, such strength. She is Ronan through and through. She is a *Drew* through and through.'

Cath shook her head with a sad smile. 'I guess that's where I don't fit in, isn't it? Why I just don't understand it all. I may be a Drew by name, but I've never been blood.'

'You're *family*, Cath,' Lily replied. 'And that's all that matters. But you need to stop fighting Scarlet's choices. She is where she wants to be. No one forced her here, but she's *here*. And whether you fight everyone around you or not, that's not going to change.' She sighed. 'That girl is going to replace me, one day, you know. She's going to take this firm to new heights, heights even I haven't taken it to.' She smiled. 'I can see it, the potential in her. It's already coming out, but in time it will grow into such brilliance this world won't know what's hit it.'

Cath looked up at her, defeat in her eyes. 'I hope you're right, Lily,' she replied flatly. 'Because if you're not, this world will just end up killing her, like it did Ronan.'

They fell into silence for a few moments, before Lily straightened up in her seat and glanced at the clock. 'Cath, why don't you go home and get some rest. I've got things I need to do here and it's best if you're not around.' Plus, the last thing she wanted was for Cath to hear the gunshot when Scarlet finally pulled the trigger.

Part of her wanted to go back down there, to help her through what she needed to do. But another part of her knew Scarlet needed to do this on her own.

Cath shook her head. 'I can't sleep tonight. I'm too het up, I need to see Scarlet, make sure she's definitely safe from this Jasper. Just for tonight.'

'I assure you, she most definitely is,' Lily replied.

'How can you assure me of that?' Cath countered. 'How, Lily?'

'You don't want to know that, Cath,' Lily warned.

Cath bit her lip. 'Actually, tonight I think I do,' she said bravely. 'With everything that's going on right now, I just need to know the things you usually hide from me.'

Lily felt her insides constrict. 'You really don't want to do this, Cath. Don't make me tell you, for your sake,' she said in a low voice. Her brown eyes held Cath's, pleading with her to go home.

Cath shook her head. 'No, I need to know,' she said.

Lily fought the urge to lie. It would be so easy to lie, to let Cath go out on some wild goose chase and smooth it over in the morning. But that went against who she was. She didn't lie to family, not when it came to things as serious as this. If Cath wanted to know then she had every right. But Lily knew it would kill her.

'Last chance to go home, Cath,' she whispered.

'Tell me,' she replied.

Lily took a deep breath in and set her hands down slowly on the arms of her chair. 'I can assure you that Scarlet is safe from Jasper, because right now he's tied up in the basement. And she's down there with him.' She heard Cath gasp and looked up into her eyes. 'And after tonight, he'll never be a threat to anyone else, ever again.'

CHAPTER SIXTY-ONE

Scarlet looked down at the man she used to think was so attractive and felt sick. The hazel eyes she'd thought were bright and interesting were nothing but flat pools filled with lies. He'd pretended to like her, had asked her out, laughed with her as if the world was a normal place. But it wasn't a normal place. It was the darkest most dangerous nightmare she could have imagined, and it was that way because of him. Ronan was dead because of him. An image of her father walking down an alley and Jasper coming up behind him with a knife flashed before her eyes, and she squeezed them shut as she tried to force it away.

'Could you spare me that?' he asked again. 'Just a few sips of water?'

'No,' she heard herself say, in a hard tone.

The situation she was in was so surreal she felt almost detached from herself as she stared down at him. So many feelings raged through her body. Hate, anger, confusion, sadness, shame and fear all fought for the top spot, and she wasn't sure which was winning. She glanced over at the gun her aunt had left on the table. She'd never fired a gun before. She knew the basic concept – take the safety off, point and pull the trigger. It seemed an easy enough process. But could she do that whilst it was pointed at a person?

'OK, well, at least grant me a few more minutes with you?' she heard him ask.

She turned back to him with a snarl. 'Why?' she demanded. 'So you can try and guilt me into not doing to you what you did to my dad?' She swallowed. 'This isn't exactly what I had in mind for tonight, you know.' She turned and began to pace again, trying to quell the adrenaline that was coursing through her body and making her shake. 'But at the end of the day, this is the life I chose. And like my dad, when I commit to something, I commit to it fully.'

She nodded to herself. It was time. It was best just to do it and not think of the after part. She'd known about the darker side of her family her whole life. Ever since the day she'd watched her aunt shoot that man in the living room. This was part of who they were, the Drews. And it was part of who she was too. You couldn't have a life full of roses without also taking the thorns. This man had killed her father and he needed to be repaid. It was only fitting, as she took her place in the firm he'd built, that she was the one to even the scales.

'Stop,' he called out suddenly.

She paused and turned with a quizzical expression.

'Stay right there for a moment,' he continued.

'Why?' She narrowed her eyes, but as she realised he'd stopped her on the other side of the room from the gun, it was too late.

Jasper sprang up from the chair and pulled his arms forward, the severed tape still stuck around one of his wrists.

Scarlet dived towards the table with the gun, but he leaped into her path and pointed the small knife at her menacingly. She immediately pulled herself short and began backing away, her hands rising slowly up into the air. There were a few feet between them, but nothing else around, and she began to panic as she realised there was nothing she could grab to defend herself with.

'Shit,' she cried.

'Yes, shit indeed,' Jasper replied with a cold smile. 'Bad move on your cousins' behalfs really, not checking me when we got here. I guess they'll feel pretty bad about that when they walk in later to find you dead, won't they?'

'Why would you kill me?' Scarlet replied, trying to think of a way out whilst keeping him talking. She realised, with irony, that this was exactly what he'd been doing to her just moments before. 'You just told me you didn't want to kill my father, that you hated yourself for it, so why would you want to kill me?' Maybe if she pulled on his guilt a little it would confuse him just enough to give her time to figure it all out.

Jasper laughed. 'Of course I told you that, you silly little fool,' he said tauntingly. 'A man facing the end of a gun will say anything to get out of that situation. But just so we're clear' – he moved closer and she stepped back again – 'I don't hate myself at all for killing your father. In fact, watching him bleed out on the ground with that confused look on his face was one of the highlights of my entire year,' he sneered.

Despite the danger she was in, Scarlet felt her anger flare higher, and her blood began to boil into a ball of rage in her stomach. 'You piece of shit,' she spat.

'Now, now,' he mocked, 'that's no way to talk to the man holding a knife to you, is it? Thing is,' he continued, 'I've actually dreamed of doing that to someone since I was a little boy. Fucked up, I know, right?' He chuckled at himself. 'But it's true. So when I got the go-ahead to finally do it, it was like all my Christmases had come at once. Honestly' – he stepped forward again, and she tried to edge around to the side – 'there was none of this angst you've been displaying. No psyching myself up – I was just ready. I actually had to hold myself back so I didn't jump in too early and fuck it all up,' he admitted. 'It was so easy to get him there too. Your laundering issues are no big secret. I dangled a huge opportunity in front of him, and he couldn't resist looking into it. It was him who asked if we could keep our meeting quiet, just until we'd settled the terms. He knew your aunt wouldn't like the precious Drew family doing business with a Snow.' He snorted. 'Perfect, really. No one had a clue. At least until now.'

Scarlet glanced at the gun. If she could just edge round a little more, she might be able to make a run for it.

'I wouldn't bother if I were you. If you try to run, I'll just make it more painful.' He shrugged with a smile. 'More fun for me, less so for you.'

'My cousins are right outside,' Scarlet warned.

'No, they're not,' Jasper said calmly. 'If they were just there, you would have already screamed and they'd have already come in and overpowered me at the very least. They left a while ago, because their job was done, wasn't it?'

Scarlet bit her lip. There was nothing for it – she was going to have to take him head-on. She weighed him up and her heart dropped. He was taller and stronger than she was; there was no escaping it. Plus he had the knife. But she had to try. She wasn't going out without a fight – it wasn't in her to do so.

Something in her expression must have tipped him off because his gaze tightened with suspicion and he set himself into a boxer's stance, tensing his muscles with a cold smile. 'Come on then, princess,' he said softly. 'You want to try me, go for it. This *is* going to be fun, after all…'

Locking her jaw, Scarlet stepped back with one foot ready to push forward, but as she did, the door swung open and hit the wall with a bang. Seeing who it was, Scarlet's expression fell into a confused frown, and she blinked for a moment but swiftly realising that Jasper had also swung round, she jumped to the side and began to run further into the dark basement.

He was caught off guard, twisting round to see where she'd gone, not expecting her to go in the other direction. 'Hey!' he yelled. He had no idea who the woman who'd just walked in was, but it wasn't Lily and so right now he didn't give a shit.

'Mum, the gun!' Scarlet yelled as she reached the wall and circled round to run towards Cath. Jasper had already changed course and was catching up to her. There was no getting away from him trapped down here. She stopped in her tracks as she realised she was only closing the gap between them and began to panic once more as he lifted his arm, the blade glinting in the dim light from the centre of the room.

'Get the *fuck* away from my daughter,' Cath screamed.

Scarlet jumped and gasped as the sound of the gunshot reverberated around the basement. For a moment everything seemed to stop still, as though time itself had decided to take a pause. Jasper's eyes were still trained on her, but his expression changed from that of a manic psychopath to one of surprise and shock. As she watched, he slowed and fell forward, crying out in pain.

Not sure exactly what had happened, she didn't move for a few moments, rooted to the spot in confusion. Then Cath's voice broke through the mist.

'Scarlet!'

She looked up into the terrified eyes of her mother as Cath dropped the gun. 'Mum.' She skirted round Jasper and ran across the room to Cath, her concern redirected immediately towards her. 'Mum, are you OK?' she asked.

'Me?' Cath asked, in a high pitch. 'I'm – I'm…' She stared at the gun she'd just shot in shock. 'Are *you* OK?' she asked, shakily.

Jasper began to wail and curse on the floor, and Scarlet turned her gaze back towards him.

Lily came running into the room and quickly assessed the scene. 'What happened?'

'Jasper had a knife,' Scarlet explained hotly. 'He got out. Mum shot him in the leg.' She didn't bother with the rest of the details – Lily would be able to work that out herself.

'Shit,' Lily muttered under her breath.

'Yeah, that's what I said,' Scarlet replied, glaring at her aunt. 'They couldn't have fucking searched him?' she asked accusingly. 'He nearly fucking had me.' Grinding her teeth, she turned and picked up the gun.

'Well, you're taking it well,' Lily remarked.

'I'm a Drew,' Scarlet shot over her shoulder. 'It's what we do, right?' In truth she wasn't taking it as well as she was displaying, but she could dissect her feelings later on in private. Right now, she had to finish the matter once and for all. And suddenly she realised she was ready. As she wrapped her fingers around the gun, she felt as though she was standing in the eye of the hurricane, in a centre of perfect calm, whilst the chaos continued to rage all around her. She was ready. It was time.

'You shot him?' she heard her aunt ask in surprise as she walked away from the pair of them.

'I might not be a born Drew,' her mother replied, 'but I am a mother. And that makes me just as dangerous as any of you.'

Scarlet crossed the room to stand over the man now dragging himself across the floor in a feeble attempt to get to the door. She kicked the hand still holding the knife – hard – sending the weapon clattering across the ground. He looked up at Scarlet, panting with the pain, resentment in his eyes.

'Guess it's too late to pretend I feel bad again, yeah?' he said mockingly.

'Yes,' she replied simply. 'It is.'

Her fear gone and nothing but cold resolve in its place, Scarlet lifted her hand, cocked the gun, pointed it at his head and pulled the trigger.

CHAPTER SIXTY-TWO

Lily and Scarlet walked into the busy toy shop side by side, stepping around the smiling children choosing their treats and their tired-looking parents. The cashier tried to stop them as they opened the door to the hallway that led to their destination.

'It's OK,' Lily said to her with a smile. 'We're old friends. Harry is expecting us.'

The cashier smiled in apology and went back to serving the excited seven-year-old buying an Action Man.

Harry's bodyguards were posted outside his office door and immediately stood up as they approached.

'Tell your boss Lily Drew is here,' she demanded. One of them disappeared into the office and the other smirked at her. She smiled back. They still thought they had the upper hand, but she was about to disillusion them, so the smirk didn't bother her at all.

The door was opened and they were checked over for weapons then invited in. Harry pulled back in his seat behind the desk as though he'd been stung as they entered – his usual response to people invading his space unexpectedly.

'Lily, what on earth are you doing here?' he asked, his head twitching to the side in agitation.

Lily and Scarlet sat down and Lily smiled at him coldly across the desk.

'We have some news for you,' she said. 'And I thought it best to deliver it myself. Phone calls are so impersonal, don't you think?'

Harry's gaze narrowed. 'I rather prefer them myself,' he replied coldly.

'Oh well,' Lily said dismissively. 'I just thought you should know that as of about twenty minutes ago, our goods were liberated from *the shed*, the storage unit you so generously held them in for us.' Her tone was as mocking as her smile. 'Thank you so much for that, by the way. Saved us a fortune in storage costs, didn't it, Scarlet?'

'Oh it certainly did,' she agreed.

'Also, in case you wondered, we've had that little glitch that affected all our stall licences rectified.' Her smile dropped. 'So in case you wondered, if any of your men are found anywhere near my stalls from tomorrow morning, they'll be swiftly dealt with, with a baseball bat. So I suggest you make sure they ain't seen around our area again if you want them to continue enjoying the use of their legs.' Her dark eyes flashed coldly at him across the desk.

Harry glared back at her, clearly fuming that she'd managed to outsmart him. She could see the cogs in his brain turning, trying to work out how she'd located her goods. In truth it was mainly down to luck. If Ruby hadn't overheard them talking that day, they would never have known to ask around for the shed. Ray had been the one to bring the location to light, in the end. He'd called a couple of days before, having finally remembered where he'd heard of it. It had been a job he'd done a few years ago and Harry had offered him several storage options. That had been one of them. From there, it hadn't taken long to work out how to steal it back. That was, after all, one of their specialities.

'Right, you've had your fun, Lily,' Harry said with a sneer. 'Now get out.'

Lily and Scarlet turned to each other and pulled a face. 'Not very cordial, is he?' Lily said, standing up.

'It appears not,' Scarlet agreed. 'Goodbye then, Mr Snow.'

As they turned to walk out the door, Lily paused and turned as though something had just occurred to her. 'By the way...' She tilted her head to one side. 'You must give our love to Jasper, next time you see him. Don't forget now, will you?'

Harry's gaze immediately sharpened as he picked up on the undercurrent in her tone, and the corners of her mouth pulled up in a cold smile. Giving him one last long look, Lily followed Scarlet back out through the shop and onto the street.

As they reached the car and slipped into their seats, Scarlet turned to her aunt. 'When will the police find him?' she asked.

It had been a bit more difficult than expected, setting the scene as a suicide. Mainly because of the extra shot in the leg. That was going to cause the case to be looked at a little more closely perhaps, but Lily had high hopes that they'd put it down to a misfire in the end. They'd dumped his body in the river underneath a disused dock, purposely trapping his leg in some old fishing net so that it stayed where it should. There was a suicide note neatly encased in a sandwich bag to keep it dry, in his inner jacket pocket, explaining that he could no longer live with himself after taking Ronan's life and placing the blame on his father, who had organised all the details of the murder. Finally they'd placed an anonymous call to the police from a nearby payphone before they came to see Harry. By now they would be dredging him out and soon Harry would be arrested, and no doubt put away for a very long time.

Lily didn't agree with bringing the police into the wars between rival firms of the underworld. It went against all their most sacred laws. But Harry and Jasper weren't part of the underworld. They were merely unscrupulous businessmen who'd dabbled in their waters with no regard for their rules. So in this case, she had no qualms about laying things out the way they had.

'We should call Ruby,' Scarlet said, her tone resigned. 'Without her we would still be very much on the other end of this fight.'

Lily nodded. 'Very true. It will be nice to be able to praise her for a change,' she added.

Reaching forward, she pressed the screen on the dashboard and flipped down through her contacts. Finding Ruby, she hit the call button and waited.

*

Ruby glanced back over her shoulder and picked up her pace, shoving her hands down into her pockets. The shrill ringing of her phone made her jump, and she dove into a side alley to silence it and see who it was. She saw her mother's number and frowned. Why was she calling? She cut it off and peered around the corner, tentatively.

Her small brown eyes darted around, searching the street for the man she'd seen following her. He didn't appear to be anywhere, but that didn't mean he wasn't out there still, hiding, lurking, ready to grab her at any moment.

She couldn't work out who he was. She was sure she hadn't seen him before, but that didn't mean he wasn't working for one of the men she owed money to. Blowing air out of her cheeks, she waited another minute or so, but he didn't appear. With a sniff, she pushed her frizzy ginger hair back off her face and turned to walk further down the alley. Just because she couldn't see him didn't mean he wasn't still out there. It would be safer to come out the other side onto the next street and carry on down to where she was headed from there.

As she reached the end of the alley, she turned to check she hadn't been followed one last time. It was empty and she began to relax. But as she turned the corner, a rough hessian sack came down over her head and the world turned dark as someone grabbed her roughly from behind.

CHAPTER SIXTY-THREE

One week later, as Ronan's body was finally laid to rest, a strange calm rested over the whole family. It had been a long time coming and a whirlwind of a journey to get to the point that they could even get his body released. Jasper's 'confession' had helped, and although the case of his suicide was still open due to the suspicious circumstances, the note had prompted a search of his personal belongings and the police had been able to match the small piece of lint to one of his suits. It had been enough to get Ronan's body released and the case of his murder put to bed.

The family stood together in unity through the ceremony, and London's underworld turned up in force to pay their respects to a man most of them had liked very much. It was a fitting tribute, and as they moved on back to the house for the wake, Cath seemed suddenly much more together than she had since the day they'd received the news.

As the guests ate and drank and shared stories of Ronan, Lily made her way to the kitchen where Cath was dishing up yet more food from the oven. 'You know that's what we're paying the caterers for, don't you?'

Cath looked up at her and pursed her lips for a second. They hadn't spoken much after the great argument that had occurred after dealing with Jasper. Cath had launched an absolute tirade at Lily at the danger Scarlet had ended up in, only pausing when they'd had to focus on sorting all the last-minute funeral arrangements.

'Well, you know that cooking relaxes me, Lil,' she said in a clipped tone. 'Always has.'

Lily nodded and put her wine down on the side next to Cath's. Cath had started drinking again once they'd been told they could finally plan the funeral. Lily and Scarlet were keeping an eye on it, but so far she hadn't disappeared into the black abyss the way she had before, so no one had said a word.

Reaching into the towel drawer, Lily pulled out the spare apron.

'There's no need for that, Lily, I'm fine here on my own, thank you,' Cath said curtly. She turned and placed the dish of mini quiches on the breakfast bar, which was already laden with enough food to feed a small army, then reached for the tomatoes.

Lily ignored the dismissal and picked up a cucumber and a knife. 'That's OK,' she said stubbornly. 'You know what they say. Many hands.'

The two women exchanged a look for a long moment, and then Cath broke it off with a sniff. 'Chunks, not slices,' she said gruffly. 'I'm making a Greek salad.'

'Lovely,' Lily replied. 'One of Ronan's favourites.'

As they chopped in strained yet companionable silence, Lily watched Scarlet out of the corner of her eye. She was staring out of the window, her gaze glazed over as she got lost in whatever thoughts were running through her head. She'd been a lot quieter since the night it had all gone down. And that was to be expected, Lily reasoned. She'd already been through so much, and crossing that final line into the dark world in which she'd now planted the seed for her future wasn't an easy step.

As she watched, Scarlet turned and met her gaze. Her big grey-blue eyes were calm enough, but Lily could see the steel that had been born behind them. Breaking away, she turned and walked into the lounge to continue seeing to their guests.

The girl was going to be alright – there was no question about it. Scarlet was strong, stronger than even she knew herself. She was the future of this firm. The future head of the family. And when she finally grew into herself, Lily knew already, that girl was going to light a fire the likes of which the London underworld had never, ever seen before.

CHAPTER SIXTY-FOUR

Ruby leaned over the bucket on the floor and retched into it once more, the contents of her stomach long gone, but bile still making its painful way out.

'Please,' she cried out pitifully. 'Why are you doing this?'

She leaned her burning head against the cool plaster of the wall and sobbed with the little energy she had left. She'd been calling out for days, maybe even weeks – she wasn't sure anymore. Time seemed an alien concept right now. Food and water arrived, and the bucket was emptied regularly by people she didn't know and who wouldn't speak to her, but other than that and a mattress to sleep on, there was nothing else in the room. Blood was caked around her fingernails where she'd clawed at the door and at the wood so strongly nailed over the window, but neither had budged. She was in so much pain from withdrawal she had no idea how her heart was still beating. It had come to a point where she just wanted to die. But she couldn't even manage to do that.

A pair of shoes thudded dully as they made their way down the hallway outside, and she opened her eyes to stare at the door, wondering half-heartedly who it was and what they were doing here. It wouldn't be anything exciting, another meal perhaps. But it wasn't food she wanted. It was heroin.

The door opened and light from the hallway shone in. She squeezed her eyes shut and pulled away for a moment. When nothing else happened, she forced one eye open again to see why whoever it was had stopped. When she recognised the visitor, she gasped and her jaw dropped in shock. Tears of confusion began to fall from her eyes as she stared up at him.

'Why?' she asked, in barely more than a whisper. 'Why are you doing this?'

Ray walked into the room and stood a few feet away from her. 'Because…' His deep voice filled the room as his dark gaze bored into her. 'There was no other way.'

A LETTER FROM EMMA

Dear Readers,

I hope you enjoyed this first instalment in the Drew family series. If you would like to hear more about the series, sign up here. Your email address won't be shared and you can unsubscribe at any time.

www.bookouture.com/emma-tallon

Lily Drew has been a character who's played on my mind now for a couple of years and she's been begging to be let out! She's hard as steel but with a heart of gold and I just can't help but love her – though I certainly wouldn't want to get on the wrong side of her!

With her at the forefront of my mind, I gradually built the rest of the family around her and I'm really pleased with how they've turned out. There is so much ahead for them all. Scarlet, in particular, is someone I'm really looking forward to writing in the next couple of books, seeing how she develops and grows into her role in the family.

For those of you who have read the Tylers series, I hope you enjoyed the crossover! This series is still very much part of that same world, so there will be a fair few crossovers and mentions of old characters as the books continue. You'll remember Freddie, Anna and Bill, but do you guys remember Ray Renshaw's first appearance in the Tyler series? If not, check out *Boss Girl* again, when you get the chance.

I hope that you're looking forward to reading the next book in the series as much as I'm enjoying writing it. I'm working hard on it already and hope to get it out to you later on in the year. In the meantime, stay safe, stay well and in the words of Ronan Drew – *may the road rise up to meet you, may the wind be always at your back and may the sun shine warm upon your face.*

All my love,
Emma X

 emmatallonofficial

 EmmaEsj

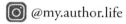 @my.author.life

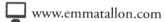 www.emmatallon.com

ACKNOWLEDGEMENTS

Firstly, I'd like to acknowledge my amazing editor, who takes my crazy ideas and helps me mould them into great stories. I'm so glad to have found someone I enjoy working with as much as I enjoy working with you, Helen. And to have found someone who takes all my randomness in her stride. This wouldn't be half as much fun without you.

I'd like to thank all my incredible author friends who are always there to listen and help and support through every step of the process, in particular Angie Marsons and Casey Kelleher. You guys are worth your weight in gold and I'm so glad to have you in my life. Don't ever change.

And I have to thank my husband who, although eight books in, has still not read a single one of my novels, shows endless belief in me and is always by my side through the highs and lows of writing them. It can't always be easy being married to a writer. Writers can remember the shirt you wore and the song that played on a date five years ago but forget things like what day of the week it is, or that we were supposed to take the rubbish out. We live on a beautiful carousel of chaos. But yet you love me anyway, Richard. And you make sure to remember all that I don't, when I'm lost in the world of my characters. So thank you.

Printed in Great Britain
by Amazon

39325498R00185